Forgive Me

T0352179

Forgive Me

ELIZA FREED

**FOREVER
YOURS**

New York Boston

Forever Yours

Hachette Book Group

1290 Avenue of the Americas

New York, NY 10104

Hachettebookgroup.com

Twitter.com/foreverromance

First ebook and print on demand edition: November 2014

Forever Yours is an imprint of Grand Central Publishing.

The Forever Yours name and logo are trademarks of Hachette Book Group, Inc.

The publisher is not responsible for websites (or their content) that are not owned by the publisher.

The Hachette Speakers Bureau provides a wide range of authors for speaking events. To find out more, go to www.hachettespeakersbureau.com or call (866) 376-6591.

ISBN 978-1-4555-8355-3 (ebook edition)

ISBN 978-1-4555-8356-0 (print on demand edition)

To John, the adventure continues.
And to Jill and Kate,
Christine and Jenn,
Thanks for using words like cockamamie and
behaving improperly.

Acknowledgments

I'll be thanking people for the rest of my life in regard to this story, but these few are at the top of my list:

With all my heart, thank you to John, Vivian, and Charlie. You've excused me from my daily roles and let me fly far, far away.

To my parents who've taught me they will always love me, no matter what. (Putting it to the test here a bit.)

To Robin Smith, whose professional editing was the equivalent of a masters-level course in writing and publishing.

To the early readers from far and wide. You cannot comprehend how terrifying it is to hand someone the first book you've written. Your kind words and thoughtful questions carried me over the doubts, the frustrations, and the lonely days. I hope someday to return the favor.

To Nicole Warner and M.A.D. for helping me fill my own "Crazy Ass Shit about Rodeo" folder.

To Rutgers University for opening my eyes.

To Salem County and the fine state of New Jersey. Let's just keep this between us, okay?

To Lauren Plude, and the rest of the insanely talented people at Grand Central, thank you for hearing Charlotte's voice every step of the way.

And finally, to Tricia Steiner who literally willed these books into the universe. For a woman who has never coveted the title cheerleader, you are one of the finest I've ever known – and I know a lot of cheerleaders.

Forgive Me

~ 1 ~

"My soul is forgotten, veiled by a boring complication"

My foot will bleed soon. Judging by the familiar curve in the road, I'm still at least two miles from home. Of course I end up walking home the night I'm wearing great shoes. The pain shoots through my heel as the clouds flash with lightning in the dark sky.

Maybe I'm bleeding already. I mentally review the last few hours. Anything to distract me from the agony of each step. The texts, the endless stream of drunken texts, run through my mind.

We're soul mates. I roll my eyes. Brian deserves a nicer girlfriend; someone sweet like him. Someone who doesn't roll their eyes at this statement.

We belong together. Bleh.

What does it say about my relationship when the only thing I ever tell people about my boyfriend is, "He's a really nice guy"? And how, after two years of being apart, did I ever take him back? The last three weeks have felt like years, years I was asleep.

We're perfect together. My mother thought we were perfect. Hell, this whole town thought it.

No one is ever going to know you the way I do. He was watching me as I read this one and I had to work hard to keep a straight face. At the time I wasn't sure why, but here on this deserted road, in the middle of a thunderstorm Brian would never walk through, I know it's because he never knew me at all. Or my soul. It's not his fault. I'd nearly forgotten it myself.

I stop to adjust the strap on my sandals and two sets of eyes peer out from the ditch next to the road. They're low to the ground, watching me. I've always hated nocturnal animals.

"Anyone else come out to play in the storm?" I say to the other hidden night life. I move to the edge of the shoulder, facing the nonexistent traffic, and give my new friends some room. I wince as I step forward, and watch as a set of headlights shines on the road in front of me and the scene around me turns mystical. The steam rises off the pavement at least five feet high before disappearing into the blue tinted night. The rain only lasted twenty spectacular minutes, not long enough to cool the scorched earth.

I'm lost in it as the truck pulls up beside me, now driving on the wrong side of the road, and Jason Leer rolls down his window. I glance at him and turn to stare straight ahead, trying not to let the excruciating torture of each step show on my face.

"Hi, Annie," he says, and immediately pisses me off. I might look sweet in my new rose-colored shorts romper, but these wedges have me ready to commit murder.

"My name is Charlotte," I say without looking at him, and keep walking. The strap is an ax cutting my heel from my foot. *Why won't he call me Charlotte?* Of course the cowboy would show up. What this night needs is a steer wrestler to confound me further. The same two desires he always evokes in me surface now. Wanting to punch him, and wanting to climb on top of him.

"What the hell are you doing out here? Alone—" A guttural moan of thunder interrupts him, and I tilt my head to determine the origin, but it surrounds us. The clouds circle, blanketing us with darkness, but when the moon is visible it's bright enough to see in this blue-gray night. We're in the eye of the storm and there will never be a night like this again. *God I love a storm.* The crackling of the truck's tires on the road reminds me of my cohort.

"I'm not alone. You're here, irritating me as usual." I will not look at him. I can feel his smartass grin without even seeing him, the same way I can feel a chill slip across my skin. It's hot as hell out and Jason Leer is giving me the chills.

Lightning strikes, reaching the ground in the field just to our left, and I stop walking to watch it. Every minute of today brought me here. The mind-numbing dinner date with Brian Matlin, the conversation on the way to Michelle's party about how we should see other people, the repeated and *annoying* texts declaring his love, and the eleven beers and four shots I watched Brian pour down his throat, all brought me here.

"If you're trying to kill yourself by being struck by lightning, I could just hit you with my truck. It'll be faster," he says, stealing my eyes from the field. His arm rests out his truck window and it's enormous. He tilts his body toward the door and the width of his chest holds my gaze for a moment too long.

"Annie!"

I shake my head, freeing myself from him. "What? What do you want? I'm not afraid of a storm." I am, however, exhausted by this conversation.

I finally allow myself to look him in the eyes. They are dark tonight, like the slick, steamy road before me, and I shouldn't have looked.

"I want you." His voice is tranquil, as if he's talking the suicide jumper off the bridge. "I want you to get in the truck and I'll drive you home." Thunder growls in the distance and the lightning strikes to the left and right of the road at the same time. The storm surrounds us, but the rain was gone too soon. Leaving us with the suffocating heat that set the road on fire.

I close my eyes as my sandal cuts deeper into my foot, and Jason finally pulls away. My grandmother always said the heat brings out the crazy in people. It was ninety-seven degrees at 7 p.m. The humidity was unbearable. Too hot to eat. Too hot to laugh. The only thing you could do was talk about how miserably hot it was outside. By the time Brian and I arrived, most of the party had already been in the lake at some point. Even that didn't look refreshing. The sky unleashed, and Michelle kicked everyone out rather than let them destroy her house.

I stop walking, and shift my foot in the shoe. The strap is now sticking; I've probably already shed blood. Jason drives onto the right side of the road and stops the truck on the tiny shoulder. He turns on his hazard lights and gets out of the truck. *He's a hazard.* I plaster a smile on my face and begin walking again. As soon as he leaves I'm taking off these shoes and throwing them in the pepper field next to me.

Before I endure two steps, he's in front of me. He's as fast as I remember. Like lightning: always picked first for kickball in elementary school. His hair is the same thick, jet black as back then, too. The moonlight shines off it and I wonder where his cowboy hat is. He's too beautiful to piss me off as much as he does. He blocks my path, a concrete wall, and I stop just inches from him.

"I'm going to ask you one more time to get in the truck." A lightning strike hits the road near his truck and without flinching he looks back at me, waiting for my answer.

"Or what?" I challenge him with my words and my "I dare you" look on my face. He hoists me over his shoulder and walks back to the truck as if I'm a sweatshirt he grabbed as an afterthought before walking out the door.

"Put me down! I'm not some steer you can toss around," I yell, as I fist my hands and pound on his back. He's laughing and pissing me off even more. I pull his shirt up and start to reach for his underwear and Jason runs the last few steps to the truck.

"Do you ever behave?" he asks, and swings the truck door open. He drops me on the seat and leans in the truck between my legs. I push my hair out of my face, my chest still heaving with anger. "Why the hell are you walking alone on a country road, in a goddamned storm, this late at night?"

My stomach knots at his closeness and this angers me, too. Why can't Jason Leer bore me the way Brian Matlin does? Jason raises his eyebrows and tilts his head at the perfect angle to send a chill down my spine.

"Brian and I broke up tonight."

"And he made you walk home?" Shock is written all over his face. Brian would never make me walk home. He is the nicest of guys. Not great at holding his liquor, but nice.

"No." I roll my eyes, calling him an idiot, and he somehow

leans in closer, making my stomach flip. "He proceeded to get drunk at Michelle Farrell's party and I drove him home so he didn't die." I think back to all the parties of the last six years, since Jason and I entered high school. Besides graduation, we were rarely in the same place. I've barely hung out with Jason Leer since eighth grade. At the start of high school everyone broke into groups, and this cowboy wasn't in mine.

"Why didn't you call someone for a ride?" He breaks my revelry.

"Because apparently when Brian gets drunk he texts a lot. My battery died after the fiftieth message professing his love for me."

"Poor guy."

"Poor guy? What about me? I'm the one who had to delete them, and drive him home. I thought he'd never pass out." I'm still mourning the time I lost with Brian's drunken mess.

"Why didn't you just take his car?"

"Because I left him passed out in it in his parents' driveway. I got him home safe, but I'm not going to carry him to bed."

At this Jason lowers his head and laughs. My irritation with him twists into annoyance at myself for telling him anything. For telling him everything. I want to punch him in his laughing mouth. His lips are perfect, though.

"It's not easy to love you, Annie."

"Yeah, well I've got fifty texts that claim otherwise. Judging from the fact you can't even get my name right, everything's probably hard for you." Jason leans on the dash and his jeans scrape against my maimed foot, causing my face to twist in pain. Before I can regain my composure, his eyes are on me. He moves back and holds my foot up near his face. He slips the strap off my heel and runs his thumb across the now broken and purple blister. I close my eyes, the sight of the wound amplifying the pain.

"My God, you are stubborn," he says, his eyes still on my foot. Thunder groans behind us and he straightens my leg, examining it in the glimmer of moonlight. I'm not angry anymore. One urge has silenced another, and awakened me in the process. He pulls my foot to him and kisses the inside of my ankle, and a chill runs from my leg to both breasts and settles in the back of my throat, stealing my breath.

I swallow hard. "Are all your first kisses on the inside of the ankle?" I ask. His hands grip my ankle harshly, but he's careful with my heel.

His eyes find mine as he drags his lips up my calf and kisses the inside of my knee. I shut up and shudder from a chill. There are no words. Only the beginning of a thought. *What if,* arises in my mind against the sound of the clicking of the hazard lights.

The lightning strikes again and unveils the darkness in his eyes. He lowers my leg and backs up, but I'm not ready to let him go. I grab his belt buckle and pull him toward me. Jason doesn't budge. He is an ox. His eyes bore into me and for a moment I think he hates me. He's holding a raging river behind a dam, and I'm recklessly breeching it.

With a hand gripping each shoulder he forces me back to the seat and hovers over me. Even in the darkness I can see the emptiness in his eyes and I can't leave it alone. He kisses me. He kisses me as if he's done it a hundred times before, and when his lips touch mine some animalistic need growls inside of me. He's like nothing I've ever known, and my body craves a hundred things all at once, every one of them him. With his tongue in my mouth, I tighten my arms around his thick neck and pull him closer, wanting to climb inside of him.

Jason pulls away, devastating me, until I realize there are flashing lights behind us. His eyes fixed on mine, he takes my hands from behind his head and pulls me upright before the state trooper steps out of his car and walks to our side of the truck.

* * *

"Charlotte, honey, are you going to get up? I heard you come in late last night."

I roll over and put my head under the pillow. I don't want to get up. I don't want to tell my mom that I broke up with Brian…again.

"Is everything okay?" She's worried. I take a deep breath and sit up in bed. The sheet rubs against my heel and the pain reminds me of Jason Leer.

"I broke up with Brian last night."

"Oh no. I have to see his mother at Book Club on Wednesday."

"I can't marry him because you can't face his mother at Book Club."

"I'm not suggesting you marry him, just that you stop dating him if you're going to keep breaking his heart." My mom leaves my room. Her face is plagued with frustration mixed with disappointment. I climb out of bed and lumber to the bathroom. My green eyes sparkle in the mirror, hinting at our indelicate secret from last night. I wink at myself as if something exciting is about to happen. My long blond hair barely looks slept on. I think breaking up with Brian was good for me.

* * *

"Jack, she broke up with Brian again." I catch, as I enter the kitchen.

"Through with him, huh?" My father never seems to have an opinion on who I date as long as they treat me well. Brian certainly did that.

"Dad, he just didn't do it for me." Jason's eyes pierce my thoughts again, haunting me. The trooper sent us home and I left him in his truck without a word. There wasn't one to say.

"Do what? What did you expect him to do for you?" my mother spouts. She's not taking the news well.

"When he looks at me a certain way, I want to get chills," I start, surprised by how easily my needs are verbalized. "When he leans into me, I want my stomach to flip, and when he walks away I want to care if he comes back." My parents both watch me silently as if I'm reciting a poem at the second-grade music program. They are pondering me.

"What? Don't your stomachs flip when you're together? Ever?"

"Does your stomach flip when you look at me, Jack?" she asks.

"Only if I eat chili the same day," my dad says, and they both start laughing.

"Charlotte, I remember what it was like to be young. And your father did make my stomach flip, but I think you're too hard on Brian. He's a nice boy."

"Yeah yeah. He's nice." I butter my toast and move to sit next to my father at the table. *He is nice*. For some reason Brian's kindness frustrates me. He's a boring complication. "I ran into Jason Leer last night." *And he kissed the inside of my leg.* I smile ruefully.

My mother's eyebrows raise and I fear I've divulged too much. My father never looks up from the newspaper.

"Butch and Joanie's son?"

"That's the one." I try to sound nonchalant as a tiny chill runs down my neck.

"I haven't seen him since Joanie's funeral. Poor boy. She was lovely. Do you remember her?"

I nod my head and take a bite of the toast. "From Sunday school."

"Jack, do you remember Joanie Leer? Died of cancer about a year ago."

"I remember," my dad says, and appears to be ignoring us, but I know he's not. He always hears everything.

"If you don't want to be with Brian, that's fine, but please not a rodeo cowboy," my mother pleads, not missing a thing.

"I only said I saw him. What's wrong with a rodeo cowboy?"

"Nothing. For someone else's daughter. I really want you to marry someone with a job. Someone that can take care of you."

"Can't a cowboy do that?" *From what I've seen, he can take very good care of me.*

"Charlotte, please tell me you're not serious. They're always on the road. Their income's not steady. It's a very difficult life." My mother's stern warning is delivered while she fills the dishwasher, as if we're discussing a fairy tale, a situation so absurd it barely warrants a discussion. She's still beautiful, even when she's lecturing me. "I know safe choices aren't attractive to the young, but believe me you do not belong in that world and he'd wither up and die in yours. Do not underestimate the power of safety in this crazy life."

"How do you know so much about rodeo cowboys?" I ask.

"Yeah, how do you know so much?" My dad asks. He stares at her over the newspaper.

"Is your stomach flipping?" She asks, and gives him her beautiful smile she's flashed to quell him my entire life.

"Yes," he says, and winks at her.

"I run out of the water, swallowed by complete devastation"

Noble?" I stare out the window as we pass field after field and lose my attention to the crops. I follow them to the horizon, the only boundary between the earth and the sky. The perfect blue meets the green fields as if it's watching over them. This is Noble's world.

God's country.

"Yes?" He brings me back to his truck. I turn to him, and watch him drive with the ease that's always a part of him.

"Would you say I'm your best friend? That we're best friends?" Noble takes his eyes off the road to meet mine. I've seen this look before. He's not sure whether to laugh.

"Are you going to give me half a BFF necklace, or something?" He asks as if I am the most ridiculous person he's ever known.

"I was just thinking about how things change."

"Charlotte, what's going on?" He's listening closely now. We pass the cornfields, almost knee-height. How many corn crops have I passed in my lifetime?

I shake my head. "I was just thinking."

"About what?" *About what?*

"You are one of my closest friends. You, Margo, Jenn, and Sam. And at Rutgers I can't survive without Julia, Violet, and Sydney."

"Where are you going with this?" Now he's worried. Noble turns left and a new set of fields draws my attention.

"What happened to the others? Jason, and Ollie, and Possum? Where are Heather Miller and Dana Davino? Why aren't we friends with them anymore? I went to Jason Leer's birthday party every year of my life until we hit high school, and then I never hung out with him."

"Charlotte, things change—the passage of time, circumstances—but people don't. We're still friends, just old friends. Jason was into the rodeo, and we weren't. We just went in different directions."

Noble turns onto the farm lane leading to his house and crosses the railroad tracks that sever it. An acre and a half back, we pass Jason Leer's house on the left. His truck is parked near the barn separating his and Noble's yards. I swallow hard at the thought of my ankle in Jason's hand.

"Wait here," Noble says, and pulls up near the side door of the farmhouse.

"Why?" I ask, knowing my cheeks are probably flushed. Noble notices and seems confused for the second time today. I'm not making any sense.

"Because my mother will interrogate you about my love life at Rutgers and we'll never make it to Jenn's." Noble's easy smile lights up his face. *He is my best friend.* "Just wait here, okay?"

Noble leaves me, and I can't take my eyes off Jason's truck. I wonder what he's doing today, what Jenn and Margo will say if I invite him to the lake house with us. The door to Jason's house swings open and hits the side of the house. Anyone else exiting a house that way would indicate anger, but Jason smiles as he strides over to his truck. I watch in delight. Everything is so powerful about him, and I can't take my eyes off him. A chill runs down the back of my neck and I tilt my head to thwart it.

Jason reaches for his truck door and glances back. At the sight of me, he stops. The smile drains from his face. It's replaced with something else. Something coercive. I should lean down in the truck. Crouch down and escape his gaze, but that would be cowardly and something about Jason Leer brings out the best and worst in me, neither of which is anywhere near fear.

He takes one step toward me as Noble practically skips out of his house. He breezes to the truck and climbs in carrying cucumbers, without even noticing Jason. As he pulls away he waves at Jason, and I sit in awe of him. We drive a few miles, me trying to understand what Jason does to me, and Noble singing along to music without a care in the world. He lowers the volume and examines me.

"Charlotte, what?"

I release myself from all things Jason Leer.

"What if the person you're supposed to be with you've known your whole life? What if they're an old friend?" Noble's gaze is serious, and that's terrifying.

"An old friend or a best friend?"

"Old, either, does it matter?" This line of questioning is not relaxing him.

"Is this about Brian? Are you second-guessing breaking up with him?"

"No. This is absolutely not about Brian." Noble studies me.

"What you're talking about will change everything. I'm not saying it never happens, just that if it ends, it never ends well."

"Have you ever been with someone you know in your heart is the exact right person for you? That everything swirling around you just moves you closer to that person?" Noble takes his eyes off the road and looks at me as if I have a unicorn horn growing out of the center of my head.

"Did you get high before I picked you up?"

"No," I say, and lower my head. I'm not making any sense today. None of this makes sense.

"You're scaring me a little."

"I know," I say, and drop the subject. It's a stupid one.

* * *

The drive to Jenn's lake house is about a half hour. Noble and I spend it with the windows down and the music playing. We pull down the long gravel-cut lane winding through the woods and park behind Jenn's and Margo's cars.

A day on the lake is the perfect end to June, I think as I jump out of the truck and grab my bag. The cloudless sky agrees with me. This will be the last summer we're all home together. It seems everyone branches out after their junior year. Jenn has already said she'll be on a beach somewhere full-time and Margo wants to stay at school and take summer classes. I'm not sure what I'll do, but it's not going to be in Salem County if these girls don't come home.

I hand the bag of cucumbers to Jenn and she starts washing

them. "Compliments of Noble Sinclair." I give credit where credit is due.

"Oh, Mr. Sinclair? You don't say? I love that you still call him Noble after all these years. Can't just commit to Nick like the rest of us," Jenn says.

"She's stubborn," Noble concludes.

"It's nice to know a farmer. I'm going to make you cucumber salad as thanks," she says.

"I was going to bring some tomatoes too, but they're about a week out."

"Let's meet back here in a week. I'll make a tomato salad then," she adds and begins cutting the cucumbers.

"Sam should be here any minute," Margo says, and grabs a cucumber. "Why don't you guys take out the canoe? It's covered in spiders. I couldn't get within three feet of it." I look out the window at the lake. It's completely still, no signs of life.

* * *

Noble and I sweep the interior of the canoe for webs before pulling it to the water's edge and placing the paddles inside. We step into the water and gingerly board the canoe. We almost tip at Noble's entry, but we right ourselves and set off on our sail with Noble at the bow. His neck and shoulders appear enormous from this vantage point. As he pulls the water with his paddle his biceps bulge. When we exit the shade of the coast, Noble takes off his shirt and I am in awe.

"How come you don't have a girlfriend?" I ask, and Noble keeps paddling.

"What makes you think I don't?"

"You wouldn't keep something like that from me, would

you?" I'm wounded at the suggestion. Noble turns around and his warm, inviting smile confuses me all the more. Why is he alone? Or is he?

"I'm just waiting for the right girl," he says, and paddles with deep strokes that push us from shore. "Until she comes along I'm trying to meet as many wrong girls as possible," he adds with the naughtiest grin.

"Sounds like a great plan to catch something nasty."

"That's very romantic, Charlotte. Just because things aren't swirling around me, or whatever the hell you were saying earlier, doesn't mean I'm a venereal disease waiting to be contracted."

"Says you," I retort, and continue paddling the canoe. The river is completely empty except for Noble and me. We row close to the shore of a tiny island with no beach. The trees hang over into the water and there are sounds of bugs, and birds, and God knows what else inhabiting it. Noble takes his paddle and pushes us away from the island just as I duck under a branch and we row back to the open water.

"How deep do you think it is here?" I ask.

"I can throw you in so you can find out."

"That won't be necessary," I say, and push my paddle straight down to the bottom. It touches nothing but water. "Deep," I say, nodding my head. Noble rocks the canoe from side to side, coming within a few inches of taking on water each time. I don't say a word. I will not give him the satisfaction. Instead I tilt my face to the blue sky and let the sun warm me. It is the most beautiful day. Almost too bright to face it even with my eyes closed. The glare is blinding. Noble bores of tormenting me and begins to row back to the house. I match his paddling and between us the canoe is charging toward home.

I stop rowing as I see Jenn, Margo, Sam, and…Sean standing on the dock.

"What's your brother doing here?" Noble asks, his voice filled with the doom I feel.

"I don't know. Keep rowing." Dread settles at the bottom of my stomach.

When we get close to shore I can see them clearly, each of them staring at me with unspoken sadness. Their faces scream at me to row the other way. Something horrible has happened. I lay my paddle across my lap and listen as the devastation in Sean's eyes cries out to me. Noble rows us to shore and gets out first, immediately turning around to help me. I run out of the water and face my brother's stricken face.

"Mom and Dad were in a car accident. A delivery truck t-boned them on the Swedesboro Road. Mom was airlifted and is being operated on now." *Where's Dad?* "Get your stuff."

"I'll follow you guys," Margo says.

"I'll drive, Margo. We'll follow you, Sean," Noble says to Sean, and I grab my shoes and climb into Sean's truck. We pull onto the lane, the one I rode in on an hour ago, and everything has changed. None of it for the better.

~ 3 ~

*"Abandoning my anger, trying numb for a while
It may serve me better than a dead hearted smile"*

I'm really sorry about your parents," Kevin says. He graduated with Sean and now he's an undertaker.

"Thanks, Kevin," Sean responds, and I barely look at either of them. This cannot really be happening.

"I know they airlifted your mom. We were all pulling for her." *Shut the fuck up, Kevin.* I roughly run my hand up and down the side of my face.

"Her injuries were too extensive," Sean says, and pulls out a chair for me. Even with my high wedges on, I'm nowhere near his height. Sean's a big, burly, Irishman with the same green eyes as my own, except mine look like that of a dead person now.

Sean and Kevin work through what appears to be a list of things people need at a funeral: caskets, obituaries, memorial cards, flowers. I barely listen to a word of it. *What day is it?*

I'll bet it's written on the top of Kevin's form somewhere. He seems very organized. I always liked him. Not feeling him today. I try and focus on the top of Kevin's papers as he plays with his pen cap above them. I wonder if my obvious hatred is making him nervous. None of this is his fault. I smile sweetly and even that seems to make him uncomfortable. If I'm killed in a car accident tomorrow, is Kevin going to have this conversation about me? How many times a day does he have this conversation? He should have studied statistics at Rutgers like me. Rutgers was a million years ago.

"Have you thought anything about the service?" Kevin directs his question to Sean. I am clearly scaring him.

"We're headed to the church next."

Great. I definitely want to take this show on the road.

* * *

"Are you okay, Charlotte?" Sean asks as he opens the truck door for me.

"I'm dead inside. Maybe it's shock or something, but I cannot seem to figure out anything but how much I hate people. Kevin seems like a nice guy."

"He is."

"It took all of me not to reach across the table and strangle him with his own tie."

Sean stares at me, completely disturbed by my statement. "Okay…" he manages, and closes the truck door.

"How is it you are so mentally stable? Both your parents were just killed in a horrific car accident. Poof! Gone. What the fuck, Sean?" His eyes widen and I note that I need to take it easy on him.

"I'm working through the process. Planning a funeral, calling relatives, meeting with the police and fire officials, dealing with the hospital and insurance companies, driving my crazy-ass sister around. You know, the process." Sean starts the truck and looks behind us to back out. We drive the three minutes to the other side of town in a hysterical silence.

***

Pastor Johnson leads us back to his office and Sean motions for me to take a seat first. This is Kevin's office all over again, but Pastor Johnson's office is full of books and it reminds me of the thing I love most about him. He is intelligent. His sermons always make me smarter. Sean and Pastor Johnson speak of memories of our parents as anger burns inside of me. My mom loved this church her whole life, and now it's betrayed me. She should be planning refreshments for someone else's funeral. I look up and realize at some point the conversation switched to music.

"She'll want 'In the Garden' sung at the funeral," I say.

"Who will?" Sean looks like his mute sister just learned to speak.

"Mom. She'd want 'In the Garden' sung. It's her favorite hymn." I lower my eyes to my hands in my lap. "Was her favorite." Pastor Johnson pauses, waiting for me to say something else, but I have nothing else in me. It's all dead, too.

"I want you both to continue attending services," His directive catches my attention. "It's important. Not because it's what your parents would want for you, but because it's what you both need. In the darkest moments of your life you should not stop worshipping." *Is this the darkest moment of my life?*

What does that mean? Is there some qualifying ribbon I receive for hitting the darkest moment?

"Even in this horrible time, God knew it beforehand." This statement completely pisses me off. My hands begin to shake at the suggestion that my parents' accident was part of a divine plan. "It's not a surprise to Him. He knew it before you were born."

"Oh yeah, well fuck Him and fuck you, too," I say, anger searing me.

"Charlotte! What the hell are you saying?" Sean is wild-eyed as he yells at me, before realizing he's now cussing in the Pastor's office, too. "Sorry, Pastor."

"It's okay. Charlotte, it's okay." I have no idea what else he's saying. I can no longer listen to a word of it.

"Would you excuse me for a minute?" I smile out of habit and walk out of his office. I sit on the front steps of the church and wait for Sean. I should be crying. I should be flat on my stomach on the lawn of the church, banging my fists and feet into the ground as I sob uncontrollably. But I'm not. I don't even feel guilty. I'm not sure I feel anything. Maybe some anger. *That's a good sign, right?*

Sean is pissed, I'll bet. I remind myself again, I have got to go easy on him. He's all I have left now.

* * *

Shockingly, Sean doesn't include me in the rest of the planning. Instead I am "watched" by my sister-in-law Michelle, or by my Aunt Diane at all times. It's like they're completing a nurse's log about what I eat and drink, always begging me to eat more and get some rest. *What the hell do I need rest for?* I think I can talk about the shittiness of my parents' death without a full eight hours.

After two days I abandon my anger. It's pissing me off, too. I try numb for a while. I walk through the grocery store aisles like a zombie searching for crackers. I pause in the makeup aisle, because I am a masochistic zombie, and remember all the times my mom let me wear makeup as a little girl. I'm sure I was the only first grader wearing eye shadow in the class picture. I can barely concern myself with it now.

I walk down the ice cream aisle and pick out my father's favorite, mint chocolate chip. My mother used to tease him that he only stayed with her because she kept the freezer stocked with ice cream. I drop it in my basket and lumber to the register to pay.

"Charlotte, I'm so sorry about your parents. We're gonna miss seeing your mom in here every week," the cashier says, and I just look at her with my dead green eyes. *Say something, Charlotte.* This interaction is going to be retold seventeen times today.

"Thanks," I manage, and walk out of the store. I throw the ice cream in the trashcan by the door. Maybe this is why cutters cut themselves? I've never understood it, but now I can't remember what it's like to feel something.

Mrs. Kathryn (Whatley) O'Brien, 53, and Mr. Jack O'Brien, 54, of Salem County, New Jersey died in a car accident on Wednesday, June 27, 2007. Mrs. O'Brien was the daughter of the late Elizabeth and Wyatt Whatley of Salem County. Mr. O'Brien was the son of the late Elizabeth and Hank O'Brien, also of Salem County. Married for 27 years, they leave behind their son, Sean Martin O'Brien, 26, of Salem County and his wife, Michelle, and their daughter, Charlotte Anne O'Brien, 20, a student at Rutgers University in New Brunswick, NJ. Mr. O'Brien is survived by a sister, Diane Randall of Quinton, NJ and 3 nephews. Mrs. O'Brien was sister to the late Robert Whatley and James Whatley. Mr. O'Brien was a chemist at DuPont. A memorial service will be held on Saturday, June 30, 2007 at the Salem County Presbyterian Church in Salem County, NJ at 11 a.m. Friends and family are invited to visit at 10 a.m. In lieu of flowers, memorial contributions may be made to www.WoundedWarriorProject.org.

~ 5 ~

"No idea how to get home, relinquishing prayer"

W ould you like to get out of here?" he asks, as he leans into me. His skin is hot on my own and a chill travels through my entire body. I look around the room and make eye contact with my aunt Diane. She looks as if she could burst into tears at the sight of me. It's a look I've seen repeated over and over again today. From the grave sites to the luncheon—pity pulling everyone's face into a grotesque glower.

I look up and our eyes are almost at the same level. Jason stands in front of me broad and solid, his eyes asking me a thousand questions. "I would love to," I answer to each of them. "I have to tell Sean I'm leaving." Not because it's the right thing to do, but because he's all I have left, and I'm trying not to add to his misery.

I stay still, leaning back on my mother's countertop, and never release Jason's eyes. I've seen them my whole life and right now I want to crawl inside of them and never come out. He doesn't smile, he doesn't say any of the useless words the others have tried to soothe me with, he only sees right through me. I take a deep breath and turn to find my brother.

Sean's talking to some firemen, still trying to digest the known details of the accident. I overhear them saying how awful that crossroad is. The land is flat and barren there and that somehow adds to the number of accidents. People drive right through the stop sign, not expecting it. Another fireman chimes in the drugs and alcohol in the truck driver's system didn't help either. The company's words of apology and concern over how damning it is to Speed Demon Delivery's reputation churn in my stomach. The firemen pat Sean on the shoulder as they all decide my father being killed instantly was some kind of a blessing.

I have to get out of here.

"Shame about your mother, but at least she didn't suffer long either," one says, and I want to be angry, but instead I smile with all the emotion of a piece of plywood. As I approach, the firemen disperse, escaping the inevitable discomfort of figuring out what to say to me.

"Sean, I'm going for a ride with Jason Leer." It occurs to me that leaving my parents' funeral with a classmate, for lack of a better term, may not be appropriate. The look in Jason's eyes told me everything I need to know today. *Run.*

Sean looks straight at Jason without smiling. "Good. Get out of here before these people try to adopt us. They're all so supportive it's depressing."

I nod and move toward the door, where Jason is waiting for me. My heart beats faster as I acknowledge the rescue operation. In just a few steps I will not be in this horrible luncheon anymore. I'll be with Jason Leer somewhere. I don't care where. A new purpose is coursing through me—to escape the living. I wave to Margo on my way out, sure she'll pass word to the others that I've deserted but provide no explanation; I have none to give her.

Cars are lined up in makeshift rows, covering the entire bulging hill that is my parents' front yard, and it's quite a walk to Jason's relic of a blue truck. We're halfway there when he grabs my hand. It's so small in his, so fragile. Jason opens the door for me and it lets out a loud, sharp groan, a battle cry for our retreat.

I take one last look back toward the house before attempting to climb in the truck. The dress I bought yesterday, to wear as I buried my mother and father, is a fitted black sheath and I can't spread my legs far enough to step up. Without a word he lifts me and I wrap my arms around his neck, hiding my face behind his ear. I shamelessly inhale the kiwi smell of shampoo mixed with cigarette smoke. The combination, or something else, makes me run my fingers through his hair. Jason places me on the seat and slowly moves away from me, never breaking his focus. His gaze steals the breath from my mouth and I'm thankful when he shuts my door and walks around the truck to the driver's side.

There's a cooler on the seat between us. He takes out a beer, opens it, and hands it to me. *Does no one care about driving sober?* Thanks to a delivery guy whacked out on pain pills, I don't care anymore either. He opens one for himself and starts the truck without speaking. It answers with a roar and begins to vibrate under me. The beer is ice cold and I hold it in both hands to try to combat the heat I feel from Jason touching me, but it has little effect.

The familiar fields are foreign as he drives a few miles down the road and turns right onto Stoners Lane. The entire world is different now. The lane ends where the trees open up to a circular gravel area about a half-acre wide. It backs up to a few acres of fields and the entire clearing is surrounded by woods. Stoners Lane was always a place to go when there was no place else. Day or night you could come back here and not be seen from the road; the enclave's only drawback is the single entry and exit. When the troopers would come to break up parties, it was impossible to get out unless you crawled through a soybean field.

He stops the truck and silences the engine; we're alone. I take a long drink of my beer and look out the window at the clouds rolling past. They barrel in from the west and roll to the east, and begin to darken on the edges; the rain will arrive before the day is over. My grandmother's words pour into my head: *Happy is the dead the rain rains upon.*

Today is different from my grandmother's funeral. We were so alike, two comrades laughing through life, but when she became ill, watching her die silenced the laughter. By the end I wanted her to go. I would sit by her bed in the middle of the night and pray she died. She shouldn't have been alive without being able to laugh.

Today though, today there is no sadness, and there is no prayer. Just two dead eyes watching the world with only a void to process the information. I don't care. I don't care about the service. I don't care about the luncheon. I don't care about the rain. I'll never again care about another thing in this life. *God, let it be a short one.*

Jason gets out of the truck and opens my door. He lifts me out and stands me up, my back to the truck. The air smells of the coming rain; it's just short of a mist. It's probably already raining over the river.

"I'm sorry this is happening to you, Annie." My middle name from his lips feels right today. My mother "tried it out" for a year as my name, and switched back to Charlotte. It always stuck with the Leers and now that she's gone, it conjures up all the times I teased her I'd be in therapy by age thirty because you can't just change a kid's name.

His consuming stare is burning holes into me. He leans toward me, placing each hand on the truck by my head for support. My breathing quickens and I can think of nothing else but the chill I feel standing this close to him. There's something in me that knows I should speak, but instead I arch my back, my breasts endeavoring to touch him for themselves. He bends his arms and comes closer to me and I sigh and raise my lips to his. Jason kisses me hard, holding nothing back.

I retaliate and force my head farther in his direction, moving my body away from the truck. He slams me into the door and the pain in the back of my head is welcome. I wrap my fingers in his hair and pull him to me, but he resists and peers into my eyes and I could scream out from the hunger in his. My open palms rest on the hot, stiff fabric of his shirt. They move to his buttons as I concentrate to undo them. With each one I struggle to breathe. My physical needs are suffocating my emotions, drowning them to the point I no longer covet my lost life.

The urge to rip it off his body is making me angry. I'm desperate to have him. The buttons are the last obstacle to touching his skin, and something in me knows he's what I need more than anything else still walking this earth. I breathe deeply as I push his shirt over his shoulders, knowing I should regain some control, but deciding there's no such thing.

Freed, his chest heaves as he inhales and I feel the wetness between my legs. In a single, frenzied push his shirt comes completely off and I stop to admire the strength of his forearms. Arms that wrestle steer, and rope cattle, and ride bulls. Impatient with my exploration, he pulls his undershirt over his head and my hands are on his chest before his arms come back down. I lean forward to take his nipple in my mouth and I lick it. The wind whips up around us, and the birds circle above, and I bite it hard. I am lost with no idea how to get home.

With a finger under my chin he pulls my face up to his and kisses me gently, sweetly, again slowing me down, and I want to punch him for it. His hard-on rests between my legs and my hips thrust toward it. He pulls back and spins me around to put both my hands flat on the truck door. He lifts my hair and kisses the back of my neck and my knees buckle. Jason catches me and wraps his arm around my waist and spreads my legs with his ankle.

My head falls onto his shoulder and I look up to the horrible sky. The clouds race from one side of the clearing to the other as he breathes in my ear. His hand reaches between my legs and trails up the inside of my thigh, dragging higher and higher until he moves my underwear to the side and teases me with the tips of his fingers. I close my eyes, abandoning the sky.

"Annie," he says as he slips his finger into me and I moan with only the birds to hear me. Jason unzips my dress and pulls it down to my waist, leaving my arms hooked in the fabric and still at my sides. He spins me around hard and stares at my bare breasts. My skin confines me as my chest heaves. Jason stares at me for an eternity and I reach out to pull him down to me but my arms are trapped.

He smiles. A tiny devilish smile, and picks me up and carries me to the back of the truck. Jason tosses me down and my head lightly bounces off the pickup bed. The pain is exquisite and I arch my back, raising my breasts to the darkening sky. He forces my skirt up to my waist and rips off my panties.

With one arm he yanks me to the edge of the truck and I want him in me. I say his name with as much sound as I can create absent of air in my lungs, and he unzips his jeans. He spreads my legs wide and my skin burns where his hands are. I want to reach out and touch his chest, but I still can't move my arms. Holding my thighs he drives into me hard and my back scrapes on the bed of the truck. He pauses, still breathing heavy, and waits for me to say something, but I can't speak. My tongue is only good for touching now. I part my lips and breathe to regain some control.

"Again," I demand, and brace myself. He comes again, and again I feel alive. Jason starts a rhythm I can barely tolerate. I'm arching my back and matching his thrusts, my body trying to protect itself and lose itself at the same time. I can see the clouds blackening the clearing. His hands are on the tops of my thighs and he pulls me toward him, maximizing each movement. I want to touch his chest, his face, and try to move my arms, but he slows and puts my arms back at my side.

I won't move again.

He cannot slow down again or I'll lose my grasp on the world and float up to the clouds. The dark, dismal clouds. He places one hand on my thigh and the other around my neck. He picks up his pace and I cannot hold on to myself. The clouds advance and I feel him one last time before I crumble around him, arching, moaning, and shivering as he continues his rhythm that is breaking me.

I whisper, "Jason," and he surrenders, letting go of my neck and falling on top of me.

And I cry.

At first only a few errant tears, but it evolves into deep sobs I can't control. He pulls my dress onto my shoulders and lifts me into his lap. Jason is silent as he holds me close, willing the pieces of me back together. I quiet the deluge and concentrate on his bare chest touching my face.

"Happy is the dead the rain rains upon," he says as he rocks me back and forth. The rain comes hard from the start and he carries me to the passenger door, placing me on the seat.

It's the most I've felt in three days.

* * *

Jason puts the truck in drive and pulls out of Stoners Lane. I try to stop crying, but I can't. I inhale deeply, which causes the sobs to catch in my throat. Jason looks at me, confirming I don't need the Heimlich before pulling onto Auburn Road. He reaches across the seat and takes my hand. His huge, rough hand feels familiar covering my own. I look out the window, but the rain is coming harder now. The windshield wipers are barely keeping up and I question where we're going and why we needed to leave Stoners. The only thing I'm sure of is he's not taking me back. We're heading in the opposite direction from home.

He pulls into the McDonald's parking lot and parks near the back of the lot. The sound of the engine cutting makes me cry harder.

"Are you okay?" he asks, with an uncharacteristically gentle voice. Even Jason Leer is being careful with me. I must be on the verge of something quite terrifying to everyone around me. His question makes me laugh and I pull my hand away and use it to wipe the tears from my face.

"No. I'm not okay," I begin slowly, but without calculation. "I'm crying in the McDonald's parking lot, with my friend, who I just fucked." At this his eyebrows raise. "At Stoners Lane, instead of mourning with my family at my parents' funeral luncheon. I would say I am definitely not okay." I have no idea why I'm clenching my jaw. What is it about Jason Leer that makes me want to hit him? And why didn't I just hit him at Stoners?

"I'm sure this is normal," he tries, and I blink my eyes in disbelief.

"Really? You think this is normal?" I'm at the edge of the cliff called Hysterical and looking down. "Is it normal to leave my brother and one hundred and fifty family and friends to bang some guy in the dress I buried my parents in?"

"'Some guy' seems a little harsh." He's laughing under his breath.

"Is it normal to have your first orgasm during said banging?" I now have Jason's full attention; the laughter gone. "And most disturbing of all, is it normal that I just told you that?" I am now screaming at him…in the McDonalds parking lot. *Shut up, Charlotte!*

"What the hell is wrong with me?" I run my hands through my hair trying to brush it, but it's knotted at the base of my head. "Do I look like I just got laid in the back of a truck?" I ask, surrendering to the ridiculousness of it.

"No," he says calmly, as if I am not on the verge of a breakdown. "Not in the back of a truck." His eyes are pacific. Gray:

the color between black and white. They don't belong in his body.

"Come here."

"No," I say, and watch the rain assault the truck window. Jason reaches across the seat and pulls me on top of him. My arm burns from him yanking on it as I lean back onto the steering wheel. *What the hell am I doing here?* The rain turns to hail and its bullets hit the roof of the truck. I look at the ceiling then back at Jason. He's waiting for me, but not for me to say something, or do something. He's waiting for me to be okay. *How long will you wait?* The thought of it makes me smile slightly and at the sight of it, he pulls me close and kisses me again.

"I'm not going to have sex with you in the McDonalds parking lot." Jason completely ignores me as he kisses me again and I forget what I was talking about. I forget to be mad; mad at him, and my parents, and God, and every other person in this world. I swing my leg over him and he pulls me close as I straddle him in the driver's seat. My arms are clenched around his neck and my lips hurt from the force of his, and I forget I'm in a parking lot.

I forget it all.

* * *

The yard is empty. All the mourners have returned to their normal lives. As Jason pulls into the driveway, I realize my normal life has no mom and no dad in it. The house looks dark except for the light my mother always leaves on in the living room window. It's been forsaken. Like me. I take a deep breath.

"Thanks for the ride," I say. It's an absurd statement. It's an absurd life. Jason gets out of the car. I follow him out and meet him at the front of the truck. "Can you come in?" I didn't think it was a possibility until I said it and now that I have, I desperately need him to say yes.

"Where else would I go?" he asks, and I almost cry with gratitude. I put the code in the garage door and lead the way into my parents' kitchen. The smell of flowers, which will now be forever connected to death, slaps me in the face when I enter the room. They are littering the counters across the entire long wall. Containers of food and wrapped desserts are on the table and the ice bucket is lying upside down drying next to drinks stacked alongside it.

The party is over.

I walk into the family room and take off my shoes and turn on the lights. When I return to the kitchen Jason is reading a note and holding my cell phone.

"Margo cleaned up. She's worried about you. You forgot your phone when you left with me," he says, as he reads the note. Why is this okay? Any other guy, at any other time, I would have something to say about him just reading a note obviously written to me. I take the note out of his hand and read it for myself. It says exactly what he said it did. "You should call your brother, too."

Instead of calling, I text Sean that I'm home, exhausted, and going to bed. I peer at Jason over the phone as I type my plan and he is quietly staring back. Sean immediately texts back his relief and an offer to come get me if I want to sleep at his house tonight. The fact that he didn't call means he's just as exhausted. I'll be fine, is all I respond. Margo will not be so easy.

I text her and within seconds my phone rings.

"Where the hell have you been? I've been worried sick," she says, before I have a chance to say hello.

"I was at Stoners and McDonalds." Jason's wicked little laugh comes from the family room.

"The whole time with Jason Leer?" She's accusing me of something.

"Yes. He's here now."

"What?" She spews, not used to being unclear on my actions or whereabouts. "Do you want me to come over there?"

"No." At this Jason looks up, interested in what I am denying. For some reason I acquiesce him. "I'm safe with him." With that I watch Jason walk to the bathroom and turn on the shower. With the bathroom door wide open, he undresses and looks in the cabinets for a towel, naked. He takes one from the linen closet and glances back at me, a naughty grin spreading across his face, before stepping into the shower. I start to sweat.

"Margo, I gotta go. I'll call you tomorrow."

"Are you sure you're okay?" Her voice is full of concern and I know she's probably already in her car on her way over here. Without Jason taking me, she never would have left. All of them, Sean, Margo, Jenn, Noble, Sam, Julia, Violet, and Sydney—my remaining family, would still be here. They'll keep me alive, but who will save me from being dead inside?

"I'm not okay, but I promise, I'll make it through tonight. Thanks for everything." I pause, not knowing what else to say. *No one knows what to say.* I never thought the day would come I didn't know what to say to Margo. The bags of rolls on the counter catch my eye. "I'll call you in the morning and we'll have lunch together. I have tons of food here. Tell Jenn and Noble and everyone else, too."

"We'll be there at twelve. Call me before then if you need anything. Do you hear me?"

"Yes. I love you."

"I love you too, Charlotte. Try and get some sleep."

I'll try.

I take off my dress in the kitchen and throw it in the trash before walking to the bathroom and joining Jason Leer in the shower.

~ 6 ~

"To exist in silence as I lay my soul bare"

And so it goes. The days are blurs of Sean, Jenn, and Margo helping me with the administration of my life. There's a will, a house, cars, belongings. Too much to comprehend. And my nights are Jason Leer.

He comes when the others leave; always here within minutes of loneliness setting in. He saves me from my thoughts and my memories. Two days ago I showed him the key under the turtle rock and now he no longer knocks. Knocking would imply asking permission to come in and he's already here.

Something's different about tonight, though. Sean and Michelle brought dinner over and drove Dad's tractor back to their house. They left an hour ago, later than expected, and he's still not here. I haven't slept without him since the funeral and now that he's absent, the depth to which I need him scares me.

I look in the mirror as I brush my teeth and my face is

distraught. I refuse to let myself consider why. Too afraid it has more to do with Jason's absence than with my parents. That's impossible, though. Did he say he had something to do tonight? Did he say anything? Do we ever say anything? I thought I understood. Until tonight. Now that he's not here the last week no longer makes sense.

I button the last button on my favorite nightshirt and climb into bed. It's enormous and cold without him. The silent darkness allows the memories to seep in. The moonlight invades my room and everything is gray and sad. *Why?*

Why did you die?

Why aren't you here?

Where the hell is Jason Leer?

Tears fill my eyes, and I roll onto my stomach and bury my face in my pillow. I can't be without them. They have to come back. I hear the truck tires on the gravel of my driveway and hurry out of bed. His truck door moans as he closes it and I go to the back door to meet him. I open it just as he's fitting the key into the lock.

His smile fades as the look on my face registers. He steps to me and wipes the tears from my face, which makes me cry a little more.

"I'm sorry I'm late," he whispers, so as to not disturb the quiet that's descended on the house. He smells of cigarettes and dirt. Actual dirt. And I'm so thankful he's here.

"I was worried."

"Worried I wasn't coming?" Jason moves closer to me and I lose my breath as he pins me up against the wall. I nod my head slowly, my eyes never leaving his.

"I came as soon as the rodeo ended."

"The rodeo."

"Did you forget the rodeo?"

"No. I know the rodeo is on Saturday." Jason's face turns to confusion. "I didn't know today is Saturday," I say, and my complete disconnection from the living makes me start to cry again. If my parents were alive, I would know what fucking day it is.

Jason pulls me close to him and kisses the side of my head as he runs his fingers through my hair.

"I need a shower," he says, but I can't be concerned with what he needs.

"I need you."

I lay my soul bare; Jason's, to do with what he wants because I can't seem to care about it anymore. He forces me back to the wall and presses his body against mine until I can feel him. Until I can feel something.

Jason's kisses weaken my stance. I wrap my arms around his neck and pull his hair as I devour him. He reaches down and rips open my night shirt, flinging buttons across the room. I hear them hit the walls before scattering across the floor. His hands cup both breasts and his fingers squeeze my nipples until I bite his lip for him to stop.

He relents, and licks his sore lip. Jason lifts me up and carries me to the bathroom, kissing me the entire time. He turns on the shower and sits me on the counter. I unbutton his belt buckle and his jeans, and tear off his shirt as I smile evilly at him. It's about time someone else's clothes are ruined. He laughs, already knowing what I'm thinking.

I watch as Jason takes off the rest of his clothes and I wonder how I got here. How I got here each of the last seven days. The answer slips through my grasp as he spreads my legs wide and enters me. My head falls back as the deep breath replaces my lost thoughts. There is nothing gentle about Jason Leer. He pulls out and grabs my hair at the nape of my neck, tilting my head toward him.

"I want you to watch," he says, and my heart races. He loosens his grip and tilts my head down as he comes into me again. I've never seen anything like it, and it's making me sweat. Sex with Brian was a moment spent on the seesaw, and this—this is—I swallow hard and look up to see Jason watching me. His eyes never leave me, and his body never stops. He's not sad, or happy as he continues to take me. He possesses me. He is dangerous and I should run from him, from this, but I look down again and watch as he comes in and out, and in and out, and I am lost. I watch as a chill rises up inside of me and I feel it spreading throughout my body as my core takes over and—I lose it and come without ever taking my eyes off Jason Leer inside of me.

He pulls my thighs with every thrust and I lean back on the counter to avoid falling over completely. I look up just in time to see his face contort as he comes in me for the last time and then he slows.

He stands still and ponders me.

"I like it when you watch," he says, but it's like he is talking to someone else. I'm floating above us with his dick still in me. "I thought about having you naked all day." I blush at his words. I didn't even have enough thoughts to figure out it's Saturday. "Annie, you're going to be okay." I hop off the counter and start to walk away. Jason grabs my wrist in his death grip and I look at the cuff before meeting his eyes. "Do you believe me?"

"I want to," is all I say as I walk out of the bathroom and into my bedroom.

***

I sit up and a pain jabs from my neck down between my shoulders. I roll my head as I pinch the muscle on both sides. The kink will take days to come out. It's from attempting to sleep on the concrete wall that is Jason Leer's chest. He is painful. But the thought of sleeping without him sends a chill down my spine. Watching him sleep, his black hair circling his face, makes him seem so gentle and calm. He looks sweet in his sleep, but Jason's not sweet. He's some force between good and evil that whisks me away from everything I'm afraid of.

We should be talking more, though. We exist in silence. No one has sex this often without speaking. I'm not sure what has to be said, but I think everyone else is talking about something. The world is communicating. Jason rolls onto his side. He reaches out and grabs my hip. Without opening his eyes he slides his hand up my side until he comes to my breast and there he rests his hand as he smiles. My stomach flips and I cannot help but smile, too. This cowboy is doing something to me. Jason's eyes open and rise to me, his hand never leaving my breast.

"What's your favorite color?" I ask.

Jason seems frustrated, or amused. For Jason, the two emotions might be the same.

"You've known my favorite color since we first learned the names of the colors," he says, sitting up.

"Red? Is it red?"

"Are you thinking, Annie?"

"Thinking about what?"

"Thinking in general. Trying to figure this out? Trying to make sense of everything. It's probably the reason we've never been together before last week. The entire world doesn't have to make perfect sense."

Fuck. You.

I take a deep breath. Why does he piss me off so much?

"I can tell by your anger I'm right," he says, and pulls me onto his lap. He throws one leg over the side of his body and I'm pretty sure he could hog-tie me if he wanted to. "My favorite color is red."

"Do you think you're falling in love with me?" I ask, afraid of the answer.

"Definitely not."

"What are you doing with me then?" I need to know, but panic seizes me. I need him so much.

"Surviving." I look down at his chest. My hands find his nipples and with both between my fingers I consider pulling until he yelps.

"I don't understand," I say, barely above a whisper.

"Falling in love with you does not begin to describe what's going on." Jason tilts my chin up so I'm forced to see his gray eyes. "I felt like I was walking around dead from the day my mom died until I drove you to Stoners Lane." He pauses and I remember how he stole me. "You are the only thing I need. The only thing I want. And you consume me every minute of every day. With you, I am alive. Without you, I am not," he says, and the weight of his words crushes me. "'I love you' just doesn't properly convey that."

"Oh," I say.

"Stop thinking. Give your mind a break and just be with me." I slide closer to him and kiss him. By the time he bends me backward onto the bed I forget what we were even talking about.

"Amid promises not to think and others to comply"

I have something for you," Jason says as I walk him out to his truck.

"A new wardrobe?"

"Your wardrobe looks fine to me." Jason appraises me in my robe.

"You're decimating it. In the seven days we've been…together, you've ripped three shirts, one dress, and broken the zipper on my favorite pair of jeans." Jason reaches into his truck and pulls out a cowboy hat. He twirls it in his hands as I go on. "At this rate I'll be out of clothes by Labor Day."

"Maybe you should wear fewer clothes," he says, and places the hat on my head.

"I think there are laws associated with that type of behavior." I take the hat off to look at it. It's chocolate brown with a band around it embroidered with turquoise flowers. On the front a brass oval with turquoise flower petals anchors the band.

"Turquoise is my favorite color," I say, and continue to marvel at the hat.

"I know," Jason says, and lifts my lips to his. "Don't overthink us, Annie." He kisses me again and I want him to come back inside with me. I tell him with my body as I lean into him and grab him with my free hand. Jason laughs his evil little laugh.

"I have to go to work," he says, but his hard-on in my hand is telling a different story.

"You can work on me."

Jason gives in. He backs me into the garage and bends me back onto the trunk of my mother's Camry. *Sorry, Mom.* I unbuckle his belt and realize I'm holding my breath. I release it as I release him from his jeans. And here, with the garage door up, and my new hat on, I have Jason Leer for the twenty-fifth time over the last eight days.

I will not think. I will not think. I will not think.

* * *

Jason leaves just in time for me to shower before Sean arrives. He's been calling me every day and every day I promise him I'm okay, but I never mention Jason. When he called this morning he asked if I was alone and I realized I'm not hiding a thing from Sean. I've never been able to keep anything from him. I hear the garage door rising as I throw some lip gloss in my bag.

"Is this really necessary?" I ask as I climb in Sean's truck.

"You need a car. Unless you want to use Mom's Camry." I

watch the garage door lower on the Camry. It's not a bad car. "I'm not always going to be able to drive you to and from Rutgers." The now familiar weight of concern replaces Sean's easy nature.

"Noble always takes me," I answer, debating for no good reason.

"It's one of the things you need. If you have no parents you should have a car." With that we drive to Delaware in silence, both of us considering all the things we "need" since we have no parents. I'm sure our lists are completely different. Sean's is probably full of practical items, mine's inhabited solely by Jason Leer. He's my only life-sustaining device. Sean pulls in front of the Hummer dealership and my confusion renders me speechless.

"You ready?" he says, noting my paralysis.

"Ready for what? Why are we here?"

"To get you a Hummer. You need something safe."

"Sean O'Brien, you have completely lost your mind if you think I am going to drive around in a Hummer."

"What's wrong with a Hummer? They're very safe." I continue shaking my head. "After this we'll test drive the Suburban."

"It won't even fit in my driveway at Rutgers. Where the hell am I going to park it? You do realize there is only one of me?"

"Yes, and if you hit something in this vehicle I need you to walk away from it." Sean's jaw is tight, a sure sign he's not backing down.

"I get the idea." I start, trying to be considerate. "I don't want anything to happen to you, either. But this vehicle is not coming home with us. Ever."

"Are you going back to Rutgers?" *Where the hell else would*

I go? I'm beginning to think the stress is taking a toll on Sean.

"Why wouldn't I?"

"I don't know. You've been spending a lot of time with Jason Leer. I'm afraid you're going to do something crazy, like follow him to Oklahoma or something." My chest tightens at the thought of Oklahoma. A salesman walks out of the dealership and adjusts his shirt in his pants. He walks toward our truck and tears fill my eyes. *He can't go.* "Mom and Dad would want you to get a degree."

"Fuck Mom and Dad. I wanted them to live."

"Well, I'm alive and I want you to finish school!" Sean yells, and the man stops mid-step, realizing now is not a good time. "What the hell, Charlotte? They died. I get it. But you can't let it kill everything else in your life. Something has to keep going." He's calming, but the thought of returning to Rutgers, of leaving Jason, is making me angry. I'm trapped in my brother's logic and it makes me want to break the window next to me. The man walks back into the dealership, and Sean starts the truck and heads back east to New Jersey.

We drive in silence over the river. The bridge is down to one lane and the traffic slows just prior to the causeway. Sean turns up the radio, opens the windows, and turns to me with his "this is stupid" look, and I'm reminded of Sean's complete inability to maintain anger.

"Just stick with the plan," he says as he switches lanes. *Oh yes. Everything is going exactly as planned.* "If in a year you still want to do something rash, you can."

"Doesn't a rash decision, by definition, require a lack of thought? Not a year's worth?"

"Just keep your head on."

After that Sean doesn't say another word.

* * *

About a quarter mile from our parents' house, I can see Jason's truck in the driveway and my heart races with the anticipation of touching him. I hope Sean doesn't want to come in. Sean sees the truck, too. I know because his jaw clenches again, but he says nothing.

"This was fun," I say as I hop out of the truck.

"Good times," he adds, never taking his eyes off Jason's truck.

"Careful going home."

"You too," he counters, and slowly backs out, leaving me alone in the driveway.

And I was trying so hard not to think.

~ 8 ~

"Civility, gentility, can't survive without the lie"

He's gone. I know it before I open my eyes. They may as well just stay closed now. I roll over to his pillow. How long does it take to get your own pillow? If you're Jason Leer, and in my bed, apparently it takes a few hours. What must his father think? Does he even know he's here? He must think I'm a whore.

None of it matters.

I open my eyes and see a small piece of paper propped up against my lamp. In handwriting I haven't seen in years it says:

Today is Saturday.
Come to the rodeo.

Do orphans go to the rodeo? I have no idea who goes to the rodeo. I haven't been to it since I was a little girl. I text Jenn and Margo.

Will you go to the rodeo with me tonight?

From Jenn I get:

> Just because you are getting your
> cuckoo clocked by the cowboy every
> night does not mean I'm spending
> Saturday at the rodeo. But I'm glad
> to hear ur up to going out.

And from Margo:

> Of course we'll go. I'll tell Nick
> and Sam to take us.

* * *

Sam pulls into my driveway in his new Ford Expedition and Noble holds the back door open for me.

"Nice hat," he says.

"Thanks, Noble." I'm unable to keep a smile from him.

"Glad to see you out." He closes the door after me and climbs back into the front.

Noble lights a joint and we take the long way to the rodeo. When it's passed to me I hand it to Margo on my left. She takes it without a word. It's too soon to get high. I'm barely treading water at low.

My party of five is plenty high by the time we park at the Cowtown Rodeo. They giggle the entire way to the line, which by now is a few hundred people deep. As the funky bunch collectively tries to figure out the last time we were all at the rodeo, I scan the landscape for Jason Leer.

Cars and trucks are pouring into the entrance. The crowd is immense. I hear the ticket collector say they expect over four thousand people tonight. *Where are they coming from?* Their appearances offer no clues to their origins. There are families everywhere—black, white, Mexican, Puerto Rican—the children are adorned with new cowboy hats and stuffed horses. Some have wooden guns that pop when you pull the trigger.

"Good luck finding a seat tonight," the ticket collector says, and I try and figure out why I haven't been here since my childhood. Sam walks ahead and finds the end of a bench for us to share. It's actually a set of makeshift bleachers built into the side of a hill. The grandstands line both sides of the arena with primitive box seats at the top. There's a country band playing and an announcer saying something I can't quite decipher. On the other side of Jenn a Mennonite boy chews and spits tobacco directly onto the ground. The lady in front of him doesn't seem to mind. There are men and women lining the walkway behind the seats, all smoking cigarettes. It's as if we've stepped back in time, but I was never alive when this time occurred.

Jenn sits close on my left; her crazy, curly brown hair blows over my face when she moves. Margo to my right is the exact opposite. She has straight blond hair and a slight adherence to rules. Jenn reaches in her camouflage tote and pulls out a beer. She cracks it open and smiles at me.

"What are you doing?" I ask in complete disbelief, unable to take my eyes off her beer.

"Quenching my thirst," she says, and takes a long gulp. Her complete disregard of the legal drinking age, and her not having reached it, remind me of how my mother used to yell, "Do not get arrested!" every time Jenn and Margo would pick me up. And she didn't know the half of it. I close my eyes and shake my head.

The announcer welcomes us to the "greatest show on dirt" and names each branch of the military, inviting servicemen to stand for our applause as he does. The crowd is speckled with servicemen and women who are met with cheers and screams. The children all join in, having no idea what they're cheering for as the announcer explains, "Without the sacrifice of these men and women, none of us have the right to be here."

We turn our attention to the far gate as a woman in a bright red, sparkly shirt comes speeding into the arena on a galloping horse. She carries the American flag in one hand and turns the horse on a dime, heading back toward the center of the arena. *I don't ever want to be on a horse going that fast, and damn that flag must be heavy.* The announcer asks us to continue standing and bow our heads as we exercise our freedom of religion for the cowboy prayer.

At this, I almost take the beer out of Jenn's hand and down it. Rutgers, in all its diversity, has reduced public prayer to an awkward ritual. The student population is rich in cultures, races, and religions. I've flourished there, and learned more about the world in two years than a lifetime of study other schools could provide. But I've also learned to listen more than I speak, and respect others views by not always expressing my own. This public display of Christianity has become foreign to me in two short years. Intellectually it is uncomfortable, but in reality the sense of community and shared purpose warm me.

Until I bow my head and realize I'm not talking to God any-more. Not on behalf of these cowboys, not for Jason Leer, and not for myself, because he took away the two people I should never have to live without.

Our gracious and heavenly Father, we pause

The words over the speakers turn in my stomach and I defi-antly open my eyes. I look toward the arena and directly into the eyes of Jason Leer sitting on the fence fifteen feet from us. He holds his head high under his giant hat, his eyes are fixed on me, and rather than praying he's looking straight through to my soul.

We only ask that you help us to compete as honest as the horses we ride and in a manner as clean and pure as the wind blows across this great land of ours

With that a breeze blows, pushing my hair across my face. The air makes me realize how hot I was under Jason's stare. As I push my hair back and place my new cowboy hat back on my head Jason smiles a devilish grin. *What the hell are you doing to me, Jason Leer?*

These things we ask. Amen.

The girl on the horse takes off toward the gate and the rodeo begins without enough warning. Out of the first gate a bull rider is released with the bull bucking into the air. The cowboy holds on until the horn blows, signifying the end of his eight-second ride. He lets go, falls on his feet, and runs and jumps on the fence to avoid being impaled by the bull. The rodeo clowns distract the bull and the cowboy runs out of the arena.

"It's so fast," I say to no one in particular.

"The most exciting eight seconds in sports," Sam says, and I shake my head. Why on earth would anyone want to compete in this arena? Five more bull riders take their turns on bulls randomly picked and named such things as Guacamole, Zoro, and Beasty Boy. The bulls and the cowboys all manage to survive and I relax, the danger averted for now. Jason is nowhere to be found. I lost sight of him when the bulls came out.

The announcer focuses our attention on the near end of the arena for steer wrestling. According to my program Jason is the second competitor. *Or is it wrestler?* The first wrestler, Brad Riley, rides his horse out of the chute and follows the steer right out of the gate on the other side of the arena.

"What happened?"

"He didn't catch him in time. He has to dive off his horse onto the steer," Sam explains.

"Too bad, folks. Let's show Brad some Cowtown love. He just spent the $100 entry plus gas to get here and is going home empty-handed," the announcer says, as we all clap for Brad.

I can see Jason on his horse inside the gate farthest from me. Between us is another guy on a horse. Ollie, I think. The gates open and the steer runs out first. Jason chases him and dives off his horse onto the steer. My eyes never leave Jason's body as he digs his heels in the dirt until the steer stops, then twists the steer until he falls onto his side and back. Jason stands up as the announcer says, "How about a Cowtown hand for our local boy Jason Leer and his outstanding 4.4-second run that puts him in first place."

Jason turns toward me and I let the air out of my lungs. How long had I not been breathing? Four-point-four seconds, I guess. The bull riding frightened me, but watching Jason steer wrestle does something completely different to me. I take a deep breath and watch him walk out of the arena.

"Damn, Leer kicked that steer's ass," Sam says.

"Yes he did," Margo adds, and we all stare at the arena as the next wrestlers take their turns, none of which are able to beat 4.4 seconds. Just like that. He won.

We stay seated, my friends' high dissipating as Jenn drinks her purse beers. We watch the Bareback Riding, which is right out of the Wild West. These guys are getting their asses kicked and still don't let go until the horn. Saddle Bronc Riding is next and seems only slightly more civilized. There are fewer entrants than Bareback because really, why use a saddle if you're into this in the first place? Next on the program is something called Tie Down Roping. A cowboy on a horse chases a calf and then lassos him. The calf looks like it's choked out as the cowboy jumps off his horse, throws the calf down and then ties three of its legs together.

"Oh God. How barbaric," I say, my face trapped in horror for the calf.

"It's not as bad as it looks," Sam says, as the calf gets up and prances out of the arena as if it's had the best night of its life.

"Yeah, if you're an animal in Salem County you'd rather spend your Saturday nights with the cowboys than the hunters," Jenn adds.

"I guess. I'm going to go to the bathroom." I need a break from the rodeo before God-knows-what event comes next.

"Don't get lost. I think we're leaving soon," Margo says, and it sounds like some other warning.

I climb over Margo and Noble, and make my way to the bathrooms. There's a short line in which I say hello to Mrs. Heitter and Ms. Cioffi. They both have no idea what to say to me so instead of searching for the right thing, just stumble over their condolences and end it with a big hug. *I don't know what to say either.* I stand facing the empty bathrooms alone, and cry for my mother. She didn't want me in this world, I think as I look around the arena without an ounce of guilt.

I didn't want her to leave mine.

***

When I come out Jason is leaning on the fence railing directly across from the bathrooms. He's alone and appears to be waiting for me, but how did he know I was here? I walk toward him and stop about three feet away, which he apparently finds hilarious.

"That might have been the most impressive thing I've ever seen," I say, bursting with admiration.

"More impressive than when I took you from behind last night? I saw you watching in the mirror."

My mouth falls open and my cheeks burn. *Appropriateness, respect, manners, tact, civility, gentility—ever heard of them?* My eyes harden on him. He is so awful, and yet I want to throw him to the ground and climb on top of him. He's the most beautiful torture I've ever known. Jason stands up straight, watching me with his playful gray eyes reading the code of my DNA.

"Save the silence for someone else," he says, challenging me. "I know you've got plenty of words in there. You can say one." Images of last night flash through my mind and a light sweat covers my body. I swallow hard at the memory of him…hard.

"Decorum," I say, still not moving any closer to him and the smile that crosses his face sends a chill down the back of my neck.

"Oooh, a big one." Jason holds out his hand and I take it and let him pull me toward him as his lips find my ear and he says, "I love it when you watch." I kiss him because he's depleted all my control and because he has to stop talking. At least like this. We are, after all in public. He kisses the side of my face as his hand threads into my hair and pulls it. His lips move to my ear again and his breath there buckles my knees. Jason holds me up and I open my eyes to center myself.

"You smell like smoke. Are you high?" He asks.

"No," I answer without thinking. He pulls me back to see me.

"No?" he asks again, doubting my answer.

"I already answered the question," I instinctively say, and he laughs a little and returns me to him. Almost as abruptly, he moves me away and looks over my shoulder, annoyed.

"Hey Leer, that was awesome," Sam says, and breaks Jason's spell on me. Is that why he's annoyed? Noble, Jenn, and Margo follow Sam and all express their astonishment over Jason's "sport."

"We're headed out to Stoners Lane after this if you want to come hang out," Noble says to Jason, and I watch him, curious for his answer.

Without even a glance in my direction he says, "Thanks, but I've started a new nighttime routine recently and I'm committed to it." I lower my head so no one can see me. I'm sure my cheeks are turning purple.

"I'm actually not in the mood for Stoners. Can you give me a ride home?" I ask Jason, and suddenly, I have everyone's attention.

"I'll give you a ride," he says, and all four thousand people in this arena disappear. I am ready to throw him down right here. Him and the shit-eating grin splattered across his face.

"Oh no you don't. It's Saturday!" Jenn practically shouts.

"It's okay. Let's take it easy. It's only been a few weeks," Margo says as she grabs Jenn's arm. "We'll call you tomorrow. Get some rest." She collects them all and leads them away without anyone seeming to even notice my absence.

* * *

"I want to tie you up," Jason says without taking his eyes off the road. I stare at his profile, the oncoming headlights illuminating it in a dark rhythm. He turns off Route 40 and we're completely alone on Auburn Road. Completely alone.

"Then you should."

His wicked smirk barely moves his face, but lights up his eyes. "Have you ever been tied up before?"

"No," I say, unaffected, and this makes him smile. I amuse him.

"Were you telling the truth when you said you'd never had an orgasm before?"

"Is that something people often lie about?" I ask, and tilt my head to see the stars. There are millions, as far as I can see, and I try to comprehend how I ended up here, in this truck, with this cowboy. According to Pastor Johnson it was planned before I was even born. The sharp pain of guilt stabs me in the stomach. Can someone be forgiven for giving God the big F-U?

"Do you ever lie?" Jason's voice soothes me and I turn toward him and move across the truck seat. He lifts his arm and wraps it around my shoulders. He smells of cigarettes and dirt and the combination is beginning to appeal to me. I slide my hand between his thighs.

"I'm rarely in a situation where lying is necessary."

"Didn't you have a boyfriend at Rutgers?" he asks, and his question is so innocent. It's as if we're on a first date.

"No. It all seemed very immediate, and temporary." I think back over all the conversations I've had with guys at college. Noble is probably the most meaningful male relationship I've had there. "Violet's had a boyfriend since freshmen year. She's the boyfriend type. The rest just have different levels of entertainment."

"Surely you've at least hooked-up with people."

"A few here and there. Formal dates. Very randomly, but once in a while, someone piques my interest at a party." Jason kisses the top of my head. His gentleness seems so distant. "Mostly they make fun of my southern accent and my height. Tall blondes aren't as common in North Jersey as in South Jersey."

"I wouldn't call you common in any region," he says, as he pulls into my parents' driveway and those are the last words he speaks.

* * *

I turn my head toward the morning light and see my belt still hanging from the corner post of my headboard. Without looking I know there is a matching one on the other side. I swallow hard at the memories of last night. My cheeks burn as I remember crying out as I came, blindfolded and bound. This cannot be wrong. God would not have created something in this universe that's this good and then made it wrong. His words, whispered near my face, again ring in my head, "I'm only going to leave you blindfolded for a while. It's not the same for me without your green eyes, but I want you to feel it." I shiver and curl my knees to my chest. I am sore from my ankles to my wrists. Even my lip hurts from when he yanked it with his teeth. He is an animal. I am fucking an animal. The chill moves from my cheeks to my chest and travels down as I roll toward him. He smiles without opening his eyes and seems like the gentlest beast in the jungle. I climb on top of him, straddling him as I kiss every inch of his neck with tiny, sweet kisses. By the time I'm able to see him, he is practically laughing. I squeeze my legs around the enormous width of his waist and kiss him fiercely; more his pace. I stop and look into his gray eyes, now completely void of humor.

"I love you, Jason Leer." It's like old habit. How long have I loved him?

"I know." He sits up, still beneath me. He kisses me and his hard-on jabs into my leg. Without thinking, I rise up and guide him into me. *That's better*. There's no need for provocative foreplay with Jason. His very presence renders me ready, up for anything. He raises me up with his hands supporting my bottom. He pulls me down hard and the air is forced from my chest. Even on top, I surrender to him. He is always in control, and it's so good. I ride Jason until the images of last night enter my mind and I close my eyes and raise my face to the ceiling. He slows his pace.

"What are you thinking about?"

"Last night," I say, and verbalizing the words sends a chill to both nipples. I open my eyes and look down. *You love it when I watch*. I watch as I again begin to rise and fall on top of the great Jason Leer. I forget to blush, forget to be embarrassed, and forget I am an orphan as I come with Jason Leer in me for the thousandth time.

* * *

I wrap my arms around his neck and Oklahoma crashes into my mind. I hold him tighter, willing him to stay with me forever, and he pulls me back to face him.

"I'm right here," he says, and I start to cry. He lays me down next to him, his hand on my breast, and curls up at my side. He nuzzles his face in my neck and whispers in my ear, "I will always be right here, Annie."

~ 9 ~

"What have you lost, my soul begs me to see"

I'll pick you up at seven. Wear your dirty shoes," he adds and I shake my head slightly in confusion.

"I don't have dirty shoes," I say before I have time to figure out why anyone would have dirty shoes.

"What?" He asks, equally confused.

"If they were dirty I would either clean them or replace them. I don't have dirty shoes."

"Don't you ever walk through the fields around here?"

"Rarely anymore."

Jason considers my statements. I assume most of the girls he hangs out with have dirty shoes. For some reason, out of all the differences in our lives, this distinction makes me insecure. Not enough to own dirty shoes, but it's an odd longing.

"I'll figure something out," I say, and he walks out the door. I run after him.

"Jason!" He turns to me, halfway to his truck already. "Call me if something comes up." He's never called me. How is it possible in the past month he has never called, never texted, not once? Jason walks back, his gray eyes lit; they are almost blue in the morning sunlight.

"Are you concerned I never call you?" *No, I'm concerned you always know what I'm thinking.* "Because there's no need to call you."

"What if something happens? Things do happen."

"Nothing will happen. If I say I'm going to be here, I'll be here." *Right.*

* * *

I stress about dirty shoes all day. Surely, in the wake of my parents' tragic death, I could find something else to stress about. Even beyond my own personal strife there's world hunger, terrorist organizations, and ship hijacking. All kinds of screwed-up stuff, but nooo, it's dirty shoes that occupy my mind.

I settle on a white eyelet dress. It's a tank top with a full skirt that hits mid-calf. It will hopefully hide the green Hunter boots I'm sporting beneath it. In the mirror it's fine. The dress is so pretty it draws the eye up, but my reflection is funny. And I know it. These boots can survive just about anything, though. They can get as dirty as he wants. That idea gets me hot. I finish brushing my teeth as I hear his truck door close. He appears in my bedroom doorway as I'm looking for my denim jacket in my closet. I don't think I took it to Rutgers.

"Hey," I say, and hold my breath. I defiantly let it out. These boots are only going to work if I force them to.

"Hey yourself. You ready to go?" he asks.

"Where are we going?"

"A Jackpot. Out by the Harrison farm," he says, and begins to study the pictures on my dresser. Most of them are from high school. He pauses at a picture of Margo and me from a swim meet. We're in our swimsuits and caps and hugging each other as if the end of time is near. "How come you didn't swim in college?" I stop searching, but don't turn to him. "You're picture was always in the paper for winning."

"Did you like those? Was it the sexy suit or the goggles?" I ask, blushing from his memories.

"You didn't answer me." *I hate you sometimes.*

"Can we talk about something else?" Jason moves from my dresser to stand directly in front of me. He's close and I reach out to him from habit. The habit of wanting.

"There's nothing you can't say to me," he says, and I feel the truth of his words in my bones. He grabs my wrists and I wince at the cutting pain. He freezes and examines each one as he rubs his thumbs over them. They are red and bruised and my right one has a small blister on it. Jason's face is stricken.

"It's not about not telling you. I'm pretty clear on your complete lack of boundaries." He brings each wrist to his lips and kisses them, running his lips back and forth over them. I watch in awe as the chill runs through me.

"Never again," he says.

"It was the opposite of hurting me." I see my denim jacket hanging out of the corner of the blanket chest at the end of my bed. I pass Jason, expecting him to stop me and force a response from me regarding the swim team, but he lets me go. I grab the jacket and walk out of my room.

Jason follows me to his truck and passes me right before I reach the passenger door. He opens it and takes out a pair of cowboy boots. They're light tan with turquoise and red throughout.

"They were my mom's," he says, with an unspoken question.

"I would be honored," I answer, and relief spreads across his face. I take off my Hunters and throw them back into the garage and put on his mother's boots.

Jason backs out of my driveway and onto the road without stopping for the nonexistent traffic. He puts the truck in drive and reaches out to me. He pulls me to him by the wrist and I yelp in pain.

"We need to take better care of you," he says, without a hint of guilt.

"I'm in awe of the care I'm receiving." I rub my wrists. "Perhaps something softer than a belt would help."

* * *

Jason pulls off the road onto a dirt lane just east of the Harrison Farm. We drive a half mile before I can see anything but pastures, fence, and fields. As we hit the peak of a hill there are lights in the distance. It looks like a football field lit up for Friday night about five acres away. Jason pulls next to a line of trucks and hops out.

"What is a jackpot?" I ask, remembering for the first time since Jason arrived at my house where we're supposed to be going.

"This one is like a one-event rodeo, in someone's backyard. They're not all the same." Jason grabs the cooler between us and jumps out of the truck. "Let's go take these cowboys' money." I follow him and try to take in the sights. There's one field surrounded by fence and lit by huge, mobile lighting rigs.

It has a chute at one end and people lining the fence on all sides. Jason greets Possum, who smiles warmly at me.

"Hey, Charlotte."

"Hi, Possum. How's it going?"

"Pretty good. You thinking of switching from swimming to bulldogging?"

"Bulldogging?" I say, hoping this arena has nothing to do with dogs.

"Steer wrestling," Possum says. "Who's hazing for you tonight?" He turns his questions to Jason.

"Ollie is supposed to be out here."

"He just pulled in about fifteen minutes ago. Good luck," Possum says, and I see Jason hand him fifty dollars.

Jason deposits me halfway along the fence and takes out a beer. He opens it and hands it to me. The air is still and the night is warm. I left my jacket in the truck and I'm glad I did. The crude benches of the Cowtown Rodeo seem like a VMA production compared to this jackpot. It is literally in someone's backyard. He opens a beer for himself and practically downs it.

"Should you be drinking before…" I pause. Before what? What the hell is he doing? "Before wrestling steer?"

"I'll be all right."

"Weren't you offered a football scholarship at Oklahoma? What's wrong with football?" I ask, a little hysterical at the thought of him again wrestling a steer.

"Football's not physical enough. I like it rough." My breath turns shallow; I'm almost panting. Jason notes the change and leans in. "Now steer wrestling, that's physical."

We see the other cowboys lining up and Jason leaves me alone on the fence.

Ollie and Jason have known each other their entire lives. Who hasn't around here? They stand to the side talking and I can hear their laughter but not their words. Eventually, they walk farther from me and I can't see their faces anymore. The people lining the fence are in groups of two or three and all seem completely unaffected by the approaching competition. I, on the other hand, can barely keep it together. Why does he have to wrestle steer? I try to calm myself. This is what he does. It's who he is. Take it or leave it. I remember my mother saying this was a horrible life and I'm beginning to understand why. *God, I wish she was here.*

* * *

The first competitor comes out of the chute and dives off his horse. It happens so fast. I can barely keep up with my vision. On the horse. Off the horse. On the steer. On the ground. Done. I hear a guy a few feet down say he clocked him at 7.5. Apparently this Jackpot is void of the high-tech announcements and timing devices associated with the rodeo.

"Leer's here." I hear them say, but I never take my eyes off the arena, too afraid to miss him.

"Oh, well this thing is tied up. What's he doing home this summer anyway? I would have figured he'd be on the road," the guy farthest from me says.

"I heard Old Man Martin practically begged him to come home. He needed help with the ranch since his stroke. Lord knows he could be winning a lot more money on the road."

Another steer is released and two men on horses chase him. The cowboy dives off his horse and lands behind the steer, who continues to run right out the opposite gate in the fence. The cowboy's slow to get up and my dread at Jason's run quadruples. The other cowboy who rode with him gets off his horse and lends a hand to pull him up. He waves to the fence and a collective sigh is let out. I take another beer out of the cooler and drink it too fast.

I put the empty can back in the cooler as I see Jason on a horse in the gate. He's saying something to Ollie and then he's set. He nods and the gate opens and the steer runs. Jason follows from behind, catches him, dives and wrestles him to the ground.

"Holy! What time was that?" I hear, and release my breath.

"I got it at 4.8. That boy is quick." I'm smiling, but my stomach is still knotted.

***

After ten minutes, Jason emerges from the other side of the fence. There are still wrestlers competing, but most of the crowd are already congratulating him. He stops to speak to a few. I've never seen anyone more comfortable with their surroundings. He runs this place. By the time he gets to me I'm three beers in the hole. His proximity calms me and the knots release.

"I have so many questions."

"About bulldogging or something else?" Jason opens the cooler and pauses at the sight of the empty cans. He opens a beer and replaces the lid.

"Steer wrestling, although I would love to know what bulldogging is. I don't understand what's happening. It goes too fast."

"Bulldogging is steer wrestling."

"Helps. What's the point of Ollie?" Jason laughs at this.

"He's my hazer. He rides to direct the steer. He makes it possible for me to be close enough to catch him. My hazer at school's a guy named Harlan. He's the best I've ever ridden with, but he's traveling this summer," Jason says, and I wonder how little he wanted to come home and help Mr. Martin. He stands behind me and points over my shoulder to the gate. "Watch this ride. The steer's released first. He gets a head start." Jason's lips near my neck make it difficult to concentrate.

The steer shoots out of the gate followed by the two cowboys. *The bulldogger and the hazer.* The bulldogger dives off his horse onto the steer and twists its neck until it falls to the ground.

"That was a good run," Jason says, and leans back to listen to the people next to us.

"I got him at 5.8," the guy says, and Jason seems pleased.

"Do you always win?" I ask as I watch the next run.

"No one always wins, Annie. It's like life." My mouth dries as the memories of death creep up on my happiness. Jason watches me, knowing loss himself. I take a long sip of my beer and smile at my beautiful friend. He went through all this first. *I love you.*

He turns me around and kisses me, willing me to forget, at least for now. I hear the men next to us talking about the last run. I let go of our loss and remember where we are, and the fact that he is awesome on a horse.

"You seem like you're better than everyone else."

"I'm good, but there are a lot of things happening at the same time. It's not like being able to swim a race fast, in a lane, without other things going on in the environment. There's weather: it's a rain-or-shine sport. There's the fact I'm wrestling a live animal which hasn't shook my hand and agreed to certain rules prior to the run. There's also my horse, or in this case Ollie's horse, that I was riding, to deal with. There are a thousand things that can happen. Every run is different from the last." My stomach knots again. I knew it wasn't like other sports. "That's the fun of it."

"I have to go to the bathroom."

"I'm not surprised," he says, and takes a second beer out of the cooler. "A six pack might have been underestimating a bit. There is no bathroom."

"I'm not surprised. How about that tree line?" Jason motions for me to lead the way. We pass a few trucks until we're about fifty yards from the fence and all the spectators. I walk just into the woods and search for a spot. His mother's boots catch my eye. I take them off and lean them against a tree. I move three feet into the woods and squat to pee. I lean over and see Jason laughing.

"What is so funny?"

"You don't have dirty shoes, but you have no problem peeing in the woods?" he says, and I don't get the distinction.

"You shouldn't judge a girl by her shoes," I say as I finish.

I turn to Jason and walk toward the boots. He meets me at the tree and pins me between it and the wall that is his chest. With his arms at his sides, he kisses me and the chill travels through me like an infection. It invades every inch of me, debilitating my brain first. I run my hands up his forearms. They are superhuman. I stretch my fingers around the outsides. My hands betray me and jump to his zipper. They're rewarded with a bulge waiting to be released. I stop kissing Jason and look down as I slide my hand between his legs and slowly bring it toward the front again. My eyes rise to meet Jason's and he looks sad. Even this doesn't move me. I can't be considerate of his thoughts or emotions. I have to have him. I unbuckle his giant buckle and unbutton his pants. The look on his face doesn't change. I unzip his jeans and slide my hand in. My eyes close and I feel him throughout my body as I hold my hand still, gripping him. The chill pulls my chin to my chest as it rises up through my breasts. I have never known anything like Jason Leer. I open my eyes and they beg him to touch me.

"You're going to be the death of me, Annie."

Jason grabs my shoulders and forces me against the tree. He hooks one hand under my knee and raises my leg above his waist. I kiss him and pull his hair with both hands to try and hold on to something. His thick neck pulls against my hands and I gyrate on him. My body no longer belongs to me. Jason releases himself with one hand and enters me in the dark of night, against a tree on the Harrison farm. I whimper, having just enough grasp on the world to know I cannot make noise. The realization excites me further as I open my eyes and see the lights of the jackpot. He thrusts into me, and each time I want more. I'm pinned between Jason and the tree, my foot barely touching the ground. He kisses my neck and pulls at my skin with his teeth, all the while continuing to have me, and I cannot take it. I come and fall limp in his arms. Jason continues and each time he's in me I convulse. He's holding me up and fucking me at the same time, yet still barely breaking a sweat. The guy is not human.

He comes and I rest my head against the tree behind me. Air enters my chest, and I smell the animals nearby. I belong here; an animal myself. A breeze blows past me and I look up at the stars, still clinging to Jason Leer.

I look down and see Jason watching me as he zippers his pants and hooks his belt buckle. He hands me his mother's boots and as I bend over to put them on I realize my lovely white eyelet dress is covered in dirt.

"It looks like I wrestled the steer," I say.

"This is almost over. Maybe you should wait in the truck while I go collect our money."

"You think?" I ask sarcastically. "It looks like I just banged the winning bulldogger." Jason smiles at my proper use of steer wrestling vocabulary.

* * *

Jason walks into my house and straight to the shower. He turns the water on and takes a towel out of the linen closet as if he lives here. He kind of does. I drop my denim jacket and purse on the floor, and try to pull my dress over my head but it catches on something and scrapes my back. It's pinned to me. I turn on the light to see my back in the mirror. My dress is torn. There's dried blood on it and it's sticking to my back—to a cut on my back. *This is what happens when you have sex against a tree.*

"Let me see," he says, and turns me around. He pulls the dress from my back in a motion that reminds me of my father ripping a Band-Aid off, and I wince. Jason grabs some toilet paper and covers the cut. "I'm sorry, Annie." I turn toward Jason and he keeps his hand holding the toilet paper over the cut. His face is drawn with concern. "Believe it or not, I do try and control myself around you."

"Don't worry about my body." I pull his face toward mine, holding it in both hands. "It's never felt anything as amazing as you inside of it." At this Jason relaxes. "Worry about my wardrobe."

"Charlotte Anne! I thought I told you not to fall in love with a cowboy." My mother looks even prettier when she's angry. She's in my bedroom, standing over my bed, as I try to wake-up. "I know you are awake and you hear me," she says, proving she is not going anywhere.

"Mom, you can't choose who you fall in love with."

"Oh honey, you can. And you are making the wrong choice."

"Aren't you supposed to say you'll support me no matter who I love?"

"No baby, that's only in the movies. Real moms tell you the truth. I don't want you in his world and he's not going to like it in yours."

"I can't let him go. I've lost too much."

"What have you lost, Charlotte?" I try to remember what I've lost. It's been so much. I've been through so much. What is it? Why can't I think of what I've lost?

I wake up crying and frustrated. Jason rolls over and puts his arm around me.

"What's wrong?"

"I had a bad dream. My mother was in it," I say, and leave off the part about Jason.

"I still dream about my mother all the time," he says sadly.

"Was it easier that you had time to say good-bye? I wish I'd had a chance to say good-bye."

"How do you say good-bye to your mom?" Jason says, and I cry some more. He's right. Time doesn't help. You're never old enough to lose your mom.

"Annie, come to Oklahoma with me. Transfer to Oklahoma." The dream of my mother runs through my head and the words of my brother. *Be careful going home.* Jason and I are lost souls, together. I don't want to answer him. I don't want to answer myself. I want to surrender to Jason again, to go to Oklahoma with him and live this life forever, but I know the answer for now is no and it brings neither of us any solace.

I roll toward him, still locked under his iron arm, and slide down to bury my face in his chest.

"You can't hide from me, Annie."

"I know," is all I say because he knows everything.

~ 10 ~

"While all I can plead is your home is with me"

I'm folding laundry for what might be the first time all summer when my phone dings with a text from Julia. She and the rest of the Rutgers girls have been calling and texting every day. I rarely answer.

Violet and I are going to the shore this weekend. Come with us.

It's too soon.

The phone rings before I set it down. I know without looking it's Julia, unhappy with my answer.

"Hey," I say, bracing myself.

"You love the shore. Why won't you come?"

"I just think it's too soon. I'm not ready for the shore," I say, and cannot believe how weak I sound. My voice never sounds like this with Jason.

"I called Jenn this morning. She told me you've been hanging out with the cowboy. What the hell is going on?" Julia sounds pissed off. That must be some misplaced emotion, right? Can you be pissed at the girl whose parents were just killed in a car accident?

"It's been one month. What exactly should I be doing differently?"

"Look, Charlotte. We miss you. We're worried about you. Violet and I are going crazy up here; you're not online, you don't text, we never see you. Then I talk to Jenn and apparently she and Margo aren't seeing much of you either. Of course we're worried. I know this is hard, but you've got to lean on the people you've trusted your whole life, not some cowboy."

"Why do you say it as if it disgusts you? He's not *some cowboy*." I am pissed. "I've known him my entire life, too, and to date he has yet to call me and yell at me for my behavior, or lack thereof!"

"You're missing my point," she says, a bit gentler.

"No, I got your point. I'm not coming up. I'll be up there in a few weeks and I'll see you and Violet then," I say, ending the conversation. "Thanks for calling," I add, and hang up.

Now I feel completely horrible. What the fuck? And why is she talking to Jenn? It's as if my grief counseling team in Salem County is preparing for the patient transport to New Brunswick. Margo and Jenn will soon be replaced with Julia, Violet, and Sydney.

I fold the towels with a new verve and question whether Julia's words have any merit. She doesn't really expect me to be online one month after my parents' death, does she? I get up and walk to the computer to Google local grief share programs. I think there's one at my church. Maybe I should talk to someone. I have no idea what I should be doing in the wake of my parents' death. When the Google window pops up I type "Steer Wrestling" in the search box.

Images of steer wrestlers diving off horses onto steers, riding alongside, and wrestling on the ground pop up on the screen. It slows the action and I'm able to mentally connect it with the five-second memories I have in my head. I type in "Rules of Bulldogging" and expect the computer to laugh at me, but it lists different resources with steer wrestling rules. One website describes it as the Big Man's Event because many of the steer wrestlers are large, hefty cowboys. *I wish you were here.* It requires strength, speed, and timing. I Google "Rodeo's Big Man Event" and it's like I'm reading about some alien competition amongst super heroes. Articles describe the bulldogger leaping from the back of a galloping horse at thirty miles per hour onto a four hundred-and-fifty-pound steer with the goal of stopping it and putting it on its back. *What the hell is wrong with you, Jason Leer?* Maybe some perspective wouldn't hurt.

I text Jenn:

Do you want to go out?

I get back from her:

I'll be right over.

Within a half hour Jenn and Margo are both at my doorstep. They help me fold sheets and towels. *What am I going to do with all these sheets? With all these beds?* They're excited to see me, as if today is the first day I'm home from college and I realize I've neglected them. Probably Julia and Violet, too.

"So, where are we going?" Jenn asks, not hiding her excitement.

"We have two great options," Margo offers. "Sam's parents are at their shore house. We can either go there, or have a barbeque at his house here."

"Not the shore. Not yet," I say.

"It might be good for you," she tries again.

"I'm not interested in what's good for me," I say without a hint of humor. "Where do you guys think I should be one month out in this whole grief process?" I ask because every person I know must know more about this than I do. I can't remember even being sad while my mom and dad were alive, let alone working through grief.

"I don't know, but if we string twelve of these together, you'll have made it a year and that's got to be better than now," Margo says as her phone rings and she walks out of the room answering it. Jenn's phone dings with a text and I sense the momentum of a party brewing.

"Promise me this will be a small barbeque," I plead.

"No promises!" Jenn yells on her way out the door. "They're always broken in the end."

* * *

I want Jason to come with me to the barbeque. There's no reason why he shouldn't. He knows every single person there. That doesn't change the fact that if I wasn't "dating" him, he would never show up there. Even in such a small town, there are groups, cliques, fashions. Jason is absolutely from a different group. I cowardly text him:

> I'm going to a barbeque at Sam's house tonight and I want you to come with me.

It's the first text I've ever sent him. I don't even know if he checks his phone often. If he doesn't respond by lunch, I'll call him. I think the more notice he has, the better. Notice of what? It's a barbeque, for goodness sake. As I put my phone on the table it rings and my heart drops. Of course he's not going to text back. He's archaic.

"Hello?" *Why is this a question?*

"You're going to a barbeque, huh?"

"I'm hoping we're going to a barbeque." I realize now that I knew before I sent the text that Jason is not going to this barbeque.

"Call me and I'll bring you home," he says without a hint of irritation.

"Really? It might be late."

"It'll be worth the wait," he says, and I'm practically purring. This is going to be the longest barbeque of my life.

* * *

Noble picks me up first and we head into town to collect Margo and Jenn. I turn to Noble and marvel at him as he drives, completely oblivious to my appraisal. His father's farm has provided the perfect tan and highlighted his curly brown hair. Tonight the blue in his eyes is intensified by the navy t-shirt snugly covering his chest. He is a very handsome boy.

"Julia called me today," he says, and I'm not surprised.

"Did you tell her I'm going out tonight? Apparently, she is very concerned with my social life." Noble half-laughs at me and I suspect he received an earful about "the cowboy."

"She's worried."

"I'll see her in two weeks," I say, dismissing the subject. I already feel terrible about hanging up on her. I'll add Julia to the distinguished list of people I need to apologize to. She's right behind God and Pastor Johnson.

"Speaking of, when do you want to go back to Rutgers? I was thinking we could go up about a week early." His question is a small glimpse of my old life. Noble always takes me to school.

"I'm not sure I need a ride. Can I let you know later?"

"You're going back, right?" He's alarmed. They'll all be meeting with Sean soon.

"Yes. My parents would want me to." I leave it at that, not saying that's the only reason.

* * *

The four of us pull off Route 40 and the lights fall behind us. Dusk comes quicker now that summer is waning. The sky rages red in the distance. Tomorrow will be beautiful.

"Red sky at night, sailors delight," I say, and Jenn and Margo turn in their seats to see the sunset.

"Oooh that's a great one," Margo agrees.

Noble turns into Sam's driveway. His house is old money. It's one of the mansions that still have a name attached to it. The "Old McGlynn House," it's called. When it's discussed, it's followed by "you know, the one Dr. Hanson had until he died." It's brick on all sides with a front-facing garage. It's big enough that the garage doesn't have to be turned to look substantial. There are five enormous double windows on the front and Mrs. Shabo always puts Christmas lights in each one that make it look like they have five trees. Sam's dad made a fortune creating and selling a tech company during the boom and now continues to create new software and companies to sell. He's new money, but his parents loved the idea of country living so instead of buying in one of the new developments the next county over, they bought this place. I couldn't be more in love with the Old McGlynn House if I lived in it myself.

Cars pull off his driveway and onto the side lawn, which is more like a pasture minus the cattle. I don't know why we don't just park out front until I see Clint carrying saw horses out of the back of his truck to block the yard.

"Hey, Clint," Jenn yells out the window. "What's up with the parking at this barn?"

"Sprinkler system out front."

"Oh," she says. Of course, a sprinkler system. I'm guessing that wasn't here when it was the Old McGlynn House. I hear what sounds like a band warming up in the distance. The guitar chords sour as they blare through speakers somewhere behind the house.

"What the hell is that?" I moan. "A band?"

"Think of it as two guys doing an acoustical set," Margo says, and Noble starts laughing at all three of us. "Can you hand me my bag?" I struggle to hand Margo the bag as we get out of the Jeep.

"What's in here?"

"Bathing suits and towels for when we go swimming or in

the hot tub. I figured you wouldn't remember to bring one." It never occurred to me.

* * *

We walk around the side of the house and the backyard is an oasis. The entire town talked about all the work the new owners were doing on the Old McGlynn House when the Shabos first moved in. The paver patio and outdoor kitchen were big news. The idea of a refrigerator and sink built into a patio was foreign in Salem County.

There are people everywhere, but the yard is separated into sections, making it seem like the perfect crowd. Sam is at the keg station, three large tubs with a keg in each. He's pouring beers and entertaining anyone in earshot.

Jenn and I get beers for Margo and Noble and realize after a moment of reversible deafness that we're standing too close to the speakers. Nicole Dickson comes over and quickly consumes Noble's attention. They make a cute couple. Not that he is looking to be a couple. I wish he would settle down. *Why do I care?* We move to the kitchen area, now littered with open bags of chips and a few hoagies. There's a roll of paper towels and a large knife to cut the sandwiches. It's a far cry from the spread Mrs. Shabo put out for Sam's graduation party. Then the food itself took up a quarter of the yard. What would anger her more; that Sam threw a party, or that he threw *this* party?

Margo pulls me by the arm, leading me into the house. She carries two bathing suits in her hand.

"Let's go swimming. We can kick these kids' asses in a race," she says.

"I don't race anymore." I tilt my head as if she should know better.

"Sorry," Margo apologizes for the memory.

I remember the look of disappointment on my parents' faces when I told them I wouldn't swim in college. Swimming was what I did here, and I didn't want to be here anymore. I wanted something different than my life in Salem County. I wanted to leave it all behind. They rallied, but I always felt guilty about it. Not guilty enough to join the team, but still bad. I should have just swum. Things are plenty different now.

"Hey," Margo says, and breaks my concentration. "It's okay. I didn't swim either, remember? It gave our mothers something to commiserate about."

"Why didn't we just swim?"

"Because we were sick of setting our alarms for 5:45 a.m. every Saturday morning. Ten years was enough."

Margo leads the way to Sam's room and I lock the door behind us. His bedroom is massive, taking up one half of the front of the house. There are shelves with trophies from football, wrestling, and shot put. Sam is quite the athlete. Even though he no longer plays football he's still a big guy. Big room for a big guy. His bathroom is larger than my entire bedroom.

"Wow," I say as I look around the room.

"It never gets old, does it?"

"It's beautiful. Sam's so down to earth."

"Mrs. Shabo told my mom they wanted him to go to public school with the farmers and the cowboys to help keep him grounded."

"Hicks'll have that effect on you," I say as I take off my dress in the bathroom. I look in the mirror and the hickey on the side of my stomach stops me from breathing. I run my hand over it and remember Jason's lips there. I swallow hard and examine the rest of me in the mirror. I have a bruise on my arm and one on the side of my leg, both from numerous positions in a hard truck bed, and the pièce de résistance, the two-inch long scab on my back from a tree.

"Margo?"

"Yes," she says as her head pops into the doorway. Instinctively, I cover my body and Margo steps into the room, reading by my reaction. "What's going on, Charlotte?" she says, concern mixed with confusion.

"Have you ever had rough sex?" At this her eyebrows raise and she tilts her head slightly to the side. She relaxes slightly.

"How rough are we talking?" She moves closer to me and pulls my arms away my body. Margo keeps her cool as she examines me, running her hand over the scab on my back. Her cold fingers give me a chill. "Was there any humiliation, degradation, or cruelty?"

"God no. I've never felt more wanted," I answer, scorned. Jason would never hurt me, contrary to the evidence on my body.

"I wish I could help you, but I'm a virgin." I double over with laughter. "So I don't know what's too rough. But if you're enjoying it, it's probably on the right side of the no-no range."

"I didn't know there was a no-no range."

"It's different for everyone. I would say my no-no range consists of hitting, biting, peeing on me, speaking disrespectfully, or tying me up." My eyes sink at the last one. "I'm sure the no-no range changes over time and with different people. You have to be happy, though. Sex is supposed to feel good."

"I feel great," I say, and launch into memories of the past few weeks with Jason. The thoughts stir my insides in a now familiar way. If he were here I would have to have him right now. Margo notes my walk down memory lane.

"Good," she says, and puts her hand on my shoulder. "Maybe we should skip the swim. You look like you've been in a car accident." The reference is a knife stabbing me in the heart. It pulls me from my thoughts of Jason and I close my eyes in silence.

"Shoot! Charlotte, I'm so sorry."

"I know. I know. It's okay. Just give me a minute." I pull my dress back over my head and flash Margo a smile to relieve her guilt.

* * *

As we walk out Sam's back door Clint hands us a joint and I smoke it without considering if now's a good time, or if I'm ready for such a thing. The backyard is teeming with people entertaining each other. It'll be hard to complete a thought, let alone a sad one. Clint tells us what it's like to still live at home and we share some of our college stories. He's working for a construction company building houses. He deserves to be successful, if anyone is deserving of such a thing. Clint's like home and I relax in his presence. It's either him or the weed, but I can't stop laughing. Jenn hands me a beer and it soothes my dry throat. I suck it down too quickly and go to pour another one.

Sam takes my cup and opens the tap. His face lights up when he sees it's me. He might be a little drunk. If he's been standing by the kegs the whole time he might be completely drunk.

"CHARLOTTE." He says my name too loud, and I turn to see if anyone's listening. "I am so glad you came tonight. I've been worried about you." Sam realizes he's stopped pouring the beer and stays silent to focus. He hands me the cup with a look of innocent love.

"I'm glad I came too, Sam. You always throw great parties." I walk away thinking I should keep an eye on him. He's unsteady at best. I find an Adirondack chair facing the outdoor fireplace. Yes fireplace, not fire pit—this is a twelve-foot-high brick fireplace inclusive of a hearth with large rockers and Adirondack chairs facing it. I curl up in a chair and the heat from the fire warms me. The music in the background is the perfect volume to lull me to sleep. I close my eyes.

* * *

"Charlotte!" I wake to Sam plopping in my lap and again, saying my name far too loud.

"Sam! Why are you yelling? And why are you on top of me?" I try to push him off, but he's too heavy and not that coordinated tonight.

"Charrrrlllllooote. Oh Charrrrrlllllllllote." He sings my name, and I cringe at the coming verse. "Why do you do what you do do do to me?" *Ugh*.

"Sam, seriously." Again I push him, but he doesn't budge. His arm swings around my shoulders and his hand catches on the thin strap of my dress. It tears, and I catch the fabric right before my breast is exposed. "Get off of me!" I scream. Sam has no idea he's ripped my dress. He puts his arm around my neck and anger crawls up my throat.

"Don't be like that, Charlotte," he whispers in my ear. "Be nice," he says, and I turn my head and see Noble making his way over as Sam spills his beer down the front of me.

"SAM! Get off of me!" I yell, and as the last word leaves my lips Sam flies through the air and lands in a heap about eight feet away from me. He rolls over groggy and grabs his shoulder in pain.

I look up to a wild-eyed Jason Leer standing in front of me. His eyes blaze and his chest heaves with anger. Fear of the next paralyzes me. I never let go of his eyes. Too afraid of what might happen if I release him, I stand in front of him and raise my hands to his chest. He's a bull preparing to charge.

"He's drunk," I say, keeping my voice level and calm.

"Doesn't matter." Jason is going to kill Sam Shabo.

"None of it does now," I say, and feel the tiniest release from Jason. I continue touching his chest, moving my hands slightly to calm him further. He looks past me at Sam and Noble and then his gray eyes fix on me again.

"Are you ready to go?" he asks, and I nod my head. I turn and Noble is helping Sam up. Sam is rubbing his head, still trying to decipher how he ended up on the ground. Jason walks away and leaves me staring at Noble, pleading for understanding. How can anyone understand this? I run after him, but his strides are sped with fury.

"Wait up!" I yell.

He gets to his truck and punches the quarter panel, creating a banging sound that's probably audible over the band.

"Is this how it is at Rutgers?" Jason turns his anger on me. His question is ridiculous. He's overreacting.

"Oh, and I'm sure Oklahoma is a thriving institute of higher learning and community service. He's drunk. That's all." I scream at him, trying to impress upon him his absolute absurdity.

"That's all? He was *on top of* you, Annie!"

"What is your problem?"

"I just walked up and a guy was on top of you and you couldn't get him off."

"It was Sam. He's completely harmless."

"What if the next guy isn't?" I lower my eyes. "Look at me!" Jason roughly grabs the ripped fabric of my dress in his hands as I raise my eyes to meet his. "That's my problem."

He opens the truck door for me and I silently climb inside. He slams it shut and my stomach falls to my knees as he gets in the driver's side. "I know you're not coming to Oklahoma and that's the image I'll see every night when I close my eyes." Jason starts the truck and pulls off Sam's lawn, and I don't know how to fix this.

The drive home is filled with me trying to figure out how and why I'm going back to Rutgers. If tonight is any indication, it's not going to be an easy road for us and he's all I want, all I need. Why don't I just transfer to Oklahoma? It's probably a great school. Or just quit school completely and travel, mainly through the central plains, but travel some. Would that be so unbelievable? Girl loses both parents in a car accident and takes some time off. Sounds reasonable. I see my reflection in the truck window and I look like my mother tonight. The worry on my face mimics her face at the news I'm not returning to school. She'd want me to go back. She'd beg me to go.

Jason turns the truck off in front of my garage and sits motionless. What must he be thinking? I unbuckle and climb on top of him, facing him with my back to the steering wheel. I kiss him, a desperate, greedy kiss, but Jason doesn't respond. He's erected a wall and the absence of his openness leaves me cold. There are never any boundaries. He's protecting himself from me and the idea is ludicrous. I could never hurt him.

"Maybe I should go home tonight," he says.

"You are home." I pull myself closer to him and take his face in my hands and I gently kiss his lips. "Your home is with me."

Jason returns to me and kisses me with the same voracity he always does. I'm breathless and relieved, and happy again. How will I ever say good-bye to Jason Leer?

* * *

I keep the bacon moving in the pan, fearful it will stick and burn. Bacon cooking in a house is delicious. Bacon burning in a house is reason to leave. I lift my cowboy hat and push my hair behind my ears as I look down and catch a glimpse of my naked body. I hope he's in the mood for bacon, I think as a smirk crosses my face.

"Good morning," he says, surprising me as he leans on the doorway to the kitchen.

"Yes. It is a good one."

"Giving up on clothes? Tired of me wrecking them?"

"I want you to have something else to see when you close your eyes." He moves so quickly. He's on top of me, his mouth sucking the air from my lungs, and I forget about the bacon.

~ 11 ~

"I'm through with the talking, done with the truth"

I step out of my Mom's Camry and onto the sidewalk. It's hot today. Hot like hell, which is where I'm headed for telling Pastor Johnson and God himself to go—whatever, I don't have to relive it. Actually, I do since I'm here to apologize. The sundress I picked out clings to me and I pull the fabric out and let air swirl around my legs. This sucks.

The walk through the parking lot is long and hot. Like hell. The church door creaks when I open it and I wonder if it's always unlocked. The church seems deserted and I try to remember if there are office hours, or some time frame that Pastor Johnson hangs out here. I grip the apology letter I wrote him hoping he's out so I can just leave it on his desk. Right next to the picture of Mrs. Johnson and his children. I am a *terrible* person.

"Charlotte?" I stop, dead in my tracks, and take a deep

breath before turning around. Pastor Johnson is behind me in the hallway, walking from the fellowship hall with a cup of coffee.

"Hi Pastor Johnson," I say as if I haven't egregiously offended him in the past.

"Are you here to see me?" he asks, and I realize he is one of the kindest people in the world.

"I'm getting ready to go back to school and I wanted to apologize to you before I went."

"Charlotte, you were angry. That's understandable," he says, and puts his hand out in the direction of his office. I step forward and allow him to lead me.

"But not excusable. I'm so very sorry."

"Jesus loves you. Nothing you can do will ever separate you from his love."

"Still, I'm surprised my mother didn't reach up from her grave and strangle me herself. As it stands I still wait for a tree to fall on me or some other tragedy to strike at the hand of her."

"She's not thinking that way at all, Charlotte. She's in a wonderful place. She's gone home," Pastor Johnson says, and his words turn in my stomach. How dare she be so wonderful while I'm here alone?

"Let's not push it," I say as I hold up my hand to halt Pastor Johnson's depiction of my mother's wonderful existence. To my relief he chuckles, but my sensibility pulls me toward the door.

"Is there a place you can worship at school?"

"Of course." *There's a place. I'm not going, but there is a place.* Somehow he deciphers my internal defiance.

"Here's my card, Charlotte. Call me whenever you need to.

God loves you and so does the rest of this congregation. We're all here for you." He hands me his card and pauses, hesitating. "I hear you've been spending time with Jason Leer, Butch's son. Perhaps you can come to church together," he says, and a heavy guilt envelops me as if I've joined the Bad Kids' Club that doesn't go to church when their parents die.

"Perhaps, Pastor Johnson," I say, and stand, anxious to walk out of his office. "Take care."

"Call if you need anything, Charlotte, and be careful going home," he says, and I turn and walk out. *I thought I was home.*

* * *

"Julia, hey, it's Charlotte. Can you meet us out front? We'll never be able to park the truck and someone will boost my stuff," I say into the phone, and look at Jason. He doesn't take his eyes off the road. "Awesome. We're on Route 18. See you in a few."

"Take the George Street exit," I say, and point at the sign on the right.

"You don't have parking at your house?" Jason asks, and moves into the right lane.

"We have a few spots behind it, but your truck will never fit through the driveway." Jason looks at me, confused. "You'll see. We should be able to find somewhere to put your truck, but it might be a few blocks away. You'll need to bring all your stuff into my house."

"Why?" More confusion.

"So the truck isn't broken into. This is the city." Before Jason can say anything I add, "Make a left on George Street."

Jason remains silent as I lead him through New Brunswick

in order to be on the right side of the road when we pull up in front of my house. There are people everywhere. They are brown, and black, and white. Some are covered in tattoos and others wear turbans. They jaywalk; some smoke; they are alone and in groups, and there are cars bumper to bumper along the main streets. Jason's truck is suddenly enormous, as is the cowboy hat on top of his head. We pass Stuff Yer Face, the restaurant I've been waitressing at for the last two years, and I smile at the crowd gathered at the outside bar. It's good to be back. Julia is waiting on the curb when we double park in front of the house. Cars behind us beep in anger and Jason looks at me, annoyed.

"It's fine. We'll be quick." I hop out of the truck and wave the cars around the truck as Jason starts taking my suitcases out of the back. By the time I clear the traffic he's down to a large laundry basket full of toiletries, laundry detergent, and other household items, and his huge duffel bag. I pull the duffel bag toward the tailgate and it barely moves an inch. I reach in to grab the center of the bag, but I still can't budge it. Jason bumps me to the side and lifts it as if it's weightless. I take a deep breath through my nose, but appreciate the sight of him. His body is a tank.

"Welcome back," Julia says, grinning from ear to ear.

"Thanks. It's good to be back. Julia, this is Jason. Jason, this is my roommate Julia." I present each of them to the other as if I'm introducing my new puppy to my favorite stuffed animal.

"Hi Jason. It's good to meet you," Julia says, and I think she is calming, having been let in on some information.

"Pleased to meet you," Jason returns as a car's horn makes me jump.

"We'd better go park. Can you watch this stuff?"

"Sure. Try back on Guilden, or Central. There were a few spots there earlier. Although, you might need more than one spot." We all three turn and look at Jason's truck, pondering our future difficulties. As I put the tailgate up another car pulls up behind us and beeps. I wave as I head toward the passenger side. Jason gives the driver the steely look of death as he passes.

"Where's Guilden?" he asks, still looking pissed off.

"Do you want me to drive?"

"No. I want to park my truck, spend the night, and get the hell out of here." His words bruise me. *We just got here.*

"Back up and bang a U-ie," I say, trying to keep a positive attitude. Jason turns the truck around and I watch my tiny roommate Julia climb on top of our stuff and make herself comfortable in the middle of the sidewalk. He follows my directions in silence. I can only imagine what he's thinking. We find a spot large enough for the truck a few blocks down Guilden and I release a sigh of relief as he turns the truck off and takes the key out of the ignition.

"Hey," I say. He looks at me with eyes the color of storm clouds today. "In case I forget to tell you, thanks for the ride." I let the words flow off my lips, begging him for another ride.

"How am I going to let you go to school here if you look at me like this? It's obvious you need to be taken care of on a daily basis. This separation is never going to work," Jason concludes.

I unbuckle my seatbelt and slide over next to Jason, leaning across his lap, facing him. I kiss him as innocently as possible. I have to will my hands not to knot in his hair. Even this kiss leaves me breathless.

"Not here," I whisper and lean back.

"You started this, Annie," Jason chastises, and I look around for pedestrians. It's broad daylight and Julia is standing on the curb with our things.

"You'll have me arrested. I don't think I'm the prison type." He leans his head on my forehead. His breath is hot on my face.

"You may not be the prison type, but you are the break-the-law type."

"I'm coming around to it."

"Oh, don't play innocent. Just because you wasted all that time with Brian Matlin does not make you a saint."

"Can we leave poor Brian out of this?" I say, and slide back toward my door. I open it and hop out without waiting for his answer. We reach Julia just as she is about to give up and leave my stuff on the curb unattended. Jason carries every bag up ten steps and into the house as Julia peppers me with questions.

"So, this is the cowboy. He's hot, Charlotte."

"I know," I say as we both watch Jason toss bags over his shoulder neither of us could drag. "I think I'm obsessed with him."

"Great," is all she says in response. We continue to watch Jason as a car full of guys pass and beep at us. Jason scowls as he comes back out for the last bag. "What are you guys doing tonight?"

"I'm going to take him to Stuff Yer Face."

"You're going to take the cowboy to Stuff Yer Face?"

"Yeah, and can you call him Jason?"

"I'm really not sure if I can."

"I have to resign and we have to eat, so I figured we'd go to Stuff Yer Face. Do you want to come with us?"

"Yes. This is going to be hilarious. I'm on my way to the bookstore, though. I'll meet you guys there."

* * *

I go in the house and find Jason already in my room. It's on the top floor, in the attic really. The ceiling is pitched and there are two twin beds, mine and Julia's, taking up most of the floor space. Julia convinced me to paint it at the end of last year and the light blue color she picked is smurfish, but it gives the room a cheery, if not nauseating appearance. He's looking at the necklaces hanging on the corner of my mirror. A silver heart charm on a chain. The heart has an A engraved on the back. I wrap my arms around him from behind as he holds the tiny heart in his enormous hand.

"It has an A," he says, and releases it.

"My Aunt Diane gave it to me when I was little. It's an inside joke between my mother and me. I used to tell her I'd be in therapy by twenty-five because she changed my name."

"It's never changed for me."

"I know," I say, and slide under his arm so I can face him. "You've always called me Annie. Even when I told you not to. You're a terrible listener," I say. Jason leans into me, forcing me back to the wall. I arch my back raising my breasts to his chest and try to take in air.

"Tell me something right now," he gruffly says in my ear before taking my earlobe in his mouth. He travels down my neck and back up again. "I promise I'll listen."

I can barely hear what he's saying. His hands on the wall, straddling my head, leave my head surrounded by his iron arms and I hang my hands off each one.

"Jason," I say, and try to breathe as he puts a knee between my legs and spreads them. He lifts my shirt and pulls my bra up, releasing my breasts. His lips find my nipple and he plays with it until I am on the verge of crying out. Jason returns to my ear. "Tell me, Annie."

I try to think. To think of what I want to tell him as his lips return to my nipple.

"I think your hobbies are barbaric," I say, and Jason peers up at me, my nipple between his teeth.

"Hobbies?"

"Sport, whatever," I say, and he runs his hands down my back and pulls me to him, his hard-on jutting onto my leg.

"And I don't think I can live without you," I say, and Jason stops moving and his gray eyes find mine. He stands in front of me, silent, and now that I've said it the honesty of the statement terrifies me. I look down, his stare devouring the truth of my words. He lifts my chin with his finger, delicately, kindly, and I meet his eyes once again.

"Don't look away, Annie. There's nothing you can't tell me. Don't you know that by now?" I wrap my arms around his neck, crossing my wrists as I lean into him. I feel small pressed against the front of him. He's hard on my hip and I kiss him, through with the talking, done with the truth. Let him know everything. Now I want to know nothing.

* * *

"This is a nice bed." Jason says as he lies on it, his arm behind his head as he watches me change into a sundress.

"Are you being sarcastic?"

"Yes. It's the tiniest bed I've ever seen," he says, and looks to each side of him, where mere inches remain. "Where are you going to sleep?" he asks naughtily.

"On top of you if I'm lucky. And it is a nice bed."

"It's not great."

"Any bed you're in is perfect." He smiles at this assessment.

"Let's go. I'll buy you dinner," I say, and reach out my hand to help Jason Leer out of my nice bed at Rutgers University. *My, how things have changed.*

* * *

The hostess greets me with a hug and Sydney practically climbs over her to get to me. She hugs me tightly and then holds my hand in hers.

"How the hell are you?"

"I'm okay," I say. *I am okay.* Sydney's attention turns to Jason. She appraises him shamelessly, still holding my hand, and turns to me.

"This must be the cowboy I keep hearing about." I can't help but laugh at her.

"This is Jason." I present him to her. "Jason, this is Sydney."

"It's nice to meet you," he says and smiles, and I want to capture him and keep him right here in Stuff Yer Face forever. Sydney turns to me beaming. She is classically pretty, her perfect nose and hair hiding the secret of her sweet sixteen birthday present from her parents: a new nose and chin and cheek implants. Now that's a gift I haven't heard of in Salem County. She makes me happy every time she comes near me.

"Smokin' Hot," she says, enunciating each word and showing no signs of embarrassment. I, of course, turn bright purple with humiliation.

"Hi, Charlotte." I hear and know before turning around that Barry, the side order cook, is standing behind me. I turn and look into the sad eyes of the man I befriended two years ago. He is gruff and angry and cruel to everyone, but was always kind to me. I hug him and his discomfort with the affection oozes from his stiff arms and lowered eyes. "I'm sorry about your parents and sorry I didn't come to the funeral. I don't have a car."

"I'm glad you weren't there, Barry. It's a sad memory that I don't want you to be a part of." His apology and his kindness are awkward. "I knew you were thinking of me," I add, and the air returns to normal. Barry retreats to the kitchen and I turn to Sydney who is rolling her eyes, and Jason who's rubbing his in disbelief.

"He is such an ass, but that was nice. He's always nice to you," Sydney says bitterly.

"He's just misunderstood." Jason is silent. "Can we get a table? For three; Julia is meeting us."

"Fun. Why do I always have to work? When are you coming back?" Sydney asks, and I'm sad. Now that I'm here I want to come back, but it will make it impossible to see Jason. I won't be able to get that many weekends off. It's no longer about the money. The insurance and settlement made sure it will never again be about money. Looking around at all my coworkers I realize it never was about the money. Sydney leads us to a four-top in the bar area, her section of course, and leaves us to peruse the menu I've got completely memorized. Jason doesn't even open his.

"Who's your friend?" He says, and I realize I didn't introduce him to Barry.

"I'm sorry I didn't introduce you. He's nice."

"Sydney doesn't make him sound nice at all." Jason's voice has an edge to it. As if anger is creeping in, but he's not sure where to put it.

"He's misunderstood. He's not here for school. He was born here. He's in his forties. He's lived a hundred lives, none of them very easy," I say, and reach across the table to touch Jason's hands.

"Barry has scars all over his hands and I asked him once what they're from and he said, 'knives.' His life is not that of a college student, so he has very little time for our nonsense. This is his job; it's our time to party. He walks me home every time we have a closing shift together." Jason's eyes harden, his anger finding a home. "I'm usually carrying a lot of cash. I appreciate the company."

"You check out the menu," I tell him. "I'm going downstairs to the office." Jason seems even more annoyed. "To resign." At this he softens and I get up. "Order me a drink when Sydney comes back."

* * *

I return to find Sydney sitting at the table with Jason. I have no idea what they're talking about, but she's hanging on every word. Sydney can make anyone talk. It's her gift. I sit down and they both look at me.

"Jason just told me you're resigning." I can't even be mad at him. I left him here, with her, unprotected. I lean in and try to slide past an elderly woman speaking Russian to what must be her granddaughter, but I need an inch more space.

"*izvinite*," I say in Russian and Jason's eyes bulge. The grandmother nods kindly and moves her chair in, letting me by.

"Yes. I just told Tony. I'm regrouping," I answer Sydney.

"Hey! You resigning?" Barry asks, poking his head out from the kitchen.

"For now, Barry. I might be back, but I need some time." I turn to Jason and he is staring at Barry's hands. "I'll still be in here all the time. I've got to eat," I add, and Barry huffs and retreats to the kitchen. That's about as well as it's going to go with him.

Julia comes in, toting Noble and his roommate Wes. They engulf us. Apparently, Jason met Wes in Salem County last summer so introductions are unnecessary. Sydney brings out ecstasy fries and bolis without us ordering. "I knew what you'd want," she says, and we all dig in. Noble is explaining the campus layout to Jason. He's concerned with the inter-campus bus system and any classes I might have off of College Avenue. There are plenty, most across the river on the Busch Campus this year. Noble offers to drive me, since most of his business school classes are there, too. Judging from Jason's face, this does little to appease him.

"Are you guys going out tonight?" Noble innocently asks. Why does this question feel like the start of a fight?

"I'm not sure. We've got a long ride tomorrow and the next day," I explain.

"Where?" Julia asks, confused.

"We're driving to Oklahoma. I'm flying back Sunday night."

"What? You're leaving? I thought you were here to stay. You're coming back, right?" She's just this side of frantic.

"I'm coming back." *Not because I want to, but I'm coming back.*

* * *

We walk back to my house. It's garbage day tomorrow and the businesses have the curbs lined with cans and bags. The smell mixed with the humid air form a heavy cloud of yuck over the street.

My room, our room, Julia's and my room, seems tiny with Jason in it. Every inch of him from his boots to his giant hat seem larger than life and for the first time I see him the way Sydney must have seen him. He is an amusement ride, a history museum, and a romantic movie all rolled into one.

"We can go out if you'd like," he offers, and a chill runs through me. I go to him and look directly into his eyes, just the way he likes it. I know he recognizes it's intentional.

"I think you hate it here."

"I do hate it here," he says quietly, without a hint of humor. "What I hate more is the thought of you here," he adds, and I lower my forehead to his chest. It clunks down on the rock. "But you needed to come back. You're different here, Annie, It feeds you. I can tell you love it and it loves you." I wrap my arms around his neck and rest my lips at his jugular. "I think you'll love Oklahoma, too. It's quieter," he adds as a series of sirens blare outside my window. "No matter where you are, I need you to be safe." Jason holds me tighter and I can barely breathe. *I am safe.*

~ 12 ~

"Questioning if harmony is missing from my youth"

Jason gets up early and showers, leaving me in my bed, staring at the glow in the dark star stickers Julia and I decorated our ceiling with. I needed to get away. Away from Salem County, away from their house, away from the road they died on.

Away.

He returns to my room wrapped in a towel that barely covers him and I swallow hard at the sight of him.

"How much do you pay for this place?" He runs the towel through his hair. It's the color of a wet road in the darkness.

"Five hundred. Why?"

"Five hundred? And there are ten of you?" he asks in disbelief. "And two bathrooms?"

"We don't all pay the same amount and there's a half bath in the basement. Are you trying to make some point, or come to some conclusion?"

"Ten girls, two bathrooms. I'm just not sure you're getting your money's worth." Jason crawls into bed naked, leaving his wet towel on the floor next to my bed.

"We have a long ride today," I say, and add, "Maybe we should start the day with another long ride."

Jason pulls me on top of him and I straddle him, sitting naked on top of him. Without the hat, and the belt buckle, and the boots, he could be any other guy lying in this bed. His thumb finds me and the chill runs from my groin to the tops of each of my shoulders, swirling around my nipples. I raise my head to the ceiling and open my mouth for air.

"Lean back," he says gruffly and I lean back, resting my hands on his thighs. I am exposed. Jason's thumb never leaves me as his fingers find me. He finds the one spot that promises something extreme is about to happen. But I can't stop the train from the crash. My chest heaves as I fight for air and he stops.

"No," I whimper.

He lifts me up and slides out from under me at the same time. "Make yourself come, Annie." His eyes haunt me with their darkness. He is leaving me.

"Did I do something wrong?" I ask, questioning my punishment. Jason smiles, erasing my thoughts, and stands erect at the end of my bed. My mouth waters at the sight of him. He is the devil.

"No, but I'm not going to be here for weeks at a time. You'll need to take care of yourself." The thought of being away from him for weeks rips through me. The sadness is crippling.

Jason comes to me and takes my nipples between his fingers, and then between his lips. He kisses the side of my face and trails his lips to my own. "I can't have you walking around campus angry, searching for an orgasm," Jason says, hovering above me, and his playfulness infects me.

"I often bump into people rambling around, searching for an orgasm."

"Are they angry? I'll bet they seem very angry. I don't want that for you. Now play," he commands and stands beside me again. Watching me.

I try my thumb as Jason always does, but it's awkward, as if I am not using my dominant hand. I switch to my finger and find a rhythm. Jason's eyes never leave me. Light gray this morning; they are now a deep, swirling pool of darkness. The sight of them, of him, returns the chill to my nipples and with my free hand I grab them. He watches me from the side of my bed and as I arch my back slightly, he reaches out. He returns his hand, grabbing himself. I want to touch him. I want him in my mouth. I lock my eyes on his lips and wish they were on me. I close my eyes and give in to my hands and my heart, and the memories of every orgasm before. I come as Jason pushes the hair from my face and whispers in my ear, "I almost came just watching you. You make my blood boil, Annie O'Brien."

My body shakes two more times and then I rest. My chest heaves, trying to recover, but the period is interrupted by Jason hauling me to the edge of the bed. He plunges into me without any warning.

"I can't wait," he says hungrily. "I can't wait, Annie." Jason enters again and I swallow him every time, my body needing him inside of me. The craving reminds me of the first time we were together. It has no meaning outside of a murderous need and I want to touch him. I reach out and Jason pulls me to him by the wrists. He continues and my body tenses again, bracing itself for another release.

"Lie down on the floor," I demand, breathless. Jason pulls out and carries me to the floor, pulling me on top of him. I straddle him and ride him without any consideration of his needs, my own clouding my civility. I come, exploding around him, and continue to move up and down to the extent my legs will rise. Jason's heartbeat thumps in his chest and I rest the side of my face against it.

"I'm guessing by the speed of your heart rate that you came."

"You are a greedy lover, Annie." He's right. I am. *This is the animal you've created, Jason Leer.* "I love that about you."

* * *

"How long does it take to get to Stillwater, Oklahoma?" I ask, and the hilarity of the question hits me. I laugh out loud.

"It's going to take about a day, as in a whole day. Maybe longer since first we have to get out of this hellhole you call home." The traffic on Route 1 has ruined Jason's mood. Everything happens so quickly with Jason. He reacts faster than I comprehend. I unbuckle my seatbelt and move closer to him. I buckle the middle one and lean on him, my hand between his legs. "How Great Thou Art" comes on the radio and I turn it up. It's beautiful and I close my eyes and lean into Jason as the music covers me with the safety of my past.

The traffic subsides and Jason pulls onto I-276 West, speeding away from Rutgers University.

"Have you been to church since your mom died?" I ask Jason, the song feeding my courage.

"Why are you asking that? And no."

"We went our whole lives. Your mom was my Sunday school teacher. Don't you think they'd want us to go?"

"I think I wanted her not to die." My courage retreats. Jason turns off the radio and we ride in silence.

"I'm pretty sure you're either in or you're out," I say, remembering Pastor Johnson's invitation to both Jason and me. I look at Jason as confusion spreads across his face. "You have to believe. Nothing else you could possibly do 'good' will ever replace believing. At least that's what your mother taught me, taught us," I explain, and he pulls me back toward him, kissing the top of my head, and ending the conversation.

* * *

We settle into our ride. Every four hours we stop to fill the truck with gas and switch seats. Driving his truck is terrifying. I've barely been driving anything, and certainly not something as large as this rolling house. Once we pass Frederick, Maryland, things simplify; the traffic dies, and Jason and I ride. When we run out of snacks, we stop for dinner in Columbus and Jason mounts me in the restaurant parking lot. It's still light out, but the sun is falling, signaling a new day. One less day we'll be together.

By Indianapolis, the sun has set and Jason is back at the wheel. I lean on my door and look at the stars, the millions of them eclipsed by the city lights coming into view as we head west, careening toward our separation.

"Those stars tell you anything?" His voice breaks my sadness with the reminder he's here. "I've never seen anyone look up as much as you do."

"I love the sky. It's different every day, but always impressive." I turn my head back toward it and notice the bulging moon, a few days shy of full. "I also like that it's the same moon all over the world. I like knowing Margo, and Jenn, and the rest of the world are going to see the same moon. And now I'll think the same thing about you."

"I'll never look at it the same way again," he says, looking out his window.

"I know," I say, and close the space between us, leaving the moon for the others. It doesn't compare to Jason Leer.

"Jason?" He stays silent. "Was it your intention to have sex with me the day of my parents' funeral?" Jason lets out the breath he was holding.

"No. I just wanted to get you out of there, Annie. I couldn't watch you smile at those people. They didn't deserve your kindness and you didn't owe it to them," Jason says, and I feel protected. "You're so strong. I figured if anyone could survive this, you could. But when I looked into your empty green eyes in the kitchen I realized you were as lost as I am." The tears fill my eyes. "And so I took you." His words lessen the pain. He did take me and I let him, and I would let him do it again.

* * *

We would have been here sooner. Could have been if we hadn't stopped to have sex two more times. Each time more desperate than the one before, a needy reminder I would leave him soon. We crossed into the central time zone and the extra hour did little to calm me. But when we finally arrived in Stillwater, Oklahoma, something was settling, almost exciting to me.

"It's so green here," I say, noting the lush grass and abundance of trees, both of which were not part of my mental picture.

"What did you expect? The desert?"

"Yes," I admit, nodding my head and still in awe of the scenery.

"From Stillwater east is green. Things change to the west and into the panhandle."

"Why?" All I can think of is how different north and south Jersey are, but something tells me the differences here have nothing to do with Manhattan and Philadelphia.

"The Gulf of Mexico. Its tropical, warm air flows north to Stillwater. The western side doesn't get it. The difference in the climate here is dramatic. That's one reason why we get such nasty storms."

We pass a sign: WELCOME TO STILLWATER, WHERE OK-LAHOMA BEGAN. Jason turns onto North Washington Street and I see a lake.

"Boomer Lake, huh? I like the name."

"I'm not surprised. There's Lake McMurtry not far up the road, too. Lots of lakes out this way."

"No ocean, though," I say, unsure of what point I'm making.

We pass what might be the prettiest firehouse I've ever seen. It's all brick with four big bays out front. This town is quaint. Japanese, Chinese, and Mexican restaurants line the road and Stillwater's culinary options make me laugh. The athletic field commands my attention as we pass it and I wonder again about Jason turning down a football scholarship. I look at him driving with his cowboy hat on and try to understand his passion for the rodeo. *It's better than competitive eating, I guess.*

There are people walking everywhere.

"How many students are there?" I ask.

"About 16,000. It's nowhere near as big as Rutgers."

"Few are, but anything over one hundred and seventy sounds big to me," I answer, remembering our graduating class from Salem County. I notice everyone walking the streets, at least right now, is white. Not one black person anywhere. "Everyone is white."

"What's wrong with that?" Jason's question confuses me. *What is wrong with that?* "You do realize you're white, right?"

"I do. I'm just not used to—"

"Annie, not every place in the world is your little slice of diversity heaven. The majority here is white, but there are people who are not," Jason says as if I'm ridiculous to want anything else.

"I know it sounds strange." *Not really.* "But I think the people at Rutgers are the real education."

"Are there any other languages you speak besides Russian?" he asks, and stresses *Russian* as if he's not even sure that's what I was saying.

"It was Russian and I don't even speak it. My roommate freshman year was Russian. Nice girl. She taught me a little. It comes in handy waitressing."

"Waitressing in New Brunswick. Probably not necessary here. See how much easier things are?" Jason asks, knowing I'll never agree. We pass a sign declaring Oklahoma State University a Land Grant School established in 1890. Rutgers was founded one hundred and twenty-four years before that.

"What does it mean to be a land grant university?" I ask, never having heard of it.

"It means we're good people; that we'll use our educations to improve the world." He pulls into the driveway of a small house with an adorable front porch. I'm excited to see where Jason lives. We pass the house and he pulls the truck up close to a cottage in the house's backyard.

"We're home," he says, and looks at me hungrily. I jump

out of the truck and stretch. It's mid-afternoon. We missed lunch. We missed nighttime and now my body wants to reclaim it. I look around the landscape. There's a tree in the yard of the main house. No hills, no mountains in the distance, no horns, no sirens, no airplanes in the sky, no black people. I have landed on Mars. I turn to the back of the truck and Jason is leaning on the quarter panel studying me.

"You gonna be okay?" he asks. I walk to him and lean into him, letting his body settle me.

"I'd follow you anywhere. Obviously," I say, and kiss him. "What I would really like to do is follow you to the shower." Jason throws his hundred-pound bag over his shoulder and leads the way to the front door of his curious little cottage. He unlocks it and the hot air escapes the front door into the humidity surrounding us. I follow him inside and the heat suffocates me. Jason hurries to open two windows and turns on an air conditioning unit in the third.

"It'll cool off. I'm just going to let the heat out and then I'll get it cool in here." It's one room. One large room. Directly in front of us is a kitchen, or a counter with a sink and an oven. There is a small refrigerator at the end of the counter—my instincts tell me to not open it. There are two unmatched wooden chairs and a table covered in what looks like peeling linoleum past the refrigerator. In the far corner is a woodburning stove the likes of which I have not seen since the cold winters of my childhood. There's an old television on a wooden stand awkwardly pushed against the side wall as if it's never turned on.

To our right, up two steps, is a large bed with small tables to each side of it. The lamps on each table are white with gold leaf designs and ornate fringed shades. I fall in love with them immediately. My cowboy with his fancy lamps. There's a bar hanging in the corner for clothes and a door I assume leads to the bathroom. I guess I should be thankful for the door. The entire room is covered in a musty dust, but it is ours.

"You live here alone?"

"Yes. Except when you're here. Which I hope will be often."

"I see why you were so enamored with my nine roommates."

"The number of you and the price. I pay $400 here."

"What?" I shout. I see the entire place in a whole new light. The kitchen is enormous, the table and chairs are quaint, and the bed rivals the Four Seasons.

"Four hundred dollars and I have to help with the yard work, but utilities are included and I get to use the washer and dryer in the mudroom of the main house." At this I have to sit down. I have been lugging my clothes a block away to wash them, trapped for three hours with whoever had nothing clean, either.

"Maybe I will transfer." Jason's pleased that I like, *love,* his place. He drops his bag and starts the shower and I start to salivate at the thought of him naked.

***

We made the bed and collapsed into it. And we slept. For eleven hours straight I lay curled on my side, Jason's bicep beneath my head. It's the only position I've found that doesn't leave me maimed the next morning. There's a strong possibility I never even rolled over last night, or yesterday.

What time is it? I reach to the nightstand and grab my phone as Jason rolls over and spoons me. It's 5 a.m. Friday. I have two and a half days left with him and then he'll be fifteen hundred miles away. I realize I'm clenching my teeth and relax my mouth, moving my jaw slightly.

"Why are you awake? You thinking again, Annie?" he asks, and somehow moves even closer to me.

"You would hate me if I never thought about things," I retort, taking my anger out on him.

"I love you thinking. I hate you trying to figure us out. By now, you've probably calculated to the minute how much time we have left together." Jason rolls over and steps out of the bed. The entire back of me is cold from his absence. "We both know you're going back. What is there left to figure out?" He's angry now, too. *What happened?* We just opened our eyes.

"Why do you say it as if this is my fault? You could transfer to Rutgers." He looks at me as if this is the *most* ridiculous thing he has ever heard, completely out of the question. He rolls his eyes and walks into the bathroom. I stare at the cracked ceiling and again question why I can't transfer here. The old Charlotte, *yes Charlotte*, would have thought a girl crazy for following a boy to his school, any school. But every cell in my body screams that I belong with him. That is, every single one but the ones still listening to the words of my dead mother.

I roll over and fall back to sleep until a clicking sound startles me. I walk around the room, following the noise. I think I'm close by the far window. The clicking stops, there's a pause, and then a voice fills the room. I spot an old answering machine on the floor next to the refrigerator. It's delightful and so very Jason Leer.

"LEER!" is shouted from the machine. "I know you're back in town because the steer are all cowering in the corners of the pastures. We're catching up tonight. From what you said the last time there's a lot to talk about." *What did he say?* "I'm coming to get you at seven. No excuses." The line goes dead and I wonder who that was.

* * *

"Are you sure you want to go out? We can stay in," Jason says with a devilish grin.

"I want to see what it's like." I'm also afraid the more time alone we have the more I'll have to think, and that scares me more than anything right now. "Stillwater is where Oklahoma began," I proclaim, and Jason laughs at me.

At exactly seven the door opens and a cowboy with the sweetest smile walks in carrying a 30-pack of Bud. Jason's lips are on the back of my neck as I put on lip gloss in a small round mirror hanging awkwardly on the wall.

"Oh. Sorry. I didn't know you had…" He looks at me, unable to find the words.

"Company," I offer. He relaxes and continues into the room.

"This is Annie," Jason says, presenting me to Harlan, who's still staring at me.

"You can call me Charlotte."

"Whatever you want," he says dazed, and Jason punches him. "Oww. What? I was just being polite."

"Well stop," Jason says, and turns to me. "You want a beer?"

"Sure." I sit on the edge of the bed. Harlan sits down next to me and when Jason looks like he might kill him, he sighs and stands up. He brings over a chair and faces it toward the bed, but since he's two steps down it's awkward. Jason seems fine with it.

"So you're Annie?" Harlan asks as if he's heard some magical fairytale about me in his childhood.

"Charlotte. Yes," I say, which seems to amuse Jason enormously.

"Harlan's my hazer," Jason says, and I search my mind for information. I've heard of a hazer. Harlan looks at me, gauging my knowledge.

"Oh, so you two are a bit of a team. And you have the horses." I'm sure I am saying this all wrong, but I know what I mean.

"We are and I do. Have you been going to a lot of rodeos this summer?"

"Only a few."

"Annie's turning into a city girl. She's concerned with the lack of diversity at Oklahoma."

"A student of the world. Love it," Harlan says, and takes a drink of his beer. "You in school?"

"Rutgers."

"Where the hell is that?" he asks, and Jason again laughs at us.

"It's in New Jersey. Some people call it civilization," I answer. Harlan dips his chin and lowers the corners of his mouth.

"I have heard of that before. Just the other day some cowboys were talking about some crazy place they called Civilization." Harlan says it with panache as he swipes his hands in front of his face.

"It's a hellhole and I couldn't wait to get out of there," Jason says, and I roll my eyes at him.

"So you two have been on a bit of a road trip. All the way to civilization and back. Hmph. How long are you staying?" Harlan's question torturess me and I look up to see Jason staring at me, aware of my emotions before I am.

"I'm going home Sunday."

"Well then, we need to get the hell out of here. Stillwater is a great night waiting to happen." Harlan throws his beer can in the sink and Jason and I finish ours in silence. I place the empty can on the counter and slip my hand in Jason's as we walk out and climb into Harlan's truck.

Harlan puts the rest of the thirty-pack in the back of his truck and we pull out of Jason's driveway, heading God knows where. Unlike Jason's beater, Harlan's truck is practically new. He drives slowly with little care of any road lines or signs. He's smiling and singing along to the radio and might possibly be the happiest person I've ever encountered. It's comforting to know he's here with Jason. He pulls into an apartment complex with a sign that reads THE RESERVE ON PERKINS out front. Harlan pulls to the side of the lot, not really in a spot, puts the truck in park and hops out.

As soon as I exit the truck I can hear the party, or several parties. They're spilling out of apartments and into the pool area. Some people are swimming; there are barbeques cooking, and tons of people smoking cigarettes. I follow Harlan into an apartment and am offered a lemon drop, which I stupidly do, and a Jack and Coke which I happily take. It becomes clear this is an Around the World and I don't want to ever leave this room. The shot warms me and the whiskey reminds me of home.

Jason and Harlan are celebrities with this crowd. Everyone stops by to talk to them. Jason stays right by my side as Harlan works the crowd. He introduces me to some, but I have little to say. I'm still getting a handle on Stillwater. I wonder if they call it that because there's no ocean. The lake water has no current.

When Harlan and Jason step outside to smoke, I stay behind and search for the bathroom. The apartment is spacious. Four bedrooms and at least the one I've stumbled into has its own bath. I finish and wash my hands and realize when I'm about to open the door the faucet isn't off. I turn it hard, but it's still on. My dad helped me fix the one on Hamilton Street last year with the same problem. That man could fix anything. If he was here, if he had survived, could he fix me? *What would you tell me about Jason Leer?* I'm studying the handle when the door opens, causing me to jump.

"Oh geez, pardon me. Sorry."

"No, it's okay," I say, and pull the door open farther. An enormous guy wearing an Oklahoma baseball hat, a t-shirt, and jeans is standing before me, blushing. "I was totally done, just trying to fix the faucet." At this he looks at me sideways. "I can't get it to turn off. You probably need to replace the O-rings." The giant boy's eyes bulge.

"You're not from around here, are you?" he asks, and I suddenly remember why I've been so quiet tonight. I don't fit in here at all.

"What gave it away?"

"There are too many signs to list," he says, looking me up and down. "I'm Rhett." *Of course you are.*

"I'm Charlotte. Nice to meet ya," I add, hoping to sound country.

"Do you want to get a drink? Looks like you're empty." I look down at my cup.

"Actually, my boyfriend is getting me one. I should get back." *In fact, I should be back.*

"Got it," Rhett says with an easy smile and moves over so I can pass him, but I still brush up against him on the way by. I don't look up and just keep moving back to Jason.

* * *

I exit the bedroom and return to the living room. I find Harlan and walk over to him as someone hands me a fresh Jack and Coke.

"Girl, where you been?"

"I was in the bathroom. Where's Jason?"

"He's ripping this place apart looking for you," Harlan says, completely unconcerned.

I turn to find Jason. When I do he's storming out of a bedroom, his gray eyes look black in the dim light of the hallway. When he sees me relief crosses his face. I place my hands flat on his chest and he threads both hands through my hair behind me. He fists his hands, pulling my hair and leaning my head up to his, never breaking his stare.

"I couldn't find you," he says. His breath is hot on my cheek.

"I was in the bathroom."

"Which one?" *Who cares?*

"That one," I say, and point to the bedroom I came from just as Rhett opens the door and walks out.

"Hey," Rhett says, obviously to me, and notices Jason. "Oh, hey Leer, I should have known Charlotte was with you. Northerners." Jason nods at Rhett, who is happily on his way someplace else.

"We need to go home," Jason says as if I'll protest. I lean up and take his earlobe in my mouth. I suck it, pull it with my teeth, then exhale into his ear and a shiver runs through him.

* * *

I wake to Jason covering my naked body with a blanket at the exact moment Harlan walks into his loft.

"What the hell, Harlan? You can't just walk in here." I roll over and try to remain asleep, not ready to face my last full day with Jason.

"What can I say? I'm jealous. Now that civilized Charlotte is here you don't want to go out, I can't just come and go, we haven't been riding." Harlan sounds properly upset.

"You're an idiot," Jason barks, and Harlan pulls up a chair.

"Words hurt, you know."

"My foot up your ass is going to hurt."

"Why don't you guys go riding today?" I mutter, my head not leaving the pillow.

"Because." Jason doesn't have to finish the sentence. I know it's because in thirty hours I won't be here anymore.

"Harlan hasn't seen you all summer. He misses you. And I know you miss riding. Go. Get dirty. Do whatever it is you cowboys do."

"I like this girl," Harlan says, and Jason throws his pillow at him. "I'm leaving! I'll be back at one to get you." Harlan slams the door behind him.

"He's a bit like having a puppy, huh?" I ask, and Jason laughs rather than responding.

***

"Why don't you come with us?" Jason asks as I walk outside with him. It's humid again today and the heavy air weighs on me.

"I'll be fine. I brought a few books to read for class and I haven't responded to any of Julia, Violet, and Sydney's texts and e-mails. I need to call up there or else they'll fly down here and get me. I can always catch up with Jenn and Margo, too. Really, I'll be fine."

Jason looks to the south as a wind blows past us. "I don't like the look of those clouds." I look at his view and see one large cloud, shaped like nothing more than a cloud, and see nothing to be concerned about. "We won't be long," he says, and kisses me as Harlan pulls in.

"Hey there, Jersey Girl!" Harlan yells out his window. "What are you going to do while we're gone?"

"Maybe some cleaning."

"Ahh. Women's work is never done. I got to get me a Jersey girl." *Good luck with that.* Harlan pulls out and Jason waves as they pull away.

When Jason leaves I decide to clean his house. There's not much in it. I should be able to scrub it from top to bottom before he gets home. I search under the sink for cleaners and find some dry-rotted sponges and half a bottle of Mr. Clean. I'm at least going to need a bucket. Jason's keys on the kitchen table catch my eye. I grab them and Google map Walmart on my phone. It's no surprise there is one less than five miles away. No ocean, but plenty of Walmarts.

Walmart is enormous and surprisingly nice. I find all the cleaners I need and linger in the home decorating section. I put a floor-length mirror in my cart—*I love it when you watch*—and crouch down to shop the small vases. Something for the center of his table would be nice, even if he uses it as a pencil holder.

"Can I help you find something?" a man asks from behind me.

"No, thank you." I try to lose my Jersey accent, but I'm sure

I sound ridiculous. "I was just looking at these vases. I want to find—" The man thrusts his hand in the air and tilts his head awkwardly toward the front of the store.

"Let's go," he says, and grabs me by the elbow. *Go where?* Customers begin to whiz past my aisle, all headed toward the back of the store. I now hear what the man was listening for.

Sirens.

Or one long siren that has no start or end like a fire whistle in Salem County. It just goes on and on at the same tone and something about its inability to rest is frightening. I follow the man to the section in the back where every other person in the store is crouched down. I turn toward the front where large windows, lined up like targets, frame the now darkened sky.

People are shuffling all around me, some sitting, some kneeling, and all taking cover in some way. And the thunder bellows. It's a deep, guttural growl that lasts five, maybe six seconds. The next one I'll time. It almost blocks out the siren. Almost. The sky brightens as an incision of lightning cuts from the sky to the ground. *Jason.*

And the siren keeps sounding.

"Pardon me," I try to regain some control over the situation. "I'm from New Jersey," I say to the man that brought me to the back of the store. "What the fuck is happening?" As the question leaves my mouth I can hear my words over the siren and they are filled with panic.

"Tornado," he says. My phone dings with a text.

Where are you?

In the middle of a fucking tornado! Why in God's name would anyone live here?

Walmart

I reply and look down at a baby who is obviously troubled with the sirens, or is it the deafening thunder and fear of death filling the air? It's hard to tell, but he's screeching, and it seems appropriate. I feel like screeching, too.

The thunder begins again and I count this time. One Mississippi, two Mississippi, three Mississippi, four thisisfuckedup, five whatthecrazyhell, six Oklahoma. I stop counting. What a horrible way to spend what may be my last minutes of life. I block out the baby crying and imagine my mother and father in their last minutes. I know they were laughing. They made each other happy. They made it look easy.

The thunder roars and I search my mind for stories of crowds huddled together in Walmart who miraculously survived tornados. Not surprising, I can't remember one story of tornado survivors. I sit on the floor, next to the screeching baby who also, not surprisingly, has a seat open next to him, and I put my head between my knees, my hands covering my head. Not for protection, for lack of any idea what else to do. It's my version of surrender.

* * *

"Annie," he says, gentle in my ear as he pulls me toward him. I'm splattered against his chest and I meld there, unwilling to move. "Annie, are you all right?" I hear him ask, and then I hear nothing. The baby stops screeching and the people stop talking as we all listen to nothing. The sirens have stopped. I pull away from Jason to hear for myself.

"What does that mean? Why did they stop?" I ask him, searching his gray eyes for answers.

"It turned. It's not going to hit here. Not now." His words and his arms around me should soothe me, but adrenaline trapped in confusion is coursing through me and I can't calm down. I beg Jason to get me out of here with my eyes and he takes my hand and leads me to the door. I can see Harlan is sitting in his truck at the front of the store, a light rain falling in front of lightning striking a few miles away.

"Do you have the keys?" he asks, his gentle voice scaring me. I reach into my bag and pull them out. My hand is shaking as I hand them to him. Jason watches the keys clanging, puts his arm around my shoulders, and walks me to his truck. He helps me in and I buckle my seatbelt without thinking. We ride back to his loft as the rain comes. It's nearly impossible to see out the windshield, but I'm looking through my side window searching for the tornado. Is this life? Surviving from one storm to the next?

Jason pulls into his driveway as the rain slows. I open the truck door as he puts the truck in park, and walk away without a word. I can feel him watching me as I leave him behind. The door is unlocked. I left it that way. It was maybe an hour ago, but it seems like days now. I pull off my wet shoes and place them just inside the door and walk into the room, committing every inch of it to memory. *Am I not coming back?*

I hear Jason's footsteps on the ground outside and him opening the door. Without turning around I know he's here. A chill runs up my back. The answering machine on the floor catches my eye.

"Why don't you have a phone?" I ask without turning around.

"What?" he asks, confused.

"Why do you have this old answering machine, but no phone? You can never answer a call, just get a message." As soon as I say the words out loud I understand.

"It was here when I moved in. The landlord pays the phone bill. I just never got rid of it," he says, and circles around to stand in front of me. He is so very beautiful. His rain-drenched black hair is curling around his face, one curl framing his gray eye as it peers at me.

"Does this happen here a lot?" There's no need to define it. He knows.

"We get some bad storms, especially in the spring and fall, but the sirens don't happen that often. It's Oklahoma, though. We get tornadoes." *Is this some source of pride?*

"So you wrestle animals and live in a city where sirens go off and people take cover?"

"And you work a shift that a man with knife scars has to walk you home from so you're not robbed."

Touché.

Jason takes my hand and opens it, placing it over his mouth and kissing it, and I stare at him emptily. My hand looks so tiny in his, so breakable.

"Does this feel wrong to you?" he asks, but I can't pinpoint any feelings other than want.

"It doesn't feel wrong at all, but I think it is." Jason kisses my palm again and the chill flows through me. "I never wanted anyone the way I want you." I watch as he moves his lips to my wrist and kisses me there, too. "We rarely speak. Is that because we have nothing to say? No harmony?"

Jason pulls my arm up in the air as he grabs me with the other hand and pulls me toward him. My breath catches and he places my hand behind his head. He kisses my neck and

I surrender my contention, lifting my chin to the ceiling. I shudder in Jason's arms as his hot breath flows over my neck, following his tongue from my ear to my throat.

"There's nothing that needs to be said, Annie." Jason's lips never leave my neck. "I think we have perfect harmony."

"The distance between us isn't only measured in miles," I say, questioning how we can ever reconcile our two very separate lives. Jason roughly grabs my face with both hands. He startles me, but I'm certain there's not an ounce of fear in me. Jason Leer will never hurt me.

"You're wrong, Annie. I'm right here." He kisses me and a fire wells up in me. I force myself upon him, pushing him back against the counter. I pull his t-shirt over his head and stare at his bare chest. My own heaves with anticipation. I run my hands over the front of him, stopping at each nipple. My eyes devour his chest and his thick neck as my breathing is paralyzed, still lost in the tornado siren and Jason Leer, and of what I'll sacrifice to return to New Jersey.

"I'm going to leave my heart here," I say, and the truth in my words leaves me cold. My fears the last three days bubble up and choke me.

"I know," he says, and kisses me with a gentleness I didn't think existed in this cowboy. He lifts me to him and I wrap my legs around his waist and bury my face in his neck. Jason carries me to the bed and places me on top of the covers like a porcelain doll on a glass shelf. He pushes my hair away from my face and kisses me, igniting something inside me that cares nothing for my well-being, and I reach down and grasp his hard-on in my hand. At the very touch of it, I want him naked. I pull off his belt and unbutton his pants; my tongue in his mouth the whole time.

Jason moves between my legs. He reaches up to pull me forward and grabs my arm roughly. Without a word, he loosens his grip and moves me with a kinder hand to my back. He's coddling me, the girl scared by the storm.

"Don't waste your gentleness on me. I like you rough," I say, and his wicked smile dances from his lips to his eyes.

"I know you do, Annie." He pulls me to the edge of the bed and slams into me. He raises both my legs to the ceiling and watches as he penetrates me again, and again, and again.

"Roll over," he commands and I respond with immediate execution. Jason drags my knees to the edge of the bed and pulls me toward him. He bends his knees slightly and comes into me from behind. At this position, everything is touching everywhere and I arch my back and lift my face to the ceiling. He moves his hands to my breasts and pulls me to him using each one for leverage. His hands on them burn as he squeezes my nipples between his fingers.

"Come for me, Annie," he says, and slaps my ass. It jars me from euphoria and reminds me of the No-No Zone. He's nowhere near it. Jason's pace intensifies as do the spasms deep within me. I can no longer hold on and I convulse, lowering my face to the bed for support, as Jason continues to take me. My chest shakes and he comes, and I know there is no sensation in the universe that will equal coming with Jason Leer.

~ 13 ~

"My vanished soul challenges what we owe the dead"

It's been four days since I left Oklahoma. Having to leave Jason to go through security was the only reason I was able to get on the plane. I would have never been able to walk away from him and onto the jetway. We talk on the phone. I text him, which he hates, and e-mail is apparently out of the question. I am in love, and separated from, a guy from 1965.

I'm a shadow buying books, cleaning our house, and reading as much as possible to get ahead in every class. At this rate, I'll be the most miserable 4.0 to ever come out of here. Sean came up for lunch yesterday. I think he wanted to see for himself that I came back from Oklahoma as promised. I've lost my parents and now I'm 1,500 miles away from Jason. There's not much to be happy about.

Julia and Violet completely disagree. They are insisting I go out tonight. It's some of our roommates' first night back in town and they've gathered everyone they can find. Maybe I should have kept my job. Maybe it would have done me good to be there. There's only one thing that will do me good. It's seeing Jason in six weeks. *Six weeks.* What the fuck?

I put my bag on the floor and see the envelope on my bed. It's Jason's handwriting leaping off the paper. Without even opening it, it is enough, enough to keep me going for the next six weeks. I lie down and tear it open.

August 29th

Dear Annie,

By now a few days have passed. The time hasn't improved a thing down here. I miss you in my bed. I miss you in my truck. I miss your green eyes, and your smart ass. I'm guessing it's worse for you, all the thinking you must be doing. I stayed at the airport until your plane took off, waiting for you to walk back out of security, but as usual your strength amazes me.

I had a year between my mother dying and having you. This summer was the first time I'd been really happy since all of that happened. But this is your first time alone since your parents died. I wish you were here with me. But you're not. There's only so much I can do from 1,500 miles away. I've thought of nothing but you since I opened my eyes this morning, but that's every morning.

Think of them often, but live your life. Go out. Have fun. (Please do not get so drunk you can't protect your-

self and take the mace I bought with you everywhere.)
Spend time with your friends. If you are not going to be
here with me, savor the time there. They'll have you four
years. I'll have you forever. I'll be patient, and miser-
able the next six weeks, but I won't love you any less or
guilt you anymore.

When I came home from the airport I found the
heart necklace your Aunt Diane gave you hanging on
the corner of my bed, and I realized what you meant
when you said you were going to leave your heart with
me. You are unlike all the other girls in the world and I
will love this heart and you until I see you on my birth-
day. October 10th is now my favorite day.

Don't think about us in terms of why or how we
work. Think about what I'm going to do to you forty-
two days from now. Believe me; I've got some things
planned for my birthday. I love you, Annie.

> *Your lonely cowboy,*
> *Jason*

October 14th

Dear Jason,

Well, it's official. You can put your finger in every hole on
my body. What will you do when we run out of orifices?
Will you leave me then? I'll follow you if you do. Of course
you know that, because you know everything.

It's obvious you've been transported from some past era.

As if the rodeo events weren't evidence enough, the insistence on handwriting actual letters confirms it. You are a walking, talking, (among other things) relic that I cannot live without.

As usual, I will spend the weeks until Thanksgiving wanting and missing you desperately. I'll have several days before the bruises fade and my memories of last weekend will last forever. I am a very lucky girl.

By now I'm sure you've found the birthday present. Did you think I was your gift, unwrapped by you to play with? I know you don't want a new phone, or probably any phone, but I need you to have it. It will make sharing my life with you easier. It's prepaid for two years so to keep it in the box is throwing money away.

Turn it on and go to photos. I left you one last gift.

> *The girl who has sex dreams about you,*
> *Charlotte (that's right, Charlotte)*

That should at least get him to take it out of the box. The picture of my box closely trimmed with a J shaved in it should get him to use it. I hope so. It was more maintenance than this body has ever seen, and not all that easy to pull off. Poor Violet had to make sure it was straight. Now that's a good friend. My mother would freak if she saw that picture, but I'm not completely reckless. It was from my neck down; all boobs and bird.

"Charlotte, you ready?" Violet screams up the stairs as I place a stamp on Jason's letter. I place it in the mailbox on the front of the house with half of it hanging out, and head downstairs to where a small party has gathered. Smoke creeps up the staircase and I realize I'm late. The benefit concert at Kirk-

patrick Chapel starts at seven. We need to get a move on. I
enter the room, and the circle of smokers, at the perfect spot
to be next in line for the joint.

"A whole joint. How very Salem County," I say, and look
across the room at Noble. He knows exactly what I mean. It's
always a bowl, or a one-hitter, or some other nifty concoction
here, but in Salem County we roll it ourselves. Noble smiles
back as Wes and Julia start rustling the crowd to get a move on.

I've paid little attention to what we're benefitting tonight.
Somalia, maybe. My favorite band is playing and I would see
them anywhere so when Julia asked, I gave her the money for
the tickets. The joint is passed again and now Noble helps Julia
get us moving. One more hit and I'm not going anywhere.

* * *

Fall is officially upon us. The leaves have turned and are already
beginning to float to the ground with the mid-October breeze.
The first to land crunch under our feet as we walk the two
blocks to Kirkpatrick Chapel.

"What is this thing we're going to again?" I ask Julia, who's
slipped her arm through mine.

"It's a benefit concert. There were only five hundred tickets
sold so it should be intimate." Julia says this with an air of ro-
mance. All five hundred of us are filing into the chapel at the
same time. I haven't been here since my first days at Rutgers.
It's probably similar to what it looked like in 1873 when it was
built for Rutgers students to worship.

We walk through the double doors held open by ushers
with buckets soliciting additional donations and the rose red
walls engulf the chapel. White pillars stretching to high ceil-

ings highlight the dark wood floors and the wooden pews. We file in, moving as close to the front as possible. It hits me that Kirkpatrick is the first church I've been in since the death of my parents. A cold air runs across my neck and I remember my grandmother's warnings of "catching a chill." I think I just caught one.

Within minutes of us sitting down, the lights fall and the band plays their soulful drums and harmonica-filled songs. I'm in the middle of the pew, flanked by Julia and Violet. Noble, Wes, and Sydney make up the rest of our group. More people file into the church and plead for everyone to squeeze together. We're all standing now so the number of people in the pew no longer matters. The acoustics in the chapel are eerie, designed for an organ, but equally moving with this blues rock band.

All I can think of is my mom. She would want me to go to church. I'm not sure this counts. But I haven't done anything she'd want, have I? *I have.* I came back to Rutgers. I'm studying. I just happen to be in love with Jason Leer. The one guy she specifically told me not to love. The very last piece of advice she gave me before she died.

The music and the lyrics are too much and I find myself fighting back tears. I lean over to Julia. "I'm thirsty. I'm going to find a drink."

"Do you want me to come with you?"

"No. I'll be back in a few. Save me a spot," I say, and try to appear unaffected. I slide past Noble and Wes and rush out of the chapel as I hear the last of the harmonica lightly sounding. I walk down the hill and rest my head on my arm, leaning against a tree that has probably been here since 1873 too, and I cry. I cry for my mother bleeding in a car, I cry for my father dying before he had a chance to say good-bye, and I cry for me on a tree, unable to tolerate a song about prayer in a chapel, so filled with hate for our heavenly father. *I am so going to hell.* This makes me cry even harder, which a small part of me recognizes as a good sign.

"Hey," Noble says as he turns me around to face him. "What's wrong? Did something happen?" His kindness aggravates the crying and I cover my face with my hands, too embarrassed to face him. Noble pulls my hands away and pulls me to his chest. He's so tall my face hits square in the middle of it and I wrap my arms around his back and hold on for dear life. "Charlotte, please tell me."

"I haven't been to church since my parents died and..." *And what, Charlotte?* "And I miss my mom."

"Charlotte, I'm sorry." I try to keep it this side of a sob as I unleash my utter sadness right into the center of his chest. He rubs my back and never says a word. My violent sorrow eases and Noble pulls my hair from my neck and lays it on my back.

"Noble, I'm sorry. I know I am a tremendous buzz kill." Noble keeps petting my hair.

"No, no. Crying girls are fun." No one can kill a party like I can; one more thing to feel guilty about. I try and catch my breath and calm a little.

"Noble, what do you think we owe the dead?" Noble's hands still and he lifts his face to the fall sky.

"What do you mean?"

"My mom didn't want me to be with a cowboy. She told me the day she died *not* to fall in love with a cowboy, that it's not safe. That it's not what she wanted for my life," I say, and wipe the last tears from my face. Relief courses through me at sharing my mother's words with someone else. Noble is searching my eyes for more information. "She was specifically talking about Jason." My heart breaks at the words released to the world. "So I'm just wondering what you think we owe the dead." He's silent, trying to find an answer to a question he would never have to answer if he wasn't burdened with my friendship.

"I don't think you owe the dead a thing. Not one thing more than you owe anyone else in this life. But Charlotte, you owe yourself to be happy." I consider his words. "Judging from the way you're running from churches you think you owe them a life without Jason Leer." His words cut me and I pull back a little. Noble's reflex pulls me to him again and I lay my head on his chest, considering the debt I've imposed on myself. *What if it's not a debt? What if it's intuition? What if she's right?*

"You're going to be an amazing boyfriend someday."

"Someday?" he asks, not sounding insulted at all.

"When you're ready to settle down. You'll have to stop chasing girls."

"Who's chasing who?" Noble asks, and I laugh. He's right.

"Such the victim," I add with fake compassion as Noble pulls me onto his back for a piggy back ride.

"Let's go to Olde Queens Tavern. I've had enough church," he says, as he starts to carry me down the hill.

"You're going to miss the concert."

"I know, but I'll miss you if I go back in," he says, and I ride the rest of the way to Queens in silence.

~ 14 ~

"While stars glowing brightly unravel what's in my head"

The anticipation of homecoming this year is unlike anything I've seen since I first arrived at Rutgers. Apparently Homecoming falling so close to Halloween is unusual and celebrated for its rarity. Julia and I have finished three bottles of wine as we work on our costumes and I'm hoping mine looks as good in the morning as it does through my double vision right now. My phone dings with a text and Julia throws it on the couch next to me, being careful to avoid the three jars of glow-in-the-dark glitter paint I've been using as a medium. The text is a picture of a full moon and it's from Jason Leer. A small sob lodges in my throat.

"What? What was the text?" Julia asks. I hand her the phone as I go to the front window and look at the giant moon lighting the sky. "Nice pic. I guess he's using the phone."

It's beautiful.

I text back and within seconds my phone rings and Julia says good night, recognizing I could be a while.

"Hello," I say, suddenly filled with energy even two bottles of wine can't dampen.

"Just because I'm using this fancy new phone doesn't mean I want to text rather than talk to you."

"Point taken. I'm glad you're using it."

"Had I known these phones came with naked pictures I would have bought one years ago," he says, and I laugh, completely unembarrassed. "What are you doing?"

"I'm making my Halloween costume. Are you sure you can't come up?"

"I can't miss Kansas. It's the last rodeo for fall," he says, and I know all of this. His rodeo schedule is taped to the wall beside my bed.

"I know. I can't wait until you're done and really can't wait to see you Thanksgiving," I say, and the hunger in my voice surprises me.

"Hmm. What are you going to be for Halloween?"

"Horny, apparently."

"See that you stay that way until I see you Thanksgiving," he says, not being playful at all.

"I'm a starry night."

"I should have known. Send me a picture," Jason says, and I look down at the very little black dress I have been decorating with glow-in-the-dark stars and regret having sent him the smart phone.

"Are you dressing up? Do people in Oklahoma celebrate

Halloween?" I ask, and laugh as the question comes out of my mouth.

"Yes. People in Oklahoma dress up. I don't, though."

"Well, I always picture you naked anyway so a costume is unnecessary. If you change your mind about coming, let me know. It's Homecoming here and things are going to be very crowded."

"Who's coming?"

"Jenn always comes for Halloween. It's a bonus it's Homecoming, too. I'm trying to convince Margo to come."

"Sounds like trouble."

"Takes some to know some."

"I love you, Annie."

"I know," I say, and listen to the empty phone after Jason hangs up. *Stupid cowboy. Why do you have to be so far away?*

* * *

Jenn arrives with her angel wings sticking out of her backpack. She pulls her halo out of her bag and it's bent.

"How fitting," I say.

"I'm so bummed Margo is not coming."

"I know. She just started dating some guy named Matt and they are going to a party as the girl in the shopping cart and the guy in a toga from *Animal House*. It's not as funny with only the guy," I explain.

"Certainly not. Is she going to walk around in a bra and underwear all night?"

"Not just underwear, but old fashioned underwear. She sent me a picture of her hair. She looks great. I think it's an outside party so I'm sure she'll have him wheel her around all night."

"I love that girl," Jenn says. "Your dress is awesome." Jenn admires my starry night.

"You have to see it in the dark," I say as I get up and turn out all the lights in the room. Within seconds the stars on my dress, all different sizes and shapes, take light and glow.

"Charlotte, that's awesome."

"I know," I say, very proud of my handiwork. The lights turn on and Wes is standing in the doorway.

"Hey, what are you guys doing in the dark?" he asks.

"You'll see later," I say. "Where's Noble?"

"He's going to meet us out later. He has a date."

"A date? On Halloween? Sounds serious," Jenn says, and I delight in the anticipation of making fun of him later.

"That's good. Noble would make a great boyfriend." With that Julia comes downstairs dressed as Princess Leia on vacation, complete with a Princess Leia wig and a Hawaiian shirt, and Sydney and the rest of my eight roommates come up dressed as planets. All of a sudden Wes's costume makes sense. He's the sun. Who wouldn't love this holiday?

Pictures are taken. I send one to Jason of Jenn, Julia, and myself, and one of the solar system I'm traveling with tonight. We head to the first party at the largest fraternity house on campus. The line is enormous out front, but Sydney has recently become close with a brother and Wes's twin brothers are both brothers so we're let in the back fence. The yard opens to an enormous dance floor with fake smoke pouring off it at random intervals. There is a long tube being held out a second story window with a funnel attached to the end. A ninety-pound girl is on the ground with the tube in her mouth.

"Thirsty?" Jenn asks.

"Not if I want to be standing by the end of the night."

"Oh, don't sell yourself short, Charlotte," she says, and Julia arrives carrying three beers in her little hands.

We settle in here, enjoying the clear night until Wes's friends from home arrive and we move inside. A deejay is playing in a near-completely dark room and the crowd has glow sticks moving with their bodies. My dress takes on a life of its own and I become instantly famous. Apparently, on Halloween it's okay to touch a starry night, even if you've never been introduced.

"Do you want to trip?" Wes shouts in my ear.

"What," I scream, leaning closer to him.

"Do you want a hit?"

"What?" What the hell is he saying?

"Stick out your tongue," Wes says, and demonstrates by sticking his out. I do as I'm told and Wes carefully places a small square of paper on my tongue. "Now smile," he says, and I do. We regroup three beers later, too close to the smoke machine. It makes me cough and suddenly feels scary. I lean into Wes.

"I don't like the smoke."

"Me either. Let's get the others and get out of here."

"Really? You want to leave?" I ask, shocked. My heart is racing, or is it? Wes was looking forward to this party more than anyone.

"Things are about to hit and I think we'll be better off someplace else."

"What are you talking about?"

"You'll see." Wes gathers our now small group and we walk onto College Avenue. Outside of the loud music and crowd, things appear totally differently. The street lights melt down to the street and back to the sky as I tilt my head. The cars' distance doesn't match the sound of their approach, and almost every person walking on the street worries me in some way. We stop at a side street and my inability to figure out if it's safe to cross the street, even without a car in sight, shocks me.

"You okay?" It's Jenn in my ear. I look at her and her bright blue eyes are covered by enormous pupils. "Wes told me he gave you a hit of acid." *Ohhh.* I scowl at her, accusing her of leaving me alone in whatever this is. "So I took one, too. Poor Julia, I shoved one down her throat also." I exhale the breath I didn't know I'd been holding. "Together forever," Jenn says, and I could hug her.

"Hey girls, I hear we're tripping tonight," Julia says, and puts her arms between ours. The three of us cross the street attached to one another as I hope we'll be the rest of the evening.

We wait for Wes and his friend, Michael, to go in the liquor store and buy a case of beer. By now, everything is so intense I can't imagine walking into a store. I don't know how they're navigating it but I'm staying out here. Jenn shows us a bird in a tree, which we discover is a squirrel. We decide it's the Jersey Devil, just as they finally come out of the store with their own adventures to tell us about. Wes is carrying a case of beer and three packs of cigarettes.

"It's going to be a long night," he says with an enormous grin.

"How long?" I ask, and take the cigarettes from him.

"It's 11:30 now. We could be like this until dawn," he says, and I look at him in disbelief. "At least."

"I'm glad I like you guys." A horn beeps and the sound reverberates between my ears. We hurry back to 108 Hamilton and pour into the upstairs living room as I lock the door behind us. Exactly who do I think is going to sneak up on us?

By the time I get upstairs the lights are on, the beer has been put in the refrigerator and Julia is playing music. Wes lights a cigarette and Julia gives him an old bowl lined with tin foil to ash into. The sight of it shocks me. Julia hates smoking as much as the next nonsmoker, especially in our house.

"Just this once," she sternly tells Wes. He moves to the windows and opens them.

"No matter what, stay away from the windows," he turns and tells me. Suddenly everything out the window catches my attention, especially the cool night air. I'm hot in here. "Understand?" he asks, and I nod in agreement and move away from the window.

"Is everyone tripping?" Michael asks.

"How can I tell?" I ask, still trying to figure out what is going on. Jason's voice rings in my head, "Stop thinking, Annie."

"Turn out the lights," Michael says, and Jenn flips the switch. Michael stands in front of us with a glow stick from the party in his hand. It's not completely dark in the room because of the street lights, but the little green stick is beaming. Michael moves it from side to side and we all watch in wonderment as a green line trails behind it. He moves it in a circle and the same trail follows it.

"I think I am definitely tripping," I say. Michael moves the glow stick in a figure eight symbol and the light tries to catch itself. We are all enthralled by his tricks, so much so that we don't hear the knocking on the door. The doorbell has us looking from one to another, scared to answer it.

"It's Sinclair," Wes says, and goes downstairs to open the door for him. *Oh Noble.* His smile is going to light this place up. I hope he's tripping, too. Noble and I kind of trip through life together without drugs. I can't imagine how much fun this would be with him. I listen for his footsteps on the stairs, anxious to see him. My phone rings, and when I see Jason's picture cross the screen I quickly hit ignore and turn the phone over. Julia is watching me sympathetically when I look up. It's hard to explain. I love him even more tripping, but I do not want to talk to him about it. Something inside of me knows this time needs to be protected; the way Wes moved us here from the party.

I hear voices arguing outside and that fills me with fear. I can't imagine anyone dealing with something unpleasant right now. Do I have to go to the bathroom? I kind of think I do, but I'm not sure. The voices raise and I make out Noble's. Why isn't he coming inside? I move closer to the window, but stay a few inches away, remembering Wes's warning.

"What is your problem, dude? I offered you one." Noble moves closer to Wes.

"It's not about giving me one, you idiot. It's about Charlotte. Her parents were killed a few months ago. Do you really think she's ready for her first acid trip? You're a selfish asshole." He's mad about me, about me tripping. My phone rings again and again I press ignore. If Noble has a problem with me tripping, Jason is going to implode. Jenn reads my thoughts, probably all of them, and switches the music. I lay my head back, relax, and drink my beer. The voices outside quiet, and my phone stops ringing and I watch Julia create a pattern on a piece of paper using markers and pens. The swirls keep moving after her pen leaves the paper and my amazement grows with every new color. I wave my hand in front of my face and the same trails follow it that followed the glow stick.

"Thank God we left that party."

"We would have been all right. It was just really crowded.

Hard to trip with all those people around," Michael explains, and I gather this is not his first trip.

"Is this always the same?" I ask.

He turns his head to me slowly, unwilling to let go of whatever caught his eye.

"No, but it's pretty much always awesome. The better the people, the better the place, the better the fun." I rub my thumbs in circles over my fingerprints and notice my hands are wet. Or are they? I rub both palms together and still can't tell.

"So it's just like real life," I say, and the guitar floats, literally floats through the room as I can see the music streaming through the air. I fight to keep a handle on everything and again remember Jason's plea to not think so much. The song's lyrics catch my attention. They're about a car accident. It's tragic—

The music stops. I open my eyes to see Noble pressing the buttons on Julia's iPod and I relax. Noble gives Wes the look of death and Wes closes his eyes to avoid it. Noble smiles in my direction, his warmth forced, but welcomed by me. He comes and sits down next to me, sinking us both into the depths of this old couch, and as he puts his arm around me I rest my head on Noble's beautiful shoulder.

"How you doing, Charlotte?"

"Better now that you're here," I say, and mean every word of it. I love Noble so much it's bursting from me. I let that thought go for fear I might actually see something burst from me. My phone rings and I ignore Jason's call again with Noble watching. "He's not going to stop calling," I say.

"You don't want to talk to him?"

"I don't want to lie to him and I don't want to tell him the truth," I admit, staring at my phone as it buzzes with a new message notification.

"The longer you don't answer the more worried he's going to be."

"I know. I don't think there's ever been a time I haven't answered. At least not at night, even if I can only pick up to tell him I love him and I can't talk." Noble hugs me tight and kisses my head. I write a text to Jason and show Noble for his opinion.

> I'm sorry I haven't picked up. I'm
> kind of in the middle of something. Are you okay?

Noble shrugs. Nothing is going to be okay where Jason is concerned. He's going to freak.

> If you don't answer the phone
> the next time I call I'm coming
> up there.

Yeah, he's not going away quietly. I send one last text.

> Please promise me you won't be mad. It's very important
> that you not upset me.

I show it to Noble. "Does that sound crazy?"

"Yes, but it's true. Go upstairs and talk to him. I'll wait right here. If you need me just yell, okay?"

"Yes," I say, and walk upstairs alone. I turn on every light but the one in my room. The stars are glowing on the ceiling and on my dress and I can't bring myself to ruin it with light. I hold my phone as I watch the stars move through the night and I question how anyone can be mad about this. It is amazing.

My phone rings and I can't wait to talk to Jason. That is, until I hear the complete anger in his voice.

"Where are you, Annie?" I take a deep breath and try to focus on the stars. They're not exactly the same as the ones above Jason tonight, but they are loving me.

"I'm in my bedroom, Jason." His name falling off my lips sends a chill through me. The love I feel for him travels like wet concrete and settles in every appendage and at the pit of my stomach.

"Are you alone?" He's confused. I try to think of what this must be like from his perspective, but it's unpleasant so I run from it.

"I'm tripping on acid," I say, and watch the constellations change above me.

"What?" He's livid.

"I'm lying on my bed, in my Halloween costume, alone and tripping on acid. That's why I didn't want you to be mean to me. I'll be tripping for, what time is it?"

"Annie, what have you done? It's 1 a.m. Is there anyone else home? Anyone there with you?"

"Yes. Jenn and Julia are here. Wes and some guy named Michael, and Noble."

"Are they all tripping too?"

"Yes. Actually Noble isn't and he seems upset that we are. That I am, but I don't want to talk about that if you don't mind," I say as if it's his obligation to understand. "What time is it?"

"I told you it's 1 a.m." His voice is quiet. I hope I haven't broken him.

"Still?"

"Yes, Annie. Still. What time did you take it?"

"I think around 11, maybe a little earlier. It feels like three days ago."

"Annie, I'm going to go, but I want you to know I love you more than anything in this world. Do you hear me? I love you." My smile threatens to break my lips right off the front of my face.

"I know you love me, Jason. I can tell by the way you look at me," I say, and can see his gray eyes staring at me with a glint in each one. "I've never felt safer," I say defiantly, and block out the memories of my parents. *Not tonight, Mom.*

"Don't leave your house and don't set anything on fire. Promise me you will take care of yourself."

"I will. I love you," I say, and hang up the phone. I wish he could be here, like this with me. Something tells me tripping might not be physical enough for Jason.

I walk into the hallway and Noble is waiting on the stairs. He startles me and then he warms me.

"Thanks, Noble."

"Anytime, Charlotte. You okay?"

"I'm great," I say, and my face hurts from smiling.

"I'm going to go. If you need anything, anything at all, you'll call me?" he asks, holding my face to gauge my understanding.

"I promise."

"Okay, have fun tonight. They call it a trip for a reason. Enjoy it." Noble turns to leave and I follow him down the stairs.

"Noble, I love you very much," I say, and he turns back to me with his naughty grin.

"I know you do, Charlotte. I love you too. I'll see you tomorrow, okay?"

"Perfect."

Our core group stays together the entire night. We bake cookies no one wants to eat, we watch cartoons, we attempt to play Pictionary which is utterly hilarious, and we lie still and listen to music. Around 4 a.m. I get a text from Jason.

Are you still okay?

And I respond

Peachy

Which probably pisses him off, but I'm on drugs for God's sake. I can't figure out what won't make him mad.

"What's up with you and Jason? You're so intense," Wes says.

"It's not easy to explain," I answer, leaning my head back on the couch.

"Well try. Because I would love to understand, too," Julia chimes in, and I'm shocked she really doesn't know. It's all so clear to me. I need Jason Leer to live, at least to feel alive. It's not easily explained. Ergo their question.

I stand up in front of them to try and unravel what's in my head. I take Wes's cigarette and turn off the light and move it back and forth. The glowing red light trails back and forth across the room. "See how this red light looks different tonight than it ever has before? That's how it is with Jason. Everything in the world is different, in the most enticing way, now that I have him."

I can feel all their eyes on me in the darkness. "Since I've been with him love is different, need is different, want is different, different from any of the same emotions I've known my whole life. I never knew things existed like this and I can't give them up now."

Their silence beckons me to continue. They still don't understand. I take a deep breath.

"If I stay quiet, I can be a thousand miles away from him, and shudder just from the thought of the things he does to me, sexually." I pause and regroup. "If I imagine him being hurt," I push the thoughts immediately from my mind, "I'll burst into tears. I can feel him in my soul and when he looks at me it's as if he swallows me whole," I say, and feel like I've done it justice.

They are all still looking at me. Not saying a word.

"What? Does it sound crazy?" I ask.

"No. It makes me think every relationship I've ever had has been incredibly inadequate," Wes says, and I exhale, relieved they don't think I'm insane. I turn on the lights and Julia is crying a little. I look at her, confused.

"I get it now. I get it," she says, and laughs at herself for crying.

*　*　*

By 6 a.m. things are different inside the house. We're all exhausted, but not sleepy. The trails stopped a few hours ago and we talked until we barely had voices left. At 8 a.m. Wes and Michael head back to their apartment and Julia, Jenn, and I lie on the couches unable to close our eyes. It's the Sunday of Homecoming weekend. Between the tailgate, the game and the tripping last night, I might slip into a coma if my brain ever lets me sleep again.

"Maybe we should get high?" Jenn suggests.

"Really, more drugs? Maybe we should have a glass of milk," I suggest, but I know we have not one healthy thing in this house.

"I think it will take the edge off," Julia says.

"Milk?" I ask, confused. It's going to be a while before my brain works again. I'm hollow inside. And I miss the trails. I miss the lights melting and the music floating. I hope I get to do this again someday.

We lie on the couches for too long or maybe just long enough, and I announce I am going to shower. I look at the clock above on my phone and it's 10:30 a.m. Besides the trippers, the house is completely quiet. I turn on the water and grab a pair of shorts and my Oklahoma sweatshirt. *God, I miss you Jason.*

I take off my clothes and let the water pour over me. It hits the top of my head and runs off my chin and I extend each arm and let it fall from my fingertips. I don't think I'm tripping; if I was the water droplets would lengthen and touch the floor, but things look different today. I understand why they say tripping opens your mind. It's different than anything I ever could have imagined. I would love to do it at the beach someday. Maybe with Noble. He would be great to trip with.

I hear voices in the hall. People must be waking up. I, on the other hand, will hopefully be going to sleep after this shower. The bathroom door opens and I wait for someone to ask to borrow something, but the shower curtain is pulled back and Jason Leer is staring at me. His eyes capture me and I force my brain to understand his presence.

"If this is some kind of hallucination, so help me I'm going to drop acid every day," I say as I step to him and place my wet hands on his face. Jason's eyes are dark and angry. He pulls his face back and furiously takes off his clothes off. I watch him in silent disbelief. He isn't really here. This is some insane side effect of LSD. I move to the side as Jason steps into the shower. He stares at me through shattered eyes.

"How?" I ask, but his eyes weigh on me and I stop talking as Jason grabs my face in both hands, resting his forearms on my shoulders. He looks like he might cry. His hands are crushing my head and I cover both his hands with my own and try to loosen his grip.

"I'm right here," I say, breathless. "Jason, I'm right here." I pull his left hand down and move it across my breast, and he exhales. His eyes finally release mine as he looks over every inch of me. "I'm right here," I repeat. He forces me to the back of the shower, kissing me hard, his lips on mine exploding something in my brain. I've wanted him so much and now he's here. I wrap my leg around his waist and he pulls me up his body. He's in me before I can ask for it. He's forcing me into the back of the shower as his assault continues on my lips and I just want him to feel me. He's looking down, avoiding me, as he takes what he needs.

And then he comes. He pulls out and rests his face on my shoulder. I run my hand through his hair and the burden of guilt washes over me. I have caused him tremendous pain. I circle my arms around his thick neck and kiss the side of his face. I leave a trail of blood and touch my finger to my mouth to confirm my lip is bleeding. The blood pools between my teeth and lip and I pull back from him to spit it on the floor of the shower. Jason watches it run down the drain and I pull his face back to me.

"I'll always be right here."

"You weren't last night," he says, and a fight brews.

"How did you get here?"

"Harlan dropped me off at the Kansas airport and I flew here." Jason looks around the shower and I know our time here is done. I've never been with him without having an orgasm.

Although, I'm not sure I could have one right now. There's a negative side effect. He steps out of the shower and wraps a towel around him as I watch. "I'll meet you upstairs," he says, dismissing me as he leaves. I lean back under the shower and try to decipher what I'm feeling. There's joy he's here, the need to touch him, utter exhaustion, and anger creeping up at his judgment. I didn't do anything wrong.

I dress in my shorts and sweatshirt and follow Jason to my room. It's a long walk past Julia's unconscious body on the couch. I've never felt anything but the need to run to him until this moment.

Jason is sitting on my bed, his feet on the floor, his elbows on his knees, and his head between his hands, naked. He could be a sculpture, but he's not. He's a living, breathing, angry cowboy. I kneel in front of him and pull his hands from his head.

"Tell me?" I plead.

"Tell you? Tell you what? You tell me, Annie." His anger is increasing. "You tell me how I'm supposed to stop you from becoming a crackhead from 1,500 miles away." He spits "crackhead" as if it is the vilest form of life. I pull away and anger occupies my face.

"You don't have to call me names," I say, avoiding his point.

"What would you call it, Annie? Your parents die in a car accident and a few weeks later you start tripping on acid. Does that sound healthy? This is why I don't want you to smoke pot. It's a gateway drug. Next you'll be cooking meth and shooting heroin."

It's hard to believe this is a serious conversation, at least on his end. I fight to not laugh in his face.

"You're overreacting. LSD is not going to kill me and it's not going to lead to a life-ending addiction to heroin. It's the soda and smoking that'll kill you. You should take a look in the mirror," I say, the fight back in me. "Have you ever tried to clean dried soda off a countertop? It's like glue. You want that in your body? You should smoke pot! Try something natural."

I exhale and fear I've gone too far. I'll know in a second because he'll throw my bed out the window.

"Natural," he scoffs, nodding his head as he says it. "Maybe later you and your cool new friends can take me out to the ACID HIT FIELD where you guys picked your natural drugs. Do you hear yourself?" *Do not roll your eyes, Charlotte.* I relax my jaw and take a big breath through my nose. And exhale it. I stand up and sit on top of Jason, straddling his naked body. I run my hands over his shoulders and down each arm. When I get to his hands I place each one on my ass and run my hands back up. I pull my body toward him and cross my ankles behind his back. *Now we can talk.*

"I'm not becoming a crackhead," I say, and move myself closer still. "I'm just trying some new things. I think drug experimentation is completely age appropriate, even more so if my parents hadn't died." Surely there is some study to back this up. "I need you to trust me and give me a little freedom to explore." I tilt his face toward mine. "I need you to trust me," I raise my eyebrows, begging for his understanding.

"If you want to explore, why can't you join a club or volunteer somewhere? Don't act like dropping acid is a rite of passage. It's not like a sheet of it comes with your admission letter." He's allayed. His anger lifts and I'm sure it has something to do with our bodies being this close because touching him is calming me, too.

"I love you," I say, and kiss the side of his face.

"I need you to come back to Oklahoma with me." His

words paralyze me. My lips are still touching his cheek as fear grips me. He pulls me back to see my eyes. "I'm serious, Annie. Come back to Oklahoma. You can explore whatever you want there. I just need you to be with me when you do it."

I know any protests I make now will only be met with his stubborn righteousness, so instead I suggest a nap. He's exhausted; he drops the subject, for now. He lies down with me in my nice bed in New Brunswick and I collapse into a state that no thoughts can penetrate.

~ 15 ~

"I seek out the end, what's beyond love and obsession"

November 24th

Dear Jason,

You were right (take note); I should have gone to Oklahoma. Do people in Oklahoma celebrate Thanksgiving?

When you showed up on my doorstep the night before my birthday I was in shock. After Halloween I was afraid you'd never come to Rutgers again. But you came, oh did you come. You came because my first birthday after my mom's death would be a tragedy, and seeing you on my doorstep saved me from the despair. What I didn't know was the first Thanksgiving would be almost as bad. At the time I was grateful, but now that I realize I traded my birthday *for today, I am lost. I can't sleep in my "nice bed" without you. Instead of this house being filled by you, it's overflowing with the memory of my parents.*

Sean went with me Wednesday to get my new license and took me to the Corner Bar to celebrate. It was delightful drinking during the day and I've decided if my career as a statistician doesn't pan out I will become a proper drunk. Will you still love me?

Sean also forced me to have Thanksgiving dinner with him and Michelle. I took a platter to your dad. That went probably exactly how you would've expected it to. He answered the door seemingly annoyed that someone, or maybe I, dared to knock on it. I gave him the food. He looked shocked. He said thank you and I got the hell out of there. I think he's really starting to like me.

Margo and Jenn came today and helped me sort through my mother's clothes. I felt awful for them. It was a long day of watching me cry. All that's left are her favorite scarves, and a few bags, and her jewelry. If I'm too young to sort my dead mother's belongings, they're too young to help me. I hope I never have to return the gesture.

I'm staying up late tonight, giving myself an excuse for not going to church tomorrow. The next time I see you I am going to strip you down and run my tongue over every inch of you. Our time together is never enough.

I am very, very thankful for you.

With the love of a now 21-year-old,
Charlotte

* * *

I'm shocked when I turn the radio station to Christmas music and Jason doesn't balk. We ride down Route 18 and away from Rutgers, with my hand between his legs. I'm relieved exams are over. Jason finished a week before me and has been hovering over me the last five days as I tried to study. There is no other distraction in the world that can match Jason Leer's naked body. Or clothed.

We exit the turnpike at 322 West and exit the Christmas music at the first notes of "O Holy Night." *Had enough, huh?* It's December 20th. There is never enough time. Classes at Oklahoma resume January 7th, a full two weeks before Rutgers begins. Two weeks in Oklahoma should be interesting. Two weeks with Jason will be intoxicating. I run my hand over his cock at the thought of it and he instantly responds.

"I'm going to drop you off and come back later," he says, smiling.

"Yeah right," I dismiss him as he pulls into my driveway.

"I have to go work on your Christmas present. I'm whittling you a wooden replica of my cock."

"That's what I wanted," I say enthusiastically. "A cowboy and a boy scout. Very nice." I climb on top of him. "Unless you want me right here I suggest you take me inside," I say, and kiss him. How can I need him so much? It's only been a few hours since I had him.

"I want you right here. Just like every other place, at every other time."

* * *

At 5 p.m. I sit up in bed and watch Jason sleep. He looks so young lying here, so peaceful. But he is a man at the age of twenty-one who still wrestles animals for fun.

"Jason," I say, and try to lift his arm over me. It takes my two arms to lift it and he finally wakes and cradles me.

"Jason, how long are you going to be a steer wrestler?" I ask, wondering if "this sort of thing" goes on beyond college.

"For as long as I'm alive," he says, and I wait for the laughter. The laughter that never comes.

"Seriously?" I ask, rolling over and resting my chin on his bare chest.

"Annie, are you thinking again? Can't you just live and let live?"

"That's rich, coming from the guy that wants me to be so careful I need to live with him so he can keep an eye on me." Jason sits up and I fear I've gone too far. He holds me tighter, avoiding a fight.

"Will you do something for me?" I ask, already knowing his answer. Jason nods and I get out of bed to rummage through my backpack. I find the last letter I received from him. He wrote it during his exam period. "Will you read this to me?"

"All your drug use made you dumb?" he asks as he takes the envelope from me.

"When I read it, it's my voice in my head and I want it to be yours," I say, and my honesty softens him.

"I always hear your voice. When I read a road sign, a menu, a book, it's always your voice in my head, Annie." *Sometimes you are so easy to love.* I nudge his hands, asking him to begin as I lay my head on his shoulder.

"Dear Annie, I see the extensive education you are receiving in civilization hasn't dulled your smart ass. Yes, we do celebrate Thanksgiving in Oklahoma. We are a very patriotic and thankful community. Speaking of Rutgers, I used my fancy phone to look up your local news and read how a liquor store was robbed and the cashier shot, just a few blocks from your house. I think you should take a gun back to school with you after Christmas break."

I hide my smile, not giving Jason an ounce of satisfaction.

"I'll talk to Sean about it when we get home. Right now my head is resting on the new pillow you bought me and I'm staring at the enormous picture of the ocean you hung when you were here for my birthday. What is it with you and the water? With safety in general? Can't you learn to love quilting or gardening? Obviously, you'd have to move out of civilization to actually grow anything in the ground. Even if you could find an inch of dirt to plant, someone would steal your crop.

"I looked up at the moon last night. I miss you, Annie. I'm tired of being apart. Come back to Oklahoma with me in January. You'll love it. January is storm-free and warmer than New Jersey.

"And I'm here.

"Without you.

"Without my clothes on.

"Waiting for you to come.

"Whatever is beyond love and obsession,

"Jason."

"Thank you," I say, and roll on top of him, wanting him for the third time today. It's only a matter of time before I call Oklahoma home.

* * *

"Do you want your Christmas present?"

"I thought you just gave it to me," I say, still breathless.

"No. That wasn't it. You get that every day," Jason says, and he looks happy, truly happy. Why is it so much easier when we're together than when we're apart? He walks across the room and my stomach knots at the sight of him naked. It's been six months; I hope this sensation never dies. He dives back in the bed, nearly breaking my arm, and holds out a small, square box. I hold it in my hand and stare at it.

"Don't worry. I'm going to knock you up proper before proposing. It's just a present," he says, and I laugh, more so at the fact he knew what I was worried about before I did.

"There's something to look forward to," I say as I rip open the wrapping paper. Inside the box is a circle pendant hanging from a gold chain. It's a turquoise stone surrounded by garnet rays. It looks like a sun, or—"Is this a spur?" I ask, studying the necklace.

"This is a rowel, which is part of a spur. I had it made for you. The blue turquoise is for you, your favorite color, and surrounding it are the red—"

"For you."

He had it made for me. Jason starts to take the necklace out of the box and I start to cry.

"What's wrong?" Jason asks, but the smile on my face breaks through the tears and I shake my head. "Oh geez, Annie."

"I just love it. It's beautiful." Jason tries to open the tiny clasp, but after several attempts with the giant clubs he calls hands I take it from him and put it on me myself. "Thank you."

"Merry Christmas, Annie. It's the first of forever."

~ 16 ~

"As the stubborn give in, a startling concession"

I can't wait sixty-three days to see you again," Jason says as if he's been stewing about it in Oklahoma and just picked up the phone to profess it. "You should have given me a weekend in February."

"Do you not like your Christmas present?" I ask, knowing he is going to love it once we finally get to the lake.

"A week alone with you in a cabin is the best Christmas present ever, but the thought of it is not going to replace seeing you before the middle of March."

"What about Valentine's Day weekend? That's only a few weeks away."

"Can't do it. Test Friday and two papers due Monday. No love that weekend. How about the first weekend in February? It's Harlan's birthday. He always throws himself a huge party."

I look at the first weekend in February on my calendar and that Friday night is ZTA's first date night of the semester. I promised Julia, Sydney, and Violet I'd go. When I didn't do our annual New York City Trip over Christmas break, I swore I would be at date night. There must be a way to make it up to them. A way to make up screwing up the makeup for something I screwed up in December. It makes my head hurt.

"Annie, you there?"

"I'm here. That weekend is my sorority date night. You'll have to come here," I say optimistically.

"Harlan's birthday," Jason says as if Harlan's birthday is a national holiday providing him a day off from all other obligations.

"I guess I'll see you in sixty-three days," I say coldly. Rodeo season hasn't even started and we're already too busy to see each other.

"Great," he says, and I wish I could punch him in the face.

* * *

I change my clothes and settle into bed with my *Statistics for Economics* book. I've been to this class one day and the professor is already my favorite. Noble's in there too, so I get a ride to class twice a week. No wonder it's my favorite. My phone dings with a text.

> You can't miss my birthday
> darling.

The number is unknown, but it's clearly from Harlan. Jason must really want me to come to Oklahoma to have given my

phone number to Harlan. Or he is sitting right next to him
and typed it in for him.

> Who is this?

I text back.

> Ha. It's the hottest cowboy
> in OK. The 2nd hottest just
> told me you're not coming
> and it's not flying. Bring your
> friends down here.

I drop the phone and go downstairs. Julia, Violet, and Sydney are watching the latest HBO phenomenon huddled together on the couch. I climb in next to them and wait for my
chance. The show is good; if I watched TV I would probably
like it. When it ends they start to get up and I know it's now
or never.

"Any chance you guys want to go to Oklahoma with me?" I
sheepishly ask.

"God no. I don't even like the idea of you going down
there," Violet blurts out.

"It's not that bad. In fact, it seems like lots of white people
really like it." I should have worked on some selling points before coming down here.

"I am absolutely sure I don't want to know what that
means," Julia says, and adds, "and I am not going to Oklahoma."

"Well see, it's my friend Harlan's birthday and he's throwing
himself a big party the first weekend in February, and—"

"Oh no," Julia cuts me off.

"What?"

"Don't try and act like you don't know that's date night."

"I won't have a date, though," I try.

"I don't have one either. We'll take Noble and Wes," Julia says as if it's the perfect solution. But since I tripped, Wes is persona non grata. We're going to need a Plan B.

"It's not that simple," I say, dejected. *Of course it's not.*

"It actually is," Julia says, dismissing the entire subject.

* * *

Ten days of Jason's mood deteriorating daily has been taking its toll on me, too. His tone got nastier as his calls got shorter. It's as if date night is hanging over our heads, the anticipation growing into a malignancy pinpointing the moment I chose Rutgers over him. Ten days without a letter from him. I'm not surprised. I couldn't think of a thing to write that would shrink the tumor.

Things, unrelated to each other, begin happening and change everything. Julia drops off the money her cousin owed me from the summer sublet of our room, a thousand dollars in cash. It is five months late, but he had to settle up with his bookie first. Tough baseball season apparently. I was in no rush. I've got some debts from the summer I'm not sure if I can make good on, either.

On Wednesday, we hit late night at the fraternity house down the street and Julia falls in love with one of the brothers. It may not be love, but whatever it is the guy scores an invitation to ZTA's date night. Today, Friday, I receive my second text from "The hottest cowboy in Oklahoma."

In case you come to your
senses: The Copper Penny
10 pm

But none of it alone changes my mind about going to
Oklahoma. If Jason and I are going to make it, I'm going
to have to keep a part of myself alive doing it. I shower and
dress, even add some makeup, all with a misplaced determi-
nation to succeed at being alone. When Julia and her date,
Sydney and her date, Violet and Blake, and I, walk into the
Harvest Moon Brewery I realize the place I belong on this
very night has nothing to do with New Brunswick or Rutgers.

I watch everyone drinking and laughing together, still a bit
stiff because it's the beginning of the night. The girls look
beautiful. Julia is sexy in black, Sydney is demure in blush, and
Violet is completely dramatic in a red wine dress that matches
the lipstick covering her gigantic smile. I have my picture taken
with some of the best friends a girl could ever ask for and then
they ridiculously include me in their couple's pictures. Noble,
who was invited by a sister of mine, finally saves me with a sly
wink and the flash of a Jack and Coke.

"I have to say, even with all of Julia's bitching, I didn't expect
you to be here," he says, and hands me the drink.

"I'm making some ridiculous point to no one." I smile
through my sour tone. Because it's impossible not to smile at
Noble, especially when he's in a suit. "You look nice."

"Thanks. Farmers clean up well, huh?"

"The best," I say, and realize what I really want right now is
to be standing next to Jason Leer. "Do me a favor?"

"Anything, Charlotte," Noble looks me right in the eye. My heels have me hovering closer to his 6'2" height.

"When Julia asks where I am, tell her I went to Oklahoma." Noble raises his eyebrows.

"Oh sure, get me killed." He jokes, letting me off the hook.

"Thanks, Noble. You are the best." I grab my coat before sneaking out the side door.

I hail a cab and tell the driver, "Newark Airport," without looking back at New Brunswick. I buy a ticket on my phone while careening up the turnpike. Security is a breeze. It's there I realize I have nothing but the dress on my back and the four-inch heels on my feet with me. I hold in my hand my mother's tiny evening bag with my phone, lip gloss, my license, and six hundred dollars in cash. I run into a newsstand to buy some water and pick-up a Jersey Fresh magnet with a big tomato on it for Harlan and a bag of peanuts. The rest is out of my hands.

* * *

The car service drops me off in front of The Copper Penny, completely over dressed, at exactly 10:38 p.m. It looks like any other college bar from the outside, but quiet. I guess it's early, but I thought Harlan said the party started at ten. I walk into the Copper Penny and it's not as empty as it seemed from the street. I check each face for Jason's or Harlan's but I don't see anyone that comes close. I find the bathroom and consider calling him. If I do, he'll be here within seconds. What if they changed their plans? What if they're not coming here? I decide a drink will help me decide and slide into the only open barstool between a group of girls to my right and two guys to my left.

"What'll you have?"

"A Jack and Coke, please," I say, and fold my parka on the stool before hopping up on top of it. All of this takes place under the watchful eye of my new neighbor, who looks from the top of my head to my platform peep toes and back up again. Rather than avoid, I look him right in the eye as I cross my legs in front of me. My cheeks flush and I appreciate the warmth. My strapless tube dress is not only over the top for the Copper Penny, but a little chilly combined with an icy Jack and Coke.

"Pardon me for saying," he starts, and I brace myself, "but you don't look like you're ready for a night at the Penny." This makes me laugh. Besides his obvious inference I imagine how one prepares for a night at the Penny. I look around the Penny; its wooden floors are mirrored by the wood paneled ceiling and framed by the wood paneled walls. It creates a warmth of some kind, like being submerged. There are random objects, a plastic pool, a rocking chair, a reel lawnmower, hanging from the ceiling and the walls are covered with signs relaying important sayings, my favorite of which is: NEVER UNDERESTIMATE THE POWER OF STUPID PEOPLE IN LARGE GROUPS.

"I know. I was in the middle of a cocktail party when I decided to come." The guy laughs as his face shows exaggerated regard.

"You don't say? A cocktail party? Now where did you find a cocktail party 'round here?"

"It was in New Jersey."

"New Jersey! What are you at the Penny for?" At this the girls next to me all start to take notice of me and I purposely lower my voice to deflect their attention.

"I thought I was coming to a birthday party, but I must be in the wrong place."

"Harlan's birthday?" he asks, and I nod my head. "Are you with Harlan?"

"No. Jason Leer."

The guy's face shows some level of recognition as he elbows the guy sitting next to him and says, "Yo, this is the one Leer was talking about the other day." At this I am all ears. The other guy leans back on his bar stool and has a look. These cowboys have little time for subtlety.

"What was he saying?" I ask.

"At the time I called him a damn liar for exaggerating, but now that I see you, he didn't quite do you justice," he says, and I blush at his forwardness.

"Thank you, but I don't usually look this nice. It was an important night in New Jersey," I say, and the guilt creeps in.

"Why are you here then?" *Good question.* Before I have a chance to answer, the door opens and a crowd pours in. Their boisterous energy fills the bar, immediately changing the atmosphere. Harlan stumbles to the middle of the floor and looks me up and down. He is ten feet away and obviously drunk. I look behind him for Jason.

"What has the good Lord sent me here?" he shouts with a satisfied grin crossing his face.

"Happy birthday, Harlan."

"Jersey!" he yells. "You have returned from that awful civilization, have you?" I move to stand in front of him.

"Yes," I say, and cannot help but embrace his infectious playfulness. He startles me by picking me up and spinning me in a circle. I hold on tight, afraid we might fall. I think Harlan's been celebrating his birthday for a while.

"You've grown five inches since I've seen you. Must be the nuclear plants," he says as he puts me back on the ground, right smack in front of a smiling Jason Leer. I fight the urge to attack him, and just take him in. He's penetrating, a stark contrast to the lightness of Harlan; the sight of Jason soaks deep within me and when I look in his eyes a familiar chill runs through me.

I lose myself in him and walk toward him without realizing I'm moving. With my heels, Jason and I are the same height. I might even be a little taller and I like it. I imagine raising my knee and having sex with him against the wall of the Copper Penny. He raises his left hand to the side of my face and I close my eyes and rest my head in it. Rutgers, and date night, and the last ten days disintegrate with his touch. Jason pulls me to him and kisses me. So very gentle at first, but then his hand moves to my hair and pulls at it as his tongue enters my mouth and I take him. I couldn't tell you where we are. A small part of me leaves my hands at my sides, knowing their next stop will be his shirt. Jason's tongue retreats and I open my eyes, the sight of a wide-eyed Harlan returning me to the center of the Copper Penny. I take a deep breath, so thankful for air travel.

"You don't know how much this means to me," he says, but I do. "You are so stubborn."

"I'm in Oklahoma, aren't I?" I point out, not wanting to start a fight, but also recognizing the planes fly both ways.

"Now that I see how you dress for a date night things will be different in the future."

"You'll come?"

"No, but you are not going anywhere near one alone. How did you get from the airport?"

"I took a car service," I say, confused on why this matters.

"You should have called me. I don't ever want you taking a car from the airport. It's over an hour away. Something could happen."

"I probably won't drown." Jason rolls his eyes at me and I

put both hands flat on his stomach, not wasting a minute with him on this stupid conversation.

"Leer, take our picture," Harlan says as he hands his phone to Jason and wraps his drunk arm over me. Jason pulls me to him, shocking Harlan and me. "Come on, it's my birthday. I share my team with you."

"I don't share Annie. Now get off her or I'll tie you by the balls to my truck," he says with a playfulness that surprises me. Harlan laughs and moves on. He really is great at dealing with Jason. I wonder if I start laughing and walking away when he gets all worked up how that will go.

I look up and see a girl I think is from Salem County, but that can't be. "Is that—" *What is her name?* Jason looks in the same direction.

"Stephanie Harding? Yeah. She transferred in last September."

"And is that—"

"Jack Reynolds? Yes. He's comes in to see her a lot." I can't remember a thing about him. He's at least two years older than us. Stephanie I remember, but not all that well. Salem County is small, but I never hung out with her. Birds of different feathers, I guess. My phone dings with a text from Julia.

I'm going to kill you and the cowboy. Jersey style.

Jason looks at me, concerned. It's late to be getting a text not from him.

"Julia," I explain. "She's thrilled I left date night and made it here okay." Jason pulls me to him again. I give Harlan's birthday party about thirty more minutes.

~ 17 ~

"I'm living my life, I proclaim without fear"

I am definitely not going to see you next weekend?" I ask, frustrated I'm on the phone rather than in his bed.

"Are you okay with that, Annie? I've got a lot to do."

"I'm fine. Valentine's Day is not a big deal to me. I just want to make sure. I might go see Jenn at East Carolina State."

"How you figuring on getting there?"

"The train. That's one of the advantages of civilization. Mass transit."

"Let me know if you go. Don't go by yourself. Take Julia; make up date night to her. How long is the train?"

"About seven hours, I think. It will give me time to write you."

"I'd rather have you safe than the letter."

Jenn calls with a change of plans. She convinces us to meet her at East Carolina State and drive to New Orleans for Mardi

Gras. It's more of an explicit order than a question. Jenn has a way of making things seem perfectly logical even when you know they are not. I used to always use the "if I told my mother this plan would it sound okay" test, but since she died I just go with it. Julia was on board as soon as she heard about it. The old Charlotte would have jumped at the chance, but this Charlotte has to answer to a cowboy. There is no upside to being an orphan.

* * *

I'm tapping my fingers on the car window as we cross the Louisiana state line, fifteen hours after we left Jenn's apartment. I'm glad we didn't try to do this all in one day. Margo's roommate has a friend that goes to Tulane and she thought we might be able to stay with him, but halfway here she called and said it fell through. Needless to say the hotels are booked and I am in Jenn's eight-year-old Jetta careening toward the largest party in the world with no place to stay. Jason is going to be thrilled.

"Nervous about something?" Jenn asks.

"Just figuring out what, and when, I am going to tell Jason about this," I say.

"Do you ever think he's a little controlling?"

"Yes!" Julia yells from the backseat, obviously not sleeping.

"No. I never do. He's protective of me, but in some ways we're hanging on to each other for dear life. I couldn't bear anything happening to him, either. He just doesn't understand Rutgers, or cities, or cultural diversity, or…never mind."

"Yeah, I get the point," Jenn says, and leaves me remembering how she had to pretty much force me to come here today and yet I am so excited for it. I have wanted to come to Mardi Gras since I knew it existed.

We stick to the original plan and follow the signs to Tulane University. Even though we have no place to stay here, it's the only lead we've ever had so we may as well follow it through. To nowhere, that is.

"Any suggestions on a place to stay?" Jenn asks, and we all laugh at the ridiculousness of this question just coming up.

"I could really use a shower," Julia says.

"I think you're setting your expectations a little high. We might be sleeping in this car tonight."

"Ugh. I'm not going to feel pretty without a shower." I laugh at Julia as my phone rings.

"Hello."

"Hey, where are you?" His voice across the line makes me shift in my seat. He's happy.

"I'm in Jenn's car." I look at Jenn and she's nervous for the big reveal. "We're actually looking for something. Can I call you back in a little while? When we find it?"

"Sure. Be careful," he says, completely unworried.

"Okay, 'bye." I hang up the phone. I should have written him a letter before I left Rutgers. Some news is better not told over the phone. Or ever. He is going to flip. Which is ridiculous. He goes to rodeos every weekend, driving long distances, on highways, with Harlan. I'm sure they're not one hundred percent sober every second. Harlan oozes recklessness. And I am supposed to sit in the library all day, every day. Jenn slows down at the sight of three guys walking on the sidewalk.

"Ask these guys if they know of a place to stay."

"Really? You want me to ask these three guys if they know of a place to stay in New Orleans during Mardi Gras?" She stops the car next to them and puts my window down. I slowly turn my head, glaring at her the whole time until I face the victims, then I smile my sweetest grin.

"Hey guys," I start out, and I'm sure their instincts are telling them to run. "Do you know of a place to stay for a few days around here?"

"It's Mardi Gras," the mean one says, but his friends are kinder.

"Everything is booked. Sorry."

"Oh. We were supposed to stay with a guy that goes to Tulane, but he ended up renting out his apartment. Do you go to Tulane?" They're not getting off that easy.

"Yes."

"Did you ever think of renting your place?" They look at each other. I almost feel bad for them. I'm the nice one. If I unleash Julia and Jenn on them they won't have a chance.

"How much are we talking?" I look into the car and Jenn clearly has no idea. Julia slides over to the car door and puts down her window.

"We'll give you $300 to stay until Monday."

"Follow us. We're right around the corner."

We are going to be raped and killed. Although, as we watch these three seemingly nice guys who I think I could take in a street fight, it does seem unlikely. We didn't get their names, but Jenn forced one of them to give her his key. I'm almost sure we could be arrested for some of this. It seems like we kidnapped them. It might be a hostage situation. Julia has the mean one wrapped around her finger shortly after arriving, and he is going over the map, parade routes, and schedule. Jenn's made it pretty clear we are not hanging out together, just living together. Jersey girls really are sweet. I walk out back and find a tree to sit under while I listen to Jason completely freak out over the phone. As I dial his number I hope he doesn't answer. I will cowardly leave a message and not pick up my phone the rest of the trip. He'll never find me here. For the first time I understand the ease of lying. This entire conversation would be so much easier.

I shouldn't have to hide.

I'm twenty-one.

"Hey baby," he says, and fear grips me.

"How's it going?" I ask. I'm not going to lie, but I'm not going to say anything unless he brings it up. Is that lying?

"Besides missing you, it's fine. I can't wait for our week at Cedar Creek. Less than a month left. How's North Carolina?"

"It's probably fine," I say, and I can feel his eyes turning dark, his silence conveying his understanding.

"Where are you, Annie?" he asks, his voice on edge.

"New Orleans." I brace myself.

"What the hell is in New Orleans?" I pause and he answers his own questions. "Jesus Christ, Annie. You're at Mardi Gras!" he screams, and I hold the phone from my ear. I've never heard him so angry. "What the fuck are you doing?" I take a deep breath and avoid my initial reaction of screaming at him. I know it's not going to help the situation. "Answer me, Annie!" His command pushes me over the edge. I'm not some dog.

"I'm en-joy-ing myself. I am attending one of the biggest parties in the world with some of my best friends," I defiantly spit out, and the words surprise me. "I'm living my life," I say, and exhale.

"Oh yeah?"

"Yeah," I say, and hold back the tears.

"Well, live it without me." Jason Leer hangs up the phone and I cry in the back yard of three guys I don't know, at Tulane University. How can he be so awful? I could be hit by a car in Stillwater, or killed by a tornado. He's kidding himself if he thinks this is all just worry for my safety. We are never going to make it. Julia walks out the back door and hands me a beer. I take it from her and wipe the tears off my cheeks as my breath still catches in my throat.

"I know it's different between you two," she says so tenderly for her. "But I hate that it makes you cry."

"He does too, I'm sure." I drink my beer and wonder when I'll see him again. If I could be there with him we could get through this, but without being able to touch him I have no idea how to fix it. I look at the back of this little house in New Orleans and vow to myself that I am not going to Oklahoma this weekend. It will have to wait.

Charlotte is headed to Mardi Gras.

Jenn must be manning the music because reggae floats out the windows, followed by her yelling out, "Stir it up, ladies." Julia and I exchange the look that signals it's time to buckle up. I'm sure the guys inside the house are doing the same. "We're headed to Vieux Carré!" she yells.

"What the hell is that?"

"The French Quarter, my lovely. Leave your bra at home." I completely ignore Jenn. She is insane. I consider calling Margo and asking what to do about Jason, but I opt for a good cry in the shower instead. Once dressed in the only shorts I could find in my drawer in February, we head to the French Quarter, having only images from magazine pictures to prepare us. It takes about ten seconds to discover nothing can prepare you for Mardi Gras.

There are people everywhere. As in every inch of my body is touching another person. I have never been so thankful for my height. My petite little Julia is staring straight into the shoulder blades of the girl in front of her. She gives me the "this is fun" look and I try to see if there is any relief, anywhere. I grab her hand just as the crowd begins to chant "show your tits, show your tits," toward the balcony above us. There is a group of five people on the balcony with beads decorating their necks. As the crowd reaches frenzy, two girls lift their shirts and sure enough, show their tits. Instead of shock I am in awe of the space around them. I couldn't lift my elbows to show anybody my tits if I wanted to. Beads are thrown and I catch sets for all three of us. The crowd moves down the street and we fight it until we're standing with room to breathe right behind it. The chant now focuses on a balcony a few doors down. I get it. The crowd follows the tits.

"Girls, you need some beads," an insanely inebriated man says, and tries to put a strand over my head, falling to the side in the process. I catch him right before he takes Julia down with him.

"Are you okay?"

"You're an angel," he says, and looks above my head as if he sees something. Something that's not actually there. He puts the beads over my head.

"Are you sure you're okay?" I ask again as he dusts himself off, and starts to move toward the sidewalk.

"Oh yeah. You should have seen me this morning. I was wasted!" he slurs, and disappears. Jenn walks over with three hurricanes and we all take a big gulp.

"So when's the first parade?" I ask, waiting for some floats to come by.

"Tomorrow we go to the parades," Jenn says.

"Tonight we get to know 1.2 million people better," Julia adds, and we all toast.

We hit a side street and find a man sitting on the sidewalk charging $10 to pee in his yard. Gross, but necessary. I look down at my feet in their flip flops and they are scratched up and black with dirt. When I finish I rejoin Jenn and Julia, using the Clorox Wipe that's included in my $10 purchase. There's probably a video of my bare ass peeing being uploaded to the Internet as we speak. That should placate Jason.

We walk back to Bourbon Street and buy yet another round of hurricanes. Eck, rum. May I never drink it again. *This is Bourbon Street, isn't it? Where's the freakin' bourbon?*

"Where you from?" some guy asks.

"Jersey," I answer flatly, waiting for the next guy to ask me if it's above the Mason Dixon Line. If you don't know where the Mason Dixon Line is, why do you care?

"Jersey, huh. You should wise up and come to the South. The confederates are superior in every way." *What an idiot.*

"Oh yeah, who won the big one?" I ask, and this really smart confederate has to think about it for a while.

"You need some beads," He says, suggesting something he's not going to get. I turn toward him. "How about you show me your tits and I'll give you my big balls?" He directs my attention to a strand of beads each the size of my fist. At least I think that's what he's talking about.

"Jersey girls don't do that," I say educating him on the poise and class of those residing "above the line."

"Do they do that?" he asks, pointing to Jenn, who is mooning a guy across the street. I sigh.

"Apparently."

By 4 a.m. I can barely stand any longer. My feet have been cruelly tortured and my eyes hurt from being open too long. I want to go home, or at least back to the house we've taken over at Tulane. We walk one block over and hail a cab. As soon as I close the door I lay my head on the headrest and exhale. I check my phone and there is not one text or message from Jason Leer. A crowd begins to form around the cab and the driver inches forward trying not to hit anyone. I lock the door next to me and tell Jenn to do the same. The crowd starts rocking the car and the driver continues to move forward. They are yelling something and I look at Julia between us. I can see people climbing onto the trunk out of the corner of my eye. The cab driver seems unaffected and continues. I'm reminded of the sign at the Copper Penny touting the power of a collection of stupid people. I think they're going to flip this thing and kill us in the process, but whatever. I'll be dead and Jason can write "I told you so" on my gravestone.

As the cab breaks free of the crowd—or as I call it in my head, the mob—Jenn proclaims, "I love Mardi Gras."

"Yeah and we haven't even been to a parade yet," Julia adds.

"Everyone loves a parade," I say, and wish I was going home to Jason Leer.

* * *

I rally in time to explore the city. We steer clear of Bourbon Street, expecting it to smell worse than trash day in New Brunswick, and mosey through the historic streets of New Orleans. We stop for catfish po' boys and beers when we're hungry, and as long as the conversation remains I don't think about Jason Leer. Well, I am actually consumed by thoughts of him, but if we keep talking I can keep it together.

By 3 p.m. we find St. Charles Street and realize many people are already lining up for tonight's Bacchus Parade. We find second row spots in front of a bar and decide to stake it out. Having been raised on Salem County's Fourth of July Parade, I'm not prepared for Bacchus. As in, I am in shock. The Salem County parade is fire trucks, and horses, and tractors decorated in red, white, and blue. Children line the streets, in which there is plenty of space, to catch candy thrown from the floats. It is gentle, and quaint, and entirely Main Street.

The Bacchus Parade is an entirely different animal. People perch on ladders with chairs beneath them. By the time the parade starts I can see nine people deep behind me. A family befriends Jenn and lets us into their party. It is here, amongst our new family, that Jenn broaches the subject of Jason Leer.

"How exactly do you see this ending?" She doesn't have to elaborate. There's only one thing I care about ending in the world. Not this parade, not this trip, not my life, but me and Jason Leer.

"I don't see it ending," I answer, and see Julia leaning in to hear the conversation.

"What? Do you guys have no hope this is going to work out?" I ask both of them. "I love him," I say, and the desperation in my voice scares me. It must scare Jenn, too, because she waits several minutes before she says another word.

"I just think you've already been through a lot. I will kill him if he hurts you."

"I think I'm the one hurting him," I say, unexcited by the giant Baccasaurus in front of us. "I keep telling him he's all I want, but I do things that completely contradict that statement." I'm hit in the head with beads and our new family thinks we're crazy having this quiet conversation in the midst of complete hysteria. The crowd is a steady scream as the largest and most colorful floats I've ever seen depict music, TV, fashions, and sports from the last forty years.

"Maybe things would be easier if you both realized it's possible to want more than one thing," Julia offers as a glimmer of hope. "That rarely works out, but it's possible, I guess." The gilded armor of the knights on horseback is followed by a band with flaming music stands coming down the street, each carrier with a propane tank hooked to his back, and again I marvel that I am not in Salem County anymore. I catch more beads and feign excitement as the Celebrity King of Bacchus, Hulk Hogan, hurls beads at me. The little girl next to us catches a blow-up alligator and absolutely delights in it. She wants a blow-up alligator; I want a rodeo cowboy in Oklahoma. Why's it so easy for her?

***

I sleep in Tuesday. It's Fat Tuesday, but that means little in New Jersey. We left with our tails between our legs, having a BAC of 87.9. Our Tulane housemates seemed happy to reclaim their house. It was a long journey home beginning at the crack of dawn Monday morning. Julia and I arrived in Philly late and I paid for a car to bring us back to Rutgers. I couldn't do NJ Transit at that point. I let sleep take me.

***

I stumble downstairs, my eyes only half open, and Violet looks like someone died.

"This just came for you." She's holding a business-size envelope in her hand.

"What is it?"

"I don't know. It's from Oklahoma," she says with a look of shared sorrow furrowing her brow. I take the envelope from her. It was FedExed overnight. He wanted to make sure it was here as soon as I got home. *Bastard.* I take it upstairs and brace myself for some form of hatred to reach out of it and choke the life out of me. I rip off the string and open it. Inside there is a letter envelope with "Annie" written across the front in the most comforting handwriting I know. I open it and it's a letter.

February 19th

Dear Annie,

~~You've gone too far. You are completely out of control. I can't keep dropping everything in my life to find you and make sure you're still alive. I almost killed someone when I hung up on you Saturday. I can't live my life with someone who has as much control over me as you do, pissing me off to the point of murder. I don't think we should be together. It's not good for either of us. You apparently want to do drugs and drink all night, while I want to love you and keep you safe. Why can't that be enough?~~

~~Do you not see that you are spiraling downward? I think you need to see a therapist, maybe withdraw from~~

~~school and move in with your brother for a while. Your~~
~~parents would be worried sick if they knew what I know.~~
~~If your goal is to kill yourself, I think you're on the right~~
~~track, you should be dead before you hit twenty-two. I'm~~
~~not going to be around to watch it. I can't. You'll kill me~~
~~too.~~

~~Why is it so difficult for you to understand the way I~~
~~feel? I only want what's best for you. At this point I would~~
~~take what is okay for you. As you're reading this you're~~
~~probably snorting cocaine and laughing at me. You'll be~~
~~whoring yourself out soon. Or worse, you'll just be so~~
~~fucked up some guy will climb on top of you and rape~~
~~you. When you try to fight him off he'll punch you in the~~
~~face until you're unconscious and can't scream anymore.~~
~~Is that what you want, Annie? Is that how you want to~~
~~LIVE YOUR LIFE?~~

~~You want to live your life? That's fine. I'm going to live~~
~~mine too and it's not going to include going to sleep every~~
~~night wondering what fucked-up, stupid thing Annie is up~~
~~to tonight.~~

~~Fuck you.~~

I love you and I need to see you.

Jason

Whatever about everything else in this letter. He loves
me and he wants to see me. The rest can be fixed, but only
if he'll see me. I do think he needs to cut back on the *Date-
line* episodes. I take a tablet out from under my bed and
start a letter to him, but I don't know what to say. I start as
usual.

February 20th

Dear Jason,

But I still don't know what to say.
I leave three pages blank and on the bottom of the third page I write:

I don't know what to say.
   But I love you.

Annie

~ 18 ~

"The death in my words too horrendous for tears"

Weeks of no letters. No apologies. Just the bitter cold of New Jersey's winter to not warm me. Jason calls, but he doesn't want to talk. He's different and I can't stand it. My only hope is the cabin on Cedar Creek Lake. We both seem to be clinging to it, as if it will heal us. Fix what's fractured or end, finally amputate, that which is killing us. He's been in different towns in Kansas the last three weekends for rodeos, and I've been waiting and wasting away. I considered going to a rodeo, even mentioned it to Jason, but he said he'd prefer me to just stay put. His words nearly tore me in half.

Even with all this, I won't apologize for New Orleans. I keep studying. If my grades drop I'll have to admit my mother was right and I shouldn't be with Jason Leer, or that Jason's right and I'm on a downward spiral. I will prove to both of them that I'm safe, that we can make this work. Even if it kills us.

***

The plane taxis to the jet way in the Oklahoma City airport and I take a deep breath. It's finally over. My heart races as I hear the cabin door open and the rows ahead of me begin to file out. I pull my backpack out from under the seat in front of me and walk off the plane to a reunion weeks in the making.

It's a short walk through the terminal. I take the first escalator to the lower level; Jason is leaning on the wall at the bottom of it. He sees me immediately, but doesn't smile. I can't keep one from my face. The sight of him is all I need. That and to touch him. The escalator is filled with passengers from my plane. It's an eternal ride to reach the bottom and reunite with Jason Leer.

My courage gives out as I reach the bottom and approach him cautiously. He slips my backpack off my shoulders and pulls me toward him, holding me too tightly. He kisses me and I float back to heaven. He's slow, savoring every millimeter of my mouth, and when he stops he puts his mouth to my ear and breathes, "Oh Annie," and I cry.

Jason pulls me back and wipes the tears from my face. He lingers over my eyes, reading my thoughts, reclaiming my soul, and finally he grants me a guarded grin that speaks more of his anger than screaming at me would.

"You're so thin," he says as he runs his hands over my protruding collar bone.

"It's been a long few weeks," I say, never taking my eyes off his face. He closes his eyes, hiding from me, and I want to scream at him, but there will be plenty of time for screaming. Jason picks up my backpack and throws it over his shoulder as he takes my hand and leads me to his truck. I climb in the passenger side as he throws my bag at my feet from the driver's side. He starts the truck and follows signs for I-240 East.

* * *

By the time we see the sign for I-35 South to Dallas, I am staring out the window and silently crying. For weeks I have been waiting to see him, having no idea it could somehow make this worse. The realization that something has ruptured between us, combined with the insistence that I did nothing wrong, consumes me. How can we be here, and how will we ever get back?

"Come here," he says, and pulls me toward him. I pull my arm back and shake my head no. "Annie, come here," he says again, pulling at the core of me. I unbuckle my seatbelt and move to the middle seat. He puts his arm around me and I disintegrate in his arms. "Why are you crying?"

God I wish I didn't know, but it's painfully clear.

"Because for the first time since you drove me to Stoners Lane, I'm not sure we're going to make it," I say, and stop crying; the death in my words too horrendous for tears.

We drive the next four hours in silence. He doesn't kiss my head, my hand is not between his legs, and we don't speak. It's the first time we have ever spent our first four hours together with our clothes on. It's a hideous turning point and I want to erase it from my existence.

I tell Jason the directions to the house and he follows them silently. We enter the wooded lane just before five and drive until we see a cottage with a wraparound porch lit by hanging white lights. It's still a couple hours until sunset, but the lights glow in the dim woods. Jason pulls the truck up next to the house and I get out first. I step onto the porch and through the front door of the enchanted cottage.

Soft music fills the house. It swirls around us as I step into the middle of the room. It has the opposite effect of welcoming me, it ignites the anger. *Why did you ever have me in the first place if you couldn't handle a relationship?* I know this isn't fair, but I blame him anyway. Fuck him.

I turn toward the door and he is standing there, barely inside the house, staring at me. I search his eyes, trying to understand what he's thinking, trying to decipher my own thoughts. What will become of us?

"Annie, I need to talk to you." Talk, talk, talk. I'm already tired of talking. I approach him and he moves back a step, his hands raised, denying me.

I advance and run my hands down the front of him, holding his now hard dick in my hand as I raise my eyes to him. "I need this," I say, and lean into him, my body hijacking the conversation. I don't care what he needs. Obviously. That's why we're in this position. I kiss him and he pushes me away with a hand on each shoulder.

"Jason, I need you." I push his hands down and pull my dress over my head, my bare breasts exposed. I climb up him and force my mouth on his but his response is guarded. I grab his hair and pull, and I kiss his neck. My lips attack his chin, and behind his ear. I return to his lips, where I impose myself upon him again. My skin is burning and I'm trapped between screaming out from need and trying to breathe. Jason takes my face in his hands and kisses me furiously. He throws me against the wall and is in front of me before I bounce off of it. His eyes are blazing as he roughly holds my chin and rips my panties off and spreads my legs with his knee. He's so fast. I can't breathe.

I reach up and grab his hand, afraid he might break my jaw. I push it away and punch him in the face, unsure of anything but the throbbing between my legs. I've never hit anyone before. I've never felt like this before. This is desperation.

Jason licks his now bleeding lip and pushes me back to the wall. He holds me against it by my neck and I search for his eyes, but he's too busy to see me. His rough hand covers the front of my throat as I watch him unbutton his pants with the other. I reach for him and an evil smile covers his face. He takes both my hands in his, my wrists crushing in his grasp as he holds them high over my head, and lifts my knee. I'm hanging from the wall, his grasp the nail suspending me, and I watch, not helpless at all. Jason pauses for one second then plunges into me. My chest caves in as I writhe, my body swallowing him.

"Is this what you want, Annie?" His words are filled with hatred and I don't care. I thrust forward, begging him for more and he pounds into me again. I utter some sound and face him, his level eyes not faltering.

"Again," I command, and he releases my wrists as he comes into me again. He lifts me up and holds me against the wall and I dig my nails into his back, wanting to rip the flesh from his bones. Jason never loses eye contact as he fucks me until I come, and come again.

My hip hurts, my back hurts, and I can't breathe, but he still enters me with hatred.

"Come," I say. He pauses and looks me in the eyes.

"Beg me, Annie. Beg me to come in you." I am lost, my body melting in his arms. He hits the wall behind my head with his open palm and it reminds me of who I am and where I want to be. I stare back at Jason with a renewed need.

My voice level and my eyes fixed, I beg, "Please come in me, Jason," and he surrenders to me.

I lower my leg and wrap my arms around Jason's neck. He buries his face in my neck and I can feel him. I can finally feel him. Weeks of needing him will be commemorated in bruises already beginning to form. Jason leans back and I take my thumb to his bleeding lip and hold it there.

"You're turning me into an animal," I say without a hint of humor.

"You're turning me into an asshole."

"I'd rather be an animal," I decide.

"Me too. That's what I need to talk to you about."

* * *

The night passes without us talking. We're too exhausted from the ride. Rides. I dread what he wants to say to me, but it's obvious he's not letting it go. He always sleeps flat on his back, but tonight he turns it to me and I take it, because I'll take any piece of him I can get at this point. I kiss him between the shoulder blades and run my hand down his arm and he stays still. I want to fight with him, but instead I close my eyes and let sleep have me.

* * *

"Annie, I need to talk."

"What's wrong?" I ask, surveying the strange room. *Texas, we're in Texas and Jason is next to me.* I close my eyes and fall back to sleep.

"I need to talk," he says again.

"Right now?" I ask, opening my eyes again.

"No, a month ago," Jason says, and I hear the need in his voice. Did he sleep at all? I roll over and face him in bed. He's so beautiful. I let my eyes cover every inch of his face. When they start to linger down his body, Jason interrupts. "Do you remember last summer when you asked me if I was falling in love with you?" I remember how confused I was that whole time. Jason seemed so sure of what we were doing. I was just along for the ride.

"I meant everything I said." He looks at me waiting for a response, but not asking a question. "It's not a life without you. I'm dead inside. When my mom died I learned the difference between the dead and the dead among the living, and I'll take the former." I kiss his forehead. "But Annie, you're making this impossible."

"How?" I ask, feeling unfairly judged.

"I know you love Rutgers, and the city, and all the rest of it, and I've come to terms with the fact you're not coming to Oklahoma, but I can't live this way. I am in complete misery." Jason's words tear through me. *Are you leaving me?*

"I worry about you every minute you're away. The only thing that fixes it is having you with me. This past month has been horrible, but still not as bad as the night you were in New Orleans. The hours dragged by as I imagined every possible thing that could happen to you." The cab ride out of the French quarter flashes in my mind and I fear what Jason would say if he knew we stayed with strangers.

"It's escalating." At this I have to use every eye muscle not to let them roll back in my head. I'm surprised he hasn't scheduled some type of intervention. Oh, that's right. No one would come but him.

"Did you ever consider if I wasn't a risk taker we wouldn't be together?" My mother's plea to find a safe guy runs through my head and I want to scream at him what I'm actually defying, because it's not him. He thinks he's such an obvious choice? Well, my mother didn't think so.

It's not fair to put my mother's dying words on Jason. *Is it fair to put them on me?*

"I can't spend the rest of my life worrying about you." At this I give in to the anger brewing and sit up to properly unleash on this self-righteous cowboy.

"Do you think you're the only one who worries?" I hurl at him. "You wrestle five-hundred-pound animals, for God's sake. Oh wait, after you dive from a horse going thirty miles per hour. Ten rodeos during school plus practice every day. I sit in class and *wait* for Harlan to call me and tell me you're hurt. And those are the good days. The real torture is having to attend. I use every element of my body to will you to survive. Every run is an hour long. I can't breathe, I can't watch. I can't look away." I have worked myself into a frenzy, having finally confessed my thoughts on the rodeo.

"Why haven't you asked me to stop?"

I want to say *because I love you too much to ask you to give it up*, but I know that's not the truth and it's too late to start lying to each other now.

I lower my eyes and say, "I'm afraid you'll say no." With that the tears come and I hate myself for crying. How pathetic. He should run.

Jason sits up and grabs my face with an urgency that halts my tears. "Don't look away from me," he says, and kisses me hard on the lips, forcing strength back into me. "Don't ever look away. You never have a thing to be ashamed of with me."

I climb on top of him, my lips taking from him everything I need. *I'm not ashamed*, I think as I climb on top of him. *But I should be.*

Jason is domesticated and gentle as he makes love to me and a peace fills the cottage as he fills my soul.

* * *

"I would give it up."

Would?

"I'm not asking you to," I say, wondering if I ever will. "You shouldn't have to give up something you love as much as bull-dogging for someone else. Especially not someone that loves you the way I do." I run my hands through Jason's hair and he lowers his eyes. If they were mine, he would force them back up, but I leave him alone with his shame. I happen to disagree. There are things you can't say to me.

"I know it's hard."

"Do you?" I hurl. "Do you have any idea?"

"You've got to trust that I'm gonna be all right," he says, and kisses my lips gently. "When I finish a run I'll tip my hat to you and you'll know I'm thanking you for trusting me, for believing it's going to be all right." Jason has broken my fears down into sign language. He thinks he can cure me with a tip of his hat. He has no idea what he's dealing with.

"Let's get some breakfast," I say, and Jason rubs his thighs.

"You need some. You're so skinny your hip bones bruised me. It's like fucking a skeleton," he says, and I laugh. "Have some ice cream, will ya?"

~ 19 ~

"The solace I encounter so easy to undo"

Jason and I spend our nights at the fire pit, warming ourselves and finding new ways to share an Adirondack chair. Our days we waste fishing, and reading, and swimming in the too cool lake. I play music all week that Jason hates, but only changes half the time, and we bask in each other.

I nap in the hammock and by Wednesday I'm finally rested. I wake to the sight of Jason taking his pocketknife out and carving the tree at my feet.

"Marking it. The way I wish I could mark you," he says, and continues carving until he backs up and I can see *J.L. + A.O.* carved in it.

"Who's A.O.?" I ask playfully.

"Some buckle bunny," he says, and I burst into laughter.

"What the hell is a buckle bunny?"

"It's a rodeo groupie. They travel around to different

rodeos and have favorite cowboys they root for. And when I say root for, I mean in the biblical way." I am in awe of this information.

"Why, Jason Leer, you are a bona fide celebrity, buckle bunnies and all. I'm not worthy," I say, and he smiles back at me. The smile that tells me I am the center of his universe. No one and nothing will ever hurt me.

From my shady hammock I see the sky, a perfect porcelain blue. Three giant black birds soar in a circle above us, their wings barely moving. They're a perfect pinwheel in the sky.

"Turkey buzzards," he says, and I squint to see better. I've never seen a beautiful turkey buzzard. They're always on the side of the road picking at carcasses. "They're looking for death."

"Maybe we should move around," I say, and Jason turns his gaze to me. He's the happiest I've ever seen him. "What a horrible existence," I say.

"That's how they were created." The buzzards continue in their circle and I'm mesmerized.

"They're so high you can't tell what they are. That close to heaven they're beautiful."

"You're beautiful," he says, and I release the birds completely from my gaze. "And this is close to heaven." A blue jay lands on the branch above Jason's carving. It hops and sings, and is full of life as the turkey buzzards soar above us. The little bird is simple and sweet, and steals my attention from the symbol of death.

"You can't die, Annie." I abandon the blue bird and find Jason watching me. "You can't leave me here alone. It will be hell…again."

And there it is. The answer to all our fights. Someone else

might be afraid to lose me, but the last person Jason lost, he lost forever.

"I'm not going to die. I'm as full of life as this blue bird." Jason climbs into the hammock with me and I roll onto my side, my arm across his stomach, holding him until the ideas fade from his mind. *I'm not going anywhere.*

* * *

On Thursday the temperature hits eighty degrees and we take the kayaks out and explore the lake. I've never seen a lake so big. We find an island and Jason makes love to me on the beach, and I name it "Lovers Land."

I run my hand in the water as my kayak drifts past his on our way home.

"What is it with you and the water?" he asks.

"What is it with you and the land?" I retort. "Without water there'd be nothing."

"Same with the land," he says, and I consider his point of view.

"But you're okay with lakes?" I ask.

"They're surrounded by land."

"Of course," I say, and forget his point of view. I'll have a lifetime to try and embrace it.

* * *

We return to the cottage and Jason mixes me a Jack and Coke while I make a salad for dinner. He pulls my hair to the side and kisses the back of my neck until I'm covered in sweat. He bends me over the kitchen table and takes me from behind.

He runs his tongue down my back, his dick inside of me, and I decide to drop out of Rutgers and buy this cottage. This is probably how the Unabomber started to fall off.

I straighten up. I'm swollen, bruised, and ripped apart. My nipples are so sore air touching them hurts.

"We can't have sex for a while," I say, and cut the tomatoes. Jason is standing next to me before I have a chance to gauge his reaction.

"Why is that?"

"My body can't take much more. It needs a break. I'm sure there are other things we can do."

"Annie, what's wrong?"

"Nothing. It's just a lot of activity after being completely alone for a month. I'm sore." Jason lifts me up and tosses me on the table. He spreads my legs and pulls me toward the light performing some crude OB/GYN exam and I shake my head.

"Oh. You're so red and swollen."

"I know," I say, and he lowers his head and kisses my bruised labia, causing the swelling to throb. He takes me in his mouth and sucks, and my breath catches.

"This isn't exactly"— I breathe—"The break I was talking about, but it's so good." His hand finds my breast. I lay my head back on the table and let his tongue heal me. He slips a finger in me and even this is difficult, but once in he turns it to the ceiling and strokes me. His tongue, his hand, his finger. *I am so glad I brought this up.* I reach down to touch his hair and with my other hand I cover my eyes as I come and Jason tickles me with his tongue. Screw dinner. I'm just going to lie here on the table the rest of the night.

"Let's take a bath," he says, and pulls me upright. "It'll make you feel better." I sit up and now this even hurts. Jason leads me into the bathroom and starts the water running into the enormous claw foot tub in the middle of the room. I go to the living room and grab my phone and portable speakers. I watch as he smells a jar of bath salts and pours them in with no regard for measurement as I turn on the music I'm sure he will complain about.

"Where's your lighter?" I ask.

"You gonna start smokin'?"

"To light a candle," I say, exasperated.

"I'll do it. You get in while it's hot." I undress and look at myself in the mirror. I'm well-rested and rosy-cheeked from the sun; the picture of health, until you see the rest of me. Car accident? Losing end of a paintball game? Sex with Jason Leer? I'm battered and bruised. I run my hand along the inside of my thigh and shudder at the thought of the things he does to me. Jason stands behind me and stops my hand with his own as he whispers in my ear, "Get in the tub."

I do as I'm told and climb into the tub. I lower myself until the water touches my torso and lift back up wincing.

"Too hot?"

"I just need a second to get used to it," I say, and lower myself again. I rest my arms on the sides and sink in, laying my head on the edge. Jason undresses in front of me, to my delight, and then goes to change the music.

He stands by the cabinet listening and I wonder what he's waiting for. His tolerance for any music I like is limited at best. He tilts his head and listens to the lyrics, and looks back at me. He likes the song.

"I feel beautiful when you look at me."

"You are beautiful, Annie. Surely you know that. I've heard you told a hundred times before."

"Understanding the way others view my appearance and the way I feel when you look at me are two totally different things." Jason lowers his magnificent self into the tub.

"What else do you feel when I look at you?"

"I thought you didn't want me to think about us?"

"That was then," he says with no need to finish the sentence. That was during a time when he protected me from thinking about anything. Jason's eyes tell a different story now.

"Transparent," I start, trying to decipher how I feel. "Alive. Condemned. Wanted. Safe. I feel like nothing bad can happen to me if I'm with you."

Jason holds my foot in the air and rests it on his shoulder and washes my leg with a sponge.

"It scares me, the control you have over me." This he finds humorous.

"That's interesting because it's the complete lack of control that keeps me awake at night." He places my leg back in the water and raises the other one. I could watch him touch me all night long. So gentle, here on Cedar Creek Lake in the fine state of Texas.

"What are you going to do after graduation?" The question comes out of nowhere and I have no answer.

"I'm just getting used to the idea I'm back in school. I haven't considered after. It's common to have a Masters in Statistics. Maybe I'll do that."

"So common."

"Probably not as common as Philosophy majors." I smile as I mention his major. "What are you going to do?" Fear grips me with this talk of the future.

"I won't graduate for another year."

"Why?"

"Light credits, especially in the spring. Makes it easier to miss four days a week at rodeos." Ah, the rodeo. It's not just a sport, it's a lifestyle. One that I don't understand.

"Do you ever think it would be easier to date a girl from Oklahoma?" I ask.

"Every day you're away I think it." I'm taken aback. "They're close. I could have them every day. They understand rodeo," he chides.

"They have dirty shoes," I interject.

"They listen to good music," he says, and I recognize how much easier life would be for him if he was with someone else. I stare into the bubbles in front of me. Jason slides forward and lifts my head.

"No matter what, I can't get past they're not you. You're in my blood and I'll never let you go." I should be insulted, or offended, or worried, but I understand all too well.

"Condemnation," I say.

Jason slides me around so my back is on his chest, his dick is resting between my cheeks, and washes the front of me with a light touch I didn't think this cowboy was capable of.

"Close your eyes and, if you promise not to use it against me, I'll tell you why I love you," he says in my ear, but my eyes are already closed. I lay my head on his shoulder and he kisses my neck.

"I promise."

"I love you, Annie, because when most girls would fall apart, you get pissed off. You don't understand the concept of surrender." I float up, not realizing I'm arching my back at his touch. "And you can't be tamed." He pulls me back to him "And yet I've never met someone with a greater ability to see the good in people. You are the perfect mix of courage and mercy." Jason rubs the sponge down the front of me and back up. His lips graze my neck and slide to my ear.

"Come to Oklahoma, Annie," he whispers, and I realize turning me around was a gift to one of us. He's letting me hide my eyes.

"Haven't we been over this?"

"Not now. Spend the summer there with me and move there after you graduate. Spend my senior year with me." A thousand reasons not to go to Oklahoma run through my mind. The tornadoes, the heat, all the white people—this I smile at, unsure of what my problem is with white people. No friends, no ocean. I'll be an alien there. But he'll be there.

"I'll go. I'll spend the summer there and if it works, I'll move there after graduation."

"You will?" He turns me around.

"On one condition."

"I would say anything, but it's you so I'll just ask what the condition is."

"You've got to back off of me for the next year." Jason frowns. "Trust my instincts. Believe that I'm surrounding myself with good people. Give me some credit."

"Annie, you have to admit your behavior is a little scary."

"I live smack dab between Philadelphia and New York City. If I want a tranny hooker dressed as a nurse to deliver an eight ball of cocaine to me, I can get it in an hour." Jason's eyes widen. "I'm fine. I will get high. I might try 'shrooms. I'll most definitely stay up too late and possibly not drink enough fluids, but I'm going to be okay. You have to trust me." Jason still looks like he wants to protest.

"You make me want to lie to you about what I do," I say, and it hits him like a punch to the face. He leans back in the tub shaking his head in defeat.

"All right. I'll try."

***

Our last full day on Cedar Creek Lake arrives in a flash of lightning. I lie on a towel at the edge of the dock listening to the water lap against its pilings. I want to spend every day like this. Jason's above me, holding a fishing rod in one hand and smoking a cigarette with the other. I shake my head. He's probably scaring all the fish away with the smell of burning nicotine.

"What?" he asks.

"You know you can't catch fish without water."

"You can't cook them without land," he retorts, and I lie back staring at the sky. The southern sky is covered with wisps of clouds, brushstrokes, but the sky directly above us is filled with the threatening kind, and each one blows fast to the east. Too fast. This beautiful day is moving out, like us tomorrow. I look at Jason again and he is the happiest I've ever seen him, skipping around here since the minute I said I would move to Oklahoma. I feel like I've done something wrong. It sits in me with a dull tone I can't quite pinpoint the origin of. Do I not want to go?

"What's wrong, Annie?"

"I'm not sure," I answer honestly.

"Our last day on the lake?" he asks, but he doesn't seem convinced.

"Probably."

The clouds move in and darken the north end of the lake

first. Everything is moving fast now. The winds pick up as if responding to a command in my head. The trees near the dock blow and my hair covers my face as I look to the sky.

"Is it supposed to rain today?" I ask.

"Looks it," He says, and I can see lightning in the distance, still up in a cloud, not touching the ground.

"We should go in."

"Right, you're safety girl."

Jason pulls his line from the water and fastens his hook on the pole. We settle into a large bench on the back porch of the house as the deluge arrives. The rain sweetens my mood by drowning out any hint of guilt in my head. The drops hit the leaves and fall to the ground surrounding us with its calming music. Until the thunder booms and I jump in Jason's arms. He laughs as the rest of the rumble finishes.

"Surprised me."

"You surprised me when you agreed to move to Oklahoma," he says, and I'm in shock.

"Did you think I would say no?"

"I know you love it where you are. I know how much I'm asking you to give up," Jason rubs the back of my hair and I sit up to face him.

"It's nothing compared to giving you up," I say, and kiss his lips.

"Your senior year won't be easy." Jason pulls my hair from my face and holds it in a tight ponytail at the nape of my head. "It's just us. We're supposed to be together. No one else. You're going to have to fight for us."

"I'm tired of fighting. You act like it's us against the world, as if the whole universe is conspiring against us," I say, and stare at my beautiful Jason Leer.

"You are naïve, Annie. It's the difference between belonging to each other and belonging with each other."

* * *

Jason and I ride out the rest of the storms, six hours' worth, drinking wine and playing War with a deck of cards he found in the dining room cabinet. We sit on the floor amidst candles, having lost power halfway through the night, and when I yawn, he scoops me up and carries me to bed. It's the safest I've felt since June 27th of last year and I am grateful to him for it. I fall asleep with my head on his arm and dream about telling my mom how much I love him.

* * *

"Annie." His voice in my ear stirs me. "Annie, wake up." He's not in bed with me, though. He's leaning over it, already awake. "Annie, wrap your arms around my neck." I do as I'm told and wrap my arms around Jason's thick neck. He lifts my naked body off the bed and covers me with a blanket. I rest my head on his shoulder, my lips touching his neck, as he carries me through the back door. He sits in an Adirondack chair on the end of the dock with me straddling him. My legs hang off the sides of the chair and Jason arranges the blanket to cover them too. It's a cold morning, the storm having washed away all the humidity of the day before.

"What are we doing out here?" I ask, still groggy.

"I want to watch the sunrise with you in my arms." Jason rubs my back and warms me awake. I leave my face nestled between his neck and his shoulder.

"This has been the happiest week of my life," I say, and try to recall a day I felt happier than today. My solace is a herculean feat on his part.

"Even better than when you went to Disney World in kindergarten and brought the whole class Goofy pencils?" I remember how happy my classmates were with their gifts. No matter where we end up, Jason and I came from the same place. Salem County, New Jersey.

"Yes, even better than Disney World," I say, and sit up to face Jason, fully awake now and wanting him. "And you are my favorite ride."

I kiss Jason again and make love to him on the dock of our cottage at Cedar Creek Lake while the sun rises behind us.

I will never forget you.

* * *

"My God, you're glowing. Were you plucked in Texas?" Violet asks, and I guess plucked is as good a word as any.

"Plucked, sucked, and completely fucked," I say as I float across the room, and land on the couch.

"Charlotte! The language, that's not like you. It must have been some trip," she says.

"I know you're going to think this is crazy, but at some point I'm going to move to Oklahoma."

"The way you look right now makes me want to drop Blake and go there myself," she says, and walks to the top of the stairs to yell to our roommates a floor below.

"You guys. Come up here and look at our fair Miss O'Brien. She's drunk on love. Either that or she lost her virginity in Texas."

"How was Panama City?" I ask, still euphoric. I hope this lasts until I see him again.

"Debauchery. Complete and utter. Fun like that should be illegal."

"I'm sure it is," I add.

"You're coming next year. Vegas, baby."

"I'll have to check the dates," I say, making no promises. Hopefully our deal holds up because without it I can only imagine Jason's reaction to a Vegas spring break.

~ 20 ~

"I demand with conviction No God, take me too"

I have now flown this flight enough to know the route the pilots take. I settle into my seat aware of our descent and study the landscape through my window. The amount of undeveloped land still astonishes me, no matter how many times I land here. The anticipation of seeing him feeds the hollowness inside of me. It's been almost a month since spring break and each day felt like a year. His letters came more often and his calls were kind again, and that made it a million times better than the month before. We may survive this yet.

"Your necklace is lovely. Do you ride?" The woman crammed into the seat next to me asks. I instinctively touch the rowel necklace Jason had made for me. *Not a horse, but I ride someone who does.*

"No. My boyfriend had it made for me. He's a steer wrestler," I say, watching my manners.

"A cowboy, huh? I was in love with a cowboy once." She looks up wistfully.

"What happened?" I ask, hesitant to break her reminiscence.

"I don't know. We were young and he was on the road a lot. Rodeo cowboys are born. It's not a choice for them. In the end I guess it was a choice for me." I bite my lip and crush my necklace between my fingers. Something about her is making me angry, or is that fear?

"Oh," I say, wanting this conversation to end.

"Is he in Oklahoma? Is that why you're coming here?"

"Yes. We're going to a rodeo in Kansas this weekend," I say, and wince at the similarities of her past and my future.

"Well, enjoy," she says, and the plane's wheels touch down. I'm thrust forward as the plane struggles to a stop; completely out of my control. It slows and taxis to the terminal, back to my cowboy.

***

The Tulsa Airport, like Oklahoma City, which I also frequent now, is small in comparison to Philly or Newark. It's a short walk through the terminal even if my gate is at the very end. Jason is waiting for me, as usual, as soon as I clear the security line. He kisses me and my knees give out beneath him.

"Miss me?" he asks as I open my eyes and look into his playful gray ones.

"Insanely."

"You are a sight for sore eyes, Annie O'Brien." He pulls back and looks me up and down. "And it's one tremendous sight." Jason leads me out of the terminal and we wait on the curb for Harlan to pull up.

"It's going to be a long ride. You sure you're okay riding with Harlan? It's not too late to get my truck."

"I'm fine with it if you are. I'll do whatever you want," I say, and lean into him, a naughty invitation in my tone.

The only problem with riding with Harlan is having to wait until Fort Hays, Kansas to get my hands on him. Harlan pulls up in his fancy truck with a trailer hitched behind it carrying the team of horses. I guess we're *all* headed to Hays today. Jason throws my backpack in the back of the truck as I climb in the middle.

"Hey, Charlotte. How's Jersey? Did you miss me?" Harlan asks.

"Of course. You ready to kick some ass this weekend?"

"That's the Jersey spirit I love. We are absolutely gonna kick some ass."

"What events are you in?" At this Harlan seems to hesitate. He looks out his rearview mirror and fidgets. I turn and see Jason walking to the truck door and forget what we were talking about. Jason climbs in and puts his arm around me and we ride five hours to Kansas unable to touch each other. I feel every breath he takes, every single heartbeat moving through his body, and it makes me want to jump out of this truck and haul him out with me. We finally see the signs for Hayes and I rub Jason's leg. He halts my hand and gives me a warning glare.

"You two suck to ride with," Harlan says, and I feel for him.

"The ride home'll be better," I say. "We haven't seen each other in a month."

"Yeah, yeah. Let's check in at the hotel first so I don't crash the truck into a brick wall from discomfort." *Poor Harlan.*

We check in at the Hays Super 8. It's next to the Conoco and McDonald's and on a strip with several other budget-friendly hotels. I couldn't tell you what the room looks like because by the time I take a step into it, Jason is ripping the clothes off my back. Five hours in a truck with Harlan was a mistake we are about to rectify. He turns me around and I kiss him. Oh the taste of him. This will never get old. He pulls the bedspread off the bed and throws me on top. He jumps on me and knocks the wind out of me and apologizes as he kisses my neck and starts to suck on it.

"I'm wearing a tank top tonight." Jason stops and lifts up to face me with an absolutely devilish grin.

"And?"

"And I thought for once I could go out without being covered in bruises. Maybe make a good impression," I say playfully as he proceeds to run his lips down my stomach.

"I'll stick to areas not seen in public," Jason promises with a wicked grin. He slides his arm under my stomach, arching my back, and runs his tongue past my belly button and licks each nipple. He stops and my skin wants to climb off of me and follow his tongue to wherever. Jason leans back, pulling his arm out from under me. I open my eyes and with them I beg him to continue.

Jason pulls my shirt over my head and bends down and yanks my skirt off, taking my panties too.

"I want to see you." He stands over the bed, silent and contemplating me. Jason's eyes traipse over every inch of me. They brand me, marking me for all other eyes in the future. I shiver under his stare and he smiles. He's well aware of his effect on me and he loves it. His eyes linger on my lips and finally, meet my own. A new chill runs through me and I want to reach out to him, but I stay still, a lover at his mercy.

"Annie O'Brien, you are so beautiful," he says, and I blush.

I rise up onto my knees and unbutton his shirt. It's difficult to move slowly, but I force myself as the throbbing between my legs pounds against my thighs. I push his shirt off and the width of his arms catches my eye. They're as big as my legs. I run my hands over his shoulders and down each arm. I pull his undershirt over his head and the look in Jason's eyes gives me permission, permission for an endless list of possibilities. He trusts me with his heart and I'm not going to let anything happen to this beast.

I run my hands across his bare chest and slide each nipple between my fingers. I lick them and kiss his chest between them, and the throbbing between my legs pounds away at me. I take a deep breath and exhale. What should I do to my enormous cowboy?

I undo his pants and lower his zipper with rushed hands. My body's needs are difficult to manage. Jason helps me lower his jeans and I watch as he stands again, completely erect. He is physically gifted, in every way. I swallow hard at the sight of him and wrap my fingers around his balls and run my hand up and down his shaft. I can feel it in my hand, and in my mouth, and between my legs. It's the only thing that will make this pounding stop and I swallow again at the thought of it.

His cock in my hand, I look up at Jason. His head's back, his face to the ceiling, and his eyes are closed as he breathes deeply. Even here, naked, he is utterly invincible. A god walking amongst us mere mortals and he's mine. I rise up and kiss his neck and I continue playing with him and he moans, "Ohhh," with only a tiny breath escaping him.

Jason tilts his face toward me and the look in his eyes screams at me to run toward him and from him at the same time. He takes my hand and lifts me by the shoulders as he throws me on the bed. I haven't bounced off the mattress before he mounts me and pulls my knees above his shoulders. He thrusts into me, my feet behind his head, and I cry out for all of it. The pounding takes him and releases him each time he moves and I cover my eyes with my hand, the sight of him too much to process with him overtaking me.

Jason rides me this way until my hips almost break from the weight of him and he releases one leg and the electrical current trapped in the wires of my body. I come, and come again as he continues to fuck me. I'm sure I can't see straight. I grip his biceps, my tiny hands trying to hold onto to something as Jason raises his shoulders, taking my one leg with him, and comes. He continues as his body quivers and every fear I've ever had seeps out of me, the touch of him making me brave.

God, I love Jason Leer.

Satisfied and completely spent, I lie in Jason's arms, running my fingers over his hands.

"How are you ever going to steer wrestle today?" I ask, more relaxed than I've been in a month.

"It's not the bulldoggin' I'm worried about, it's the bull riding." I must have heard him wrong. I stop caressing his hand as his silence weighs on me like a challenge. I sit up and look at him sternly.

"The what?" I ask, and he laughs, not because he thinks it's funny, because he wants me to feel ridiculous and I do not.

"I'm doing both this weekend. Bull riding and bulldoggin'. It's not a big deal."

"Yeah, it is a big deal. What the hell are you doing?" I ask, a little less cool than I would like to seem.

"It's not like I've never ridden a bull before. I just happen to

prefer bullldoggin'. The opportunity came up so I'm taking it."
Opportunity?

I lay my head back down silently. I'm going to regret anything else I say at this point. Including, *My mother was right. I don't belong here.*

"Long go-round starts soon. We've got to get goin'," he says, and pulls his arm out from under my head, almost taking my ear off with it.

"Long go?"

"Two days of long go-rounds, short go-rounds on the third day. Only the top ten make it to day three." I nod my head, filing the information away in my "Crazy Ass Shit about Rodeo" mental folder and sigh as I examine the damage to my clothes. This is why I now bring a few extra outfits with me.

***

Jason deposits me in the stands near other Oklahoma fans and hands me a sheet of paper with all the events and entrants typed on it.

"Is this my program?" I try to smile. I don't want him to trade me in for one of these chicks that obviously has no problem with him riding, catching, wrestling, or being gored by animals.

"You gonna be okay?" he asks, acknowledging that I'm trying.

"Just dandy," I say, and smile for real this time. He's awesome. This is awesome. It's all so fucking awesome. It's going to be over in a few short hours. He kisses me, too provocatively for public, but I'm probably not heading back to Hays soon so may as well ruin my reputation, and walks to the other side of the arena where all the cowboys, and cowgirls, appear to be having team meetings of some kind. The Fort Hays State University Rodeo has as much pomp and circumstance as Cowtown and the school flag is brought in on a horse. Right behind the American flag, of course. These cowboys may be crazy, but they're patriots.

A gorgeous long-haired brunette sings the national anthem from atop a horse and each school is announced. About fifteen are called, most of which I don't recognize the names of, and I remember Harlan's reaction to hearing Rutgers for the first time. Are we really that far away from each other? Oklahoma State is announced and a group of girls three rows down go wild, led by the Salem County's finest, Stephanie Harding. When she turns around I wave hello. Hopefully I'll have time to talk to her later and see how she likes Oklahoma. For now my eyes are fixed on the end of the arena where the bulls are already in their gates. Jason's listed as the fourth rider in the first event. His bull's named Rocco. Come on, Rocco. Be gentle.

The first three riders take off and I'm mesmerized. It's absolutely insane to me. I quickly gather the point is to stay on the bull eight seconds and then get the hell off as soon as possible. You don't get any points beyond the first eight seconds, so why stick around.

Jason's announced and I can make out the top of him towering above the gate, looking down and doing something with his hand as the bull moves beneath him. I feel sick. I am going to throw up all over this bleacher. The gate opens and the bull bucks out with Jason holding on above. His one hand is in the air mirroring the jerking motion of the bull as it waves in one direction and snaps back. The bull jumps, or bucks, or whatever, and throws his rear legs into the air until a buzzer sounds and Jason jumps off landing on his feet and steadying himself with his hands as the bull contemplates rushing him. Jason climbs up the wall as two rodeo clowns corral the bull. He hops down, tips his hat to me, and follows the bull out of the gate. I exhale and drop my forehead to my hand. When I look up Stephanie and her friends are cheering wildly. I'm still trying to breathe.

Bull riding, Saddle Bronc Riding, Team Roping, I'm almost relaxing as I research bull riding rules on my phone. I get a text from Jason:

I do better when you're here.

Yeah, well, I do better when I'm not. Instead I text back:

You amaze me.

Cowboys and cowgirls who have finished competing filter into the crowd and I hear them talking about the parties tonight and tomorrow night. Apparently there's one sponsored by Fort Hays the last night. I wonder if we're going to any of these. Jason'll probably find three more jackpots. That boy could compete all night long. I'm starting to understand the way he is in bed. He's just rough. In all the right ways.

The fifth event is Steer Wrestling and Jason is first. The guys that have recently joined me talk of Jason and how good he is. He and Harlan are on their horses in the chutes and I realize how much easier this is to take in now that I've seen it before. I brace myself for the next five seconds and watch Jason push his hat down low on his forehead. The gate opens and the steer runs out, followed by Jason and Harlan. My eyes never leave

Jason. When he catches up to the steer something monstrous happens. His horse misses its footing and appears to fold up on himself with Jason under him. The steer runs by stomping on Jason's head in the process and I'm left watching a motionless Jason lying in the dirt as Harlan races over on his horse.

I'm out of my seat and running toward the arena. I'm five feet from the gate when a boy grabs me around the waist and hauls me back.

"Whoa, you can't go out there."

"The hell I can't," I say, pushing him off me. He grabs my wrist and I think Jason would kill him for grabbing me this way. I look back at Jason and several people are now kneeling down to him. From what I can see, he's still not moving.

"Look. Do you remember me? From the Penny?" I follow his arm to his face and recognize the guy I'd been sitting next to at the bar. Someone from home, or Oklahoma.

"You have to help me. I have to get out there."

"They'll take good care of him. You wait right here with me. Come, stand on the fence so you can see better," he says, and with only a helpless mind to pull from, I follow his directions. From the opposite side of the arena more men come, one carrying a bright yellow stretcher, but Jason doesn't move. I hold my hand to my mouth as a dark and ugly tremor originates in the back of my throat and climbs down to my stomach. My head's in a vice, my eyes fixed on Jason and if he doesn't move soon…

They roll him onto the stretcher and secure the belts around him. Harlan gets back on his horse and rides to me standing here on the fence, with some guy from the Penny.

"Stay right here. I'll be back to get you with the truck." I just look at him.

"Charlotte, you hear me? Stay right here." I nod. Why didn't he say he's fine? Why didn't he say he's going to be all right?

The men carry Jason's body off the dirt and into a waiting ambulance and as the door closes, my head collapses in my hands and I plead out loud, "No God, take me, too."

I'm vaguely aware of an arm around me, a few steps to the side, and some guys recounting the five seconds of Jason's run, trying to determine what happened. Harlan drives his truck right up on the lawn and stops it in front of me. The guy opens the door and helps me in, and Harlan takes off without a word.

Harlan's GPS is the only one talking. It guides us through the streets of Hays and delivers us to the Hays Medical Center just as an ambulance pulls in the driveway. The hospital stands three or four stories high, with a lighthouse made out of stone at the entrance. Everywhere around us is flat, like the rest of tornado alley.

"Charlotte," Harlan starts out slow and I look at him out of obligation rather than caring what he has to say. "That steer's got nothing on him. He's going to be all right."

"I know he is," I say for the benefit of Harlan, for the only thing I really know is what it's like to sit across from Kevin at the funeral home and pick out a casket. We get out of the truck and Harlan moves to walk by my side. A helicopter is landing on the roof and I consider it a good sign. People are airlifted here; it must be a good hospital, or the only hospital.

Once inside Harlan is told to sit and wait and we do. The last time I was in a hospital I waited. Waited to be told my mother was dead like my father. Harlan's phone keeps ringing. People want to know what's going on. I hear him tell each of them what he saw in the arena and that we know nothing new.

"Send it to me," he says, and I can't imagine what's coming. When Harlan gets off the phone he walks to the window, reading his phone, or watching his phone, and I know it's a video of the run.

"I want to see it," I say, and Harlan turns to me red-faced. We're not used to taking care of each other. Jason is always firmly between us and now it's just Harlan and me.

"No you don't."

"You think I'm going to forget what I saw? That video's not going to scar me. Send it to me," I say without an ounce of emotion left in me. My phone dings with a text message from Harlan, including a link to the YouTube video of Jason's run.

* * *

As time passes, more people arrive. Jason's rodeo coach and the rest of the team file in. We all stand together in the hospital waiting room. Every footstep approaching the room, every conversation on every phone in the hall, every dinging of a bell I decipher for information of Jason Leer. Finally the doctor emerges and finds Jason's coach. We all huddle around.

He's alive.

It's all I hear, but it's enough. I lean on Harlan, who's not at all pacified.

"Awake…blindness…temporary…edema of occipital lobe… head trauma…torn bicep tendon…surgery," I take this in, and that we'll have to wait.

Several cowboys offer me their seat, but I stand by the window. I watch the darkness take over, and look for the moon. I should call Butch, I suppose. I look around the waiting room for Stephanie Harding; she's the only link to Salem County, the only stream to feed him the information and she's sitting silently with her roommates. I'll wait until Jason is awake to call him. We still don't have much information. Hours pass and some of the students head back to the hotel, opening more space in the waiting room for the rest of us. Harlan is never far from me. He looks tortured, as if he blames himself in some way.

The doctor comes back into the waiting room and approaches the coach, who is half asleep.

"If you want to go see him, we have him stabilized." The coach turns to Harlan and me.

"I'm sure you'll do him more good than the rest of us," he says, and I immediately walk toward the doctor, Harlan following close behind me. As we turn the corners of the stark hallway that I'll never recognize on the way out, the doctor provides more information.

"He's sedated. We'll keep him comfortable until the swelling subsides." Harlan nudges me forward and I linger at the end of his bed, letting the light on the wall above Jason's head tell me the unabridged story of his injuries.

Jason's arm is in a cast. His head is bandaged, and purple bruises are already forming across the right side of his face. It looks as if the steer stepped right on his face. *What did that feel like?* My bottom lip quivers and I clench my jaw to stave off the tears. I take a deep breath through my nose and close my eyes as I exhale. *He's alive.*

There are things beeping and tubes wired from him to a metal stand with bags hanging on it. A nurse is arranging his blanket around his waist, being careful of his arm. My fingers cover my still-shaking lips as my head shakes, denying the sight of him. His bed is sitting up, but his eyes are closed. A faded hospital gown is draped across the front of him. It hangs low on his shoulders, showing cuts and bruises across his chest. There's a large tube taped to his mouth with an accordion style bag at the other end of it. I close my eyes and hang my head. This isn't him. It can't be him. *God, no. Not him.*

With every image burning into my brain, sadness sets in. I'm unable to exhale. He's alive. That should be all that matters, but the knowledge is absent of relief. The thing he loves most in the world will kill him. It's only a matter of time before he dies at the hand of it, and I may be a witness.

I walk to the side of his bed, and lean over to kiss his swollen face.

"You scared me. You can't leave me here without you." I close my eyes to keep from crying. I take his hand between my own and massage it and then I remember we're not alone.

"We'll take the breathing tube out tomorrow. It helps regulate his carbon dioxide and oxygen levels, both of which we anticipate self-regulating as the swelling goes down." I run my fingers up and down his arm.

"Can he hear me?"

"We've had no indication his hearing was affected, only his sight. He'll be asleep for a while, though. His body has a lot of work to do, both now and as he rehabilitates his arm."

"How long?" Harlan asks, still at least three feet from Jason's bed.

"He's looking at a full six months before he returns to normal activity," the doctor says, and nods his head to Harlan, "especially your version of normal."

I stop listening and stare at Jason's good hand, too sickened by his beautiful face marred and bandaged. Harlan pulls a chair over for me and I lean on the metal rail separating Jason from the healthy as I continue caressing him.

At some point Harlan asks if I need anything. I'm vaguely aware of nurses checking and recording vitals and a shift change as the sun takes over for the night, but my eyes never leave Jason. I stare at his chest as every breath causes it to rise and I check off my own vital. He is alive.

The sight of his hand limp in my own brings the tears, and I squeeze my eyes together to fight them back. I rub his hand on my face, willing it to move itself. *Touch me, Jason.* Defeated, I return it to his side and hold it there. I drop my head onto the railing and let my eyes close.

"Charlotte. Charlotte, you've got to eat something. Why don't you come with me to the hotel and lie down for a while?" Harlan asks.

"I'm not leaving to get some rest or something to eat. I'm not leaving until he's able to come with me," I say, angry with myself for falling asleep. I look up and Harlan looks like he might cry. "I'm sorry, Harlan."

"I know you love him. I love him, too," he says. "He'd want me to take care of you. He's going to need you strong."

I stand and my back screams its reproach at the chair I made into a bed. *Nice bed*, I think and smile at Jason. For the first time I realize the breathing tube is gone.

"How long was I asleep?" I ask Harlan, my voice barely functioning. I look out the window as the sun sinks low in the sky for my second night in Kansas.

"Annie." The name weakly floats into the room, hooks on my ribcage, and pulls me to him. I look at Jason and back at Harlan to confirm he heard it, too. Harlan nods.

"Jason." I pull his good hand to my lips and kiss it.

"Annie, I can't see you."

"It's temporary. It's going to come back," I say, and the

sound of my name on his lips makes me start to cry. "You just have to rest and it'll come back." Jason closes his eyes and ends our conversation and the sorrow returns.

Harlan retreats to the hotel for the night and I give him my room key to bring my backpack to me. I also order food, leaving the type completely up to Harlan. I stand and walk around the room every hour, trying to fight off sleep, too afraid I'll miss him waking again. But when I pull the blanket the nurse gave me up to my chin I fall asleep in my chair, in this horrible chair, that I am thankful for.

"She might be right about this one," my dad says, and I plead with him with my eyes to disagree with her.

"Dad, I love him."

"I know you do, but he'll never love you enough for you to be safe, Annie." His words confuse me.

Why?

"Why did you call me Annie instead of Charlotte?" I ask.

"Annie." I shake my head free of the unwanted dream and realize it was Jason who called my name. I raise my head and see Jason's eyes staring at the ceiling.

"I'm right here. Not going anywhere."

"I still can't see you."

"That might be a good thing," I say, and laugh a tiny laugh.

"How long have we been here?"

"I'm not sure," I say. "I think it's Saturday. We came Thursday. Do you remember what happened?"

"The last thing I remember is having you in the hotel." *Lucky you.* His words make me cry for the memory.

"It won't be long and we'll be back there again, but now you have to rest. Repair. Doctor's orders." A silence settles between us, but I have to tell him one more thing. I want him to know that he is the only thing that matters in this world to me. That nothing, in any other state, means a thing.

"Jason," I say.

"Annie?"

"I love you," I say instead.

"I know what you mean," Jason says, and closes his eyes. He always knows what I mean.

* * *

Harlan returns with a take-out bag from Gella's diner and I completely house a Sandwich Cubano with homemade chips. I look up into the eyes of Harlan. He seems disturbed by the inhalation of my meal.

"Hard to watch?" I ask, half apologizing. "I guess I was hungry."

"Goddamned New Jersey rock head. You need to eat, girl!" he says, and I close my eyes and nod in surrender.

"Thank you," is all I offer in return. "Can you sit here while I shower?" I ask, getting up from my "bed." Harlan hesitates. "Do you not like hospitals?"

"This is the first time I've ever been in one, and I hope I never come back." When I think about it, it's only my second time.

"All the years you've been involved in the rodeo, you've never been to the hospital?" I ask in disbelief. No stitches? No broken bones?

"I've seen lots of injuries, but never been to the hospital. One guy last year got caught up in a horse and drug around the whole arena. It tore all his clothes off, but by the time we got him out he was able to limp away. I saw a guy lose his eye when I was little, but I didn't go to the hospital. I gave up bull riding after watching it."

"That'll do it, I suppose," I say, and watch Harlan carefully sit next to Jason's bed. This sport is insane.

* * *

I turn the shower to as hot as I can tolerate it. I turn my back to the spigot and let the scorching water beat on me. God, I wish Jason was in here with me. I finish and hop out. I'm sure this shower is not intended for my use, but I'm not leaving this room without him and I'll soon start to smell. The nurses have been so good to me. I need to remember to send them something if we ever get out of here. I watch Harlan stare at Jason and wonder what he's thinking, what both of them are thinking, as I brush my hair in the corner of the room. Jason opens his eyes slowly and looks at Harlan.

"Where's Annie?" I walk into view and he smiles.

"You can see," I say, half-breathless.

"I can and you're beautiful."

"I feel beautiful now that you're looking at me," I say, and lean over to kiss his still swollen lips. Harlan stands and walks out of the room.

* * *

A long ride back to Oklahoma, followed by a shower with some assistance from me, and a dose of painkillers has Jason drifting off to sleep in his own bed for the first time in six days.

I lie with him, holding his hand, and wonder at the last week. I want to fall asleep next to him, but first I have to make some calls. I've already e-mailed all my professors. They've all been very supportive, except for my favorite one who is not a fan of excuses, no matter how good. Noble's in that class, too, so I can get the notes, but it's close to exams and I'm not there to plead my case. I call Julia first.

"When are you coming back?" she says instead of hello when she answers.

"In a few days. We just got back to Oklahoma and I want to make sure he can manage on his own."

"In a few days, like when? Are you guys coming to the Spring Formal?"

"Definitely not. Jason can't fly and is in no shape to go to a dance. I might be home in time, but I've missed too much school," I say. None of this is my fault. "I know it's sold out so if you hear of anyone who still wants to go, the tickets are in my jewelry box. They can have them," I add.

"I'm sorry. It's not a big deal. I mean, I really want you to go, but Nick showed me the video and I'm sure you've had a tough week."

"Yeah. It's been a long one," I say, and look down at Jason, who even in this condition is the most beautiful thing I've ever laid eyes on. "I'll keep in touch, okay?"

"Call whenever. I'm here," she says, and we hang up.

I consider texting Noble, but I owe him a call. I've e-mailed twice from the hospital, where I never wanted to make a peep for fear of being asked to leave, but now there's no reason not to talk to him.

"Hey," he says, and his kindness holds me tight through the phone.

"Hey. How's it going?"

"Better here than there, I suppose," he says. "I talked to Professor Bryant for you. He wasn't moved until I showed him the video. Then he said since you've scored nothing below a ninety-eight all year, he would make an exception."

"Thanks, Noble," I say with heartfelt gratitude.

"When did you become so wicked smart?" he asks, laughing at me.

"I'm just a gifted statistician."

"Among other things," he says, and I forget the stress of the last week. "When are you coming home?"

"It's not going to be an easy trip," I say, and look at Jason as his eyes open slightly, his arm casted and resting on a pillow beside him. "He meets with the doctor down here tomorrow and then starts rehab. I'm going to see what that brings before I leave him."

"Exams are in two weeks," Noble states.

"I know." *I just don't care.* "Thanks, Noble," I say, and hang up, questioning if I'll ever truly get back home. Jason turns his head to me.

"Was that Sinclair?"

"Yes. What are you doing up?" I ask as I take his hand in mine and raise it to my lips to kiss it.

"He loves you, Annie."

"I love him, too," I say thankful for Noble in my life. "He's one of my best friends."

"No. He's in love with you. I can tell the difference," Jason says, and I burst out laughing. My eyes find the prescription bottle on his night stand. These drugs are working on him.

"What gave it away? The way he has been nothing but a good friend or the parade of girls he's banging at Rutgers?"

I quietly laugh some more. Noble would think this is funny, too. I've told Noble I love him a hundred times in this life. We hold hands, and play together. He's even shared my bed a few drunken nights at Rutgers, but it's never been anything but friendship. He is a teddy bear.

"The way he looks at you. It may not be exactly love, but it's something like it."

"Go back to sleep, you crazy cowboy," I say, and Jason's eyes roll shut once again. I crawl under the covers next to him and lay my head on his good arm and drift off to sleep happily for the first time in almost a week.

~ 21 ~

"I forfeit the safety of unclouded sight"

Janine has strep throat," Violet says as she plops down on my bed. I'm still getting used to being back in New Brunswick. Last week changed me, and not for the better.

"That's terrible. Did she go to Hurtado?" I ask, and try to remember if the Rutgers' health center is open on Saturdays.

"She went yesterday and they gave her antibiotics, but she's still contagious *and* feels like hell." I begin pulling my abandoned school books onto my desk, fearing I'll never catch up on the last week before finals. "So she has a ticket to the formal tonight and Nick is supposed to be her date," Violet adds. *We're still talking about this?*

"Can she sell it?"

"It's too late. But you already have a dress. And you know Nick, so it seems like the universe is telling you to come to the

ZTA formal with me tonight." Even this conversation is exhausting me. There's no way I'm up to a date night.

"I can't. Believe me, I can't."

"Is this about Jason? Because he doesn't even have to know."

"I would never keep that from him," I say sternly. Violet should know better. She's been with Blake for years. She's the girlfriend type. "And it's not about him. I'm exhausted and I have so much work to catch up on. I missed all my classes last week and now exams are going to start on Thursday." I am frantic. I looked over the notes Noble sent me, but they make less sense than I'd hoped they would. I'm going to have to teach myself the last three chapters of *Statistics for Economics*. Good times.

Julia walks in carrying an envelope for me and my dress hanging under a plastic bag. "I found this in the hall closet. I thought I'd bring it in just in case you change your mind." I roll my eyes. "I'm sure your handsome Noble can look fantastic in minutes," she adds.

"I'm sure I'm not going, but I love you for trying." I sit on my bed and open my letter from Jason. I just left today and he didn't overnight it so he mailed while I was still there.

May 2nd

Dear Annie,

I'm watching you sleep and writing this with my "good hand." You are so tired, worn to the bone from taking care of me rather than yourself. Harlan stopped by while you were at the grocery store and said he'd never seen anything like the way you sat by me for days while I was unconscious in the hospital. *Your strength shocked Harlan, but doesn't surprise me.*

You're beautiful. Even in your sleep. Your hair is hanging down your back and your lips are cherry red today and parted slightly. The covers are wrapped around your waist and I can see the side of your breast poking out from under your arm. You are my own personal work of art. As soon as you open those green eyes I'm going to figure out how to have sex with you with only one arm and on drugs. You can probably help with that. You know all about drugs. See, these things come in handy.

You're supposed to go back to Rutgers in a few days. If you're reading this that means I somehow let you go. I figure if you can return after the death of your parents, you can go back after I had this tiny little fall. But know that I've never wanted you to stay more than I do now. Not only for my own selfish needs, which by definition are at the forefront of my mind, but because I can't imagine the crazy thoughts running through your head. I won't have enough time before you leave to convince you this type of thing isn't typical. That I will probably never be hurt again. This was my "fall," and now we can move on thankful it was a mild one.

You said my name a little while ago and violently reached out and I can only guess what you must be dreaming about. Your mind tortures you. Just hang on until this summer. Try not to think too much about it. Focus on your exams and the next time I'm going to see you. I love you, Annie and I'm so sorry you had to witness what you did in Kansas. If it were you instead of me, I would never let you near another rodeo arena. But you're a better person than me.

Not really, Jason.

> *The object of your affection,*
> *Jason*

* * *

I refold the letter and place it back in the envelope. The nine other girls in my house are blowing, buffing, plucking, and fastening so loudly I couldn't study right now if I wanted to so I take out a notebook and write the most terrifying person in my life a return letter.

May 5th

Dear Object,

I stayed by your bedside while you were sleeping because I wanted to be there in case you woke up scared and confused. Unlike you, who apparently just watches me sleep in a rather creepy way.

Your "fall" hurt more than your body. It tore me to pieces that I'm still trying to fit back together. All I knew was that I had to be with you. I tried to run into the arena, but I was held back, sentenced to watch you lying still on the dirt. My heart broke as they rolled your lifeless body into the ambulance and drove you away from me.

I told God to take me too because wherever you are is where I want to be. He took mercy on us both and let you live, and now I'm left fearing what will be when his mercy is expended.

So you're wrong. It's not my mind that tortures me.

We have six months for me to cry, beg, and plead for you to give up the rodeo. All of which I already know is in vain, but for now I can't think about it. I have to pass my final exams. Don't think I don't know your letter was a poorly veiled attempt at cutting off the impending conversation about your body, your safety, and my life. You're not the only one who knows the other so well.

For now, I am going to spend the next two weeks missing you, worrying about you, and studying. After that I am going to have sex with you until I can't walk and try to identify a hobby you'll like as much as steer wrestling. I don't think we've given bird watching a proper chance.

The person plotting for your survival,
Charlotte

* * *

Fuck Annie. Charlotte's back in town. Boys start to file in and flowers are exchanged, and I'm glad I at least changed out of my sweatpants and put on some lip gloss. This scene could depress a girl. They look beautiful. The spring formal is the dressiest event of the school year and the ZTAs go all out. Their gowns range from long to too-short, beaded to simply chic, and everything in between. For a second, I think of running upstairs and donning my black maxi dress with the neckline that practically touches my belly button, forgetting everything I have to worry about for the next four hours. But even after choking in the mix of perfumes and cologne, I stay in my shorts and oversized sweater knowing I don't belong there tonight.

The crowd leaves and I can hear them all the way down the street. They have a block to walk to the bus and they are an absurd parade of high fashion and loud voices. The house is dead without them. Not an ounce of life left behind. I place a stamp on Jason's letter and walk it to the mailbox hanging on the front of the house. As I close the lid on it, I see Noble walking up Hamilton Street, whistling as he comes, with his backpack hanging over one shoulder. I smile at the sight of him and watch as he walks right up the front steps of my house.

"What are you doing here?" I ask as he hugs me tightly.

"I came to teach you statistics, and any other subjects I can help with."

"You did?" I'm frozen in a state of disbelief.

"You're a smart girl, Charlotte, but I can teach you in one night what will take others a lifetime to figure out."

"Come in, I'll order us dinner," I say, and pull Noble into the house.

***

Noble's tutelage doesn't disappoint. He's right. This would have taken me a long time to figure out without him going line by line through the notes with me. He's a patient teacher and quite hilarious, even when discussing statistics. We eat bolis from Stuff Yer Face and both lean back on the couch at the same time, full and tired.

"Do you want to smoke?" Noble says as he pulls out a joint and holds it in front of our eyes. My intuition says no, but why? I stare at the joint and turn my head to see Noble smiling at me, and then he winks, erasing my unfounded internal conflict.

"Sure," I say, and Noble lights it as I open the windows wider.

We smoke and smoke until we're laughing so hard I finally lick my fingers and pinch it out, not wanting to waste Noble's weed. I lie back on the couch next to Noble and put my feet up next to his on the coffee table.

"Have you talked to Julia lately?" I ask.

"I talked to her a lot while you were in Kansas and Oklahoma. We exchanged information daily, trying to find out what was going on with you," he says. "And Jason."

"Do you think she's mad at me for not going to the formal?"

"Probably," he says, and laughs, "but we never talked about that."

"Think she'll get over it?" I ask, hoping she already has. If they all have a spectacular time tonight maybe they won't even notice I'm not there.

"It's astonishing what a person can look past," Noble professes as if he's talking about me, instead of to me. I sit up and look at him, melting into my couch.

"Do I have some huge blind spot?" I ask with exaggerated concern.

"No. You're perfect," Noble says, and we both laugh. "Sometimes we let ourselves be consumed to the point of blindness."

"Ah, abandonment. You prefer to be tethered to reality rather than give-in to the fairy tale."

"When you say it like that it sounds boring. There's a certain invulnerability to unclouded sight," he says, and I ponder his words. Noble has always had a beautiful way of seeing things. An invulnerability, as in, incapable of being wounded or immune to the attack.

"It's safe," I say, and force myself to stop thinking about this. Safety is overrated.

~ 22 ~

"Demotion, realization, I surrender the fight"

Exams end and summer begins, but all I care about is getting to Oklahoma. It's been two insufferable weeks since I left Jason. The escalator feels like it's running backward until I see Harlan waiting for me, then it seems to stop. Fear strangles me. He sees me and smiles, and I relax a little, but I'm still confused.

"Where is he?"

"Therapy. He didn't tell you because he was afraid you wouldn't let me come get you."

"Well, this is ridiculous. It's a complete waste of your time."

"You don't have to tell me," he jokes.

"How is he?" I ask, and Harlan stops laughing, but starts off toward the parking lot. "Harlan, what?"

"He's miserable. I couldn't wait to come get you today. I'm hoping you can pull him out of this. He can't seem to accept he ain't gonna be bulldoggin' for six months."

"Would you be able to?" I ask because I'll never understand why someone would want to in the first place. Harlan ignores me and takes my backpack off my shoulder while he holds the door open for me.

* * *

We pull into Jason's driveway to the sight of him fumbling with his keys in the door. His frustration is obvious, even without stepping out of the truck. Jason drops the keys and instead of picking them up, he kicks the door in. Harlan looks at me and raises his eyebrows.

"Thanks for the ride," I say, and watch Jason take deep breaths to calm down.

"Call me if you need any help," Harlan says. "And good luck," he adds as he puts the truck in reverse and I close the door.

Jason is standing just outside the now broken door when I get to him. His cast has been replaced with the special range-of-motion brace which makes him look like he has a robotic arm, permanently bent at the elbow. I run my hand over it, barely touching him, but having to examine it for myself. Jason watches my hand move up his arm to his face where our eyes meet in a torrent of need.

"Trouble with the door?" I ask.

"No. Opened right up," he says, and we both look at the damaged trim by the lock. I walk past him and enter the loft, which looks completely different now that Jason is on his feet again.

"I would have been here sooner, but Harlan doesn't drive as fast as the car services," I say, and turn to face him. His eyes flicker with a hint of his old wicked self. I close the door, as best I can, and stand in front of him. His face is almost completely healed and I run my finger across the fresh skin covering the cuts and thread my hands in his hair at the back of his head. His chest heaves and I turn my attention to his t-shirt. I want it off of him, but guessing he feels the same way, I pull my tank top over my head and throw my bra across the room. He awkwardly leans down and takes my nipple in his mouth, licking it and sucking it as if it brings him something necessary to sustain life. I pull his shirt up and over his good arm and neck and let it hang on his left shoulder.

"How about we just leave this here? In case we want to put our clothes back on today, it'll be there," I say, and look at his smiling gray eyes again. He doesn't seem miserable at all. I pull off the sweatpants I bought him before I left and marvel at the fact he's wearing them. I've never seen him in anything but jeans. Zippers and buttons must be a particular nuisance with only one arm to work with. I kneel down and take him in my mouth, squeezing my thighs together at the taste of him. It's been too long. Jason's hand is on the back of my head, but he never moves it as I lick, suck, and swallow him whole. His body reacts to the attention and he comes, faster than he ever has before, surprising me and relieving him.

I stand up and lead him to the kitchen chair. I gingerly sit him down and retrieve a pillow from the bed to rest his arm on. Once I think he's secure I climb on top of him and ride him with my forearms resting on his shoulders, his good hand on my bottom. I am so selfish. I can't even look at him for fear he may want me to stop. I continue with my heady ride until my body reaches the release I've waited weeks to achieve. I come and continue to ride him, letting the convulsions tear through me, until my legs give out. I rest on top of him, my head on his good shoulder, my lips touching his neck, as I try and recover.

"You have no idea what that just did for me," he says, low and gruff in my ear.

"I think I have every idea."

"I've been useless. Unable to do anything here." I lean back and play with Jason's hair as I consider his sad face.

"Well, as usual, you do me just fine. Don't sell yourself short." I say, and kiss him on the lips, so thankful they are no longer cut or bruised. I kiss him until my body wants more of him. And then I ask, "Do you want to try it on the bed?"

"You're a greedy girl, Annie O'Brien." He's playful and relaxed, and I know we'll spend the day trying different places, different positions. What a great way to catch up with my one-armed man.

* * *

The ease of the first few day wilts in the summer heat of New Jersey. Jason is increasingly angry and frustrated by his lack of mobility. He's a grump and hard to be around. By the second week in June I can't even mollify him with sex. It's always been our safe place, so I'm at a loss. I hate seeing him like this—demoralized. I want the old Jason back. I want him strong and powerful. I want him to be happy. We came home because it's home and without the rodeo there was no reason to stay in Oklahoma, but even home does little to heal him.

I hear him drop something in the kitchen and by the time I get there he's throwing the frying pan against the wall.

"What is your problem?" I yell, sick of being a passenger in his misery.

"I'm a goddamned invalid, that's my problem," he says, and snorts air from his nose.

"It's not permanent," I say, and pick up the pan. "But how you're acting could leave a mark."

"You know what today is?" I look at the calendar on the wall; it's June 13th. Jason sees my probe. "It's the College National Finals. You know what I was ranked going into Kansas?" I hold still, realizing this is a monologue not a conversation. "Second, Annie. I was second going in. Well in range to take it all."

I lower my eyes to the pan in my hand, trying to think of something to say other than "Good," which I know will get us nowhere.

Instead I leave him to his misery and go back to the bedroom.

* * *

At six I find him on the back deck lying in a lounge chair and I climb on top of him. He's on his back with his braced arm resting on the arm rest, looking out at the fields, and he looks lost. To me, he is exactly where I want him to be, but for him he has no idea where or who he is. Jason looks at me with his confused gray eyes and I just want him to be happy.

"I need you to know that no matter how I feel about you getting hurt, I'm sorry you didn't go to finals," I say, and he studies me trying to judge my honesty. "I don't lie, remember? I'm not ready to see you back on a horse, but I'm also not ready to watch you decay in my house all summer." Jason starts to say something and I stop him with a kiss. One which takes on a life of its own and I wonder if I should abandon this plan and go with Plan B. I lean back and rest my hands on his stomach.

"I want you to take me to the rodeo tonight," I say, and he doesn't move a muscle, not even in his face. "I want you to go and sit with me and explain everything that's going on and what you love about it. I've been to a half dozen now, but never one with you." Jason pulls my face back to his and kisses me again, comprehending the enormity of the gift I am offering, the acceptance of a murderer.

* * *

And so I learn that college rodeo makes no distinction between amateur and pro; they compete for money at both venues. That steer wrestlers get one jump to the steer, if it gets loose the dogger may take no more than one step to catch it. That a steer is only down when it is lying flat on its side, or on its back, with all four feet and head straight, and that the wrestler must have a hand on the steer until the flag is thrown.

He explains the steer have to be a minimum of 400 pounds, but can't weigh more than six hundred and that at most of the big, televised events the steer weigh at least five hundred. I block the memory from my mind of the steer stomping on Jason's head.

I also learn the horns on the steer must be blunted to the size of a dime and this gives me some comfort. *Not really any.* The bulldogger exits from the left of the steer, the hazer to the right, and the steer gets a head start.

Jason is patient and pleasant as he explains the rules to all the events and sprinkles in stories he's collected from a lifetime of rodeos. I sit to his right and hold his good hand in my lap and marvel at the fact I've never asked him all these questions before.

For bareback bronc riding he shows me where the cowboy's legs have to be as he comes out of the chute. I'm pretty sure I couldn't stay on a horse with my feet above the break of its shoulders even if it wasn't bucking. Even more impressive is the rule that the rider's free hand cannot touch himself or the horse or else he's disqualified.

"Why are there two guys riding around in there, too?" I ask.

"They're pickup men to help him get off his horse." Sure enough, they help each rider. "I'd rather ride a bull than broncs. They kill my back." I take a deep breath. I'm here to learn, not break down in tears and beg him to never set foot in an arena again.

After team roping, we get up and walk toward the back fence to look at the cattle. I watch as dozens of fans stop Jason to talk about the rodeo and his injury. They all love him and loved to watch him compete. He's a local hero and there's not a person in this arena not pulling for Jason to bulldog again. Except for me. When he's engulfed by some of the older men I slide onto a nearby bleacher and let him bask in it. He's suddenly full of life, beautiful again. If it weren't for the brace I wouldn't know a thing has happened to him. As their conversation wears down I hear him promise to come back next week and help with some of the events. He catches sight of me while they all carefully shake his hand. He is light, and joyful. He is restored.

* * *

"Thank you, Annie." We wait for the traffic to clear out of the lots. It doesn't feel like gratitude. It feels like a clear placement of me behind rodeo on the list of his needs. I realize it's not a demotion; I've been here all along. I slide over and huddle next to him, unable to have his arm around me because he needs it to drive now.

"You know it's been over a year since the first time you drove me home from the rodeo."

"I know," he says. "You're different, Annie. You're strong again."

"Do you prefer me weak?" I ask, and Jason watches me.

"Would it matter?"

"You wouldn't want me weak, but I don't feel any stronger. I still need you as much as I did last summer." It's desperate, but true. "You know that, though."

* * *

It's an odd summer routine. We both take online classes to lighten the load during the school year; Jason in anticipation of returning to rodeo, and me with the hopes of getting an internship in the spring. Jason has lots of questions about the internship, all of which I ask him to put on hold since I've barely thought of it myself.

I meet Sean for lunch a few times, always at the Corner Bar, which seems odd. He and Michelle took Jason and me out for dinner one night, but other than that I've had little contact with the people of Salem County.

I look at my watch as I park in the lot next to the Corner and again find it strange we're here, but everything is strange these days. We sit at the bar and order hot roast beef sandwiches and fried pickles.

"Why don't you just come to the house?" I ask, and Sean raises his eyebrows as if the answer is obvious. "What?"

"Every time I go by there Jason's truck is in the driveway." I nod understanding. He doesn't want to interrupt. I should tell him he'd be okay at lunch time, but that's not true.

"Do you not like him?" I ask as our beers are delivered.

"He's fine." I stare at him, trying to pry the truth from him.

"I think you consider him temporary," I say.

"He is, isn't he? You're not planning on marrying anytime soon, are you?"

"I'm not interested in a wedding but I want to be with him." We both stare into our beers and shell peanuts. "Forever," I add and Sean seems shocked. How could he not know how I feel about Jason? Am I so accustomed to the person next to me knowing every emotion I have before it registers with me that I've forgotten what it's like to actually communicate?

"Seriously?" he asks. His voice is taut with annoyance.

"That's what I mean. You don't seem to like him."

"He's a bull rider, Charlotte." When he says it like that, yes it sounds ridiculous.

"Steer wrestler, mainly." I quiet, realizing it's a small distinction with Sean.

"Is he moving home after graduation?"

"He's not graduating. Five-year plan. I'm moving to Oklahoma in May, after graduation. Aren't you happy that's part of the plan?" I ask, hoping to pacify Sean.

"This is an actual plan?" he asks as the bartender brings out our food.

"Yes. Believe me, I don't want to live in Oklahoma, but I want him and he's there." I realize he could live in the Arctic Tundra and I would follow him there. Sean and I eat our sandwiches with only the sound of the TV behind us. He's hungry. That's a good sign. The news didn't make him sick. Although, I've never seen Sean miss a meal.

"Sean, what do you think we owe the dead?"

"The dead, or our dead parents?" He clarifies what's been torturing me. What I think we owe the dead, or what other people owe the dead, is completely different than what I owe my mom and dad.

"Mom and dad."

Sean considers the question and looks at me, searching for the least painful answer, but still unsure of the source of the question.

"I think we should spend every day trying to make them proud. The same way we would if they were still alive."

Hmmm. The problem with that is if Mom was still alive she would be pressuring me daily to find a nice accountant to marry. Her comments about the dangers of rodeo would be endless, and I might actually crumble under the pressure.

"What did they say when you told them you were going to marry Michelle?"

"They told me to make sure I treat her the way I'd want my sister to be treated." I sigh, digesting the statement, and take another pickle from the basket.

"Is this about Brian Matlin?" Sean asks, completely confused.

"No." *I wish.*

* * *

We went to the rodeo every Saturday night and it was just enough to get Jason through the week. He helped with the gates and the livestock and was behind the scenes most of the time. I took wine or beer and watched from the stands. Without Jason in the arena, I relished the excitement of each event. It became less foreign and I actually started to enjoy it.

Every week I would sit in the same place and came to know the people around me. The box seats have been in the same families for generations. It is a community like no other, but strong and welcoming nonetheless.

For the most part, I was alone. Jenn and Margo made good on their promises not to come home for the summer. I couldn't convince any of the Rutgers girls to come to the rodeo, and Noble used the long days of summer to farm with his father. He and Sam came with me to the rodeo one weekend and Jason's eyes were on me the entire night. He never said a word, but it was hard to enjoy it, especially remembering Jason's drug-induced thoughts on Noble being in love with me.

I didn't have my friends; I didn't have the ocean all summer. I wanted my mom. I wanted my dad. I wanted my friends. When I was alone the silence of their voices screamed at me. Pictures taken at the shore house Margo, Jenn, and I had rented after graduation still decorate the bulletin board in my room, and I looked from them to the mirror not believing I was capable of smiling the same way again.

I tried to convince Jason to go to the shore, but he wanted no part of it. Our only trip last summer had been a disaster. This was what it would be like if I had gone to Oklahoma like we planned. And this is what it will be like next summer and for God knows how long after that.

I had Jason, though. I had him to myself, in my bed. I had him every single day of the summer at least once. I wondered how I would ever return to Rutgers and leave him in Oklahoma. For all the things that were missing this summer, I overflowed with him and I couldn't keep myself from smiling. Confirming once again that he is what makes me happier than anything else on this Earth.

~ 23 ~

"The sound of the waves, the shore's energy transforms"

I press "done" on the computer, signifying the completion of my last final exam for the summer, and sit back in my chair stretching. This is the last weekend before we make the trip to Oklahoma. Jason starts school in a week, two weeks before I do. My phone dings with a text from Julia:

> RU Weekend in Belmar
> this weekend. Come up here.

I start to write back no, but stop. Why can't I? Jason's getting around fine on his own and he'll be entertained at the rodeo. As the thought sinks in, my excitement grows and I can think of nothing else but a weekend at the Jersey Shore.

Jason is at physical therapy for the next hour so I go to the next town over and get a pedicure. Instead of my usual OPI,

"I'm Really Not a Waitress," I opt for the pretty pink color, "The Lifeguard Makes Me Blush" in honor of my upcoming weekend. I stop and pick up the latest issue of *Vanity Fair* which reminds me I'm white as a ghost and need sunscreen. I grab self-tanner too. When I return home Jason is grilling chicken on the back deck.

"Hey," I say as I watch him turn the chicken breasts.

"I was starting to worry," he says, looking over his shoulder for a minute.

"Why didn't you call?" *Silly question.* I walk over and kiss his cheek and the heat off the grill hits me. Or maybe it's the heat off Jason Leer. "Like my toes?" I ask, flashing him my pedicure.

"In my mouth," he says, and I blush. "Yes, I like the pink."

"I'm going to the shore this weekend with my roommates." Jason stops moving the chicken around and stays still. "Julia texted me this morning. It's an unofficial RU Weekend at the North Jersey beaches."

"Are you inviting me?" he asks, finally turning toward me.

Do you go to Rutgers?

"No," I say, and wrap my arms around his waist. "You don't want to go to the shore. If you did you'd have taken me before now. You just want to go to keep an eye on me and that's not necessary." These are all great points.

"It would bother you if I went to some reunion and didn't invite you." *You do it every Saturday night*, I think but don't say a word. "You're not speaking?" he asks.

"I wasn't asking permission. I was telling you as a courtesy. I'm not looking to turn a fun, relaxing weekend with my friends into an argument. I haven't seen them in months. After next May I'll be lucky if I see them once a year." I walk into the house unwilling or unable to finish what I just started. I text Julia:

I'm in.

And she responds:

Do not back out.
I am going to start broadcasting your presence.
So excited!

I pull some dresses out as possible items to take. I haven't been anywhere since Jason got hurt. I can't remember the last time I cared what I put on. Just picking out an outfit is excit-ing. I find my camo mini skirt and hang it with a black tank top, and a long black sleeveless maxi with no real back to it. It hangs awkwardly on the hanger, unsure of how to rest. From the back of my closet I pull out silver strappy wedges that've been forgotten since last summer. This is going to be fun if it kills us.

"I'm sorry." His words break my concentration and shock me. I look up and he appears to be genuinely calm. "I don't care if you go." I look at him, annoyed. "I know you don't need my permission. Look, I'm spoiled. I haven't had to share you with another person all summer. It just took me a few minutes to get used to the idea," Jason says, and I warm to his sweet words. The camo mini catches his eyes and his face turns to stone.

"What is that?"

"It's a skirt."

"For a child?"

"For me. Don't worry. I'll wear underwear."

"Why can't you just wear what you wear to the rodeo every Saturday?"

"Because I'm not going to the rodeo," I say, and the excitement in my voice surprises even me. If Jason is hurt by my statement he doesn't let it show. He walks over to the black dress and tries to make sense of it.

"Where did you even get this?"

"Just because I don't buy my clothes at Tractor Supply does not make them inferior."

"Well, this one's missing the back. It is the back it's missing, right?" I hang the dress back in my closet and pull out my white jeans and a raspberry colored tube top. I keep the silver wedges out. "Much better," Jason says, and rolls his eyes.

* * *

I stop in Moorestown and collect Violet on my way to North Jersey. Her presence heightens the escapism surrounding my weekend. The excitement in the car builds with every mile marker we pass.

"Nice car, Charlotte. When did you get this?" Violet looks around my new Volvo SUV as if she's shopping herself.

"My brother got it for me. I had to talk him down from a Hummer, a tank, and one of those Ducks that can drive on land and in water. He's apparently quite invested in me living."

"I can't blame him. You guys have been through a lot. I think this is a nice compromise. Are you going to bring it to Rutgers?"

"I doubt it. I'm going to Oklahoma with Jason first. I'll probably fly right to Newark."

"I cannot believe you guys have made it this long," she says, and my head jerks toward her, shocked. The idea of us not making it is not one I speak of nonchalantly. "What? Have you not noticed you two were not exactly meant to be together? Not to mention it's hard to keep something going over a long distance." I shake my head confidently and she adds, "Out of sight, out of mind."

I completely dismiss Violet and by the time we walk onto the beach I can't even remember what we talked about in the car. I set my chair facing the sun, dig my toes into the sand and listen as the sound of the waves hitting the beach fills me with the healing energy of the shore. It transforms me, but from and to what, I'm not sure. I am utterly in love with the Jersey Shore. I could sit here all day by myself, but the addition of the RU girls makes it therapeutic. *I needed this.*

We linger on the beach until most of the crowd has left and around 6:30 head back to Julia's cramped house. I lay my backpack down on the floor and sit on top of it. The small couch and chair are already full of too many people. It strikes me that I am technically a millionaire, but apparently living in squalor this weekend. I pull out my phone and text Jason.

Miss me?

Doesn't describe it.

I love you.

Call me when you get home.

I'll text you. The house
is small and I won't want
to wake anyone.

How small? Where are you sleeping?

I look into a cramped bedroom with a twin bed and an air mattress taking up the entire floor. There are clothes everywhere and not one pillow.

In a cozy little bedroom with a small bed, just made for one, and a teddy bear resting on the pillow. No need to worry.

Easier said.

I put my phone away and head to the outside shower, knowing the line will be shorter than inside. It's a hot night and I'm thrilled I have my little camo skirt to keep me cool, even if my boyfriend is not. The logistics of Julia's house leave little room for primping so I throw some lip gloss in my bag and call myself "ready."

We take a cab to the Parker House in Sea Girt and find tons of people from Rutgers. Julia has, as usual, done an excellent job of spreading the word. My smile, a permanent fixture since I exited the highway, is the evidence of how much I've missed everyone, of how much I've missed the shore. At least half of ZTA is here and it's absolutely restorative to catch up with everyone.

I walk inside to the bathroom and see Noble talking to a girl I don't recognize. She's practically drooling. I keep moving, not wanting to interrupt. When I return to the back deck Julia, Violet, and Sydney are surrounded by a bunch of guys I've never seen before.

"Here's our little weather girl," she says, displaying me to our new friends.

"How many times do I have to tell you, it's meteorologist?" I say, not missing a beat. I guess it's weather girl night again. Sydney chimes in with my fake name and city, which she has, of course, already researched knowing these guys will Google me instantly. A sweet-looking girl with long blonde hair and green eyes pops up in front of a weather map and I smile at them. Tonight, Julia has promoted herself to my producer. It's fitting since she's a communications major. What's wrong with being a statistician? *It's sexy, right?*

"Is it going to be sunny tomorrow?" Noble asks in my ear and I turn to give him a big hug.

"You're smart to ask an expert," I say, and look behind him for the girl. "Where's your friend? Is she the one?"

"She is the one. The one for the next few hours. I'll introduce you when she comes back."

"Noble Sinclair, it's time for you to fall in love."

"Charlotte, I do love her. I love everything about her. It's just tomorrow I might love someone else." I roll my eyes and shake my head. He pulls me toward him as a bar back carries a bin full of ice behind me. The girls engulf us and smother Noble with their North Jersey kisses. The rest of ZTA notices and his former conquests come over to say hello. He has a rare gift for remaining friends with everyone he's ever been with. He told me once it's because he's very clear on the expectations from the very beginning. Must be his cloudless vision.

We drink more at the Parker House than I have the entire summer combined and spill into a cab to Bar-A. Here, there are several deejays. A dark dance floor inside is highlighted by glow sticks and necklaces as the throbbing beat of the music bounces off the walls. We spread out and I'm happy to be outside for the rest of the night. The crowd is a little more Jersey, but everyone's in a great mood. It's impossible not to be on this perfect summer night. Outside, there's another deejay, plus fire breathers, palm trees, and my favorite, a mechanical bull. Bull riding's a party game up here, down south it's a sport. I wonder what my cowboy is up to tonight.

It's 1:53 a.m. when the lights come on and people begin filing out of the bar. No more liquor. No more music. No reason to stay. I have Julia with me, but everyone else I know was lost a long time ago. Julia and I exit the bar and see the ice cream truck at the end of the parking lot. Not many cars are moving. Rather than scoring a guaranteed DUI, most will leave their car until tomorrow.

"Come on, Charlotte. I'll buy you an ice cream," Julia says.

"Aw. You do love me."

"I do."

We scan the pictures of ice cream treats decorating the side of the truck and look up to order as Wes sticks his head out of the truck.

"Wes! What are you doing here?" I say, completely forgetting about my Chipwich.

"It's my summer job. I drive an ice cream truck." I burst out laughing. It's fantastic.

"I've never known a real life ice cream man," I say, and can't help but smile.

"You guys going home, or do you want to hang out?" I can tell by Wes's face "hang out" means smoke and I know I should probably just go home.

"We're in," Julia says, and climbs in the back of the truck, leaving me standing in front of the window.

"Let's get out of here. The stragglers never buy. They can't find their money," he says, and climbs into the driver's seat. Julia and I stand up in the back and search the freezers for Chipwiches. Wes stops short and we fall to the front. My brother would kill me for this one.

Wes pulls into a side alley, next to a small bungalow on the beach.

"It costs me $800 more for the summer to be able to park the truck." I look back at the truck and marvel at the business expense.

Inside we find an empty house and I'm in awe. There's a small kitchen that's open to the living room, a bedroom on each side and one bathroom. And it's empty. Julia's house probably has at least ten people littering the floor by now.

"Want a beer?" Wes offers and really, what's one more?

"Sure. How many people are renting this with you?"

"There are three of us, but about ten are here this weekend. They'll be back soon," Wes says, and hands me a beer and lights a bowl. I smoke it and pass it to Julia whose eyes are already half-closed.

"Are you sure you want to smoke?" I ask, and she opens one eye to combat my ridiculous notion. Wes turns on music and reggae fills the room with a sweet kindness as Noble walks in.

"Hey girls! How's the weather, Charlotte?" he practically yells, and I realize he's drunk.

"It's still beautiful," I say as he sits down next to me. I hear my text dinging.

> I thought you were going to
> text when you got home?

I'm not home yet.

I send without a care in the world.

"Where's your girl?" I turn my attention back to Noble.

"I just walked her home."

"That's nice," I say, and study at the look on his face. There is so much more to the story he's not going to share. I suspect if it were just Wes here he would get an earful. The girl's probably a complete freak in bed. I'll bet he has bite marks all over him.

"Are you crashing here?" he says, and breaks my concentration.

"I…" I look at Julia, completely passed out on the couch next to me. "I guess so."

"You can sleep in my room if you want." He raises his hands in the air. "Like brother and sister, I promise," he says. He could be in a coma and I'm sure Jason would want me nowhere near that room, *which* is not unreasonable because I don't really want him sleeping with anyone else, either. Even if it is just sleep. "This place is going to fill up quick," Noble adds, and stumbles into his room.

I sit on the floor, my head resting on the couch next to Julia's, and close my worn eyes. The weight of my entire body rests in my eyelids and floats away as I allow them to close. Sleep will find me here, sitting up on the floor of Wes's shore house.

I half open them to the sound of guys yelling. At first I think they're outside, but I realize at least some of them are inside the house. There's laughing, so I don't think they're fighting. I make sure my skirt is covering me and lay my head back down on the soft couch. An enormous being falls on me and scrapes against my neck. I cover my head with my hands and look over to see Wes rolling on the ground next to me.

"What the hell?" I say as I grab my neck. Wes is laughing, having been hysterically thrown across the room.

"Oh hey, Charlotte," Rob says. "Sorry I didn't see you there." I haven't seen Rob since May. He's one of Noble's closest friends from Rutgers.

"I think something cut me," I say still holding my neck. Wes crawls over to me and looks, practically through his eyelids, at my neck as he moves my hand away.

"Shit, Charlotte. Something did cut you." He looks down at his chest and then over his whole body. He holds up his arm and his oversized watch now has several strands of long blond hair hanging from the crown.

"Come in the bathroom and let me take a look, Charlotte," Rob says, and although he's nice I know his offer has nothing to do with the scratch on my neck.

"It's fine. I'm sure it's fine. I'm going to bed. You guys have a good night."

"You sure you're not mad?"

"Certain."

I open the door to Noble's bedroom and turn on my phone to provide some light. He's passed out on the tiny bed. At least it looks tiny with him in it. There's just enough room on the floor between the bed and the wall for me to lie, but he's hanging off the side of the bed, not even under the covers.

Just this once...

I climb into the bed and the soft mattress and pillow under my head are like heaven. I roll toward the wall, not touching Noble at all. I can hear his deep breaths and know he'll be asleep for a while. I set my alarm for 8 a.m., netting me four hours of sleep and text Jason:

I'm home.

Just this once...

I'm glad.

Is all I get back and I happily drift off to sleep.

***

Noble stirs at my alarm, but doesn't wake up. I crawl out from under the sheets and quietly sneak out of the room. I rouse Julia, who is now lying like a princess with men at her feet everywhere I turn. After a few minutes, I drag her tiny body out of the cottage. We walk the nine blocks home still half asleep. We change into our bathing suits, brush our teeth, and head directly to the beach, where there's room to sleep and I let the beach heal me until 11:30 a.m. Until Sydney can no longer take it, and wakes me up to tell her every detail of my night after the last point she saw me.

***

The second day is more of the same, with the exception of our sleeping arrangements. Violet and Blake are staying at Violet's dad's partner's house in Spring Lake and Julia, Sydney and I quickly relocate there. Even with all three of us sharing one bedroom we still have 800 times the room we had at Julia's.

The house is magnificent. After happy hour at the Parker House, we grab food and head back to the patio to finish our Rutgers weekend. I get a text from Noble:

> Rob just told me some
> interesting facts about
> my night last night.

> If you don't remember it wasn't memorable.

> How's the weather in Spring
> Lake or are you an author of
> erotic fiction now? It's hard
> to keep up.

> Tonight Sydney made me an office manager.

> Boring

> At ESPN

> She's good.

He texts and I happily fall asleep next to Julia and Sydney in our four-post bed at the corner of Luxurious and Breathtaking in Spring Lake, New Jersey.

* * *

After breakfast I drag Violet from Blake and we head home laughing about the weekend the entire way. It has literally been months—how many, maybe six months—since I've had this type of fun. These girls are hilarious. We ride with the windows down to smell the ocean as long as possible, and switch to the air conditioning when we hit the highway. I smile the whole way home, and if it weren't for being completely exhausted I'd call Julia and relive every minute of it all over again.

Jason's truck is absent from the driveway. Maybe he went to church. I laugh a little at the thought of it as I climb into our bed and let exhaustion have me.

* * *

When I wake his robotic arm is around me and he's spooning me; two things which never happen. He missed me. And I missed him. I delicately roll toward him and he's smiling at me. I kiss his lips and savor the taste of him. I love having Jason Leer in my bed.

"You never need a nap after a Saturday night at the rodeo," he says, and I kiss him again, letting him feel my need for himself. I gingerly roll him on his back and rest on his chest. I take in his beautiful face and kiss him on the cheek and on his neck right below his ear. The wind blows the sheers from my window and I look up as they float out from the windows. Jason tenses beneath me. "What happened to your neck?" he asks with eyes that are turning black.

I reach down and cover the cut on my neck. It's really just a scrape. He's being ridiculous.

"It was an accident," I say weakly. "Wes scraped it with his watch." I watch as Wes's name registers with Jason and when I think he's fully digested my statements, I return to his neck.

"We'll talk more about this later," he says.

"That's fine, as long as we do what I want right now." I reach down and grab his already hard-on. The mechanical man laboriously rolls me back over and devours me, to my delight.

~ 24 ~

"A hope for a future between alone and vicious storms"

August 29th

Dear Annie,

Why do you keep leaving me?
How do you keep leaving me?
I wait at security for you to turn around and come out. I wait until I see your plane in the air, but you never come. Not once.

I understand you want to finish your last year at Rutgers, but now that it's almost September, and you're there, I wish I had tortured you into submission. I'm not sure I'm going to make it. Having you every day this summer has made it impossible to be without you.

Eight months and this is over. Just eight more months and you'll be mine forever.

I've been riding again. Don't freak. The doctor cleared it. No specific conditioning, just riding. I'm hoping to compete again starting in November. I'll let you know the exact date when I know. It's going to feel good to dive on a steer again. (I know that made you cringe.)

Good luck with your classes. Try not to get shot in your sweet New Brunswick. I'll be very pissed off. I'm still getting over your neck.

> *Your source of sexual frustration,*
> *Jason*

PS–Harlan is mad you were here for two weeks and didn't see him once. I told him I wouldn't let you put your clothes on.

September 2nd

Dear Jason,

I'm yours already. You don't have to wait eight months. Your obsession with location, specifically with my relocation to Oklahoma, is disturbing. Can't you love me from afar? Are we nothing without sex?

Speaking of, I think we should video us next time. Oh, sorry. My mother just reached up from her grave and slapped me. Maybe not a good idea. I'm thrilled you are

riding again. This sense of comfort and relaxation is begin-
ning to bore me and the thought of you back in the rodeo
arena will ensure less sleep and more anxiety. Really, thank
you. "Source of my sexual frustration" doesn't fully encom-
pass the depths to which you bother me.

New Brunswick has welcomed me back with open
arms. It missed me. I've purchased my books, the last ones
I'll need until graduation. Did we talk about my in-
ternship this spring? Oh well, another time. Please tell
Harlan he's always welcome to visit the northeast. We
have cheap beer here too and ours has a higher alcohol
content. He can come for Halloween. You are going to
LOVE my costume.

Your sweet and submissive girlfriend,
Charlotte

PS - I get on the plane because it's the only way back to New
Jersey. You do realize, even after I move there, I'm going to
come back to Jersey? Often.

The campus is buzzing. Halloween is one of the biggest parties of the year. Jenn is pissed she can't come this year because
it's also my sorority's date night. No outside girls allowed;
strict rules. Unlike rules, Jenn does not like to break traditions.
She took it well. She's headed to Margo. Part of me wishes they
were both coming here. Our moments together are fleeting. By
this time next year we're going to be all over the place. Jenn is
determined to find a way to Hawaii and Margo keeps talking
about skiing. Neither of them mentions settling down in Oklahoma. I guess that's too much to ask.

Jason's plane gets in at 7:30 p.m. We're going to be late for the date night, but at least it's right downtown. Noble drops me off at the airport around seven, giving himself plenty of time to get back to College Avenue and change before the party. He and Julia are going as friends, not romantic dates tonight, which is perfect for me. Jason will have another person he knows there.

I'm already in my cowgirl costume, or as Violet likes to call it, my slutty cowgirl costume. It's chilly, but even if it was ninety degrees out, I would have this parka pulled up around my neck. Jason would flip to see me in the Newark Airport in the slutty cowgirl costume. I laugh just thinking about it. A group of passengers fills the baggage claim area and I can tell it's his plane. I've already seen three ten-gallon hats and two sets of overalls.

Within seconds he comes into sight and I run to him before he clears the doorway. He catches me and picks me up with his good arm as if I'm only ten pounds. He holds me until I get my fill of his scent, having buried myself near his kiwi hair. He lowers me to my feet and kisses me. I could spend the entire night right here in his arms, but we'd probably get arrested.

"Ready?" I ask, and turn toward the exit marked GROUND TRANSPORTATION.

"Are we taking all the trains again?" he asks, wary from our prior New Jersey Transit adventures.

"Tonight we are taking a cab. I want to get to the party as soon as possible." Jason seems unenthused, but happy to climb in the back of a cab with me.

"Nice boots." He pulls my coat up and examines the boots he bought me for my birthday. When he notices the absence of pants he continues to raise my coat until he gets above my knee, pushing it up with his hot hand on my leg. It's driving me insane. "Annie, what are you wearing?"

"My Halloween costume. I'm a cowgirl."

"A naked one?" he says, and the words falling off his lips make my mouth water.

"No. In fact, I'm wearing the shirt you left here last time." Jason looks confused. "I altered it a little. Hope you didn't want it back."

"What I want is to see your costume."

"You have to wait until the party." Jason's hand squeezes my thigh and he raises it higher, still not encountering any fabric. His face is a cross between anger and obsession and I'm suddenly very hot.

"We need to stop at your house first." I look at him through my eyelashes. "I have to drop off my bag." He runs his hand up and down the inside of my thigh and the muscles in my stomach clench.

"Just a quick stop," I say, slightly out of breath.

* * *

When the cab stops on Hamilton Street a police cruiser is double parked in front of my house with its lights on. There are several people on the stoop and the front door is wide open. Julia's in her flasher costume giving the officer information. I pay the driver and run out of the cab without a word to Jason.

"Are you okay?" I practically yell at Julia.

"Someone broke into the house," she says, and I look at the door. It's fine. "They came up the rear fire escape and broke the window."

"The one by our room?" I ask, and imagine someone in my room.

"You live here?" the officer asks.

"Yes," I say, and Jason's hand lands on my shoulder.

"I'm going to need you to try and figure out if anything's missing." *Try?*

"Of course. When did this happen? Were you home?"

"Nick and I walked in on him. He ran out the front door while we were in the downstairs kitchen. It wasn't until we walked upstairs we figured it all out."

"My God, Julia. You could have been hurt."

"Or worse," the officer says. "We think he was watching the house, waiting for everyone to leave." At this, Jason's hand tightens its grip on my shoulder. This is going to be a long conversation.

I walk into the house with Jason a half-step behind me. His breath on me, angry still, is the ominous music accompanying this horror film. The back window is broken and shattered glass covers the floor. Noble is hammering a piece of plywood over the hole.

"Noble," I say, and he stops hammering and turns around. "Are you okay?"

"I'm fine. Julia's pretty shaken up. I know she wants to go to the party. It's her last one, but she's kind of a wreck," he says, and I still can't believe someone was in our house. "I'm going to nail this window shut until we can get to the hardware store tomorrow, so pray there's no fire."

I take two steps back and turn into my room. Both mattresses are flipped off the frames, the lampshades are crooked and the framed pictures on my dresser are in a pile, including my parents' wedding picture. I run my fingers over the shattered glass still covering their faces. When I look up Noble and Jason are staring at me. Noble's sweet concern is written all over his face. Jason may soon kill someone. I carefully place the frame back on my dresser.

Every single item in the room is now on the floor. Every piece of clothing, every purse, lies inside out, every wallet open, everything thrown violently in a search. I raise both hands to my mouth and breathe heavily through my nose. Jason's eyes are screaming at me, but I can't fit his issues in with my own right now.

I open my purse and thankfully find my license, credit card, and insurance card are with me. Julia and Noble follow the policeman into the room and we all stand in the thirty inches of floor that's uncovered.

"He did a number on this place. Can you tell if anything's missing?"

"My student ID," I say, and realize it has my name and my picture on it. I shiver as a chill runs down my back. I walk to my bed and drag it away from the wall. I untape the envelope from the bottom of the headboard and count the money inside. Fifteen hundred dollars. It's all here. When I look up, they're all looking at me. "What? My grandmother was crazy. She hid stuff all over the place." My heart necklace is in Oklahoma and my rowel necklace is around my neck. "I don't have anything else of value here," I say, and Jason looks like he might kill someone. I wish we were alone.

"Are you sure you still want to go to the party?" Noble asks Julia and she nods.

"I don't want to be here," she says, and I take out my phone and Google the name of the hotel the party's at. I step into the hall and book two rooms. We're not coming back here either.

We all use my cash stash to check in. Noble takes Julia to her room to get high and try to forget about the break-in for a few hours. Jason and I check in to our room and I take off my coat for the first time since I picked him up. My costume, meant to turn him on, does nothing to make him feel safe. It's shorts, cutoffs that barely cover my bottom, a giant silver buckle, and his plaid shirt hiked up to my ribs and tied in a knot. It's covering my white bikini top and my hair is in pigtails popping out from under the cowboy hat he gave me when we first got together. It would have been perfect, but now it's a blinking neon warning sign.

"I brought other clothes to change into," I say, and begin pulling things out of my bag that I found on the floor of my bedroom. I know there's a pair of yoga pants in here, somewhere. Jason puts his hand on my own to stop the search.

"Annie." I ignore him and look out the window, his hand still on top of mine. "Annie, you can't stay here." I close my eyes. *Not tonight, Jason. Not tonight.* "You have to know that. After seeing your house the way you just did, you know you can't stay here, right?" New Brunswick has betrayed me, but I'm still not leaving.

"Annie, answer me!" He's yelling now. Frantic at the thought we're not seeing this the same way, I search every corner of my mind for the words that will avoid this fight.

"I love you, Jason," I say, and turn to him. "Will you take me to the party?" I ask, and he thinks I'm deranged. His eyes seek some recognition of severity from mine, but he'll find none there. Avoid, avoid, avoid. "I want you to take me downstairs to the party and later, we'll talk about all of this. I promise."

"There's nothing to talk about, Annie. If you think there's a chance in hell of you ever stepping foot in that house again without me, you have completely lost your fucking mind." I put both hands on his chest and rub them up and down, trying to soothe him. He holds my wrists and pulls them away. "I'm serious, Annie. I'll take you to this party because it's the last one you're going to at Rutgers."

***

We take the elevator downstairs in silence, standing three feet away from each other and never breaking eye contact. If only this were a staring competition—although, he'd probably win that too.

We head straight to the bar and find Julia and Noble downing tequila shots and telling the rest of our roommates about the break-in. The girls from the upstairs triplet plan on sleeping in the basement. They'll all be in the downstairs apartment and lock the door to the upstairs. Julia and I agree it would be easier to go back if our room hadn't been ransacked. The entire time Jason stands near me, his eyes the color of a winter battle.

"Sydney still needs to be told," I say, remembering she's working at Stuff Yer Face tonight.

"I called her and told her we'd come get her after date night. She's going to stay downstairs, just needs a walk home. I don't want her going into the house alone." Julia's words make sense, but there are ten of us. At some point, someone is going to go into the house alone. I avoid looking at Jason. I already know his plan for working this out and it includes me throwing all of my belongings in a bag and flying back to Stillwater with him. Isn't there crime there?

I am becoming an expert at separating Jason's anger from the task at hand. His enormous control over my emotions cannot be the definitive factor in every situation. I move through the crowd and note all the costumes. Some of them are just hilarious. Noble has doctor's scrubs on with a button that says "Free Breast Exams," Julia's a streaker complete with a naked body suit. There's a black widow and her corpse man, the president and first lady, and Arnold Schwarzenegger and Maria Shriver. And then there are the cowboy and the cowgirl. As the twins, dressed as the Olson Twins, come up and turn me around to slap my ass for a picture, I look up to see Noble watching me and laughing.

I look to the side and Jason is watching Noble watching me. Fear runs through me. This night cannot get worse. I wink at Noble and he turns to order yet another drink as I see Jason approach Noble and say something. Whatever it was, Noble seems unconcerned. He puts his hand on Jason's shoulder and speaks calmly in return. If anyone can handle Jason, which no one can, it's Noble. They have known each other since the day they were born. Noble puts a cigarette behind his ear and Jason follows him out the side entrance of the hotel.

I order myself and Julia another drink and we watch as Violet and Blake argue in the corner, not all that inconspicuously.

"What's wrong over there?"

"Blake thinks she was flirting with one of his brothers. Or something else ridiculous," she says with all the patience of the roommate of the girl who is the "boyfriend type."

"Do you think they're going to live happily ever after?" I ask, considering my own future.

"Probably. It will just be a very rough version of the traditional fairy tale."

"Aren't they all?"

"I like to think there's something between 'alone' and 'vicious storm,'" she says, and I can see the back of Noble through the door. It's amazing how relaxed I am without the crippling stare of a pissed off Jason Leer.

"No wonder you and Noble get along so well," I say, and we drink our drinks in silence.

Jason and Noble come through the door as a slow song quiets the crowd. It reunites those separated as they find their way to the dance floor. Jason walks up and takes my hand, which stuns me. A few minutes with Noble were worth whatever fears were running through my head. He leads me to the center of the dance floor and pulls me close.

I wrap my arms around his thick neck and rest my head on my own arm resting on his shoulder, and we dance. I hold onto Jason as if this is the last dance of the night, of the year, of our time together, and I forget about my room at 108 Hamilton Street. Jason leans his face on mine and our feet slow. There's a need igniting and a chill runs to my nipples pushing my body even closer to his. He senses it, too. I lift my head and see in Jason's eyes an invitation for the rest of my life.

I grab his hand and walk off the dance floor. By the time we push the up button on the elevator I have him pinned against the wall, kissing him furiously. This should have been his welcome to New Jersey, not the police cruiser outside my house. The doors open and we stumble in, still connected in every way.

"What floor?" I ask, unable to complete a thought. Jason's mouth is on my neck, taking me away from here, away from New Brunswick. His breath hot near my ear makes me forget why I ever wanted to be here in the first place.

"Eleven." I press the button as he pulls my top down and kisses the top of my breast, just shy of my nipple. His anger

is missing, his hatred for my beloved Rutgers has left. He is
ravenous and savage, and wholly mine. The doors open, but Jason's hair in my hands and his tongue on my breast keep me
from looking up.

I hear, "We'll take the next one," from a girl.

And, "What was wrong with that one," from a guy who
sounds like he's smacked shortly after.

Jason lifts me up to straddle him. He presses my back to the
wall of the elevator and I think he is going to take me right
here, right now, but the doors open again on the eleventh floor
and he carries me down the hall to our room. We lean against
the door with him kissing me, my body still wrapped around
him, and I can't remember what he was even mad about earlier.
He is so responsive now, so obviously in love with me. Jason
could never hurt me.

I find the key and we fall into the room. Jason takes his
time unbuttoning my shirt, and I'm ready to jump out of my
skin. I recognize the mercy he has shown me over the years by
just ripping my clothes off. His tongue finds my nipple and I
moan, never wanting his lips on my body more.

"I love you, Annie," is the last thing I hear before I disappear
into the storm that is Jason Leer.

* * *

We dress and return to the party just as things are winding
down. The desserts are being packed up by the catering staff
and I ask a waitress if she would mind wrapping a cupcake for
me.

"Are you hungry?" Jason asks, as if he's imagining licking the
icing off me.

"It's for Barry. If we're going to Stuff Yer Face to get Sydney, I want to take him a cupcake."

"Why?" he asks, completely irritated. For the life of me, I cannot figure out why this would bother him.

"Because I think there's a strong possibility that Barry's never had a cupcake given to him. In his life," I say without patience or understanding, because I have none. "I don't get the sense his mom was whipping up a batch for his birthday every year," I add and Jason takes the bag from me to carry.

We collect Sydney and deliver the cupcake. Barry is awkward in accepting it even though I try not to make a big deal out of it. We walk Sydney back to Hamilton Street and make sure everyone's safe and sound in the bottom apartment and grab a cab back to the hotel. Jason looks out the window as we pass Stuff Yer Face again.

"He didn't even say thank you."

"I think gratitude is a foreign emotion to him," I say as I lean into him and he pulls me close, kissing the top of my head. "Can't you give anyone the benefit of the doubt?"

"Do you have to give it to everyone?" he asks, playful again. I never would have expected this night to be salvaged.

*　*　*

When we're tucked under the covers and whispering in the darkness of our hotel room I decide this is as good a time as any to talk about tonight. He's never going to start out gentler. I can't figure out where to start, knowing exactly where the conversation is going to end. I remember Jason's conversation with Noble.

"What did Noble say to you at the party?"

Jason's hand stops playing with my hair.

"What? Something you can't tell me?" I ask, confused by his silence.

"Sinclair warned me about pushing you," he says, and takes a deep breath. "He reminded me of how stubborn you are." I smile a little at Noble's assessment. "Do you remember in fourth grade running club when Possum told you no girl could beat him running a mile? You specifically. He said, 'No girl named Charlotte is ever gonna be fast enough to catch me.'"

"I'm still pissed about the whole thing," I say, and remember how infuriated I was at Possum.

"Sinclair and I were remembering how we'd see you out running after school every day. You hated running, but hated being told what you couldn't do more."

"I still hate running," I say, and shake my head.

"And when it came time for the race, you overtook him by the three-quarter mile mark." I remember how good it felt to run past poor Possum. "And the crowd starting chanting, 'Possum stinks. He can't outrun a girl.'" Poor Possum. "And when you heard them, you slowed down and let him win."

I look at Jason, trying to piece together exactly what this has to do with my house on Hamilton Street being broken into.

"Sinclair warned me that between your stubbornness and your kindness, there's no guarantee what happened to Possum was always going to be the outcome. That if I push you too far, you might actually run your fastest, at any cost."

I roll on top of Jason and kiss him.

"I can't lose you, Annie," he says, and runs his fingertips down my bare back. I lay my head on his chest, so happy he's here in New Jersey, with me.

"You can do anything you want. Why do you want to do nothing in Oklahoma?" she asks, and I can barely understand her through the swelling on her face.

"What happened to you, Mom?"

"I was in a car accident, Charlotte. Where have you been? Lost?" she asks with a knowing look on her banged-up face.

"I'm not lost. I know exactly where I am."

"Where are you? At the crossroads of following Jason's life and living your own? Brilliant navigating," she says, and her words sting me.

"Why do you hate him?" I spew at her, ignoring her injuries. She's ignoring mine.

"I couldn't care less about him. You think this is about him? It's about you, Charlotte. As usual you can't see yourself through him. This is not the life a mother wishes for her little girl."

"Yeah, well, I'm not a little girl anymore. If you were so concerned with my life," I scream the words at her, "my safety! Then you should have stuck around!" I start to cry.

I wake up on top of Jason, crying into his chest and angry at my mother. This is not fair.

~ 25 ~

"My life is confined to lost or lost in you"

The plane lands in Tulsa and I turn on my phone.

> Call Harlan for a ride.
> He's waiting for your call.
> Do NOT take a car.

I roll my eyes. He's so ridiculous. I was lucky enough to get on the earlier flight. I'm not going to now sit and wait over an hour for Harlan to get here. I walk off the plane and straight into a car.

When I'm safely on I-64 West I text Harlan.

> No need for the ride.
> I'm already on my way.
> Thanks anyway.

WTH CHARLOTTE!
You tryin to get me killed. He's
gonna be madder than a hornet.

I'll handle the hornet.

I wait for him to call, spewing his anger at me, but he doesn't and I remember he has his last physical therapy appointment this morning and a meeting with the doctor. His plan is to be cleared and then we're off to Alva, Oklahoma for the last rodeo of the semester. Tonight we can celebrate his return to life-threatening activities and my twenty-second birthday.

When the car pulls up in front of Jason's loft the sight of his truck weakens my confidence. I take a deep breath and pay the driver. I keep waiting for him to run out and tackle me as I make the short walk to his door.

The door's unlocked. I open it and step in, looking for Jason, listening for the shower. He closes the door behind me and I jump.

"So you do have some fear in your body?" He's so beautiful, finally completely healed. He's broad and solid, and I want to climb on top of him. He's rubbing his jaw; a clear indication he's been clenching his teeth. I step toward him and move his hand to kiss him.

"Why must you defy me?" he asks, and I lean into him and kiss him, opening his lips and unleashing my tongue.

"Impossible. You must be confused," I say, and then kiss him again.

"How's that?" Jason asks, his voice softening as my hand finds the rest of him hardening.

"To defy you would imply you have some control over me."

Jason stops my exploring hands with one of his own over them. He rests his arm on the door behind my head and stares at me until I flush. I still refuse to look away. He leans over and kisses my neck and says in my ear, "I think you've got this all wrong," and the touch of his breath on my neck and in my ear leaves me to wonder what we're even talking about.

Jason reaches his hand up inside my sweater and releases my breasts with two fingers on the hook of my bra. He leans down and takes each one in his mouth, teasing and licking them while I watch. He runs my left nipple between his teeth and when I start to fear if he's going to bite it off he looks at me, naughty as ever.

He pulls at my jeans. The button and the zipper disintegrate in his fingers.

"Fuck," I say, pissed because I only brought one other pair with me.

"Oh, we'll get to that. Don't be so greedy, Annie."

***

Alva is over two hours away, but we drive in for Thursday's Long Go-Rounds. If things go well, we'll spend the night tomorrow night. Harlan refuses to ride with us even after we promise to behave in the truck. He's scarred from Kansas. *Aren't we all?*

Jason and I barely speak on the way. What's there to say? He's excited. I am not.

When we reach Northwestern Oklahoma State University Jason parks and walks me to a "good" seat in the arena, but I can't sit yet. Nervous energy keeps me moving in small steps back and forth. I check the gates of the arena, listen for the cattle in the background, and find the ambulance parked nearby. We were very lucky in Kansas.

"Hey. I'm going to be all right out there," he says, and I just look at him. "I need you to be all right up here." I didn't come to make this harder on him. How can he not be nervous at all?

I can feel the energy coursing through him. He needs bulldogging with the same intensity he needs me. I'm not a suitable substitution.

"Don't die," I say rather than good luck, and his smile steadies my heart rate.

"Not a chance." He kisses me. It's an embarrassing display of affection that I cannot get enough of. "This will be over before you know it."

"And then we come back tomorrow."

"And Saturday. Don't forget about Saturday, Annie, because I'm definitely making it to the Short Go-Rounds."

"I may not look it, but I'm very excited," I say, and kiss his cheek before he walks away, practically skipping, and leaves me alone in the stands.

The flags come rolling in, the national anthem is played, and the arena is cleared. The whole time I feel sick. I might actually throw up. I suffer through bull riding to get to steer wrestling where a pain starts behind my ears and jabs forward to my eyes. Jason is the second run and I barely see the first, too consumed with thoughts of Kansas.

I can't see his face, he's too far away, but I can tell it's him. He's in the gate and Harlan's to his right. I'm vaguely aware his name is announced. Jason nods, and the steer runs out followed by Jason and Harlan. He dives from the horse and turns the steer over before I can hold my breath. The crowd is on their feet cheering and Jason turns to me, takes off his hat and points it at me, and smiles a smile that erases the last six months. I take both hands to my lips and blow him a kiss through flowing tears. How does he do it? In less than five seconds I relinquish every note of bitterness toward bulldogging and cheer like a common buckle bunny.

Jason stands, facing me in the arena, for longer than he took to wrestle the steer and I am paralyzed by the sight of him. When he finally replaces his hat and runs out I listen to the fans around me replaying his run and discussing his injuries. A group of girls in the front row catches my eye and I notice Stephanie Harding with them. They must travel to a lot of these. I wave, but she doesn't see me and keeps talking to the girl next to her.

* * *

Jason and I linger at his truck waiting for the parking lot to clear. Cowboys from other schools stop by to congratulate him and talk about Kansas, many of them a witness to the carnage as well. Harlan is the last to say good-bye.

"It's good to have you back," he says, and hugs Jason. "You too, Jersey," he says, and flashes his Harlan grin at me. God, I'm thankful to not be in a hospital waiting room with him right now.

It's cold tonight, only about forty-five degrees, and I pull my sweater up around my neck. I picked it because it's long and covers the top of my jeans, which are held together with a rubber band. Jason walks back to me as Harlan pulls away. He somehow looks more beautiful than he ever has before and I silently admit I am completely his. Whatever he wants.

The bats stop flying above and the moon stands still. He

commands the air and the sky and my body. When he reaches me he kisses me gently and I lean into him afraid I'll crumble under the weight of his tenderness.

"I'm better when you're with me," he says.

"That's not true. You're awesome every time you get on a horse."

"I'm not talking about bulldoggin'," he says. I close my eyes and let his voice slip past my lashes and float through my body. Jason leans over to speak directly in my ear. "I can't wait, Annie. I need you. It has nothing to do with worrying about you." His words burn my insides and I raise my hands to the back of his neck.

"It's about needing you," he says, and I tilt my head toward him, his breath on my neck too much. "And surviving you." Jason utters a sound, a slight groan, as he kisses my neck and I am lost. He moves my face so our eyes meet. "Do your internship in Oklahoma. Make this our last month apart."

I kiss him because my body is no longer interested in talking and Jason pulls away. "Not here. I want you in our bed. In our house," he says, and opens the truck door for me.

Just like that, I've gone from an animal to a lady, one he holds the door for and won't have sex with in a parking lot. I'm not thrilled with the promotion.

"He's gone," Harlan says, and turns to walk away.

"What do you mean he's gone?" I grab his arm and spin him around. He looks at my hand on his arm, and into my eyes without a hint of compassion.

"He's gone, Jersey. He didn't make it. His injuries were too extensive." I've heard that somewhere before.

"That's impossible," I say, still trying to understand

what's happening. "I just moved here. He can't leave me here without him."

"Didn't he ever tell you no one always wins?" I think he did say that, but I still don't understand. Harlan jumps in his truck and pulls away and I walk back into the loft. It's empty. There's nothing left of Jason or me.

I kneel down on the floor and cry.

"No God, take me too."

I lift my head, disoriented and profoundly sad. I can hear Jason breathing and the dim light brings his face into view. I lay my head back down on Jason's arm and kiss it. He's right here in his bed with me, in our loft. He's with me. I must have fallen asleep on the way home from Alva. I roll toward him and lean over him as I take in his beautiful face. He's here, not going anywhere.

I swallow the fact we won't always be together. Something will tear us apart. Death will be the end of us. It's only a matter of time as long as he's a steer wrestler. The idea of him leaving consumes me.

"Jason," I say, and kiss his lips. "Jason, I need you to wake up." I shake his arm and he raises his head and looks at me, confused.

"Annie, what's wrong?" he asks, still groggy.

"I had a dream you left me. You left me here alone," I say, and choke on the tears welling up in my throat. Jason pushes the hair back from my face and pulls me toward him. He kisses me and the chill flows through me. "Jason," I say, breathless, unsure if I can admit to him that which I can barely admit to myself.

"Annie, you have to believe that we are going to make this work," he says, bravely confronting my fears. He pulls me to him and kisses me again. "Do you feel that, Annie?" I nod my head in silence. "That's ours alone."

Jason rolls me onto my back and crushes me as he kisses me. His lips are intense and hungry and all mine. He sits up and pulls me up by my wrists. He lifts my sweater over my head and takes off my bra. I watch him work with the hopelessness from my dream still burying me. He unhooks the rubber band holding my jeans together and pulls them off. The night air chills me and then Jason is upon me again, warming me with his eyes, and his lips, and his hands.

I tighten my arms around his neck. I'm holding on for dear life and he lets me. He stops and looks in my eyes. His dark, colorless eyes answering every question I've ever had and I surrender to the beast. I wait for something to say, but why bother, he knows everything already. I kiss him instead. I kiss him as if this is our last night together, as if he'll be gone tomorrow. Jason sits up and pulls me on top of him. I press the front of me against him and wrap my legs around his waist as he lowers his head and kisses my neck. I raise my head to the ceiling and fight against the lack of air.

Jason lifts me and guides himself into me and I wish I wasn't on the pill. I wish I was pregnant with his baby. I want a piece of him forever. My lips never leave Jason's, my tongue exploring him while I ride him, and when I finally do come up for air he slows his pace and stops me completely.

"Forever," he says, and I nod.

With this confirmation Jason lays me back on the bed and mounts me. He thrusts into me with a violence that nearly breaks me in half. I lower my legs and put my feet on the bed to anchor my body before it shatters. Jason grabs my hair in his fist as he continues his onslaught. His lips near my neck cover me with his hot breath and I never want to leave his grasp. I hold onto his arms and watch him come a moment before I lose myself to him.

"Come to Oklahoma," he says, breathless in my ear, and I turn my head and look at the wall. I run my hand through his hair and completely avoid the invitation.

* * *

The next two days are awkward. It's the equivalent to the time your best friend drunk-texted you that he loves you and you tried to act like he didn't send it, that you never received the text, but you both know you did. Jason presented an option and I'm acting like he didn't say it.

Jason takes first place in Alva and we arrive back in Stillwater just in time for me to collect my broken jeans and head to the airport. He's quiet on the drive, finally coming down from the high of domination.

He parks as usual and walks me to the last possible step he can take without a ticket.

"Happy birthday, Annie," he says, and I can't read a thing in his eyes.

"I'm glad I was here, but I wish I was staying until Tuesday. I want to wake up on your arm for my birthday," I say, and kiss him and hold him tight, apologizing for not saying any of the things I should be saying. It's all jumbling in my head.

You're everything to me.

You are amazing.

I need you.

I'm nothing without you.

But I stay silent. My departure disputes all of them and although I know it's not fair, I know it's true.

"Call me when you get home," he says, and it might be the most chivalrous thing he's ever done.

I stumble through security and buy a plum tea at Java Dave's. I mosey to my gate and sit down. The sadness unhinges me and the tears fall down my face.

You know what, Mom? I already love him. It's too late. It might have been too late when I mentioned him to you. Maybe he's part of the master plan, too?

I stand at the announcement of my flight's pre-boarding and take my phone out of my bag. I stare at it, waiting for the right thing to say to come to me, and then I recognize the truth.

I was born to be with you.

I hit send as I walk back toward the security check point. As I cross the entryway, I can see him leaning on the window, his back to me as he reads my text.

"Can you give me a ride?" I ask, and Jason turns to me in shock. "Car services are very dan—" His lips halt my words and I give in to the knowledge that I belong with Jason Leer. Wherever he is.

November 11

Dear Jason,

I'm sure you're wondering how you're back at the airport just two days after you brought me here before. By now I've made it through security and I'm sitting alone in the ter-

minal, crying and questioning whether I've made the right decision. I couldn't leave on Sunday. I'm not sure exactly what made it different than all the other times I've departed Oklahoma, but it was. If I went to therapy they'd probably tell me it has something to do with the idea of leaving the one person that keeps me anchored to this earth for my birthday, but I suspect it's not that easily defined.

When I'm away from you I am lost.

But, when I'm with you I am lost in you.

There's no doubt of which I'd rather be, but I have an obligation, or some compulsion, to return to Rutgers. It's as if I have to complete me before delivering myself to you. I don't know if this is making sense, even to myself, but if I don't finish undergrad at Rutgers I'm afraid I'll always feel like I moved on in life without living this part.

With all that being said, leaving you drains every ounce of strength from my body. I can't wait for the day when this is no longer an issue. Please be patient with me. It's only a few more months and then we have the rest of our lives together.

Your lost soul,
Annie

~ 26 ~

"Now and forever, you belong to me too"

Jason lies in my bed watching me read for what seems like a week. Exams are hard enough without his body anywhere near me. He's happy, though. My roommates start to warm to him. He tells them about Oklahoma and steer wrestling, and how much he loves me between their exams, and they can't help but adore him.

He drives me home as snow falls on the turnpike. The garden state is in a constant state of gray now, the air permanently cold and threatening snow. I sit next to him in the truck, my hand between his legs, and for the first time since my parents died I'm actually looking forward to a holiday.

"I was thinking of taking you later to get a tree," he says, and I'm delighted.

"Really? I didn't think you cared about such things."

"I haven't, but this year I want to celebrate Christmas, with you. Properly."

"It's time," I say, nodding my head.

* * *

The tree is small, one of the only ones left on the farm, and lopsided, but it's ours. We set it up in the front window of the house and I find my mother's decorations in the attic. I hand each box down to Jason.

"The tree's not that big, you know?" He says with his head sticking up into the attic, waiting to carry the boxes down the stairs.

"You're the one who said 'properly'," I remind him and hand him the lights. I'm giddy, excited for Christmas. I hope he likes my gift. "I think we should invite your dad to Christmas dinner. The last time I saw him he seemed to hate me a little less," I say. Parents usually like me, but not Butch.

"Why would you want to eat with someone who hates you?" Jason asks, and I look at him as if it's the dumbest question I've ever heard.

"He's family. Whether he likes me or not is irrelevant." Jason shrugs and keeps carrying the boxes to the living room. "Where are you from?" I ask indignantly.

"He doesn't hate you. At least not any more than he hates every other person since my mom died. It's the way he is now."

What way am I now?

* * *

We decorate the tree and it's beautiful, at least when the lights are lit at night. Everything is more beautiful with Christmas lights. I bake sugar cookies in the shape of trees and wreaths and decorate them with green sprinkles, and Jason eats them before I can even get them cool.

"I can't remember the last time I had Christmas cookies," he says, and he's happy.

"Yes you can," I say, and the joy drains from his face. "I think we should go to church Christmas Eve." Jason looks down, as if I'm suggesting he take Russian language classes with me. "Jesus is the reason for the season," I say, and kiss him to lighten his load.

"I'm not sure why, but I don't want to go," he says, and my heart breaks for him. I know exactly why he doesn't want to go. Nothing will remind him of his mother, of the pain of losing her, more than setting foot in that sanctuary.

"It would be a way to honor her, too," I offer, but it does little to console him. "If not church, than we need to visit their graves. My grandmother's, too. They all need grave blankets."

"Okay. I'll go. No one knows how to ruin a cookie like you do," he says, and kisses me in a way that ends a conversation and starts a new one with our tongues.

* * *

We manage to hang lights on the trees out front without breaking our necks and buy poinsettias for the front porch. I stand back and admire the house. My mother would be proud.

We lay grave blankets on the graves of our loved ones. I cry like a baby in Jason's arms at the sight of my father's. Jason can barely approach his mother's. We're a complete mess, but it must be some sort of progress. He pulls me close to him, tolerating my tears like the brick wall he's become.

Sean and Michelle come for dinner and bring Auburn Road's Classico Wine and we drink too much of it. Butch even has some, citing the local winery as the only reason for his indulgence. Sean hands me a large box wrapped in silver paper and I put down my glass to tear into it. It's a gray Rutgers Sweatshirt and a gift card to Stuff Yer Face. I look at him ruefully.

"You've got a bit of Mom in you, huh?" I say.

"God help me, yes. She's been haunting me in my dreams as if it's my responsibility to keep you in New Brunswick."

"If it's any consolation, she haunts me, too."

"Not really. No," he says, and laughs as we clink our wine glasses together. I give Sean and Michelle a painting of our family's first farm house that I found in the attic and had framed, and a gift card for a hotel in New Brunswick. When Sean opens the gift card he looks at me confused.

"For the night of graduation. We're going to celebrate. You guys can't drive home," I say, and Michelle pulls the card out of his hand and lets out a big Yahoo at the thought of a night away. It's as close to tradition as Sean and I can come and I look across the room and realize Jason and Butch are even further away than we are. Will these two ever be able to heal?

* * *

Our family leaves and Jason and I are left alone by the fire. I pour the last of the open wine bottle into my glass and cuddle close to Jason on the couch. His chest, impossible to sleep on, is perfect to lean against. I inhale deeply the kiwi smell and run my nose up the side of his neck. Jason closes his eyes and leans his head back on the cushion, giving himself to me.

I climb on top of him. His face is inches from my own and I study him. My beautiful Jason, left to me on Christmas and every other day. I have to take good care of him.

"Jason." He raises his head and answers me without speaking. "What do you think we owe the dead?"

Eventually, the corner of Jason's mouth tilts up and I can see, even in the dim firelight, that he is happy.

"Is this about your mom not wanting you to be with a cowboy?" he asks, and my breath catches. Even for him this is knowing too much. "You talk to her in your sleep. You beg her to understand." My astonishment can't be hidden. I lean back, my mouth hanging open.

"How long? How long have I been saying it?" I ask, feeling betrayed.

"Since a few weeks after they died. I think it was right around the time you could start forming a thought. You used to think so much back then. Torture yourself, even in your sleep."

"Why didn't you ever tell me?"

"It's a conversation between you and your mom. Just because I overheard it doesn't mean you're ready for me to listen." I pull him to me and hold him. My arms wrapped around his neck can't save me from the tears that overcome any safety I know. Jason runs his hands down my hair and rubs my back. He kisses my head and holds me until I quiet down.

Jason takes my face in his giant, rough hands and says, "Annie, honoring the dead can't mean sacrificing the living. I belong to you." He reaches to the side table for his Christmas present. "Look at your face in this picture," he says, and holds up the frame. It's a picture of me hugging him and the look on my face exalts pure joy. There is no doubt from this image that in his arms is where I am the happiest. "Now and forever. You belong to me, too." I kiss Jason on the lips and try to imagine how he's felt all these months listening to me beg my mother for understanding.

"Besides, you never listen to a goddamned thing I tell you. Why would you listen to her?" he asks, and I laugh. He and my mother could discuss my stubbornness at length.

* * *

We package everything back up. The decorations, the doubts, and the memories of the dead and begin to deal with another separation. Jason and I join Margo, Jenn, and Noble at the Pedricktown Christmas Tree Burning. The whole town piles their trees on the lawn of the fire house and then set them on fire. It's a giant bonfire complete with hot dogs roasting and hot chocolate and yet one more memory of my parents I fight through. They took me every year when I was a little girl. I watch the fire burn the hotdog on the end of my stick as Jason wraps his arms around my waist and rests his heavy chin on my shoulder.

"Four more months, Annie." His is a one-track mind. He kisses my neck and I amend, *two-track mind*. "No excuses come May. I've been very patient."

"This is patient?" I ask, and flip my dog over, black bubbles forming on the one side. "Six weeks of rodeos should keep you busy while I work in New York City."

"Why does it have to be New York? Can't you do statistics anywhere?"

"Because people come from all over the world to work in New York City and I can just hop on a train and get there every day. It's a gift."

"It's a curse," he says, and kisses my neck.

"Hey, you two, Mrs. Shabo invited us over for hot toddies tonight if you can tear your bodies apart long enough to drink one," Jenn says. I'm going to miss them, too.

"We'll be there," I say, and Jason groans on my neck. "We have all night," I whisper in his ear and he gyrates a little into the back of me.

"Promise we won't stay long. I still haven't given you my gift," he pleads and I nod, filling with anticipation of his present. I breathe deeply and the smoke-filled air invades my lungs.

* * *

"That was nice," I say, satisfied with Jason hanging out with my friends. Mrs. Shabo seemed excessively pleased with the idea of a real cowboy on her estate. I was surrounded by the best life has to offer and Jason was at the center of it.

"It was long," he says, and walks out of my bedroom. I climb into bed and listen to my heart race as I wait for his return. He falls on the bed with a flat box, obviously wrapped by a female, in his hand. "Merry Christmas, Annie," he says, and his face is utterly wicked. I take my time unwrapping the paper, and pull out the most beautiful blue silk scarf. I spread it out across the bed and realize it's the ocean and the waves are painted in such a way the water actually appears to be moving.

"It's beautiful," I say, and look at him confused.

"It's to replace the belt." *What belt?*

Jason takes the scarf and wraps it around each of my wrists

in a figure eight and raises them above my head. My racing heartbeat sinks to the throbbing between my legs. My breathing is shallow and rapid, but I manage to get out, "Merry Christmas to me," just before he pulls me toward the headboard by my bound wrists.

~ 27 ~

"I'm overwhelmed with you, my doubts I ignore"

Julia graduated in December and lucked out in the poor economy by landing an entry-level job at Condé Nast. "It's like barely in the door, entry level," she told me, but I'm still proud of her. Lots of degrees are hitting the streets, which are already filled with overqualified candidates. She insists she was making more money by not working, because the cost of the commute is killing her.

We walk to the New Brunswick train station together every cold, gray morning and she buys a coffee at the Dunkin' Donuts stand while I jockey for a spot on the platform. Rarely, we get seats; usually I try to use my height to block us off a little space. The heels help. I typically tower above a large percentage of the commuters. We ride to Penn Station and switch to the subway headed uptown. Our offices are within four blocks of each other. They're some of the most grueling and exhilarating days of my life.

I drink in every element of it: the smells of the city, the languages being spoken on every corner, the crowds, and the bitter cold. Julia takes it all for granted and complains as we drudge through the streets day after day, but I know I'll never have it again and I won't squander a moment of it.

* * *

I become fast friends with the receptionist, an over-the-top, bilingual—obscenities being her first language—girl whose name is Renee, and within minutes you know she would take a bullet for you if necessary.

"What the fuck's up, my little Jersey buttercup?" she greets me with in the morning, or some other completely inappropriate verse. Once I look past her colorful use of curse words in all sentences not related to business, she becomes my closest friend at the office.

My boss is a man about my height, bald before his time, a badass named Bruce who inspects me immediately and clearly likes what he sees. *The HR gods have shined on you this semester, Bruce, because I'm a really hard worker, too.*

"So what are your plans after graduation, Charlotte? Is a career in statistics your goal?"

"Definitely. I'm here to learn as much as possible," I say, and Bruce is delighted.

"You'll learn a great deal during your time here. The best way to open doors is to provide results. It's tough out there right now, but interns at Robertson are given first consideration when a permanent position opens. You make your own opportunities." I'm excited by his words, swept up in the concepts of success and contribution. I want a permanent position. I want to beat out every other candidate.

* * *

I work myself to the bone. No assignment is too difficult, no hours too late. I can feel the pride rising from my father's grave. That man defined work ethic. He was of another generation, one that appreciated the company they worked for and considered a job a gift for their family.

Bruce and his peers are openly complimentary. I make sure Bruce looks good with every assignment I turn in, and quickly become his go-to employee, taking on more than actual paid statisticians. It's the perfect arrangement for everyone involved, except Jason Leer.

He absolutely hates me working in New York. The long hours are killing him. He worries about me every day of the week. Several days I think about lying and saying I'm home when I'm not yet, but it's a line if crossed I'll never return. He abhors Bruce's attention and finds his praise to be more related to my legs than my actual work product, which demeans my efforts and hurts my feelings.

But I keep moving. I listen to his complaints and patiently try to appease each one while Julia and I go to happy hour and have lunch near the park. We are a walking, talking, dress-up game for little girls and I'm not going home from the play date early. No matter who comes to pick me up.

* * *

By the first weekend in February, Jason is threadbare. I detox the entire plane ride and as we touch down on the runway, I'm confident I can seem properly unexcited about New York City. As I walk through the security barrier, I realize I have nothing to worry about. The sight of Jason, standing by the pillar, takes my breath away. Without a plan I run to him and throw myself against his body and he wraps his arms around me and buries me within him. It's the closest thing to the truth I know.

"Annie," he says, and kisses my cheek with an unshaved face that scratches me. I leave my head exactly where it is, unwilling to release him. "You okay?" he asks, worried by my reaction.

"I'm overwhelmed with you," I say.

"It's my goal to overwhelm you," he says playfully. "And overtake you, and overcome you."

"I get the picture." I lean back so I can look into his light gray eyes. "Did anyone ever tell you your eyes darken with your mood?"

"My mother. She used to say they were not of this earth. Whatever that means," he says, and picks up my bag, flinging it over his shoulder as he grabs my hand and starts walking toward the parking lot.

"I think it means they're of the atmosphere. A storm one day, cloudless sky the next," I say, and he turns toward me.

"Have you been attending a lot of hippie dippie poetry readings in New York, or something?"

"Yes," I say, and climb into the truck next to him.

***

We head west to Stillwater and somehow the land looks twice as flat as when I left it. I wonder how many miles ahead I can see. I think of the three inches, if I'm lucky, I can see ahead of me on any given corner in Manhattan. How can a few hours on a plane be the only thing between these two regions? They're foreign to each other in every way.

I spend the rest of the ride considering the similarities of the two places. Both Oklahoma and New Jersey have rodeos, but that's really only South Jersey. The farms, the land, the openness of Christianity, that's all Salem County. I realize Oklahoma is not that different from home, but it is a world away from North Jersey and the New York City Metro area. Perhaps that's why I love Rutgers so much. It's different from home. And that's probably why Jason hates it so much. He doesn't like different.

Jason pulls into his driveway and I smile at the loft sitting in the backyard of its house. I reach down to pick up my bag and see Jason watching me from the corner of my eye. He's been quiet the whole ride.

"What?" I ask.

"I'm glad you're here, Annie."

"Me too," I say, and jump out of the truck.

Jason opens the door for me and I step inside to a five-by-five picture of the New York City skyline. It's anchored by the Empire State Building in the center with other unidentifiable buildings surrounding it. The picture was taken at dusk and there's a pink hue lying around it like fog. I walk in and stand in front of it. It's enormous, taking up almost his entire side wall. I imagine him affixing it to the wall with multiple nails and dread creeps up within me. There is something desperate about the picture and the thought of him hanging it, as if he's spending his time searching for ways to make me like it here.

It's cold in the loft and Jason throws two logs in the woodburning stove. He comes to me and stands behind me, his heat warming my entire back. He wraps his arms around my waist and rests his chin on my shoulder as we look at New York City together. Is this how it will always be? Jason and I looking at the skyline from inside his bedroom in Oklahoma because he'll never want to visit with me?

I notice a pile of papers on the table with my name written across the top. I leaf through them and find job postings and campus job fair flyers. *How long have you been collecting these?*

"I know you love it there. There's nothing here," he says, and the cold reality of his statement drains me.

"You're here." I reach back and run my hand through his hair as he turns to my neck and kisses me there. He's hungry and I pull on his hair as his breath on my neck sends chills throughout my body. I bend my knees slightly and caress the front of him with my rear. Jason reaches down and slides his hand into my pants, finding a wetness that disputes his version of what's here.

"Annie, you're always so ready," he says, and I turn around to face him.

"You don't have to try so hard. I am, and will be, happy here." I kiss him to force the truth into his mind. He has to know that whatever is not in Oklahoma is far outweighed by the fact he is.

"I know you can do anything, but the sound of your voice when you tell me about New York scares me. You're never going to sound that way talking about something here, about the rodeo, or the lake. I won't ever be able to give that to you. It's not in me," he says, and the sight of desperation on his face curls in the back of my throat.

"Let New York give it to me. You just worry about being in

me." Relief crosses his face and he picks me up like a pillow and throws me on the bed and dives on top.

* * *

Jason's fears were justified. On the car ride back to Rutgers from the airport I search for Statistician jobs in Stillwater, Oklahoma. I'm excited to see forty-three come up on the results, but I curl my lip as I realize not one is a real statistician job. They include plant manager, customer service representative, and several tutor positions. Just to torture myself I run the same search for New York, New York. There are 36,757 jobs listed for statisticians in the New York Metro area. I'll bet Jason's already done these. One step ahead in the bad news parade.

I close the window on my phone. One thing at a time. I'll finish this internship and then figure out a job. I don't want Jason to think I hate it in Oklahoma. I don't know why. He clearly doesn't mind telling me what he thinks of New Brunswick. It's the difference between temporary and future. The driver pulls onto Hamilton Street and I'm home. Students are walking, talking, and avoiding cars that don't care if they hit them. This town is alive and it shoves the life back into me.

"How was Tornado Alley?" Julia asks.

"A whirlwind," I say, and can't believe I'm back already.

"Are you going to expect me to come visit you once you move there?" she asks as she plops down on our couch.

"I'm expecting to be back a lot, but I'm trying not to create an idea of what it's going to be like. I don't want to be disappointed."

"Me either," she says, and I know that's true. "He's from

New Jersey, for God's sake. It's not like you met him in North Dakota. Can't he move home? Salem County's so much closer than Oklahoma."

"I don't think Salem County has what he needs," I say, and recognize he's outgrown it.

"It has a rodeo. Which, by the way, no one up here believes exists in New Jersey."

"I know, but I think he's out of that league now. He's too good. He's going to have to travel around the country competing on a bigger stage."

"Like how much? How often is he going to be on the road? Are you going to be hanging out by yourself on the great plain?" Julia asks, and I'm frustrated by her obviously intelligently thought-out questions. AND she reminds me of my mother.

"I don't know. I haven't figured it all out yet."

~ 28 ~

"Your presence a promise, no one could love you more"

So tell me about Vegas," Jason says as he walks into my empty house on Hamilton Street.

"What do you want to know?" I'm guessing he wants to know nothing, but is compelled to know everything.

"Did you have fun?" he asks, suspicious of my aloofness.

"Don't you always have fun when you go to Vegas? The entire city was conceived with amusement in mind."

"Annie, what is going on?" he asks, and I realize why I never lie. I am terrible at keeping something from him, especially something he is obviously going to find out about anyway.

I push him back into the couch and he doesn't move at all. I sigh at my concrete wall. "Sit down," I instruct and he laughs before giving in and sitting. I stand in front of him and take off my boots and pants. His face changes, morphing from happiness to anticipation. I smile weakly, expecting the worst, which he notices and furrows his brow.

"Before I take off my sweatshirt I want you to promise me you won't freak out," I plead. Jason rubs his jaw but remains silent. I lift my sweatshirt over my head and watch as his eyes take in my breasts and rest there, and then travel down. I can see the blood rushing to the surface of his skin and see his fist clench. I bite my top lip, wishing the next ten minutes were already over.

"Annie, what did you do? You branded yourself?"

"It's just a tattoo," I say, already combating his over-the-top reaction.

"Your initials were permanently affixed to your skin by some guy with a needle in Nevada," he says, and pulls my naked body to him. A chill runs through me as he wraps his hands around my backside and tilts my hip toward him. He is within inches of the tattoo and reminds me of the closeness of the artist, which I'm sure will be the worst part of this conversation. He runs his thumb across the still sore tattoo.

"It's still healing. It's going to take a few more days before it returns to its original glory."

"Were you naked when he did this?"

"No." I roll my eyes. "I pulled my pants down on one side. The rest of me was completely clothed. He couldn't see anything and believe me, in Vegas, I didn't have anything all that interesting to see."

Jason continues to study it, a pissed off expression taking over his face.

"It's a mermaid's tail," I say, and he studies it again. "In the shape of my initials. It's just like you to see me first. Most people only see the mermaid's tail."

"Most people?" he screams and the tides turn back to the typhoon that was approaching.

"Julia, Jenn, Margo, Violet, Sydney; most people. Of course I showed my friends. All females. You're the only guy who's seen it."

"Who will ever see it?" he asks, and I can't think of a person, but I'm assuming this was a rhetorical question. "It's like you get off on pissing me off," he says, and I can hear him calming slightly. I exhale.

"On the contrary. A weaker person might actually let the fear of your wrath ruin their fun, but I persevere." It's not easy, constantly preparing for the storm that is Jason Leer.

"Do you like it?" I ask, collecting my courage.

"Do I like my girlfriend's new tattoo that she pulled her pants down low to get?" he says, and I push him back on the couch and climb on top of him. I grab his face in my hands and force his eyes off my hip.

"Yes. Do you like it? Since you're the only person that's going to see it from now on, it means a lot that you like it," I say, and kiss him. I can feel him on the back of my thigh forgetting about the tattoo and pull myself closer to him. I would climb inside of him if I could.

"It's going to take me some time to get used to it. You're going to have to stay naked until your roommates come back in three days."

"That sounds like a deal," I say, and kiss him. "I want you to be comfortable, so if me being naked for days on end is what it takes for you to be comfortable, I'll sacrifice for you."

"Sacrifice, huh?"

"You are a horrible burden, Jason Leer," I say, and kiss him for being him and for surprising me by barely yelling at all, and because the anticipation of what he is about to do to my body would make a condemned woman smile.

* * *

He walks around my room and my eyes remind my body exactly what he does to me. Jason Leer drives me wild. He lingers at the mirror resting on my bureau and examines the Mardi Gras beads hanging on the corner of it. He turns to me, his lips pursed, his mood soured. I should probably leave them in New Jersey when I head to Oklahoma.

I lift the covers on my tiny bed and beckon him to me. Jason walks over and takes up almost every inch of space in it. I roll on top of him and lay my head on his chest and I listen to the most beautiful sound I've ever heard, Jason Leer's heart beating.

"Jason," I say. I've been waiting for the perfect time to ask him and it's not going to get better than right now. "I want to take you to New York tomorrow," I say, and wait for him to complain.

"Okay, Annie," he says, and I can hear him smiling in his voice. "You can take me to New York City on one condition." I lift my head to see what he's talking about. "You don't get your hopes up that I'll move there," he says, and I rest my head back on his chest. I was worried he wouldn't even visit with me. Not in my wildest dreams is Jason Leer moving to New York City.

I spend the rest of the day trying to figure out what to do on our day trip to New York. Every detail I consider. Is the train going to confirm every worry he's ever had? Is my driving into the city going to scare him more? Should he see Times Square or will the sight of the Naked Cowboy push him over the edge? I know I'm getting only one shot at this apple.

We head out as soon as the morning commute has cleared. I decide to drive in, saving myself the analysis of every detail of my commute from the New Brunswick train station to Penn Station. I suspect Jason is on to me when he mentions wanting to experience my typical day, but I ignore him.

Jason's shocked to see we park in midtown just forty-five minutes after leaving Hamilton Street. I hand over my keys to the parking garage attendant and collect Jason, who's already looking up at the buildings on the edge of the sidewalk. I slip my hand into his and we turn right at the next corner.

"I want to take you to my office," I say, and he raises his eyebrows.

"What? Are you surprised?"

"Yes, but I don't know why," he says. He's patient and relaxed and each time we're bumped or beeped at I turn to him worried he's already tired of the city, but he gives nothing away but mild curiosity.

We walk into the lobby of the building that houses Robertson's Reports, a survey creation and interpretation company, and I explain that we don't own the entire building, just some of the floors. This is a new concept for Jason, but what isn't here? We pass through security and Jason starts toward the lower elevator bank. I steer him toward the set marked Floors 35–64. Now he's completely confused.

"There are so many people that come in and out of the building at the same time, it makes the process more efficient if we designate elevators. Those in that bank," I point to the set he was about to enter, "won't go all the way up to my floor."

"What floor are you on?" he asks, fascinated.

"The fifty-fifth." This is going well. The city seems absurdly peaceful with him here. The door opens to the lobby and I show Jason the view from the window. It faces the street and the buildings on the other side. We're so high, it's a vantage point we probably won't get the rest of the day. Jason smirks as he takes in the view.

"I see why you are always so shocked by how flat it is in Oklahoma."

"Crazy, isn't it? Can you believe this is less than two hours from Salem County?"

"I can't believe it's on the same planet."

We walk into the receptionist area and are met by the shrill voice of Renee following her big boobs in their march toward us.

"All right! The fucking cowboy came to the city," she says, and looks around to confirm we're alone. She smiles widely at me and I beam with pride. "You're twice as smokin' hot as Charlotte here describes you. I'm Renee," she says, and holds out her hand as she gives him her best side glance. Jason can't hold back the laughter as he shakes her hand. You really can't properly explain Renee to someone; she needs to be experienced to understand.

"Pleased to meet ya," Jason says, I think playing into the western bit a little.

"Please tell me that you brought another cowboy to ride with you."

"Renee!" I yell.

"Sorry, sorry. It must be a terrible burden fucking the virgin Charlotte," she directs at Jason, and he looks at me with sex in his eyes.

"It is," he says, and I know it's time to save us.

"Is Bruce here?" I ask as I pull my employee badge out of my bag and open the security door behind her desk.

"He is," she says, still not taking her eyes off Jason. It must be the hat.

***

I show Jason around my windowless office and he's satisfied with his representation. I have three pictures of him around my computer and my calendar print out is littered with Oklahoma State's academic calendar and rodeo schedule. He sits in my chair and stares at me and I wish he could be here with me every day I work.

"Charlotte," Bruce comes in and stands too close to me.

"Hi Bruce, I want you to meet my boyfriend, Jason. I'm showing him around the city today." Bruce looks up and notices Jason at my desk. He doesn't miss a beat as he warmly offers his hand to Jason who shakes it as if sending a message.

"Well, I've got a meeting in ten. Enjoy the rest of spring break. I'll see you Monday?"

"I'll be here," I say, and Jason looks as if he's biting his tongue. The thought of his tongue makes me want to throw him on the desk and rip his shirt off.

***

We have lunch at the pub with the best burgers I know of. Jason even admits they're good. The bar is dark and quiet, and I again revel in having Jason all to myself. I hold his hands when the waitress takes our plates and wonder if he'll ever tell me what he really thinks of the city. Or maybe I'm hoping he never does.

We stop at a newsstand and pick up drinks and newspapers.

I get a magazine I never have time to read and we head south. It's an unusually warm day so we walk to Bryant Park and lay out the sheet I brought. We waste the last sunny hours of the day lying on each other and reading. It's a strange respite from the city. The two of us floating in the center of the park as the epicenter of the world produces around us. A few times we share what we're reading, but mostly it's enough to be touching, his head resting on me as we read.

Jason's head becomes heavy on my stomach so I sit up and shift it to my lap. I lean back on my hands and admire the architecture surrounding Bryant Park. I'm facing east toward the New York Public Library. Someone told me when it was built it was the largest marble structure ever attempted in the United States. It's no less impressive today. To my left is the W.R. Grace building, which somehow slopes down as if it's made from water instead of glass, and to my right stands my favorite building in all of New York City, the American Radiator Building. It's now home to the Bryant Park Hotel. The black brick and gold accents must harbor some dark and romantic stories. I look down at my dark and romantic story and he's staring at me, his silent gaze full of love and appreciation.

"What?" I ask, and run my hand through his hair. Jason rolls toward me and sits up to face me. I wish I could capture his gray eyes and keep him here, in the city, forever.

"You're so happy here," he says, and lightly kisses my lips.

"I'm happy wherever you are," I say, dismissing the city even as the American Radiator Building stalks above me belying my words. Jason kisses me again and looks at the hotel, too.

"That's your favorite?" he asks, nodding to the hotel. I'm now used to him knowing everything, no longer surprised by his ability to read me.

"You're my favorite," I say, and kiss him again.

When the sun wanes, we move to the Southwest Porch. I order us beers before joining Jason in the hanging porch swing. We watch the employed return home to their families as the lights of the city turn on, and swing in our tiny corner of Bryant Park.

"It's not that different from Oklahoma, you know?" he asks, and I practically spit out my beer.

"I was just thinking the same thing," I say.

"There's cattle being moved for several different means of profit," Jason observes. I look at the people walking on the street, stopping at the lights when directed, and moving forward again.

"The burgers are good," he says, and I beam with pride.

"And the girls are beautiful," Jason concludes, and kisses me on the lips. The chill runs down me and back up again.

"I feel beautiful," I say, again warming under his stare.

"You should. No one could love you more, Annie O'Brien."

"They might call me by my name, though."

"Annie is your name," he says, and I roll my eyes before resting my head on his shoulder once again.

~ 29 ~

"From one storm to the next, I search for that which I forgot"

It's been four weeks since Jason and I were in New York and a peace has settled between us. No longer is the city something that belongs to me alone; he shared it with me and created some shared understanding that settles us. It's been a lonely, but tranquil month.

The weather finally breaks for good and we have warm afternoons greeting us as we file out of our skyscrapers. Julia and I meet as often as possible for happy hour and take the train back to New Brunswick together. Today is different, though. Jenn and Margo are flying in and we rented a hotel room. Tonight's happy hour could last until brunch. Since March, when we all met in Vegas for spring break, Margo and Jenn have been dying to come to the city. And now that they are, it's better than a birthday.

Julia and I check into the hotel and head to the lobby

bar for drinks. We're almost done with our second martinis when Jenn rolls in, followed by Margo within forty minutes of each other. They run their stuff up to the rooms and we're off.

We stop in the first bar we see for food and beers to take the edge off and devise a plan. Something touristy to remember the city by is in order. We head to Rockefeller Center and do the Top of the Rock. The sun has already set; the view is magnificent.

"It's hard to believe this is all resting on an island, and unbelievably we don't sink," I say, looking out at the enormous steel structures.

"Oh, I think lots of people sink here, Charlotte. It's just not in your nature," Margo says, and I see the city in a different light. It's seven-thirty and I know there's someone out there already too drunk, and the person that just got fired is sitting next to them. The betrayed, the abandoned, and the forgotten. The homeless man begging for money to take back to his homeless wife. A mother dying, and a drug addict buying. I look at the twinkling lights of the buildings beneath me and am in awe of life.

Why am I on the top of the world this second and others are not? *Why did my parents die?* How is it possible that I can be happy for even a moment without them? I think of Jason. I didn't sink because he pulled me up when they left. He held me there until I could stand on my own. He saved me.

I take a picture of the skyline with my phone and text it to him with the caption: *I'm on top of the world and all I can think of is how happy I am because of you.*

He'll probably write back some ridiculous statement about safety and asking all kinds of questions about our plans for the night. Julia recruits a man to take our picture with the skyline behind us, a shot I'm sure will not turn out but I'll cherish it anyway, and we bid farewell to the view.

"Well, that concludes our tour today, girls. Now it's depravity time," Julia says as we take the stairs to the subway and take the M train to Broadway–Lafayette, leaving the workday far behind. We go to the Swift Bar in NOHO on Renee's recommendation. She said, "It's like a finger up the ass. The first time you're a little hesitant and then you just keep going back." Julia wasn't exactly sold on the recommendation, but I explained Renee's relationship with the English language and she agreed to try it. Renee promised to meet us there later.

The Swift Bar welcomes us with two hanging baskets confirming spring has indeed sprung. We walk into a beautiful, quaint room with wood paneling and a long bar. There are chalk boards advertising the endless selection of great beers, and warmth emitting from all the patrons. It's decidedly not midtown. We walk to the back where there are long wooden tables and booths made from church pews and a pulpit. *Now this is the type of church I can attend.*

We settle on a table, and Jenn and I order the $12 oysters and Guinness special. Julia and Margo cozy up to beers the waiter recommended based on their favorite flavors while the cool night air is trapped behind the walls leaving us to perfection. We toast to Manhattan, and I add "to good friends that last a lifetime," and then we drink.

We drink our way through three rounds.

A table of beautifully dressed late–twenties sits down next to us and as we bask in our pew, we overhear them pine over the lost real estate market. While New York is apparently still an expensive place to live, there are some deals currently on the market they haven't seen the likes of since they've been in the business. The more they drink, the greater their angst, the more enticing the sales pitch.

"We really should buy something," I say, and Julia laughs as if it's the funniest thing she's ever heard.

"Like a Statue of Liberty snow globe?" she asks.

"No. An apartment. Someplace we can come and hang out in. Or maybe stay over instead of trudging home on the train." I lean back in my chair and take in the bar. No one here is rushing to take a train home. Staying in the city, living here, is a gift. Even if I'd only be taking advantage of it once in a while. "Where are you going to go come May?"

"I haven't figured it out yet. I can stay in New Brunswick, but that's still temporary. I was considering Hoboken. The rents are cheaper than the city, and the commute is better than New Brunswick."

"We should buy something and when I come to visit I'll have a place to call home, too. We don't have to keep it forever. Just until the market recovers. Then we can sell it for a profit. Use the money as a down payment on a colonial somewhere near the carpool line."

"God. This is depressing," Jenn says. "Not the New York part, but do we have to discuss kids? I'm far too young; just a child myself," she says demurely.

"Are you growing a money tree in Oklahoma that you haven't told me about?" Julia asks, and the mention of Oklahoma sobers me and dampens my thoughts of real estate purchases.

"I have a huge settlement from my parents' accident." My voice loses its excitement. "But it's probably a crazy idea."

"How huge?" Julia asks, still not believing me.

"Sean and I each got 7.5 million plus our inheritance," I say, and they put down their glasses and blink their eyes at me.

"Seven-point-five million dollars?" Margo asks.

"Yeah. Apparently it's expensive to have your employee high on drugs and killing people in a work truck."

"Well, that changes things," Julia says, and looks at the candles surrounding us.

"It changes everything," I say, and order another Guinness.

* * *

Renee tumbles into the Swift Bar around one, astounded we're still here. Our plan was to find a new place, but this one seemed to have everything a girl could want. The food was inviting, the drinks were kind, the atmosphere was delicious, and the boys were strong. Or whatever; by now I'm starting to feel it, all of it.

"What are you 'hos doing here?" she asks, and I'm confused since she recommended the bar. "This is NOHO. You all should be checking out SOMEHOES, or maybe FOUR-HOES." Renee is cracking herself up. I give her a hug and head to the bathroom.

When I come back Renee's explaining to the others, "Now all we have to do is convince this brainwashed bitch to pull off the cuffs and the blindfold and take advantage of the job."

"Talking about me?" I joke, assuming they are not.

"Yes, you 'hobag," she starts. "As the receptionist I happen to be entitled to some early information about a job posting that I think you would be perfect for. In fact, it's basically the exact same thing you're doing now." I look at her, confused.

"Apparently, you're doing such an awesome-ass job Bruce has decided he needs someone to make his dick look this big for all of eternity."

"What?" I ask, trying to decipher her rant.

"He's going to post your job and I want you to apply for it." I take a deep breath, finally understanding. I signal the waiter we need another round.

I can't take a job in New York City.

I'm moving to Oklahoma.

***

I wake up on the very edge of the bed with Julia pressed up against me. She has ninety percent of the bed and she's at least six inches shorter than me. Life is not about proportions. I grab my phone from my bag and see the tiny number four in the envelope icon and I dread pressing the screen. I don't think I called last night. I usually call when I get home, but not last night. I scrunch up my face to brace myself and open one eye to read the messages.

> Thanks for calling. You are
> a drunk and so are your friends.
>
> You're probably dead in an alley
> right now and the police are reading
> this.
>
> Why must you stay out until dawn?
> Isn't your body allowed to sleep?
> You should look into rehabs.

> Tell your friend Renee I'm not
> impressed with the job.

The last one punches me in the face and I swallow the fist down to my stomach. Oh God, what did we say? There is a very real possibility we were belligerent. And what am I going to say now to get me out of this? I set the phone on the table and go to the bathroom. When I come back I slide in on Julia's side and now have more than half the bed to fall back asleep. I'll save dealing with Jason for when I'm rested, or at least not so hung over I want to jump out a window.

* * *

We head to brunch and I try to piece together our night.

"What did we say to him?" Margo's eyes widen and she blows air out of her puffed out cheeks and I can tell she's hiding something. "I know you remember something, Margo. Tell me, now."

"I don't know if I dreamt this or actually remember it, but I think Renee might have made up a song she was singing loudly as you were trying to talk to him."

"Oh God. No."

"Oklahoma, has no boner," Jenn sings as she holds her glass of ice water to her forehead and continues to squint through her sunglasses.

"So New York should be home to the stoner," Margo continues and I hide my head in my hands.

"Fuck the cowboy, fuck the horse," Julia picks up. "'Cause

Charlotte only comes in the back of a Porsche. Maybe? Or something like that."

"I want to die."

"Shouldn't be a problem. He's probably on his way here to kill you," Jenn concludes.

"What about the job, though? What did he hear about that?" I ask, now frantic.

"I don't know."

"Me either."

"You're fucked," Julia closes the conversation as our eggs are delivered.

* * *

Jason doesn't take my calls, which I would find juvenile, but songwriting while drunk is not exactly the picture of maturity. I chastise Renee when I get to work on Monday and she seems completely unaffected.

"If he can't take a little fucking humor after thirteen rounds, he's not the cowboy for my girl," she says, and I realize I'm getting nowhere. I hide in my office and try to sort it all out in my mind. I asked Julia if she wants to buy an apartment. Renee told me Bruce is about to post my job. Both of which I may have shared with my slightly insecure boyfriend in Oklahoma while drunk, and singing.

I bring up my calendar on my computer and see Thursday's rodeo is at Oklahoma Panhandle State University in Guymon. *Where the hell is that?* I type it into Google maps and discover it is in fact, in the panhandle of Oklahoma. *Brilliant, Charlotte.* It's almost five hours from Stillwater.

Shockingly, there are no direct flights to Guymon from Newark.

I text Harlan.

> Are you with Jason?

> Oooohh Jersey, just talking to
> you could get me killed. I just
> saw him throw a car at some boy
> that asked if you was coming down
> here this weekend.

I take a deep breath and exhale.

> That bad, huh?

> You best show up naked next
> time you come.

> When are you leaving for Guymon?

> Thursday morning. You coming?

> I'm trying.

> Oh goodie. He bulldogs better when
> you're in town. Lmk if you need a ride.

> Lol

I'm going to have to fly into Tulsa and ride with Jason to
Guymon. Which means I am going to have to take off Thursday and Friday of this week. Which means I now have to talk
to Bruce and ask for the first two days off I've ever asked for.

I hear Bruce walk into his office and listen to his messages on
speaker phone. I wait until he has deleted them all and walk in.

"Charlotte, just who I wanted to talk to. Come in." I take a seat in the chair in front of his desk and my stomach knots. "Before we get to that, what can I do for you?"

"For me?"

"You did just come in here for something, didn't you?" he asks, looking through his top drawer for something.

"I need to take off Thursday and Friday," I say, and the words sound absurd coming from my mouth. I don't take days off. Especially not days used to go make up with my boyfriend who is pissed at me.

"Wow. I didn't see that coming. Is everything okay?"

"Yes. It's my boyfriend's last rodeo of the season, and this weekend I realized I don't want to miss it." I say, and it's very close to the truth.

"Okay. Take it off," Bruce says as if it's absolutely no big deal. Which I guess it's not since Robertson's doesn't actually pay me any money.

"Thanks." I start to get up.

"Whoa, wait one minute," he says, and hands me a packet of papers stapled together.

"What's this?"

"Something to read on the plane. It's a job I'm about to post that I think you're perfect for. I want you to interview for it," he says, and I want to drop the papers like burning cinders.

"Bruce," I start searching for the words to come out of my mouth. "My future plans are not exactly definite, especially when it comes to location." Bruce raises his hand, halting me.

"One day at a time, Charlotte. Read the posting." I nod and walk out of Bruce's office.

* * *

Jason still won't take my calls. I hold my breath every day for the arrival of a nasty gram, but none comes. Could he possibly be so pissed he won't even yell at me anymore? Is it normal to fight like this? I consider Violet and Blake. They fight all the time. Maybe it's age appropriate.

I pack a small overnight bag, happy to have switched to warm weather clothes, and haul it to New York with me on the train. Julia and I score a seat and she hands me condo listings to review. None of the details, pictures, or prices move me. They are the most depressing things I've ever read.

"I don't think I can talk about this right now. I have to get things settled down in Oklahoma first," I say, not wanting to hear Julia's thoughts on Jason.

"You know." I brace myself because I am going to hear them anyway. "Sometimes I think Jason is over the top, but I would have been pissed, too, if I were him." Somehow her taking his side is twice as annoying as usual.

"Thanks," I say, and we both laugh at my predicament.

* * *

By the time I get to the airport, I'm already exhausted and my feet hurt from my heels. The wrap dress I chose hangs off me as if I slept in it, and my face feels like I've slathered New York on it. After security I go to the bathroom and change into jeans and flip flops and wash my face. Work attire will only serve to piss him off further. I text him:

I'm coming to Tulsa on the 9:30 tonight. If you're not there I'll take a car.

To which he doesn't respond. *This is fun.* I hope they didn't leave for Guymon a day early. By the time they call me to board my flight I'm starting to lose my nerve. Maybe a few more weeks apart would be better.

* * *

The landing is rocky to say the least. There's turbulence the entire way in and the tiny man next to me is praying with his eyes closed. I'm certain I'm not dying in an airplane. Car probably, but definitely not an airplane, so I just watch the poor little man as he grabs the cross around his neck. Hopefully he's including all of us in his conversation. He's sweating and bright purple when the plane hits the runway hard. We're all flung forward as the brakes are applied. The lights flicker and several overhead compartments open on impact, littering the aisles with bags of different shapes and sizes. None of this affects me. I watch the spitting rain and the lightning in the distance as I walk through the terminal and hope my storm is here.

I exit the secured area and see Jason leaning on a pillar. The little man gets down on all fours and kisses the ground near my feet. His family runs to him, hugging him as I watch them like a bad movie. Jason walks over and takes my bag off my shoulder.

"Rough flight?" he asks, and I shrug. *Not because of the weather.* I can't tell what Jason's thinking. Partially because he hasn't made eye contact with me since I first walked in. I guess it'd be too much to ask to settle this whole thing quickly, here in the Tulsa airport, and just enjoy our weekend together. Jason takes off toward the exit, leaving me to follow, and I realize it's way too much to ask.

He climbs into the truck and I watch from the curb. When I don't climb in too, he sits in the driver's seat, waiting, not saying a word, and not turning around. I feel like a child and even though I acted like one last weekend, I don't like being treated like one by him. Anger is growing inside me and I take a deep breath, trying to remember that useless saying about cooler heads. I open the door to the truck but don't get in. He turns toward me, his eyes dark and angry even as he smiles.

"Don't you have anything you want to say to me?" I ask, unable to hide the edge in my tone. This amuses him.

"I have lots of things I want to say to you, Annie, but I realize you won't listen so I'm done saying them." I look around and realize I'm not getting anywhere in the airport parking lot. I climb into the truck and we ride to Stillwater in complete silence.

* * *

Jason opens the door to his house at 11:15, 12:15 my time. I've gone from New Jersey to New York to Oklahoma and worked a full day in between. The sight of my pillow draws me to it until I notice the picture of New York is missing. In its place is a hole in the wall. I look at Jason and see his right hand is bruised and cut. *Poor wall.*

"I have some things I need to talk to you about," I start, even though what I want to do is throw a screaming fit like a child. How ironic.

"Something other than what you told me on the phone last weekend?" he asks, letting the disdain fall off his tongue.

"I don't remember what I said last weekend," I admit, and he snorts a little as he shakes his head in disgust.

"I'm thinking about buying a condo in New York City with Julia."

He picks up a plate and throws it at the wall behind me. Cold runs through me and settles in my chest.

"You flew all the way to Oklahoma to tell me you're not coming back here? You should have just texted."

"Let me finish," I say, trying to keep my voice steady. Crying is not going to get me out of this one. Jason pauses and stares at me with hatred in his black eyes. "I'm still coming to Oklahoma. This is where I want to be. The condo would be an investment, not a place for me to live." Jason finally raises his eyes from the floor.

"What else you got to get off your chest?" he asks, still hating me.

"I'm going to apply for a full-time position at Robertson Reports." Jason walks over to the table and sits in a chair. With his elbows on his knees he lowers his head into his hands and stays there. "I'm going to work there, hoping if I do a good enough job they'll let me do it from here." Thunder booms outside the window followed by its wicked sister, lightning. "I need some more time, though."

At this he raises his head. His tortured eyes confirm I am breaking his heart. This is everything he has worried about, coming true. To Jason, I'm choosing New York over him. He lowers his face to his hands again without a word.

"I'm still coming," I say, and move to him. I kneel down below him and pull his hands down, but he still hangs his head. "Jason," I beg, and he looks at me.

"It doesn't sound like you're coming, Annie. Why can't you just tell me you're not coming? How long are you planning on stringing me along while your friends make up clever songs?" He stands, ready to fight now, and his anger sears me.

"You need some more time?" he mocks me, nodding his head as he picks up steam. "How long should I wait, Annie? Six months? You need six months? How about a year?" He throws the chair against the wall and it crumbles from the impact.

"I need until August. Maybe before, but I can be here by September," I say, kidding myself that he's actually listening to me.

"Annie, you are the strongest person I have ever met." It's a small glimmer of regard. "So why don't you fucking speak your mind? Tell me you're not coming so I can stop thinking we're going to be together." I hear the words. They slip past my ears and into my brain, but I can't properly process them. Is he talking about us not being together ever? Anywhere?

I will never drink again.

I could use a shot right now.

The fragments of the plate, and the chair, litter the floor and I know they're in better shape than Jason and me. *We're not going to be together.* I start to cry and walk out of the house. From one storm to the next, the rain pelts me and I cry until the sobs come from deep within me and my stomach churns up my lunch. I walk to the other side of his truck and lean on the bed. My eyes travel down it to the spot where he held me in the rain the day of my parents' funeral and I hide my face in my hands. I collapse with each mangled sob and finally crouch down next to the wheel and cry.

Why is this so hard? Why can't I just move here and take

a tutoring job? I have enough money to buy a condo in New York, but I'm determined to have a job? What the hell is wrong with me?

The rain is pooling, soaking my feet and my jeans. My shirt sticks to me and I'm cold. I cover my head with my arms, and lie on the ground as the lightning cracks above and the thunder bursts into my head. But still the crying doesn't stop.

Jason and I are not going to be together.

He lifts me up into his arms as the wind blows the new leaves off the tree next to us. I grip his neck as if I'm falling from a cliff and sob onto his shoulder, my body convulsing as it comes to terms with his thoughts. Jason's house is now dark, the power gone with the last bolt of lightning. He stands me up on the floor and undresses me as a whimper escapes my lips. He carries me naked to his bed and lays me down and covers me. He goes to the bathroom and gets something out of the cabinet and hands it to me with a glass of water.

"Take this, Annie." He places a pill in my mouth and I down it without question. He leans away, starting to get up, and I grab his arm.

"Don't leave me." I plead for more than the right now. Jason leans back and pulls me to his chest. The touch of his coarse hand rubbing my arm and the feel of his lips on my hair are the last things I remember of my first night back in Stillwater.

* * *

I wake up and look at my watch. I've been asleep over eleven hours. *What did he give me?* Light fills the room, the storm having moved east, and I wonder where my other storm is. I roll over and listen to the shower running. I step out of the bed and into the bathroom. It's filled with steam, the heat from the shower covering the room in a mist. I pull back the curtain and see Jason leaning on the wall, the shower head pointed at his back. He looks at me without a hint of strength left in him. He's broken.

I step in and let the scorching water touch my legs.

"This is not over," I say. My eyes insist he believe me. I lean into him and hold his face in my hands. The kiwi smell of his shampoo surrounds me and I'm intoxicated with Jason Leer. "Far from it," I say, and he kisses me. He's hesitant and cautious, and then his eyes turn and he's no longer careful. He is desperate and ravenous and holds my face in his giant hand as he swallows me whole. His hands run down my body and over each breast, and between my legs. It's the first time, and the last time, he's ever touched me and I let my head fall back as his tongue and mouth are on the side of my stomach, and my hip, and the rest of me.

Jason stands back up and kisses me again and I might cry out from needing him, today and forever. He raises my knee to my arm and rams himself into me. He pulls out taking my concept of reality with him, and I lower my eyes to watch as he comes in me again. When I look up he is watching me, watching. I wrap my hands around the back of his neck and beg him with my eyes to continue. I look down, my leg hooked on his elbow. Jason bores of this position and hooks both his arms under my legs, supporting my bottom with his hands. He forces me to the back of the shower and hangs me up on his arms. I'm suspended as he continues his rhythm. I lose myself and grab the shower above me, my hands barely able to hold on and when I look down again I come, grabbing a hold of him and saying his name as he finishes.

I am hanging off of him, my arms and legs wrapped around him, and I cannot loosen my grip. Neither of us is going anywhere. I don't know how or when this is going to work, but I'm determined to make it. I haven't been this sure about something ever, and even if he has his doubts I'll carry us both through it.

Jason puts me down and I hold his face in my hands.

"I love you," I say, but it never seems like enough.

"I know." His eyes lighten and they almost match the steam around us. Jason steps out of the shower and leaves me alone.

* * *

When I'm done, I throw one of his shirts on, button it to the top, and come outside to find him reading something on his phone. Please God do not let it be messages from me last weekend. I straddle him and he puts the phone down. His hands rest on my thighs and it's impossible not to smile at him. He's so beautiful; his black hair and gray eyes, the constant mystery of a black and white photograph. He raises his hand to my face and I take it and examine the scratches from the wall again. I kiss it and rest his palm on the side of my face.

"I can't keep doing this, Annie."

"I know that." I didn't fully understand it until last night, but I get it now. He's at the end of his rope with this arrangement.

"It's not even about me anymore. I can't keep doing this to you. I'm ripping you in half. It's not fair to you." I raise my hand to protest and tell him for the hundredth time this is what I want, but he stops me. "You're a different person up North."

It's time to lay it all on the table.

"Jason, I love it there. I love New Jersey more than any place on Earth. I love the fields and the woods and the ocean and the sand. I love that it's a short trip to D.C., Baltimore, Philly, and New York. I love that the people are loud and funny, and irreverent. And yes, it's different than it is here, but I'm not the first person to consider living someplace different because someone they love is there." He looks completely unmoved by my statements.

"I think you're having such a hard time accepting this because if the situation were reversed, if it was me asking, you wouldn't be able to move there." I say it, and Jason lowers his eyes. "Look at me." I kiss him and slide closer still to his body. I want him to feel me when I say what's next. "Last summer I had a difficult education in what the rodeo means to you. I know exactly who you are and what you need, and I'm okay with where I stand in that order." He shakes his head, denying it.

"If I can accept it, you're going to need to. It's in your blood. I'm good at statistics. I like the study. It's not the same. And I love New York, but I'll love it when I visit, maybe even more so than spending every day there. And I'll love watching you bulldog because I'm in your blood now, too." Jason runs his hands up and down my thighs as he sighs deeply.

"Don't not fight for me to come here because you know I'd never win if we switched sides, because I'm not some naïve little girl who doesn't understand her place in the world. I'm a rock head from New Jersey fighting for her spot." Jason's face shows no signs of relief. He either doesn't believe me or there is something else weighing on his mind. He kisses me gently on the lips.

* * *

The weekend passes with lots of hand holding and long gazes. Harlan can't decide if he prefers us in love or in hate. He seems to lose either way. Jason takes first place and continues his domination of the Central Plains Region. The entire weekend, there's talk of an enormous graduation party for the outgoing cowboys and cowgirls. Several people ask me if I'm coming for it and I hear Jason tell a few we'll be there. I don't have the heart to remind him it's my spring formal. The one we missed last year because of his injury. The last one I'll ever go to. There will be plenty of time to work it out. Tonight we celebrate the finest bulldogger ever to cross my path.

~ 30 ~

"For with you I am alive"

I watch the terrain as we approach the city of Tulsa. A few buildings climb above the flat earth, reminding me of New Brunswick. It's a small city, too. The highway is lined with trees, ripe with leaves this month, but it's still not home. The hill-barren land still feels foreign and I am an alien in it. With less than ten miles to the airport, Jason mentions my return next weekend for graduation and I'm forced to remind him of my spring formal. It never occurred to him, never mattered.

"Come on, Annie. You're coming to Oklahoma," he assumes, and I can't understand why he doesn't view the formal as important. We've—apparently *I've*—planned on going the entire year to make up for the one I missed last year.

"I don't think I am. You're coming to New Jersey. I need my date. It's a formal and it's my last one," I say as delicately as possible, but I can tell he's quickly losing his patience with this conversation. His jaw is tense and so is mine. "Let's talk about it later. I don't want to waste our last few minutes together with details."

He still seems annoyed.

"We'll work it out," I add, and he smiles as if I've relented and it's settled that I'll come to Oklahoma. I've spoiled him by coming so often.

* * *

The week passes without a word from me about the interview, or the condo, or the formal. Jason brings up the graduation party a few times and when I repeat how important my formal is to me, he becomes frustrated and we get off the phone. There's little time to commit to the conversation because I'm preparing to interview for a job he doesn't want me to have. It's strange to be doing so many things at once he's not excited about. Actually, that he is completely against and angry about. But I trudge forward, hoping he'll come around, and knowing it's going to work out. I keep telling myself he loves me.

"When's Jason coming?" Julia asks as we collapse on our beds. Today was a very long day at work.

"I don't think he is." It's the first time I've let myself accept he's not coming.

"You're going to miss the formal?" She's appalled.

"I don't know what to do. I don't want to miss it, but he's not coming and I don't want to go alone either."

"Take it from me, a lot of these people you'll never see again. Things change quickly in the real world. It's barely possible to hold on to the people closest to you. All the others who've cracked you up the last four years will be lost."

* * *

Julia leaves to pick up dinner and I find my phone in my bag. I tell myself he'll be fine with the decision, but I know it's not going to be fine. I'm so tired of fighting with him, especially over stupid stuff. *If it's so stupid why don't I just go to Oklahoma?*

I find his gorgeous face attached to my contact and press the green phone button. It rings twice and a glimmer of hope that he's not available shines, but then—

"Hey, Annie," he says, sounding ornery.

"Hey, where are you?"

"I'm helping decorate for the graduation party. When are you getting here?" he asks, and I hear the need in his voice even after only a few days apart.

"Jason, I want to go to my formal." He's silent. "With you. I want you to come up here tomorrow, like we planned, and take me to the formal. It's important." My words trail off. If it's so important why am I not yelling it at him? Too exhausted? Too depleted?

"Annie, it's just a dance. You've been to tons of dances. I've waited long enough. Now you want more time. The least you can do is come out here this weekend and give me something to make the wait bearable." I try not to hate him. It's not just a dance and for once, this isn't about what he needs. He would keep taking from me until there's nothing left.

"It's not just a dance."

"Annie, I'm sorry. It's not just a dance. But it doesn't change the fact that I really need you here."

A thousand different ways to reinforce the concept of its importance, and his importance to me, jump into my mind and float around. Instead of hooking one I blurt out, "I think we should separate for the weekend."

There's a morbid silence on the other end of the phone. I hear people around him disappear into the background as a door slams which I assume is Jason finding a new place to talk, one in which he can freely express his opinion of my plan.

"It's the best solution I can come up with," I say.

"That's your best? It's not even a solution, Annie," Jason yells into the phone, and I pull it from my face. His reaction is making me angry and I resent having to dread calling him. He's a spoiled child who only thinks of himself. *Don't you want to ask about my interview?*

"We want to do two different things this weekend; both of them are important. Is it so wrong that we separate for this one weekend and both do the things we want to do?" I try to share the logic.

"Except yours is a formal, requiring a date. Who the hell are you planning on taking, Annie? Some drug addict asshole you've been hanging out with? Or maybe some cool new song-writer friend from New York? Who exactly are you going to get all dressed up for?"

"Fuck you, Jason," I say without much emotion left in me. "It's you I want to dress up for, but you're choosing to spend the weekend with other people in Oklahoma. I'll barely know a handful of people there, and I want to say good-bye to the hundred girls I'm friends with here. Is that so hard for you to understand?" I scream as if he's the dumbest ass in the barn.

"No, I get it, Annie. I gotta go."

"Go decorate some more?" I ask, and my utter hatred for a graduation party in Oklahoma oozes out.

"Fuck you, Annie." He hangs up, leaving me regretting almost every word I said. I really can be an asshole.

I'm tired, exhausted, actually. My interview was with Bruce, his boss, and two of his peers. Even though this new job was created using my internship as a blueprint I still spent hours preparing last night. I was articulate, intelligent, and poised, and Bruce beamed proudly when he walked me out of the conference room. But the process drained me and left little energy to manage my cowboy.

* * *

I sit in the last row for our last sorority meeting. The incoming president is going to do a fantastic job. She's sworn in and gives a speech brimming with excited anticipation for the coming year. I'm consumed with doubt. Doubt for next year, doubt for my next conversation with Jason, doubt for tomorrow night's formal. Every single girl around me is buzzing about her dress, and I'm sitting here disgusted.

I marvel, one by one, at each of my friends. My heart bulges with love for these girls who have endured the last four years with me, the best and worst of my life.

They're beautiful.

There's the naïve tender heart that's been taken advantage of, but will have the last laugh as a wealthy trader.

The Phish follower who'll excel in law school and spend her life negotiating divorces.

The girl with the beautiful hair who cut it off because it annoyed her.

The exhausted, the wealthy, the confused.

The crazy chick from North Jersey who kept me sane on late shifts at Stuff Yer Face.

The virgin, the whore, and the "maybe just tonight."

The lesbian, the Buddhist, the scarred.

The twins who will become physicians, but in the meantime try and lift my skirt in a picture.

The one who held my hair while I threw up my freshman year.

The teacher, the mother, the loved.

The little sister, the big sister, and the sister who will lose both her breasts to cancer before we're thirty.

I see them all so clearly as they live their lives without the knowledge of death, and the fear of screwing up the living. May they never know the loss Jason and I have. May they never be lost.

They don't owe a thing to the dead.

And neither do I.

Tomorrow is Friday and it's probably not going to be much better than Thursday. Unless of course I board a plane to Oklahoma, which I don't want to do. The dull tone in the pit of my stomach, always the tell something is very wrong, sinks me down into my chair. I gaze out the window at the dark night and remember the night Jason first kissed my ankle. I knew that night I would belong to him forever.

My eyes close and I embrace the sinking feeling. It's my soul's declaration; he's all I'll ever want. I know, as sure as I'm sitting here, that it's never been a question of giving up, or giving in, but of giving myself to the one person I already belong to. It doesn't matter if Jason is at the formal; he's in my heart. He rescued my soul when it tried to follow my parents and he brought it back to me. It will forever want him more than anything else on this Earth and I'm not going to fight it. I walk out of the room, leaving my sisters to finish the important business of ending, and dial Jason's number.

I'm not surprised when he doesn't answer. I listen as his voicemail picks up. He won't listen to the message. I call his house and leave one on the answering machine. It's late, and we've been through a lot. There was a time when the bulk of it wasn't at the hands of each other. It'll be like that again soon. As soon as we can be together.

"Jason, it's Annie. I love you. I'm sorry I'm not there. I'm sorry for so many things. I've been so afraid of losing me, terrified I won't be Charlotte anymore if I give in...if I surrender to you, that I almost lost you. But tonight I realized I'm nothing without you. You are the only thing I need. The only thing I want. And you consume me every minute of every day. With you, I am alive. Without you, I am not." I can't keep the smile from my face; the choice so obvious, and the fight within me won.

"I may not belong with you, Jason, but I belong to you. I'll be home soon. Call me when you wake up in the morning."

* * *

Day breaks without a word from Jason. I've been walking around all day as if this is settled; my mind put at ease by the realization he's all I'll ever want. There's nothing more to fight about. I have a quick celebratory drink with Julia before leaving the city. My hard work paid off and Bruce offered me a full-time position with Robertson's Reports effective May eighteenth. It's more like a prison sentence imposed than a position earned. Julia comments on my sorrow-drowning and reminds me to have fun at the formal tonight.

"Are you sad you're not going?" I ask, still not accepting the fact she graduated in December and that she *and* Jason will not be at my last formal.

"Not at all. I have a date tonight," she says, and takes a gulp of her drink. "I know it's hard to believe, but Rutgers will fade fast. It all does if you keep moving forward. I'm building something new now and come May eighteenth you'll start some construction of your own."

"You're so profound," I say, and finish my own drink. "I've got to get home. As it is I'm showing up late, without a date, for my last ZTA formal."

"It's a tragedy in so many ways," Julia says, and hugs me.

* * *

I feel absolutely ridiculous climbing into the cab with my turquoise sequined dress hugging me. Without time for a proper hairstyle, I let it dry wavy and pulled a small section back from my face. It at least looks like some effort was expended. I'm rushed, disheveled, and exhausted, but I'm on my way. It's probably better I don't have a date. I don't mean that. I wish Jason was here.

The site of the formal is thirty minutes away so I settle into the ride and take out my phone to call him. I meant to call all day, but I never had a minute to myself. With the cab driver sitting two feet from me, I'm finally alone. It's 7:45 in Oklahoma. We never got to the details of the party so I don't know when it's supposed to start. The idea of calling him annoys me and I wish we could just fast forward to the next time I see him. It's always easier when we're together.

I put my phone away and lean on the window. The sky is black, not a star visible through the cloud cover, not a sliver of the moon to be seen. I wonder what it's like in Oklahoma tonight.

I pay the driver and step out of the car, stone sober and stone faced. The mansion before me is immense and I regret my stubborn insistence on attending. I turn to ask the driver to take me home as he pulls away, leaving me facing the street, my back to my last formal at Rutgers.

The enormous wooden doors of the rented hall amplify my sense of foreboding. I push one open and hear the sounds of ZTA. It's a mix of raucous laughter and music that immediately puts me at ease. I walk down the hall, not really knowing where I'm going, and stop short at the doorway on my left. The party's liveliness equals that of a thousand people. They're gorgeous, all dressed to the nines, and they are everywhere. I should have forced Julia to come.

One hundred girls exactly and ninety-nine boys; those without a lover at least having a friend. And there's me, reveling in them for the last time and grateful I walked through the door.

Above the heads I see Noble's blue eyes fixed on me and I can tell he's smiling without seeing his lips. He walks over as a slow song begins, and stops three feet away. I blush as he appraises me in my short, sparkly gown, and laugh hysterically when he dramatically reaches out his hand in an offer to dance.

I take it and Noble leads me past the crowded bar and onto the dance floor. It begins to fill, but I'm the center of attention, because I'm with Noble. Wherever he goes, he commands the floor. He's mine. Just for right now.

"I figured you'd be on a plane by now," Noble says, and stares down at me with pride. "You never cease to amaze me, Charlotte."

"Funny. I amaze you. I infuriate our other friend from Salem County," I say, and place Jason between us.

"Can you blame him? You're stunning." Noble spins me and pulls me back to him. "I wouldn't want you alone here either."

"Then he should have come with me. He was invited and certainly wanted here," I say, ending the conversation. Noble pulls me to him and we dance like children without a care in the world, but I haven't been that person for almost two years. Without my parents, life has been one care after the next.

"When are you moving to Oklahoma?" he asks. His voice is low and morose. I'm going to miss Noble.

"Not until after the summer. I was offered a job in New York today and I accepted it." The words pour out, finally accompanied by pride and joy. My excitement touches Noble and he smiles as well.

"Congratulations! But, how?" He doesn't have to finish the question.

"I don't know. I haven't figured it out yet. I'm just trying to…"

I have no clue what I'm trying to do. And neither does Jason, which is scaring the hell out of him. Noble pulls me to him and we dance to the end of one song and when the second one starts, he doesn't let me go. This will probably be my only dance of the night so instead of doing the proper thing, returning him to his date, I savor it.

"Did you ever figure out what we owe the dead?" he asks, still holding me close to him.

"I don't know." I shake my head and rest it on his shoulder.

"But it can't be more than we owe the living. Life's too short to live it by someone else's rules." I feel safe with Noble. *They'd want me to be happy.*

* * *

The song ends along with the portion of the night I'm allotted for dancing. Noble stands still and I bring my hands back to my sides.

"It's time for a drink. Or are you getting ready to run off?" he asks as he leads me to the bar, and orders me a Jack and Coke.

"Not tonight. No big gestures tonight," I say, and watch as the bartender places my drink on a bar napkin with my sorority's motto printed on it: *Seek the Noblest.*

* * *

Noble leaves me to fend for myself at the perfect time. Enough alcohol's been consumed to separate those who aren't going to be together by the end of the night. It leaves plenty of people to mingle with and not be so absurdly alone.

As our new president takes the stage my phone rings. I silence it before getting it fully out of my purse and see it's Jason. My heart stops for a moment.

I need him here tonight. Every night.

"For some of us, this will be our last party together," our new president says, and it's impossible to comprehend. My phone vibrates in my hand.

I need to talk to you.

"Hug your sisters now, because you never know if tomorrow will come."

I'll call you when I get home.

"Nothing lasts forever, including our time together." She pulls out every cliché, and all of them fit. Tonight is as much about grief as it is gaiety.

I'm going to call back
in a minute. Pick up.
Please

I rub the screen with my thumb and close my eyes. I can't deny him now, or ever. The phone vibrates with his call and I walk to the back door. I follow the smokers out back and find a garden no one else has discovered. I look up at the now shimmering stars. There are a million. They shine on me with a calmness that sinks into my soul, and I answer his call.

"Hello."

There's silence on the other end of the line. I check the screen, making sure the call connected.

"Jason," I look back at the sky. It's an incredible night.

"Annie." His words come from behind me and a chill runs through me. Tears fill my eyes. I am frozen by his voice.

He wraps his arms around me from behind, and I let my head fall back to his shoulder.

"You're here."

"I should have been here all along," he says into my ear, and I inhale deeply to steady myself. "I'm sorry, Annie." I lower my head to the ground. I'm the one who should be sorry. The months of torture I've put him through to finally realize no fight is worth losing him.

Jason turns me around and kisses me with a tenderness that rarely exists between us. He holds me at arms' length, staring at me with sad eyes. His face is drawn and masked by exhaustion. Large dark circles anchor his bloodshot eyes and sorrow has replaced any emotion I used to feel from my beautiful Jason Leer. I'm terrified I've actually beaten him down to the point of not fighting anymore. His chest is caved in and he's small, a mere fraction of the Jason I'm in love with. It's as if he's given up, and the surrender has weakened his core.

He takes my face in his hands and his gaze, through battered gray eyes, scares me. For the first time in my life, he looks weak. He places his lips on mine, barely touching, and he starts to shake. Something is very wrong with my Jason Leer.

"Annie, I don't deserve you," he says, and it's as if someone beat it into his head with a hammer last night.

"Clearly," I joke, but Jason doesn't laugh.

"I have to tell you something, Annie." I kiss the side of his face, barely listening and surer than ever we'll always be together. I can't believe he's here. "Something awful, Annie." I look at him again. Love, hope, admiration, need, all flow through me. I've put him through so much. I run my thumb across his lips and watch him lower his eyes and hide from me.

"Forgive me," he whispers.

"There's nothing to forgive." I shake my head, and kiss him.

"Annie—"

"Coming here tells me everything I need to know." I take his hands from my face and wrap my arms around his neck, and kiss him with the fire that keeps us together. Jason responds and lifts me to him and I can feel him. I can feel the old Jason coming through, and all my fears melt away at the presence of his lips on mine. He sets me back on the ground and I run my hands through his hair. "I love you. You're all I'll ever need, and nothing you say will *ever* change that."

"Annie—" I kiss him again. Through with the talking, done with the truth. I love him.

"Do you feel that, Jason?" He nods his head in silence. "That's ours alone." Jason stares into my soul, working through the internal conflicts of our relationship. He is silent, and then his face changes and he pulls me to him. His arms around me so tight I can barely breathe. "I promise I'll keep you safe." He is squeezing the life out of me. "I promise," he says, and kisses me, his body remembering my own.

"I know you will."

I answer myself, and my mother, and Sean, and anyone else who questions exactly where I belong in this life. "I've always known I'm safe with you."

* * *

I pack my bag the next morning to the sound of horns blowing on the street as one person has pissed off another with their driving. I drink in the yelling; the free driving lessons offered in North Jersey. The idea of moving, packing my things and really moving, to Oklahoma excites me. The thought of waking up on his arm warms me, and however the rest works out we'll be together. The horn beeps again and this time profanities are included.

I'll be back, my sweet Jersey. As often as I can.

"Without you I am not."

W hy the fuck is it so dark in here and what is that clicking? I think I'm going to throw up. Annie has to stop, or I'm going to throw up. I'm so cold. Annie's so cold. Something's wrong with her.

"Jason, it's Annie," the answering machine in the corner says.

I look at the person on top of me. Her breasts hang low and bounce from side to side as she rides me. She swings her head back at the voice on the machine and I see it's Stephanie Harding.

"Stephanie?" I say, and try to remember how I got here.

"I love you," Annie's voice fills the room and I'm sure I'm going to be sick.

"I'm sorry I'm not there." That's right. She didn't come; had to stay for her formal. "I'm sorry for so many things."

"I've been so afraid of losing me, terrified I won't be Charlotte anymore if I give in…if I surrender to you, that I almost lost you. But tonight I realized I'm nothing without you. You are the only thing I need. The only thing I want. And you consume me every minute of every day. With you, I am alive. Without you, I am not."

Her words grind my stomach and I throw Stephanie off me as I run to the bathroom and gag into the shower, throwing up the tequila I poured down my throat tonight. The smell of it causes me to retch even with nothing left in me. I crouch on my hands and knees and I beg Jesus to make this all a bad dream.

"I may not belong with you Jason, but I belong to you. I'll be home soon." I hear float into the bathroom, and I want to die. How could this happen to Annie and me?

"Call me when you wake up in the morning."

The smell of vomit is everywhere. I hang my head and realize there's throw up all down the side of me.

"Jason, baby? You all right?" Stephanie's annoying voice cuts me and I retch again.

No, I'm not all right.

Lost Soul

My soul is forgotten, veiled by a boring complication
I run out of the water, swallowed by complete devastation

Abandoning my anger, trying numb for a while
It may serve me better than a dead hearted smile

No idea how to get home, relinquishing prayer
To exist in silence as I lay my soul bare

Amid promises not to think and others to comply
Civility, gentility, can't survive without the lie

What have you lost, my soul begs me to see
While all I can plead is your home is with me

I'm through with the talking, done with the truth
Questioning if harmony is missing from my youth

My vanished soul challenges what we owe the dead
While stars glowing brightly unravel what's in my head

I seek out the end, what's beyond love and obsession
As the stubborn give in, a startling concession

I'm living my life, I proclaim without fear
The death in my words too horrendous for tears

The solace I encounter so easy to undo
I demand with conviction No God, take me too

I forfeit the safety of unclouded sight
Demotion, realization, I surrender the fight

The sound of the waves, the shore's energy transforms
A hope for a future between alone and vicious storms

My life is confined to lost or lost in you
Now and forever, you belong to me too

I'm overwhelmed with you, my doubts I ignore
Your presence a promise, no one could love you more

From one storm to the next, I search for that which I forgot
For with you I am alive. Without you I am not.

Please see the next page for a preview of the next
book in the Lost Souls series

Redeem Me

~ 1 ~

Beyond Recognition

The pain in my head won't stop. It's a hammer pounding on the sides of my skull, gutting my existence. I wrap my arms around my head, holding it tightly, trying to thwart the pain. The room is completely black, but the hammering doesn't mind the darkness.

I rock back and forth repeating, "Please, God, just make the pain stop. I'll do anything if you just make it stop."

Like a hammer that breaketh the rock in pieces...

Thanks be to God.

~ 2 ~

A Slow Death

The roar of the plane about to hit my house wakes me. It won't actually hit because the pilot will pull up just before impact and descend again on the other side. It's deafening and somewhat frightening, even though I've heard it my whole life and know it won't crash. It always reminds me of what WWII bombings must have sounded like. If only this crop duster would drop a bomb on my house.

The windows are open, the temperature having dipped into the low seventies last night. The breeze is still present this morning and the sheers covering my windows billow out on one side of the room and are sucked in on the other. I close my eyes and roll onto my stomach as the attack continues. Fertilizer, pesticides, fungicides...whatever it is...I should go out there and open my mouth. Drink it in. It's better than opening my eyes. My stomach churns. It's either a response to utter despair or the mere concept of another day beginning. When will the daybreak finally break?

The house phone rings, it must be 8 a.m. Every morning his calls begin at eight. As usual I don't pick up, but the machine does.

"Annie," my middle name on his lips cuts through me and I begin to cry again, "please pick up the phone." His voice is low, tormented. "I love you." I run to the bathroom and make it to the toilet just in time to throw up, a little bit getting into my hair. I can still hear his voice, but I can't make out the words. My back aches as I try to stand and catch a glimpse of myself in the mirror. My reflection is simply horrifying—bloodshot eyes, mangy hair, and dry, cracked lips. I look like I have a serious drug problem. I shrug at the fresh idea and go to my parents' room to search their medicine cabinet for any kind of painkiller. As I walk into the hall I hear, "Not knowing where you are is killing me. I need you. I need to talk to you. I need to feel you, Annie."

"Fuck you, Jason Leer," I yell at an outdated answering machine.

No pills here. I wonder how difficult it would be to establish a "drug connection." Apparently lots of people are hooked on drugs. It shouldn't be too hard to get an addiction started. If I'm not going to kill myself, I'm going to need something to help me cope. This house is like walking around in an old photo, except my parents missing from the picture for the past two years.

I've always blamed the delivery truck driver for what happened, but everything's different now. I completely understand the desire to be out of my mind on something. Perhaps the driver discovered his reason for living had sex with someone else, and he only knows about it because there's a baby on the way. For the first time in two years I feel some empathy for him. See...there is a bright side.

I head back to my bedroom, but it's just another source of agony. Last summer Jason spent almost every night in that bed. It's still a little lower on the top left corner from the time we broke the frame. I walk over to the headboard and begin to untie the scarf he gave me last Christmas. It's never been worn except on that first night when he tied my wrists to the bedpost with it. A dull aching in my pelvic bone subsides and I put the scarf in the pile on the floor with my semiformal dress, my Oklahoma sweatshirt, and some pictures of Jason and me.

I walk to the garage and get a screwdriver. The headboard detaches more easily than I thought it would. I put it next to my mattress with the other things that need to be destroyed.

"I hate you, Jason Leer." This is my new daily affirmation. I should be looking in the mirror when I say it, but after that first glimpse, I can't stand the sight of me.

I fall back on my bed and switch on my laptop; the homepage announces it'll be sunny today with a big, happy sun. Yippee! It's August 21, officially seven days since I heard the outstanding news, and I'm still not recovering as well as my brother would like.

I Google "Stages of Grief." There are five, there are seven, there are none. There seems to be some dissent in the grief community. *Can nothing be easy?* I click on Elisabeth Kübler-Ross's five stages. It's somewhat comforting she's decided on only five stages of grief—less anguish on my part hopefully.

Stage One—Denial. I think I'm well past that. No denying Jason had sex with Stephanie in May and now she's having his baby. I like to punch myself in the face with that fact every day. I wouldn't want to feel anything but hatred for him. Moving on to the next stage.

Stage Two—Anger. Yeah, no shortage here.

Stage Three—Bargaining. Does asking God to terminate a pregnancy count? I should be disgusted with myself, but I'm not. I haven't actually bargained. I've made no promises in return, I just asked Him to do it because I want him to. So selfish.

Stage Four—Depression. Right.

I leave the computer knowing I'm nowhere near the last stage, Acceptance. I'll never accept what he's done. What he's done to me. He was supposed to protect me, to keep me safe. I walk to the mirror in the bathroom again, this time wanting to sadistically bask in the effects of Jason Leer's actions. "What? I look awesome," I say sarcastically as I wince at my reflection.

I am gross. My emerald-green eyes replaced by blood-drenched circles surrounded by black shadows. My hair, once long and lustrous, is a matted web atop my head. I think there's a hair tie in there, but I'm no longer sure. There's barely a trace of its former bright, blond color. Angry, selfish, and gross. No wonder he cheated on me with Stephanie. Oh yeah, and depressed. I can't even move through my stages in an orderly fashion. Angry, selfish, gross, depressed, and disorganized. Wretched in general.

My pep talk is interrupted by a knock at the door. As is my new system of communication, I ignore it completely. Whoever the hell it is can continue to lead their life without interrupting my progress through the stages. I yawn and my lip cracks and starts to bleed.

I return to my computer and Google "Signs of Dehydration." This is fun. Much better than moving all my things to Oklahoma to be with the man I love.

Loved.

Hate.

Want to set on fire.

I have one more week off from work for the move. A move from a city I love and an office I love. Six months it took. Six months of working insane hours with impeccable results to sell my boss on the idea of me telecommuting from Oklahoma. Now I'll have the pleasure of explaining why I'm still in NJ. First I'll have to figure it out myself because when I can complete a thought it's usually, "What the hell am I doing in my hometown? *Our* hometown. Mine, Jason's, and that whore Stephanie who's carrying his baby's hometown." I think I'll just quit my job and focus full time on working through the disputed amount of grief stages.

The knocking stops and I head back to bed, exhausted by Day Seven of my new life.

* * *

"Hey, it's your brother." Sean comes into my room the same way he's come in the last ten days, without me answering the door. "I heard you've been starting fires," he says as if this is normal. "Camping out?"

"How did you hear that?" I sneer.

"By living in Salem County, that's how. What are you burning?"

"Old clothes." I don't bother to even lift my head off the pillow. From this vantage point he looks much taller than his six-foot-one-inch height. Sean goes silent and I assume he gets the nature of the fire.

"Do you have any other old clothes to burn?"

"Am I breaking some sort of ordinance or something?" I mock.

"Actually, yes. The state of New Jersey is under a water-emergency restriction because of the drought. You can't go around starting fires. You'll burn the whole town down."

I resist the urge to roll my eyes because, even though I couldn't care less how many towns burn down, I do care about Sean. He's already lost his parents; he doesn't need a bitch for a sister as well. I sit up in bed and my beautiful appearance registers on his face.

"Man, you look rotten."

"Rotten or rotting?" I enunciate the last syllable. "Because I think I'm both."

"Come out to the kitchen and eat. Michelle sent soup. She's worried sick about you."

I lower my eyes to my blanket in guilt.

"I wish she wasn't. I wish neither of you were," I say rather than I'm sorry because I'm a selfish beast. I follow Sean's bear-like self to the kitchen. His usual lighthearted expression has been replaced with one of debilitating concern.

"Eat," he says as if he's not leaving until I do.

The soup is still warm and it burns the crack in my lip. The pain feels good. Maybe I'll start hiring some of those people who will come to your house in leather and beat you.

"Look," he starts, wringing his hands, "I have no idea how this feels, but I'm starting to grasp that it's beyond shitty." I nod just to help him out. "You've got to start showing some signs of…recovery."

I keep eating silently.

"I've started researching facilities to send you to if you can't turn this around. I don't know what else to do. You won't talk to anyone; you won't take care of yourself." Sean runs his hand through his blond hair and I become distracted looking at my own mange—it used to be the same color as his.

Angry, selfish, gross, depressed, disorganized, and crazy. It's a new low. I like it.

Sean leaves. I promise to shower every day and head back to bed as I hear the phone ringing.

About the Author

Eliza Freed graduated from Rutgers University and returned to her hometown in rural South Jersey. Her mother encouraged her to take some time and find herself. After three months of searching, she began to bounce checks and her neighbors began to talk; her mother told her to find a job.

She settled into Corporate America, learning systems and practices and the bureaucracy that slows them. Eliza quickly discovered her creativity and gift for story telling as a corporate trainer and spent years perfecting her presentation skills and studying diversity. It's during this time she became an avid observer of the characters we meet and the heartaches we endure. Her years of study have taught her laughter is the key to survival, even when it's completely inappropriate.

She currently lives in New Jersey with her family and a misbehaving beagle named Odin. An avid swimmer, if Eliza is not with her family and friends, she'd rather be underwater. While she enjoys many genres, she has always been a sucker for a love story…the more screwed up the better.